FOLLOW ME TO GLORY

A Novel by Will Hutchison

Copyright © 2006 by Will Hutchison

ISBN 0-7414-3560-8

Published by:

INFINITY
PUBLISHING.COM

1094 New DeHaven Street, Suite 100
West Conshohocken, PA 19428-2713
Info@buybooksontheweb.com
www.buybooksontheweb.com
Toll-free (877) BUY BOOK
Local Phone (610) 941-9999
Fax (610) 941-9959

Printed in the United States of America

Printed on Recycled Paper

Published March 2007

WHAT THE READERS ARE SAYING......

"In the warrior's footsteps of Cornwell's Richard Sharpe, Patrick O'Brian's Captain Jack Aubrey, Tom Connery's Markham of the Marines, and Forester's Hornblower, so travels Will Hutchison's hero, Ian Carlyle, the young Scottish nobleman and Guards officer. Hutchison's portrayal of life as an officer in the Crimean War is riveting. He has described exactly how it was…a dirty war fought by pomp and circumstance. This is a first class and extremely accurate historical portrayal of the Scots Fusilier Guards, and a terrific tale of adventure from beginning to end."

Kevin Gorman, BA (Hons), Regimental Historian
Headquarters, Scots Guards, Wellington Barracks, London

"I congratulate you on a fine yarn, well-written and packed with action. Your clear passion for military history and meticulous research make the tale rich with historical detail and a very good read."

Major Colin Robins, OBE FRHistS
Editor Emeritus, 'The War Correspondent'
Journal of the Crimean War Research Society

"Meticulously researched, moves fast and furiously, providing an intriguing history of the Crimean conflict in 1854 and 1855. The combat sequences are gripping, forceful, and highly personal. The author has clearly been in harms way, himself, a time or two. Looking forward to the sequel, where Will Hutchison's hero is drawn into the American Civil War."

Michael Vice, Historian and Curator (Ret),
Gettysburg National Military Park

"A compelling weave of tactics and character. Amid the expert detailing of troop movements, ordnance and military command, are personalities cleverly developed – you cannot help but invest emotionally in their wellbeing. I would feel comfortable climbing out of the trenches and following Ian into battle. In Will Hutchison's easy, energetic style, it's clear that the author cares about his characters as well. I couldn't put it down. Not only a good story, but a story well-told."

B.J. Small
Editor, *Gettysburg Times*

Follow Me To Glory is dedicated to my wife, Rosemary, for her love, support and patience.

ACKNOWLEDGMENTS

This story is set in the years prior to and during the Crimean War. To tell the tale properly, I conducted meticulous research and made singular efforts to remain faithful to history. You will find the events as they unfold, the lives of the real people, uniforms, equipment, weapons, tactics, and regimental histories as accurately portrayed as was possible to present them in the context of the story itself.

The fictional characters are surrounded by real historical figures, and the events of an extraordinarily bloody, disease-ridden, incompetently managed war. I have attempted to create dialogue and minor encounters, within the context of major historical events, which bring life to these figures to allow them to play their parts in the story. To the degree I have succeeded, I give thanks to a kind providence.

Lieutenant the Honourable Ian David Carlyle, Scots Fusilier Guards, second son of the Earl of Dunkairn, exists only in the mind of this writer, as do many of the other major characters. Dunkairn Hall, the manor house and estate located near Kilmarnock, Scotland, also exists only in the writer's imagination, although there are similar wondrous beautiful places throughout the splendour and majesty of Scotland.

The Scots Fusilier Guards as a regiment does most assuredly exist today, although in 1877 the name was restored to its present title, the Scots Guards. The exceptional deeds of this glorious regiment speak for themselves, and continue to epitomize professional soldiering today, as it did back then. I was proud to make this the regiment of Ian Carlyle, whose character was modelled after the exploits of three actual Scots Fusilier Guards officers who fought in the Crimea.

A kind, generous, and highly successful author of historical novels, Jeff Shaara, suggested I bring forward two points to the reader. First, the characters in this story have English, Scottish, Irish, Italian, or even Turkish accents. In order that the reader will not be forced to wade through my ponderous efforts to reflect such marvellous accents as a "thick highland brogue," I have kept such effects to a minimum, trying to add a taste here and there to keep the reader mindful of them.

Second, during the period to which this tale pertains, the manner of speaking and the usage of words were different. In some cases it was more formalized, in others more colourful. I have attempted to flavour the dialogue with hints of these differences, as well, but for the reader's sake, have kept such manners of speech to a minimum.

Among so many obligations, this writer owes a debt of gratitude to the officers, non-commissioned officers and other ranks of the Guards, who graciously gave their time, energy, and knowledge to aid me in this endeavour. In particular, I'd like to mention Captain David Horn, Curator, Guards Museum; Captain Robert T. Clarkson, Project Officer, Scots Guards Archives; Major R. Clemison, Record Officer, Scots Guards; Mister Steven Richards,

Assistant Curator, Guards Museum; and Mister Barry MacKay, Chief Superintendent, London Police (Retired), formerly Scots Guards.

For their patience and kind assistance, I would also like to thank Ms. Rebecca Hunkin, Visits Manager, Eton College; Ms. Penny Hatfield, College Archivist, Eton College; Lieutenant Colonel Will Townend, Curator, Firepower, the Royal Artillery Museum, Woolwich; Mister Arthur Jugg, Site Manager, Royal Military Academy, Woolwich; Mister Richard Dunn, Director, the Royal Engineer Museum, Chatham; Ms. Beverly Williams, Curator and Archivist, the Royal Engineer Museum, Chatham; Captain Harley Nott, former Royal Engineers, and his gracious wife, Ms. Meena Nott.

My thanks to Peter Culos, a fine artist, for his splendid artwork, and to Curt Musselman for his outstanding maps.

Above and beyond the call of friendship, I would especially like to thank Steve Hanson, whose editing skill was essential and invaluable; Lieutenant Colonel Wade Russell, former Royal Tank Regiment; Kevin Gorman, Scots Guards Archivist; and Mister Nigel "Spud" Ely, former 2nd Parachute Regiment and Special Air Service, now author. Their assistance and encouragement were priceless.

Lastly, I will never be able to repay my debt to the amazing and passionate historians of the Crimean War Research Society. To name but a few who helped me: Lieutenant Colonel Peter Knox, David Williams, Rod Robinson, Captain Pete Starling, David Cliff, Brian Abbott, Evgeniy Dubovic, and Bill Curtis, whose knowledge and collection of Crimean weaponry is without equal. I would respectfully and gratefully add Major Colin Robins and Michael Springman, who critiqued the final draft and helped me "de-Americanize" the narrative and dialogue, where necessary.

The cover is a portion of a painting entitled 'Scots Fusilier Guards Saving the Colours at Alma' by Lady Elizabeth Butler. It was commissioned by the Scots Guards in 1899, and it is by their kind permission that it is reproduced here. It depicts Captain Robert Lindsay of the Scots Guards advancing with the colours, which were shot through and the staff broken. For his bravery and example, he was awarded the Victoria Cross.

It is my fond hope that you enjoy reading this tale as much as I have enjoyed writing it.

Ian Carlyle

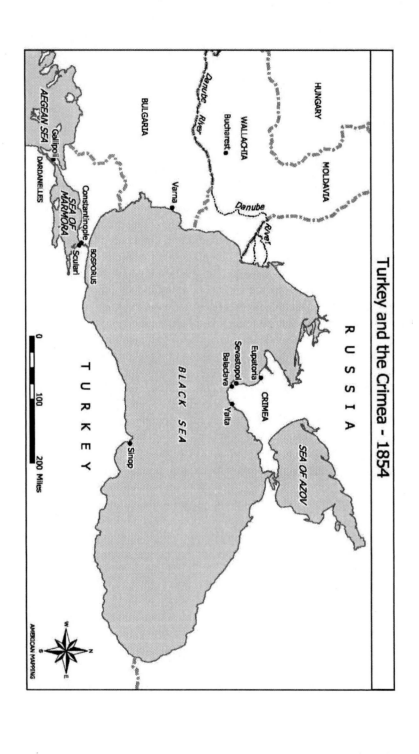

Turkey and the Crimea - 1854

Chapter 1

Ian felt the shuddering blows strike his horse a tick after the two not-too-distant musket cracks. He heard the awful thwacking sounds as the lead balls hit flesh. The gallant animal collapsed on his left side, pulling Ian down with it, into the muddy ground below, pinning his left leg under hundreds of pounds of horse and a tangle of saddle and stirrups.

The pain was knife-sharp, deep, and unbending. *Bloody hell,* he thought, *if it's broken, I'm a dead man.* He struggled to free himself from the numbing weight, which pressed the leather straps and sharp brass buckles of the harness into his leg.

Ian stretched his neck to look over the dead horse's back, through the mist and rain, saw them coming at him, fast. There were six riders thundering down, Cossacks by their long cherkeska coats, cartridge loops across the chest, and grey fur caps. Some carried long deadly lances pointed his way, others brandished large curved swords. Ian knew he hadn't long to live unless a miracle happened, knew these fearsome warriors would show little mercy.

The miracle was standing over him, preposterous in its elegance. He looked up and saw his friend, Captain Lewis

Nolan, calmly and stylishly astride his mount, gazing with haughty distaste at the oncoming attackers.

Ian shouted, "Lewis, for God's sake, give me some help here. I'm a bit stuck-in."

"A moment, Ian," Nolan said, deliberately removing his huge Deane Adams .50-inch revolver from its holster. He carefully aimed at the charging, screaming Cossacks. Since it was not necessary to cock this revolver, he slowly pulled the trigger. The pistol bounced abruptly in his hand, firing with a distinctly loud bark.

Ian stretched his neck again, saw the lead Russian's horse crumble to its front knees, the rider flying over its head, arms flailing wide apart, as though he'd grown wings. He struck the ground face first, slid grotesquely in the mud and decay of the forest floor, then lay motionless.

The Cossack behind him, riding at full gallop, crashed into the stumbling lead horse. The second Cossack was thrown off his mount sideways, and trampled by the oncoming horsemen. Two were on the ground with one shot. Ian was amazed. Nolan looked decidedly amused by it all.

They were closer now, the other four, still coming. Ian could see their distorted faces. If he didn't free himself, he'd risk capture and an unpleasant death.

Ian crawled, clawed, and kicked his way clear. He scrambled to his feet, ignoring the fierce pain in his leg, and looked up again at the stoic Nolan sitting on his mount almost casually. Ian said, as calmly as he could manage, "Lewis, I should think it time to leave, or we might be spending the rest of this war eating borscht in some filthy, rat-infested Ruskie prison."

Nolan would have none of it. Without looking at Ian he replied, "Please, Ian, you're spoiling my sport." With that, he carefully placed the Adams' long barrel in the crook of his left arm and aimed. The pistol bucked again, his horse moving ever so slightly at the piercing crack of the revolver, Nolan in complete control of weapon and animal. Ian saw a small black hole appear in the forehead of the closest Cossack, and watched as the dead Russian, feet rising in the air, rolled off the back of his horse.

Three were down now, three angry charging Russians left. The downed Cossacks were lancers. The three getting dangerously close were circling swords above their heads, screeching like banshees.

Ian jerked out his own smaller American Colt Revolver, wiping off the mud as best he could with a braided tab from his once blue, now ugly, wet-brown frock coat. The pistol remained by his side as he stared at the closing Cossacks. *It's been a short war,* Ian thought, with surprising calm.

Nolan said, "I say, Ian, shall we leave here with a bit of dignity?" He grabbed Ian's arm, swung him onto the back of the saddle, and spurred away with ease. He almost lost Ian as he pulled effortlessly left, then right, in an agile zigzag pattern.

Ian was barely able to stick his pistol in his belt, as he hung on for his life. Nolan wove the mount skilfully around scrub bushes, trees, and large boulders. He was a magnificent horseman, but with two riders the borrowed mount was tiring. Ian looked back, saw the Cossacks gaining, heard the pounding of hooves getting closer.

Ian's world seemed to move more slowly, as he realized the danger approaching. His mind flickered back to their landing, which had been a farce. The combined French and British armada boasted a fighting muscle of eight triple-decked ships of the line, twenty-two double-decked battleships, seven frigates, and thirty of the newer steam and paddle-driven warships. All of these were bristling with naval guns of every size. In addition, there were several hundred sail and steam transports, like so many lazy fat whales, ready to disgorge their men and supplies onto the hostile shore.

On the British side it was a mismanaged mess, the beach area a circus of misdirected supplies. Commissary and quartermaster personnel had been running around, bumping into each other. Soldiers wandered about searching for their companies, trying to form up.

Lord Raglan wanted a reconnaissance, and Lord Raglan would have what he wanted. Wishing to know if there were Russian infantry to their front, he'd ordered Captains Ian Carlyle and Lewis Nolan of his staff to find out. They'd just managed to stagger onto the beach south of Eupatoria, along the Crimean Peninsula, when His Lordship gave the order.

Nolan's horses were not yet landed, and Ian's were unsaddled. He and Nolan quickly borrowed two saddled cavalry mounts from a young, confused 11th Hussars cornet, and were off, moving inland down a dirt path to get His Lordship's answers.

Now one of those borrowed horses was dead, the other exhausted, and the two young officers were in grave danger of being captured or killed…or both.

Nolan shouted over his shoulder, "Doesn't look good, old man. Horse won't last much longer."

Ian could almost smell the Russians moving in for the kill. He looked back, saw the leading Cossack raise his sword high in the air. The head of the Cossack's horse came even with him. The giant sword would be coming down. Ian tried to pull the Colt revolver from his belt with his right hand, while his left arm clung desperately to Nolan's waist.

There were several distinct cracks, and bullets buzzed by Ian's head. He thought: *These Cossacks are rather spectacular shots…from galloping horses.* He chanced another look back, half expecting to feel the Cossack's sword slicing down to cleave off his head. To his surprise, two more Cossacks had fallen from their horses, including the one close by. The last Cossack picked his best, and only option. He swerved expertly away, heading back from where he'd come, leaving his five companions bleeding bright red onto the Crimean soil.

Ian's puzzlement overcame his enormous relief. He looked in front. There, emerging from a clump of trees ahead was a group of grinning, green-jacketed riflemen, reloading their weapons as they moved. Their Minie´ rifle muskets had done their deadly business well. Ian and Nolan knew how close they'd come, and waved thanks as they rode past the smirking riflemen, who were convinced these two bumbling 'staff officers' had merely gotten themselves lost and ended up in front of their advance post.

Later, their horse rested, the two made their way to the landing area to find Lord Raglan's headquarters. It was still raining…but more vigorously.

"Christ," Nolan said, "we'll never find His Lordship in this sopping mess. Look at my uniform, will you."

"Not to worry," cut in Ian. "The Army landed without tents, remember, the headquarters should be an easy spy." He was right. The only tents visible were His Lordship's headquarters, and were rather conspicuous in the middle of 27,000 soldiers bedding down on barren fields of wet, mushy ground with only their greatcoats for cover.

Ian remained highly agitated from their narrow escape. He was trying to get past how close they came to death, without much success. *What am I doing here?* He asked himself. *How in God's name did I get here? I was to be a scholar, don the academic robes at Cambridge.*

He glanced about at the soldiers trying to find comfort amid the mud and downpour. He could taste the remains of his terror, sand-dry mouth smacking when he opened it. There was an odd feeling, though. He found himself almost sorry the excitement was over, thinking: *My blood is still racing. My heart's beating faster than I care to imagine.* He laughed to himself. *You bloody fool; you've answered your own question, haven't you? It's the destiny you've always wanted... Captain Ian David Carlyle, Scots Fusilier Guards, meeting the enemies of the queen...and that, indeed, is why you're here.*

As the two officers picked their way through the waterlogged red-clad regiments, Ian focused on the day, now coming rapidly to a close. He had changed. He knew that, but he didn't know how.

Ian reflected: *A very long day, indeed. Lewis and I ran from the Russians, yes, but it was our only choice. I was afraid, God, I was so afraid, yet it didn't stop me. In fact, it was exhilarating. I never felt so alive. No, by damn, it wasn't that bad after all, and I acquitted myself rather well, considering. It all happened so quickly...so very quickly.*

Chapter 2

The landing had indeed been a comedy of magnificent proportion. Ian remembered bits and pieces of the farce as it progressed. They came ashore among the vast dumps of piled biscuits, barrels of salt meat, sacks and tins, ammunition boxes and various other equipment spread all over the beach in stacks of confusion. Ian recalled a quartermaster officer shouting and carrying on about some miserable civilian sod dumping commissary boxes among his stores, while an engineer officer shouted, "What dumb bastard parked artillery equipments right in the middle of the only damned track off this bloody beach?"

It was approaching dark when Nolan and Ian rode their one exhausted horse down this same muddy track and into Lord Raglan's headquarters camp. Nolan reported, "Your Lordship, we saw no sign of infantry at least five miles inland."

"Thank you, gentlemen. It's been a rather arduous day. I'm going to retire, and I suggest you do the same," he said in dismissal.

Ian found his servant, the former Sergeant Angus MacLean, smoking a long clay pipe, trying to keep his brown tweed coat dry under an odd bit of canvas. As a private, Angus was soldier servant to Ian's father, the Earl of Dunkairn, at

Waterloo, and later, after the Earl retired, became his personal valet. The old Highlander practically raised Ian and his brother, Peter. He was often more a father to the boys than the Earl, himself. Ian was astonished and pleased when the Earl allowed Angus to accompany him to the Crimea as his own valet.

Ian's small single tent, which reminded him very much of a dog kennel, was set up, and ditched all around to stop the rainwater saturating the ground from coming in. It was dry inside. Angus must have done it before the rain started. Angus' own canvas shelter was a discrete distance to the rear. Since these tents hadn't been carried ashore, by His Lordship's order, Angus must have acquired them from the ship in some fashion. *Don't ask*, Ian thought.

He was pleased to see both his horses, Savage and Packey, tied to a line. Angus said, "What say you to a bit of food, sir?"

Ian almost cried. "As always, MacLean, you are a wonder...as soon as I've checked the horses."

Angus smiled, "Aye, sir, they've been watered and fed, but you see for yourself. An acceptable piece of beef will be waiting, with a wee bit of cheese and a rather nice port I found lying about." Ian smiled to himself.

Angus was well pleased with his charge, thinking: *His father and I taught the lad well, "Horse first, then the man."* In the Carlyle family, it was a horseman's duty to tend personally to the animal and companion who served him.

Savage, Ian's favourite, was a 16 hands, silken chestnut thoroughbred, with a white stocking on his right foreleg, and a blaze on his forehead. He was arguably one of the very best jumpers in all England. Packey was an all black 'stayer,' smaller and shorter in body length than Savage, but very fast, with the stamina of ten horses. Both of these marvellous animals had refinement, endurance, speed, and, most of all, heart.

Ian gave them some extra feed, then combed and brushed them, knowing Angus had already done so. He thought: *The other officers are still trying to sort out their tents and gear, including the ever-resourceful Nolan, while I'm about to enjoy a leisurely meal before retiring. Good old Angus.*

Ian's few personal items were laid out with precision neatness in the tiny tent. His Hussar Pattern "Hungarian" saddle, saddlecloth, bridle and a set of horse furniture were protected from the rain under a piece of canvas next to the horses. His German-made 1796 light cavalry sabre, which had belonged to his father, was hanging from a black leather sword belt with snake buckle around his waist, wet and muddy from his recent adventure.

Ian took the mud-encrusted pistol, which he had almost been forced to use, from where it was tucked in his belt, and the sword from its scabbard. He pulled the .36-inch lead musket balls from the pistol's six chambers, removed the six percussion caps, and emptied the damp powder. He then cleaned and wiped sword, scabbard, belt, and pistol, until they gleamed. This was another series of chores he preferred to do himself. Finally, Ian re-loaded the pistol and laid his weapons within close reach inside the tent.

It hadn't been raining when he and Nolan left for their reconnaissance, so he hadn't brought his blue cloth cloak, which he carried rolled in an India-rubber waterproof sheet strapped to the front of his saddle. He was now soaked through and caked with mud. He also hadn't bothered to carry a blanket ashore, assuming the cloak would do.

Ian's other personal items came ashore in a valise strapped to the back of his saddle: toilet articles, writing materials, an extra shirt and a pair of sturdy wool stockings. Ian brought along a full canteen and a leather double-bag haversack. The haversack contained three days' rations of salt pork and biscuits, an old briar pipe, a pouch filled with Cavendish tobacco, matches, a silver cup, a plate, and eating utensils.

The rest of Ian's belongings remained stored in his chest, left aboard the *Caradoc*, the ship that had brought Lord Raglan and his staff from Varna to the Crimean coast. With luck, he might someday see his things again.

Ian stretched, and looked about him. He really wasn't hungry. He moved to the fire, and said, "Angus, don't bother with the food."

Angus mumbled, "Ye really must eat, lad, ye'll need energy tomorrow."

"Perhaps later," Ian replied.

A short distance away was a rather extravagant cluster of tents. Curious, Ian walked over to them. He recognized Major Antonio Capecci, a Sardinian liaison officer he met on board the *Caradoc* on the way from Varna.

Capecci was a short, thin, rather compact officer with thick black hair and a large moustache. He was smiling. He was always smiling.

There were no Sardinian troops with the Army of the East as yet, but in advance they sent Major Antonio Capecci to serve on Lord Raglan's staff. He brought with him his considerable personal establishment: a valet, two grooms to care for his several horses, and a rather large cook. They were all scurrying about nearby trying to arrange for the major's comfort.

Ian thought, but not unkindly: *Perhaps the dapper major, with his moustache, immaculate uniform, and his many servants, was enough to help England and France to victory over these annoying Russians. Capecci is, after all, one of Sardinia's elite Bersaglieri.*

Even in the fading evening light, Ian could recognize the dark blue tunic and gold-fringed epaulettes. The major looked proud and elegant as a peacock. His black-felt wide-brimmed hat, huge plume of ostrich feathers hanging off to one side, just touched his right shoulder in perfect symmetry. Feathers and all, his flamboyant appearance was not in the least unpleasant, quite the opposite. He had a warm, self-assured smile, and a most pleasant air about him.

Although Ian was rather taken with him, he couldn't help but wonder whether such be-plumed soldiers could stand the strain of a long campaign and the terror of close fighting. Of course on these points Ian wondered the very same thing about himself, every minute of every day.

The major asked, "Would you happen to know where Lord Raglan is at the moment, Captain?"

"Yes sir. I just left him in his quarters, but I believe his intent was to retire early."

The major thought a moment, said, "No matter, I'll see him tomorrow."

Then he looked questioningly into Ian's eyes. "Understand you had a close thing today."

Damn Lewis, Ian thought, irritated that his friend Nolan talked too much. He replied, "A bit, yes."

The major asked, waving his right hand about elegantly as he spoke, "Captain, would it not be more fitting if you and I were leading a company of infantry, rather than accompanying these fussy old staff officers?"

"You read my mind, sir. Exactly where I intend to be, with luck. I'll ask to be returned to my regiment in the Guards Brigade as soon as possible. You, sir?"

"Ah, well, I'm content to serve on His Lordship's staff until my countrymen arrive, then I'll have a battalion to command."

Ian beamed, "If my luck holds, I too will lead men in battle. I think it is my destiny."

Major Capecci frowned; his hands stopped moving, "Use caution with your dreams, Captain. In my experience the reality often falls short of the mark."

Ian saw Angus MacLean walking briskly toward them, mysteriously carrying two steaming cups. MacLean, as was his habit when doing something unaccustomed, lifted his left eyebrow and looked squarely at Ian, then at the major. Ian immediately understood what was happening, solved the cup mystery, and thought: *Good old Angus.*

Ian's voice became cheerful as he turned the conversation, "What say you, Major, to a hot cup of strong tea before we meet the enemy?" As Ian said this, MacLean came next to them, handed each officer a cup, and stepped back quickly to stand at a relaxed parade rest nearby.

Somewhat surprised, the major took the offered cup, "Captain Carlyle, you English and your servants. How do you train them so?"

Ian's smile disappeared, then quickly returned, as he said, "If you'll pardon me, sir, you're mistaken twice over. I'm not English. I'm a Scot, and proud of it."

"Of course you are, do forgive me," said the major. "I forgot how particular you Scotsmen are about your heritage."

Ian's smile broadened, "...and this, sir, is retired Sergeant Angus MacLean, much more than my servant. MacLean is a Waterloo man and a warrior in his own right. Although in this world he attends my needs, he's far dearer to me than a mere servant. What I know of life, I learned from him. I would be much the less without his companionship and wise counsel."

Angus, close by, cleared his throat, but said nothing. He remembered what he considered the four most important dates in his life: When Lord Dunkairn officially retired from the army on 22 March 1820; 12 January 1822, the day of His Lordship's marriage to the wonderful Lady Harriett, whom Angus loved from the first time they met; 12 October 1828, when their first son, Peter, was born; and 22 August 1830, when the young Ian exploded on the world all hands, feet, eyes, and smiles. From that moment, although Angus loved and was devoted to Lord and Lady Dunkairn, and Peter, the "wee bairn," Ian, had completely and absolutely captured his highland soul.

He couldn't have been prouder at hearing Ian's words to the major. Had someone looked closely at that craggy war-marked face, huge pork chop sideboards just touching his thick moustache, they would have seen a wee tear forming beneath his right eye.

The day was finally over. Ian was exhausted. He bid the major goodnight, and crawled into his small tent. He discovered that Angus had placed a layer of dry straw and moss on the earth, covered by a spare India-rubber ground sheet he'd acquired – somewhere. Amazingly, he discovered a warm goose-feather comforter, as well. From where these things materialized was just another example of the Angus mystique. Ian was merely thankful.

Over the next several days, while the army ponderously prepared to advance, a small group of comrades formed among Lord Raglan's junior staff. There were five of them. They banded together for a number of reasons, not the least of which was Lord Raglan's rather maddening proclivity to let as little information out to his staff as possible, thus making their individual functions that much more difficult. By talking among themselves, each adding a piece to the continuing puzzle into which this campaign had materialized, they were able to keep abreast of the changing scene.

They had something else in common. They were not the privileged members of His Lordship's inner staff circle, which was made up of those related in some fashion to Lord Raglan or his family, or those of general officer rank.

This merry little band of somewhat outcast staff officers placed their tents in close proximity. They messed together, rode together, shared cooks, grooms, food, firewood, and servants. The most senior of the group, although you would never realize it by his quiet, sociable demeanour, was Major Capecci, who grew to be a close friend to Ian. The major added an air of international sophistication, as well as a bit of colour with his Sardinian Bersaglieri uniform and round-crowned, feathered hat.

Next was Ian's comrade, Captain Lewis Nolan, the young flamboyant cavalry officer who had saved his life. Nolan was a striking fellow, but not handsome, the only officer in the Crimea from the 15th Hussars. He was unusually slim, with a dark appearance, curly hair, a long thin nose, high cheekbones, and sharp features. He and Ian had much in common. They were both trained as engineers, and shared an uncommon affection for horses.

Nolan was an aide-de-camp to Quartermaster-General Sir Richard Airey, who served as Raglan's Chief-of-Staff, as well as the Army's Quartermaster. Nolan was certainly the most outspoken member of the group. Other officers seemed jealous and resentful, perhaps because of his Hungarian Army education, possibly because he was an accomplished horseman and a published author of a book on cavalry remounts, or perhaps due to his extensive active service in India. Interestingly, this resentment did not extend to the rank and file who came in contact with him. They held him in high esteem as an officer; another reason Ian found him a good companion. They had been friends since Nolan's arrival at Varna, months ago.

Nolan was not an easy friend to have, as Ian found out quickly in the officers' mess at Varna. Resentment toward Nolan was exacerbated by his frequent unsolicited lectures on his favourite subjects, the general mishandling of cavalry mounts, and the tactical misuse of mounted troops. When not engaged in such tirades, he could be quite charming, socially.

After Capecci and Nolan came the group's own personal intelligence source, Captain Leicester Curzon. Curzon was a remarkably bright officer of the Rifle Brigade, and still wore their dashing green uniform with black trim. He was of medium height, with brown hair and eyes, and was rather ordinary looking. He was brought on the staff by special request, because of his well-known skills in organization and administration. Curzon was the assistant to Colonel Steele, His Lordship's Military Secretary. In that position, he was frequently privy to information shared by Lord Raglan only with the most senior of his staff officers and division commanders.

The most junior of the group of comrades was a gentle, circumspect little man who reminded Ian of a tough tree stump. Lieutenant Antoine Piccard's regiment was the Chasseurs d'Afrique. He was a French liaison officer, who spoke exceptional English, having spent many years in America. Piccard had short black hair and sported a narrow moustache, carefully pointed at each end, with the barest bristle of chin hair sticking out impertinently from under his lower lip. He dressed in by far the most colourful uniform in the group, that of the Chasseurs, a red kepi with light blue headband, a light blue waist-length jacket with black lacing down the front, and red pantaloon trousers.

Then, of course, there was Captain Ian David Carlyle, himself. Ian was of medium height, his ramrod posture making him look much taller. He had a delicate face, like his mother's, with the straight nose, high cheekbones, and strong chin of his deep highland roots. Having been brought up largely in London, he had only a trace of Scottish accent, unless he chose to charm or mock someone. At those times his brogue became as thick as porridge, a useful skill he could turn on or off like a water spigot.

Ian had dense sandy-brown hair, which appeared red in bright sunlight. The hair complemented fashionable side-whiskers. Ian's clear blue eyes, when focused, could soften the hardest heart. These same eyes could also turn to iron straight away, and cut through the resolve of most opponents in an instant, another useful skill.

Ian carried himself with the decisive and confident demeanour of a military officer. He wore this bearing like a badge of honour. This, like so many aspects of Ian's character, was his father's and Angus' influence. Ian was, after all, the second son of the Earl of Dunkairn. He was in the Crimea at the end of a long personal struggle, and wanted this war badly, to pursue his dreams of glory.

His personal motives aside, Ian was thus far totally unimpressed by the political logic of the war. In private, he often thought: *Matters not that the Russian army had already been beaten by the Turks at Silistria...withdrawn back within their own borders. Matters not that the situation had been stabilized. After all, our French allies and we are here, now, to fight a damned war. Wouldn't it be a terrible waste of such pretty armies to go home now? That wouldn't do at all. More to the point, the people of England and France wanted to see blood, and you certainly couldn't disappoint the people, especially if you were a politician in England today. It would put them in a right black dudgeon, wouldn't it?*

Ian's father, Lord Richard Carlyle, Earl of Dunkairn, a former Army officer, was now one of those same politicians. He could recall his father wearing the old scarlet and gold uniform of the Grenadier Company, 3rd Foot Guards, while Ian proudly held the gigantic black bearskin cap, nearly larger than he was. He'd beam, as he handed it to his father. He could still smell the stale musty odour of the soft fur. As far back as Ian could remember, he wanted no more from life than to wear that bearskin cap, and lead men in battle against the Queen's enemies. Games he played with his older brother, Peter, books he read as a child, endless fantasies and dreams, all focused on that vision.

His father, no longer the gallant soldier of Waterloo fame, had taken up his seat in the House of Lords before Ian was born. His Lordship was a strong-willed man, and, as Ian grew, the severe old Earl systematically shattered the young lad's vision of being a soldier as surely as if he slashed it into tiny bits with his long shiny sword.

He would lecture Ian constantly, "You think too much, boy. Will never do for an officer to worry on things. Gets in the way. Be thankful you have a brain. Use it. Follow your brother's example. Wipe this soldiering nonsense from your mind once and for all. It will not happen. Never, you hear me, boy, never."

Around his father's disapproval, Ian wrapped layers of uncertainty about his own self-worth. It was the horror of disappointing his father, disgracing the family, and an enormous fear of failing to live up to his own expectations of the perfect officer, leading the perfect soldiers. This dread was sometimes reinforced by vivid sweating nightmares in which he lay in a dark hole, curled up like a coward to avoid the blasts of war, or, even more devastating, leading a charge, sword in hand, screaming, "Who will follow me to glory!"...Only to look back and find no one was with him, alone, marked forever as an officer whom men would not follow.

Now, Ian was a soldier of the Queen, and an officer. Glory was within his grasp, if only he could prove himself.

Several nights after the landing, the five comrades were finishing a rather simple meal, relaxing around a small communal fire within their gathering of tents. The rain finally stopped. By the flickering light of the fire, Ian attempted to scribble a letter to his father, who had long since become exceedingly proud that his son decided to defy him and become an officer in his old regiment. Ian ended the letter:

...I would like to report our fine progress and a rush to glory, bands playing, flags unfurled, but nothing could be further from the dismal present reality.

Lord Raglan has worked tirelessly day and night, and it is through no fault of his we are still bogged down here where we landed. He is stymied at every turn, if not by the slowness of our French friends, then by an incompetent commissariat, an overwhelmed quartermaster, an ill prepared medical staff, or an apparent lack of interest in London.

We may march tomorrow, or the following day, but I do not hold out much hope. With God's kind help, we will prevail, and be at them soon enough.

I will post this in the morning, and try to make my letters in future more positive.

Your Most Loving Son,

Ian

"Ian, old man, what the devil are you about?" asked Nolan. The officers gathered around a fire were each in their own thoughts, watching the crackling sparks fly from the flames like fireflies, only to burn out forever a tick of time later.

"Just topping off a letter home, Lewis. Say, you wouldn't have a drop of that port you smuggled ashore?"

Curzon entered the light of the fire and interrupted, "It's tomorrow, gentlemen. We will march tomorrow."

Piccard laughed, "Oui, mon amis, and pigs fly. I fear we shall winter on this wretched beach. We've been here a week...it seems like a year, no?"

"Where is that port, Lewis, my dear friend. If we are about to die as the gallant and all-knowing Leicester Curzon suggests...we should have a salute." It was the major's slightly accented voice. He always kept them smiling.

"No, it's true. It's on. I was at the meeting," Curzon said. He was usually right, and there were mumbles and nods around the fire.

Nolan rummaged through his haversack, stopped abruptly, looked up, and smiled at the circle of friends. "I've enough for a dram for us all, if we're careful." He pulled out a small dark bottle, removed the cork, and passed it around the fire. Tin, pewter, and silver cups came clanking out from hidden accesses, faces brightened.

They drank in weary silence, watching the crackling fire.

Later, the port gone, and the fire having turned to a bed of coals, there was a round of quiet good nights, as each man drifted to his tent. With no wood to keep it burning through the night, it was left to crackle, pop, and die.

The camp became quiet. The exhausted officers fell asleep in their own thoughts, some dreading the dawn, others, like Ian, excited by its uncertainty. He watched the occasional travelling sparks make their jagged way, trying so very hard to stay alive. The thought came to him that on the morrow they all might be as these bright red dots...trying hard to stay alive.

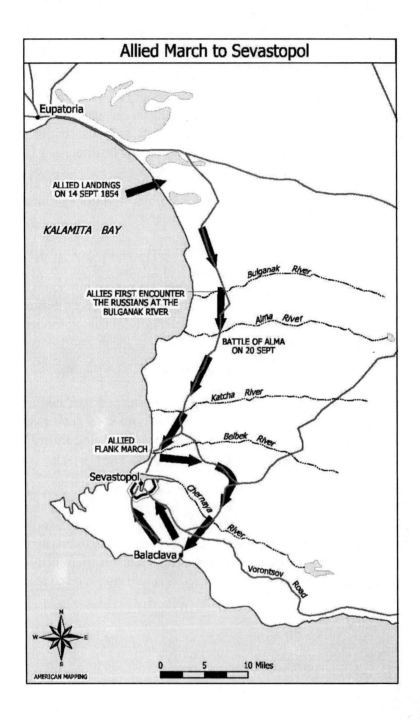

Allied March to Sevastopol

Eupatoria

ALLIED LANDINGS
ON 14 SEPT 1854

KALAMITA BAY

Bulganak River

ALLIES FIRST ENCOUNTER
THE RUSSIANS AT THE
BULGANAK RIVER

Alma River

BATTLE OF ALMA
ON 20 SEPT

Katcha River

Belbek River

ALLIED
FLANK MARCH

Sevastopol

Chernaya

River

Balaclava

Vorontsov Road

N W E S

AMERICAN MAPPING

0   5   10 Miles

Chapter 3

"Tea or coffee, sir," asked Angus, as Ian struggled out of his small tent, yawning and stretching, luxuriously. Reveille was to be sounded at 3 a.m. Lord Raglan's staff officers and clerks were being awakened an hour before that to prepare orders to the division commanders that the army was advancing.

"Coffee, I think."

"Sir, would you know what the day might bring?"

"The rain's stopped. We're drafting orders for the march. I'll take Packey to the front of the column or wherever Lord Raglan is riding. You should remain with Savage and the baggage train in the rear."

Angus was feeling a bit stiff this morning, but otherwise quite fit. He said, "Aye, sir, I'll put our kit on his back, since we've no carts. He won't mind."

"Good, I'll see you when the day's march is over. In the event I haven't mentioned it, Angus, it's very fine to have you with me, very fine indeed."

"Thank you, sir, now drink yer coffee, before it gets cold…uh…sir."

They marched off at 9 a.m., leaving a brigade of infantry and a detachment of the 4th Light Dragoons behind to clear the beach. They also had to tend to several hundred new cholera victims. The widespread cholera, which plagued the armies since their staging area at Varna, remained with them. To make matters worse, the army's tents, which finally arrived a few days after landing, were left behind for lack of transport, to be loaded back on the ships.

The French were on the allied forces right with 30,000 infantry and artillery. A Turkish force of around 9,000 was attached to them, with the combined allied fleet and the sea protecting their right flank. The French had been irritatingly ready to march well before the British. The British were inland on the left of the advance.

Lord Raglan feared a flank attack, and kept his infantry in a compact mass, two columns of infantry divisions with artillery to the right of each division, Rifles in advance and as rear guard. The cavalry, consisting at this time of only the Light Brigade, the "heavies" having not yet arrived, was dispersed to the far front, on the left flank and well in the rear. Behind the infantry columns came the army's meagre transport of equipment and stores in rickety country carts, pulled by bullocks or the small local horses, and a scruffy herd of cattle and sheep. Then came the civilians, some wives who drew lucky and accompanied regiments as laundresses and the like, wives of select officers with their servants, and the odd adventurous tradesman, photographer, journalist, or sutler.

The day began with the army's spirits high, bands playing gaily, flags flowing, men singing bawdy verses to the marching tunes. This lasted about an hour. The ground marched over was flat, smooth, covered in grassy scrub, and exposed to the sun, without a jot of shade to be found anywhere. The heat moved from tolerably hot, to intolerable, to unbearable, as the morning sun rose higher.

One at a time, within an hour or so, the bands ceased playing. The marching men, drenched in sweat, began gasping for any bit of air. They began discarding shakoes, bearskins, bonnets, and even greatcoats and blankets. They would miss the headgear. As awkward and hot as the shakoes were, they were protection from the blazing sun. With quartermaster stores a mess, they would sorely miss the greatcoats and blankets in the cold nights and freezing weather ahead.

Stragglers appeared in growing numbers. Then it began...slowly at first. A man would be talking to a mate, or drinking from a canteen, go suddenly quiet, a drawn look coming over him. Then a bluish tinge would appear around the lips, throat choking with vomit, face blackening. He'd fall by the side, crying for water, his mates whispering, "Cholera...it's the cholera." They'd fear to help him, to touch him. He'd be dead in three or four hours.

Even this was not the most insufferable hardship for these sweat-soaked men. It was the thirst they found intolerable. Most had been unable to get sufficient water for days. Wells dug at the beach gave up only brackish water. Water discovered as they marched proved undrinkable. Extended deprivation made the men confused and delirious, causing ordinarily strong soldiers to drop in their tracks. The army couldn't travel for more than half an hour without halting. Resuming the march became increasingly difficult as time passed.

Ian was in his place with Lord Raglan's staff behind the advance guard, at the head of the infantry columns. They were moving south toward Sevastopol. It was close to one p.m., the sun sweltering hot. By this time Ian was leading Packey, girth loosened. He gave him as much of his own water as he could, a bit at a time, pouring it from the canteen into his forage cap for the sweating horse to drink. Packey looked right done in. Ian pinched the horse's skin, and by its slowness in smoothing out knew the animal was dehydrating, needed more water. He didn't have it to give.

He spoke softly to Major Capecci, walking his own horse, "Antonio, this march is destroying us. There's a report that men are even discarding their weapons. How much farther do you think?"

"I shouldn't think too far, at least to the river we saw on the map, the Bulganak."

Ian started to say something further, when a horse pulled up next to him. The rider was leaning down to speak with him. Ian looked up. With the blazing sun in his eyes he could barely make out Lieutenant Piccard.

Ian said, "Antoine, what is it?"

"Pardon, Captain Carlyle, I didn't know if you'd been told."

"Told what, Antoine? What is it?"

"Your man, your servant."

"MacLean, yes. What about him?"

"He's down, mon ami. Fell to the ground, without so much as a whimper. I was riding next to where he marched, saw him weave a bit, then fall like the stone. One of the bandsmen was tending him when I left."

Ian froze. He could barely think, *not Angus, surely not. He's a rock. Must get to him quickly.*

Major Capecci overheard Piccard's words about MacLean. He at once moved to Ian's side and began tightening Packey's girth straps. Capecci said, softly, "Go, Ian, see to him. Go my friend. I'll make your apologies to His Lordship."

Ian snapped back quickly, was on Packey the next instant, and away, as Capecci and Piccard watched. Piccard said, "It is the cholera, Major. It has taken so many of my own countrymen. I recognized it at once."

The major said, "That's a great pity, Antoine. Those two, they are very close."

Ian pushed Packey as much as he dared toward the rear of the column. He spotted the gaudy silver and red jacket of a bandsman, saw Angus on the ground, his head held up by the very young musician.

No! Not Angus. He's strong. Always been there…for me…for Peter. Will always be there. Ian's heart was pounding, stabbed by pain…as he rode closer, now at a gallop, his head filled with a thousand memories from his childhood.

Chapter 4

Ian and his brother Peter were raised between their Dunkairn estate and London, where the Earl sat in Parliament. Angus saw to their every need and their worldly education, while Lady Harriett, their quiet, loving mother, saw to their more formal education through various tutors. Lady Harriett loved Angus, but was always admonishing him not to teach the boys the ways of violence, fighting and such. The Earl wisely remained silent on this subject, deferring to his wife.

Ultimately, Lady Harriett made Angus, who could never refuse her anything, take a blood oath on it. She would tell the boys, "Use your minds, not your fists. Be careful, and always remember you are gentlemen. Above all, remember that the answer to a difficulty is never violence, never."

This philosophy was fine with the quiet, intellectual Peter, but did not sit well at all with the wilder Ian. Angus merely held his own council, but, as a prideful highlander, kept to his oath to Her Ladyship.

Ian's awakening to the real world came at Eton College, where he arrived at age eleven, two years after his brother, Peter.

Peter was worried about his younger brother. That wild streak would be trouble. It wasn't easy getting along at Eton.

In the past few years he'd certainly had his share of problems. Now Ian had come, all wide-eyed and hopeful.

"That was heavy," Peter said. He was winded after they'd dragged Ian's huge trunk from the coach stop to the rooms at Dame Vallencey's lodging house along Baldwin's Shore, near Eton High Street.

Ian hardly listened, as he looked with wonder around the rooms they'd now be sharing for the next several years. He saw a common room with a fireplace, two desks, and a table where he imagined they would eat and talk of weighty things on into the night. Two tiny bedrooms sandwiched the common room like neat little bookends, each containing only a bed, not much wider than Ian himself, a small closet, a chest of drawers, a mirror, and a washbasin. The "facilities," shared by thirty other boys, were in the yard outside.

Spartan as the rooms were, Ian was beside himself with joy, "Marvellous, Peter, bloody marvellous."

"Ian, we must have a chat, old boy. You need to know the rules around here. Better we do it right off."

"Good. Let's do, while I sort out my things." He opened the trunk and began moving odd bits of clothing into the modest closet in the empty bedroom.

Peter was annoyed. This was serious and important. It upset him that Ian would be moving about while he listened, as usual doing two things at once. It was so like Ian, that it soon made Peter laugh at his own annoyance. This was one of the many things he loved about his brother.

Peter began, "Ian, the knowledge you can acquire here will serve you well. You must listen and learn, my dear brother, listen and learn." Although moving about, Ian was, in fact, listening intently. He adored and respected his older brother, thought he was the most intelligent person on earth.

Peter Carlyle was tall, bony, and looked like he hadn't had a nourishing meal in weeks. His clothes always appeared to be hanging from his body, as though if he stood rigid-straight and shook himself, they might fall off in a heap at his feet. Peter was the eldest son of the Earl of Dunkairn. He accepted his birthright as heir to his father's Earldom without pretension or care, distaining the courtesy title of Viscount.

Peter's mind was excellent, a true scholar, but his knowledge came exclusively from books, not experience. He read voraciously, and collected that knowledge like a miser collects coin. Like the miser, it was indeed a massive accumulation, but very little would ever be spent. There was not much risk, and no adventure in Peter's life or future. He was content to hoard the knowledge, while folding himself in the family name and all that went with it.

Peter stayed close to Dunkairn Hall as they grew, while Ian preferred to journey off, casting about nervously for his next quest. He explored everything with a feline-like curiosity, was always into some mischief or other. Ian had escapades, and Peter lived them vicariously through him, sharing Ian's audacious deeds only in spirit. He was constantly asking Ian to describe his adventures.

Whether it was throwing stones at the old Baron's windows down the road, or stealing fruit from the Vicar's trees, Ian took great pleasure in telling Peter these tales of derring-do in the most excruciating particularity. They would often talk in shouts, as they rode their father's horses across the moors that abounded at Dunkairn, Ian always wanting to ride faster, Peter always trying to slow him down.

In their rooms at Eton, Ian's reply to Peter's plea to listen and learn was typically arrogant, "Peter, you know this isn't what I wanted, but the Earl would have it no other way. I'll do my best. If I must be a scholar, I'll be the best damned scholar there ever was, and you can count on that, dear brother."

Peter laughed again, "That's the spirit I expected, right enough, but you now reside in Dame Vallencey's house, and senior boys run the houses where Oppidan students live, especially this house."

Ian carelessly tossed his black beaver top hat on his bed, and continued unpacking. He said, "Oppidan?"

"Students not selected as King's Scholars. You and me, whose parents pay their way and who live outside the college grounds."

"Where do the 'scholars' live, then? What do they pay?" Ian hung his one black frock coat and trousers in the closet, as Peter watched, becoming impatient.

"They have rooms within the college, pay nothing. Ian...stop interrupting and listen to me, it's important."

"Sorry, Peter, do go on."

"The Dame is away most nights. I suspect she drinks, and who knows what else. She won't dally close to here for fear of running into someone who knows her, so she travels to nearby towns. The senior boy, as the house captain, runs things around here. Name's Fairbain...a real swine...but he's cock-o'-the-roost within these walls. That's certain."

"Wait, you mean the schoolmasters don't run the school?" Ian paused, then carefully placed two stiff white linen undershirts in a drawer, and went back to the trunk for more.

"The Head Master and the others are in charge in the school and classrooms, but not so much out here, off the grounds. That's my bloody point, Ian. There are traditions. Many fall heavily on the younger lads like you. You must accept these things and get along."

Ian nodded pensively, said nothing, but stopped abruptly after putting two black neck scarves in a drawer. He plopped down in a chair across the table from Peter.

Peter, pleased to at last have his attention, said, "Damn it, Ian, I know your temper. You'll lash out at the first bugger who offends your sense of honour or fair play. Obey the rules, obey the house captains, or you'll be severely punished, flogged, I dare say…worse, you'll embarrass me, father, and the family name."

Peter had perked Ian's intense interest. He knew Ian too well.

"Ian, you must above all else understand the 'fag system.' New boys, serving senior boys," Peter paused.

Ian's eyes narrowed, perceptibly.

Peter continued, "Small things, really, tending to their needs, fetching fuel, making beds, cooking, serving meals, and the like. Don't do as I did. I fought the system. It got me absolutely nowhere, and was a complete distraction from my studies."

Peter waited impatiently for Ian's response, but there was none.

"I became an outcast. I still am. Best to merely go along. It only lasts till you're in Upper School, then you can be a 'fag master,' and have your own servants. You see?"

Ian snapped back in disgust, "I see I'm not going to do well with this lot."

"Yes, that's my worry. You must get on. I've already done enough damage by fighting it. Made myself the perfect target for the bullies that abound, and they are plentiful, right enough.

"I'm asking you, Ian. Control your anger and your pride. Play along for both our sakes, and for the family name. What you can learn here far outweighs any of this rot. Besides, our own father went through this same thing years ago. For that matter, so did Sir Arthur Wellesley, the Duke of Wellington, himself."

Ian cared little what the Duke went through, and found it a tough proposition imagining the Earl of Dunkairn being someone's "fag." He thought about it, as Peter looked at him, anxiously.

"All right, Peter, relax, I'll do my very best. I'll play silly buggers with them if I must. I won't like it, but I won't embarrass you, father, the family, or the school."

Peter sighed, unconvinced.

Chapter 5

As Ian laboured with his classes and his future, he developed an interesting hypothesis. Peter always thought Ian created this concept because he wanted justification for not following his dream of becoming a soldier, other than merely respect for his father's wishes. Ian explained his theory to Peter over and over, fleshing it out each time he told it. He honed the concept to a fine sharpness.

On many cold nights, warmed by their fire, Ian would stand before Peter, tall as he could, right hand placed just so on his chest, clasping his robe's collar, every inch the profound thinker. Looking off into space, he'd begin, "You see, Peter, it's my belief that the really big cats, lions, tigers, leopards, and such, are simple, pure creatures. I rather envy them that. They sleep, eat, reproduce, and when in peril, they fight like the very devil, or take flight in order to survive. When necessary they kill, without hesitation.

"Within each of us there should be such a beast, a leopard-like creature, poised, ready to strike." Ian read stories in the Eton library about the leopard's prowess, written by worldly explorers of dangerous and mysterious places, like Africa. He relished the journals and wondrous drawings of

Scotsmen like James Bruce and Mongo Parks. Thus, he embraced their powerful image of the big cat in his theory.

"This giant cat only asserts itself when anger or terror or some other primitive emotion overpowers our reason," Ian would say.

"Then our cat-brain is called forth and takes command. We either flare back in a rage, like the leopard springing and striking from its hiding place, or we flee to survive, the leopard carrying us with it to some safe haven. Should inflicting pain or killing be required to get through...so be it."

He'd pause for effect.

Peter would say, "Mother would certainly disapprove. Ian, I see the concept, but what's this to do with your decision not to become a soldier?"

"Everything. It has everything to do with it, don't you see? The ideal soldier, the one I'd have to be, just to please father, could, would, and absolutely should live by these sorts of instinctive urges like eating, sleeping, the odd tumble with a lady. More important, though – fighting, withdrawing where prudent, killing where necessary...I think too much, Peter, as father says. I have an uncommon thirst to know all there is to know about all things...all the answers – the 'hows' and the 'whys' of everything."

Ian would stop to think it out more clearly before continuing. Peter would wait.

"I don't see this leopard inside me, I really don't. I can't react instinctively like that. I would question, and give an enemy time to react. I'd be getting men killed by my damned hesitation...my men. No. Father is right, as usual. I could never be that sort of unquestioning soldier, dedicated to duty and obedience, acting on pure instinct alone."

Peter accepted the logic, but was sad for his brother. He didn't see Ian as Ian saw himself. Peter saw the wildness, saw the leopard, but could do little to convince his brother that he was wrong, that he should follow his dream.

Chapter 6

For the two brothers, the next years at Eton were filled with acquiring knowledge of the highest order. To Peter's surprise, Ian even managed to live with the fagging system and the hazing of new boys.

The times the two boys were at home on holidays made any problems at school more tolerable. They spent the halves with their parents, Angus, the horses, and the familiar hills of Dunkairn. These were times of laughter and warmth, but there was trouble ahead, building in intensity.

Whether or not Peter accepted it, his father had ensured that Peter's written title in the Eton records was Viscount, as the eldest son and heir to the Earldom. There were other nobility at the school, of course, but they assimilated readily into the college culture by excelling in football, cricket, water sports, and the like. Peter was frail, not a sportsman at all. He spent his time at his studies, shunned social and sporting activities, fought the fagging system, and was seen as an anti-social recluse.

Peter's refusal to fag for the senior boys in his early years was considered very bad form, a slap in the face of school tradition. Peter stoically accepted his classmate's occasional insults, abuse, blanket tosses, and other bullying, maintaining his refusal to be anyone's "fag." However, dealing with these situations did take much energy away from his scholastic pursuits. Ultimately, their taunts and abuse overwhelmed him. A day came when he succumbed, agreed to do their bidding, just so that he could concentrate on his studies.

Unlike his brother, Ian was naturally agile. After settling in at Eton, he quickly learned to love the competitive sports. He became an undeniable scrapper in the Eton Field Game, and most any sport he tried. This gave him an acceptance, which eluded his older brother.

On the other hand, Ian was seen to spend countless hours alone with Peter in their rooms, talking and pouring over books. This placed him squarely alongside his brother in the sights of the unsavoury element in the college and within their own house. The enemies Peter acquired over the years now began to focus their venom on Ian, as well.

As in most public schools, there were toughs at Eton who took advantage of the way things were done and forced others to follow like sheep in taunting their weaker or less assertive Lower School classmates. The ruling bully, and the head fag master, as well, was a senior boy named Roger Fairbain. Peter had warned Ian about him.

It is a tremendous asset when a bully is big enough to intimidate by size alone. Being both tall and exceedingly wide (no one would dare call him fat, even in secret), you could easily describe Fairbain as formidable. He used his size like a giant hammer to club and cower all that crossed him by the sheer menace of his presence.

Fairbain's face wore a perpetual mask of meanness, which he had perfected over the years by practicing diligently before a mirror. He had straight, dark, stringy hair, which fell over one eye, giving him a sinister, almost piratical appearance. His collar was always askew, his clothing dishevelled. In contrast, his shoes were immaculately shined. So much so, that it was sometimes difficult to take one's eyes off them. This brilliant shine was the result of hours of polishing by Fairbain's fags. He saw to it that every student at the school knew exactly why they gleamed so.

To add to his power, he was acknowledged by Mister H. Angelo, a small nimble Italian, and Eton's renowned fencing master, as his most promising pupil. Mister Angelo used Fairbain as an assistant fencing instructor for slower students. Even he was astounded by the large heavy man's speed and dexterity with a foil.

Those classmates Fairbain could not intimidate by his size and bluster, he certainly could coerce with his fencing prowess. It was his habit when disobeyed to have a Lower School boy held while he expertly carved a tiny set of his initials, RF, in the lad's rump with the bare point of a foil.

Like many of the young gentlemen at Eton, Fairbain's family had money through industrial and mercantile investments. Although wealthy, his family was not of the aristocracy, as was Lord Dunkairn and his offspring, gentlemen by right of birth. Fairbain's father would never attain that exalted status, no matter how affluent he became, and Fairbain knew it too well. This was the breeding ground for the jealousy and pure venom, which consumed him. He had grown to despise anyone who was in any way connected to real nobility.

With his common background, it was unusual that he gained the power he had in the school, but understandable when his size was considered. There was no one who chose to oppose his tyrannical influence. He would say to his toadies, "We must put these awistocwatic bastards in their place." Fairbain spoke with that odd deliberate speech pattern of softening some letters, like "r" into a "w."

Soon after Fairbain established residence with Dame Vallencey several years ago, he discovered her secret life and love of whiskey. He began following the Dame on her nightly visits to various out of the way public houses and other questionable establishments. He was then able to use this information, which could ruin her with the college fellows if brought to light, as power over the Dame. Fairbain could get just about anything he wanted from her, and did.

Fairbain's chief toady, fag master of many Lower School boys in the Dame's house, was a chubby, ferret-faced, spineless boy named James Smyth-Foster, who made certain that Peter, and later Ian, received more than the usual share of taunting and hazing. Ian became a fag for Smyth-Foster, who tormented him relentlessly, under Fairbain's tutelage. Nothing in their early training prepared the boys for the terrible savagery coming their way.

Chapter 7

They came in the dark of night. "Get the little bastard. Quickly now." Shocked by the ferocity of the attack, Ian was unable to cry out. They slithered into his bedroom at two in the morning, wrapped him in a sheet, and carried him off.

The huge house was nearly deserted. Most of the students were home on holiday. Peter and Ian decided to remain behind a day or so to catch up on their studies with their tutor, and were soundly sleeping in their rooms. Dame Vallencey had also gone on holiday.

As they dumped him on an unyielding dirt floor, he heard muted sounds, like pleas for help, and knew he was not the only victim this night.

A chill crept through him, like ice-cold water moving slowly over flat rocks, as he recognized the muffled cries of the other victim. It was Peter. Something was very wrong. Peter was now a senior boy himself, and should have been well beyond hazing and school pranks. He began to be afraid.

His head was still covered, but he heard a familiar voice order, "Wemove the sheet."

Rough hands tore the sheet away, and Ian found himself on the floor, staring at a pair of large shoes, their shine reflecting even in the low flickering candlelight within the room. Ian looked up as best he could to see five shadowy creatures circling around him. Peter was on the floor nearby in another sheet, tied around several times with sturdy rope, crying softly inside his white cocoon.

As the creatures above him moved in and out of the scant light, he saw both Roger Fairbain and Smyth-Foster. He didn't know the other three by name, but their faces were now stone masks inside his head.

Peter's whimpers came from within the bound bundle. He feared the frail, withdrawn Peter had already given up. Ian needed to protect his older, but more fragile brother.

With great effort, Ian staggered to his feet, calculating odds. He recognized the room, knew it was in the deep cellar of the house. He doubted a cry for help would do any good from this inner sanctum. More to gain time than by any plan, he shouted at Fairbain, "What do you want?" He choked back the urge to add, *You fat bastard.*

Fairbain and the others said nothing in reply, still circling around Peter and Ian, chanting mumbled unintelligible phrases. It was like some ghastly religious ritual.

Ian thought about his options…*I could fight or somehow run. Peter will be of no help. We don't know much about fighting, anyway. Running for help won't do, either. While they're circling there's always one or two between me and that door. Peter surely can't run, and I won't leave him, even to go for assistance.*

Then, calmer, he thought of what his mother had said a thousand times, "Use your wits, Ian, be careful, and always remember you're a gentleman. The answer to a difficulty is never violence, in spite of what your father or Angus might have told you."

Aye, that's the very thing, by God; I'll use my wits and talk us both out of this mess. This was his last deliberate thought before being struck down with a heavy blow from behind. No talking, no reasoning, no negotiating, just mindless vicious force applied instantly.

Dazed, but not destroyed, Ian clenched his fists and flailed out at his assailants in all directions, hit nothing. He was struck repeatedly until he fell, first to his knees, then to the floor, senseless.

He tried to talk...get up on his feet...felt kicks to his stomach...fragmented thoughts. *Wasn't supposed to be this way...Mother...Angus...should be able to reason through it. Get clear...but they're so...violent.*

Dizziness, nausea, pain, tiny spots of brightness in the murky sinister void closing in...*What did mother say? Violence...is...never...the...answer.* Then a shroud of blackness oozed over his confusion.

At some point later, through the dark thickness and the pain, he heard Fairbain say, "Bind his hands behind, and blindfold the little bastard...quickly now, chapies. Haven't got all night."

As his minions roughly obeyed their master, he felt only sickening terror. He could not make his arms or legs move to escape them, to flee. He was soon helpless. The black spread over him again, heavier this time, like syrup, a sweet, sticky, dark thing, yet a release from the pain.

Peter. Peter, I think I've fallen. I'm under my horse. Get him off me. Help me, Peter. Where are you? It hurts so much. Then it came back, hitting him brutally as he remembered. *We aren't in the fields. There are no horses. Peter is here, but in trouble somehow. The pain is real, from having been beaten and kicked. I'm lying face down on the floor – not at Dunkairn.*

Ian felt the sharp numbness of stomach-tightening terror grip him, vice-like. It was fear over what had happened, and what was about to happen. His eyes were covered, mouth gagged, ankles and wrists bound, unyielding. He tasted the metallic bitterness of his own blood, smelled it, mixed with the cutting odour of decaying earth. Ian could feel the dirt and tiny stones jabbing his skin. He heard shuffling, felt movement in the room. More panic. *What's happening now?*

Then Fairbain's peculiar voice said, "So, you puny fag, you think you're better than the west of us? Well, let's just see what sort of man you weally are."

Ian was still. No one came to him or touched him. He made the connection. Fairbain was talking to Peter, not to him, but he could no longer hear Peter making those sounds. This frightened him more. He was shaking uncontrollably. His movements drew Fairbain's attention.

"Wait," he said. "Take the blindfold off that little bastard. He should see his arrogant bwother's shame, and his own fate."

Ian's blindfold was torn off. He was struck dumb by the spectacle before him. The attackers were in a circle around his brother. They obligingly opened the circle so that Ian could see from the floor.

Peter, naked, was being forced to his knees, struggling feebly. Fairbain was standing in front of him, feet apart, trousers around his ankles, a fencing foil held carelessly in his right hand. There was no protector on the point, making it quite deadly. Fairbain toyed with the foil, jabbing it offhandedly into Peter's chest, causing tiny painful cuts.

Peter's eyes glazed over in terrified disbelief, as he was pushed forward. He uttered small sounds as the foil pierced his skin, over and over. Fairbain visibly savoured the pain he was causing. He flicked the foil several times, deftly engraving two letters, "RF," at least two inches high into Peter's bleeding chest.

42

Peter pleaded with his captors, "Please, no more." Fairbain cupped his left ear, leaned down to Peter, said, "What say, old fella, can't quite make you out. Do twy to speak up. Won't do to mumble." Then he giggled, an odd high-pitched malicious giggle, almost a cackle.

Fairbain paused, apparently for effect, to heighten the terror of the moment. He succeeded. He said slowly and carefully, "Wight. Pull his head back by the hair, and you...open his mouth, fowce it open."

Peter looked as though sanity was deserting him. He tried to scream. It came out a muffled choking sound. Ian would never forget that sound. He shut his eyes as tight as he was able, but it was too late. The scene was seared on his brain, as though with a scalding iron, forever.

Ian heard the insane mocking laughter of their tormentors, as he struggled with his bonds...no use. He opened his eyes, and saw the evil smile on Fairbain's face. He felt gorge rising from deep in his stomach.

Chapter 8

Perhaps it was triggered by Fairbain's insane laughter, perhaps the malevolent smile, or it may well have been the awful gurgling, choking sounds Peter was making. Ian never knew where it came from or why. He didn't know if it was good, or evil, but at the time, he didn't care. He had somehow summoned it, willed it to come to him. It was no accident.

It moved through him, gradually at first, scaring him. It felt like a burning iron fist was curling around him, some mythical giant's huge hand – closing. He may have willed it to come forth, but he was captured by it, as well.

He no longer felt disgust or humiliation. He felt only an infinite all-consuming, ever-growing anger in the pit of his soul. Was this the beast rising? *It is in me after all. I feel it. I can feel it.*

As his anger became a release from the pain of what he saw, Ian transformed himself in his mind into the leopard being, felt the tall wet grass around him, lying unseen, intently staring at his prey. He could feel the muscles of the beast inside him, now his muscles, as they rippled, burning while the anger grew.

The next few minutes passed like hours. *My life is changing. I will never know more of childhood than what I have already known. From this day, everything is different. I will move past this, bring Peter past this. Then it will be my turn.*

He knew it now. He could survive. He knew he could do what had to be done, knew with cold certainty that nothing the gods could throw at him could be worse than this...and, he would conquer this. Through the mind-numbing pain, there was an absolute freedom he had never felt before.

Fairbain was laughing at Peter. The other four began beating and kicking Peter to the floor, each taking his turn. They left him lying helplessly bound face down, whimpering, in a pool of his own blood. Ian watched, holding back tears for Peter and suppressing his mounting anger with a massive effort.

Their attention deliberately refocused toward Ian. They were about to begin the taunting game with him when Fairbain noticed something was wrong. He made the mistake of looking into Ian's eyes.

Fairbain pulled back, brusquely. He didn't see the expected fear, or the terror he so relished in his past victims. He did see the cold deadly eyes of the beast, unblinking, burning a hole through him, as though through the tall grass, hungry.

The others began uncomfortably shuffling their feet. They saw it too. Fairbain said, "Bastard," then flicked the foil at Ian's face, leaving a deep, inch-long cut below his left eye, a blood-red tear.

The eyes that responded to the cutting were animal fierce and unflinching. They seemed to reach down into Fairbain's stomach, and twist his insides.

Fear was reversed. They wouldn't have been able to explain it, but they felt it pulling at them, urging them to leave, quickly, before it was somehow too late, before it devoured them. They began to mumble in false bravado about having had their fun, and drifted out of the room.

Ian watched it work, intellectually fascinated by the power he felt within. He was defining the beast, the big cat, the leopard. He didn't understand it yet, but it was coming. It was an inner strength that allowed him to overcome the immediate horrors, harden to them, and prevail at any cost. Was this the warrior's spirit he thought for so long he was lacking?

He wasn't analyzing the situation, or dissecting it. What Ian most wanted to be at this moment was an instrument of destruction, of retribution, pure, simple. He wanted to fight, not flee, and he wanted so very badly to kill. It wasn't an intellectual process – it was a passion.

No, he thought, *not now.* With an intuition born of a thousand years of highland blood, he knew that this was not the time. *Patience. Must wait. It'll be worth the wait. It is so hard to do nothing...so hard, but Peter and I will survive. These five men are doomed. They will pay beyond their wildest imagination for what they did this night.*

Chapter 9

Left alone in the cellar at Dame Vallencey's house, Ian worked free of his bonds and went to his brother. Peter was lying motionless, eyes open, staring at the floor as though an infinity away.

Ian suspected that the bruises from the blows and kicks, and the cuts from the fencing foil were not that serious, only the carved initials would leave a physical scar on Peter to remind him of the incident forever. Ian's real concern was for Peter's mind. It was that distant sightless stare. Ian wept softly, and placed the sheet over Peter's naked form.

Peter looked up only once, still unfocused, sobbed in anguish, "Ian, you saw. You saw it all. I am so ashamed, so sorry."

Peter gazed off at some unknown object, stunned numb within his shattered world. Ian spent hours on the dirt cellar floor holding his brother, soothing him with gentle words.

As dawn approached, Ian guided Peter like a ghost up the stairs and back to their rooms, "Come along, Peter, we have to clean a bit." Peter rose unsteadily, moved mechanically wherever Ian pointed or placed him.

Ian used an unsoiled bed sheet to make bandages for Peter's cuts and basin water to cleanse the bruises. He laid Peter in bed in a fresh nightshirt, his touch tender, tears tasting of salt. He smoothed his brother's hair. When he was certain Peter had drifted into a restless sleep, Ian curled up on the floor beside the bed where Peter lay. His own bed, only a room away, seemed too far from Peter's side.

A fortnight later, during the early morning hours, Peter packed his belongings and left Eton College, unnoticed by anyone, including Ian. He found a train north, toward Scotland, toward their beloved Dunkairn. He would never leave there again.

A note was on the table in their common room:

My Dearest Brother,

I am so very sorry. I cannot bear to talk to you. My shame is too much. I shall not stay here any longer. I must go home. I was never as strong as you. You must now be the man for both of us. It was my duty to protect you. Forgive me for failing you.

I love you,

Peter

Ian cried. It was too late to stop him, even if he'd wanted to. He felt he must let Peter fight his demons his own way, but he immediately wrote Angus MacLean a long letter. He didn't spell out the grotesque details of the incident, describing it as "an embarrassing hazing by fellow students, which effected Peter very strongly." Ian also failed to mention that he was there, badly beaten himself, and forced to watch. He told Angus that Peter would need all his wonderful skills to build back in him strength of purpose and a will to carry on.

Ian had to face his own demons, and his future, but he was like the leopard now, quick, gaining confidence, stronger each minute, each hour, each day. With the fading of his childhood trepidations came the recognition that this inner strength was indeed the spirit of his destiny, a spirit that drives men, guides them through danger, and he possessed it. His intellect wasn't in his way; it was showing him the way. Ian determined to act: *By damn, I'll be a soldier. I'll lead men against the Queen's enemies, and to bloody hell with anyone who tries to stop me. I'll use my intellect to advantage, to become the best of all possible officers. I swear it.*

Ian welcomed his new freedom, but there were many matters needing attention before he could truly set out to fulfil his dream. He must complete his studies, for the family's sake, and there were scores to settle, for both him and his brother. He couldn't move forward until this was achieved. This was now part of his destiny. What he wanted, simply, was revenge. *And I will have it, by God. For Peter and all the victims. I will have it.*

Chapter 10

The secrecy behind Peter's return home alone in mid term intensified when he announced at dinner the first night, "Father, Mother, I've something to tell you both. I'm done with formal schools. I'll not return to Eton, and I'll not be going to Cambridge. I'm almost eighteen and old enough to make my own decisions, and that's my final word."

They were in shock. Even his father was speechless. He composed himself, said, "Damned odd, Peter, damned odd."

Peter must have thought then of all the plans his parents had for him, because he added, "I know this is a fierce disappointment to the both of you, but I hope you'll come to accept it."

His Lordship said, "What the devil's going on, boy?" This was the reserved son, the one who was never any trouble, not like his wild brother. They'd have expected this from Ian.

Peter would tell them no more. His father and Lady Harriett were perplexed at this sudden departure from their grand design for the eldest son. They ultimately credited Peter's abrupt change and subsequent mood swings to a growing phase. They decided he would come to his senses eventually. There was time for him to go on to university. Cambridge would still be there. He merely needed time, a rest.

Angus knew better. *Peter is never going to attend university. There's something bad wrong, and I must find out. Aye, I must.*

Angus received Ian's hastily written first letter, but accepted its contents with reservations. With Peter's strange behaviour, he realized that this was far worse than a mere "hazing" by fellow students. Peter had either leaped the fence of sanity forever, or the road back from whatever strange and lonely place he was in would be long and painful.

Angus then received a second letter from Ian, with no further mention of the hazing incident. Ian asked news of Peter, then told Angus of his plans to pursue his dream of soldiering, and gain a commission in the Scots Fusilier Guards, the new name of the 3rd Foot Guards, his father's old regiment. Ian asked Angus to recommend the best way for him to learn the skills of a soldier while he was continuing his formal education in the classics at Eton.

Angus was not taken in by the blandness of Ian's written words. He was too clever a Scotsman not to put Ian's change of direction and Peter's abrupt homecoming together. *I know Ian too well. Whatever other reasons he has for deciding on the military, there is a connection to Peter's condition. Aye, Ian's a shrewd lad, and he's going about this cautiously, but I smell something in the air. I need to find out the truth of what happened to Peter.*

Late one night, several weeks after Peter came home, Angus was making rounds within the manor house to be sure all was snug and safe. In passing Peter's bedroom, he heard a piercing cry of pure anguish, and the sounds of crashing furniture.

Fearing there was an attacker of some sort, Angus rushed into Peter's room. He found the room a shambles, and Peter, alone, raising a chair over his head, apparently to throw it at a mirror. Peter froze on seeing Angus. He dropped the chair, broke down in tears, collapsing to the floor. Angus went to him, touched his shoulder gently, and waited for him to collect himself.

It all came out. The years of taunting and humiliation at the hands of Roger Fairbain poured out of Peter like a toy wooden boat in a rushing stream. He described every detail of the constant ridicule and harassment, day after day. When it came to the incident itself, Peter was forthright and accurate, to a fault.

On Angus' face were huge great tears, and the enormous heart of the tough old highlander was breaking. Peter said, "Ian was forced to watch the whole thing, Angus. I'm so ashamed. I was supposed to be the older brother, protecting him. In the end, I think he protected me."

Angus began to talk, his soft gentle Scottish brogue soothing Peter's anguish, some English, some Gaelic. Peter cried for hours letting it all surface. Angus was patient and constant, guiding him through his pain.

Peter fell into a deep sleep. Angus tenderly placed him in bed. He sat by Peter most of the following day while he slept.

At first Peter remained too ashamed to communicate with Ian directly, but often asked Angus for news of him. Angus told him of Ian's change of heart, and the secret, that he was going to become an officer after all. Peter was more pleased with that turn of events than anything that had occurred since that horrible night.

Eventually, Peter began to emerge from his self-imposed prison. He began to help his father with correspondence, took part in the daily affairs of managing the estates, and from time to time attended one of Lady Harriett's endless social occasions at Dunkairn. He would never be the old

Peter, but the new one was slowly materializing, with Angus' wise and gentle assistance, and the patience, if not understanding, of both his father and mother.

Ian received Angus' letters describing Peter's progress with much joy. He and Peter began corresponding from time to time. It seemed an unwritten understanding, as only close brothers might have, that the incident was never mentioned.

Angus knew what he now must do for his "wee bairn." *Ian is the strong one all right. It's not just for his future that he'll be learning the skills of fighting. Ian's blood is up. He's seeking justice, an affair of honour. He must settle the score on those bastards who devastated his brother, and, by God, I'll help him, somehow.* Angus had a plan, which had been waiting for just this occasion. He needed to find an old friend from his warrior days, a man he could trust with a most important mission.

Chapter 11

Ian was walking to his house down Baldwin's Shore, coming from a class, absorbed in thought. It was several months after the incident. He spotted a smallish man, clothes of a workman, walking toward him in the opposite direction. As he came closer, Ian was somehow taken by his style. He seemed stocky, but without fat. Under his loose clothing, Ian thought he detected compact shoulders and an overall tautness. He could see the man's thick tightly corded neck. There was something familiar about the way he walked. It reminded him of Angus and his father, the purposeful smooth stride of a military man, a bundle of energy waiting to explode.

The man wore a leather cap at a jaunty angle, rather shabby yellowish wool trousers, and a weathered green corduroy coat. A brightly coloured scarf was tied loosely around his neck, over a rough-hewn reddish undershirt, open at the collar. Ian saw no hair under the cap. He assumed the man either shaved his head or was bald. He also wore a huge sly engaging smile. Ian thought: *The best way to describe this man would be "a cocky little bastard."*

As they closed upon one another, the man came to a halt directly in Ian's path, forcing him to stop. He stared up at Ian, asked, "Would ye be the young master, Ian Carlyle?"

"Who's asking?" *An Irishman*, Ian thought.

"Billy Murphy's my name, and proud I am to meet ya Master Ian. I'm a friend of Angus MacLean."

"Angus?"

"He saved my worthless hide a time or two, in another life. He sends his regards and asks ya to be kind enough to spare a few moments, private-like, where we might talk, man to man."

Angus hadn't immediately replied to Ian's written appeal for help, but if Angus sent this man, there was good reason. He didn't want to take him to his rooms, too many curious classmates. Ian made the mistake of choosing a small seedy back street public house, down off Eton High Street near the bridge. This place was frequented exclusively by local toughs and labourers. Students were not welcome. For privacy, they moved past the bar to a table in the rear.

Ian bore the brunt of a serious scowl from the barman, and intense stares by two locals leaning into the bar. As they sat, the men were still staring, talking in low tones, looking meaner by the minute. When the barman came to the table, Ian ordered coffee. His new acquaintance ordered a dark, thick Guinness beer, which he downed almost as soon as it reached their table, leaving a tan froth moustache on his upper lip.

Billy wiped his coat sleeve across his mouth with relish, pulled his chair back, looked Ian over, head to toe, slowly and silently. He said, "Let's see what we have to work with here."

"What do you mean by that?" Ian replied, somewhat annoyed.

"Well now. Angus tells me ya might be needin' to learn a thing or two about fightin'. Well, I've been a soldier all me life. Fought for two or three countries in me time, including this here England, to my everlasting shame. I've been in the infantry and done a stint in the hussars. (He pronounced it – Hoozars.) My last rank, just so ya know, was sergeant major. So, young master, the short of it is...I'd be knowin' a thing or two about fightin'."

Even knowing Angus had sent this tough-looking little man, Ian was a bit sceptical. He was, after all, much smaller even than Ian, and looked too young to have seen much of the soldier's life, let alone so much active service. It was hard to tell, though, because this was one of those men who looked ageless, like Angus.

As Ian contemplated those thoughts, he heard, "Hey boy, we don't allow no bastard rich brats from that fancy school in here. Do nothing but cause trouble, you do, looking down yer ruddy noses at us working folks. You get out...now!" The two locals from the bar moved in front of their table. Ian was shocked and speechless. He'd never before encountered such impoliteness in the businesses around the college.

Billy's head rose slowly up to look at them from where he sat. He said quietly and conversationally, "Well now boyos. Ya've got two terrible faults against ya already. First, yer rude...and second, yer bloody English...but I feel kind today. So what I purpose is that you boyos go about yer business, we'll finish our drinks, then we'll be off, quick as yer hat, and no harm done. What say ya to that?"

"Fuck off, ya paddy bastard."

Ian was looking right at Billy, yet he never saw it coming. He only saw one of the locals fly upended from a standstill as if by magic, and slam down again onto a nearby table, crushing it. He twitched, then lay still. Billy had torn a small rug out from under him in one lightening movement without ever signalling his intent.

Billy flew from his chair sending his left elbow up into the face of the other local. The sound of it connecting with the man's chin was a sickening crack, and no doubt broke the jaw. Billy grabbed the man's coat front with his right hand, pulled him forward and down, smashing his right knee into the poor devil's groin. The man came off his feet at the force of the knee, then went down screaming in agony, clutching his crotch and mumbling strange sounds.

It was over in seconds. Ian was still seated, and Billy was calmly standing over him. He said, "I'm thinking we might be taking our leave of this place. The beer is terrible awful, and the service, not worth the mention. What say you, young master?"

Ian stood and stared at him in disbelief for a split second, then his eyes focused and opened wide. He picked up the empty beer glass and threw it at Billy's head. Billy, caught off-guard, barely ducked from its path. He heard the glass hit something, a thud behind him, followed by a choked cry, then glass shattering on the floor. Billy whirled around in time to see the barman, a giant club slipping from his hand, blood streaming down his face from a gash on his forehead. The barman fell straight back, unconscious before he hit the floor.

Ian had seen the barman about to club Billy from behind, by pure reflex he'd picked up the glass and threw it, no time to warn Billy. If he'd waited, Billy would be the one lying on the floor with a cracked skull. Connecting with the barman's head was sheer luck. It amazed Ian as much as it surprised the barman.

Billy looked directly at Ian for a long second, then said, "You'll do young master...by God, Angus was right, you'll do nicely. Now let's be off before there's more trouble." They left at a fast walk and cleared the corner at a dead run. As he ran, Ian silently thanked Angus. *I'm going to learn a great deal from this little Irishman.*

Chapter 12

Billy found modest lodging and a job, coincidentally as a barman at a public house, but across the bridge, up the hill, in Windsor, beyond the castle, a fair distance from the establishment where their recent encounter occurred. They settled into a routine quickly. Billy set his working hours to correspond with Ian's classes. Nearly every waking hour, otherwise, they were together.

Ian studied his school lessons, Latin and Greek mostly, because they were required to remain at Eton. These subjects came rather easily to him. He cut out many of the outside tutored classes he had been taking in mathematics, French, and drawing, to devote most of his time to studying in altogether different subjects. Ian rarely went home on holidays, spending them learning the arts of war. Billy found Ian an apt pupil, with lightening fast reflexes, excellent balance and coordination, as well as a passion and will to learn surpassed by none in Billy's memory.

Ian learned "a bit about fightin'." Billy was patient, but his lessons were long and difficult. He brought to the classes all his considerable skills learned growing up in the slums in Belfast, during a tour in the 15th Hussars, a very long time in the 23rd Regiment of Foot, and fighting as a mercenary for Sardinia, and a few other countries.

"Ian, me lad, we'll start your learning with the toughest part for most men, close-in fighting."

"Billy, my father and Angus did teach me a little about boxing, until my mother put a stop to it. Is that what you mean?"

"No, Ian. What I mean is learnin' to use both hands and feet, without rules, for the purpose of doing serious damage to the other fella, if not actually killin' him. I also mean the dangerous and bloody art of handlin' a knife. Then there's sabre fightin'…to kill Ian, not for sport. Ya'll learn a bit about pokin' a man with a bayonet, followed by me own personal favourite, the upward stroke with the butt of a rifle in the balls. When I finish, Ian, lad, you'll never come up short against yer fellow man again."

So it began, day after day, month after month. Billy taught Ian to use and shoot both the musket and pistol until he was exceptional. Ian was already an accomplished rider, but one day Billy rented horses from a local stable. Ian was curious, asked, "Since I can already ride, Billy, would our time not be better served in other areas?"

"Not on yer life, boyo. Ya only think ya can ride. Now ya've a whole new world to learn. I'll teach ya how to shoot, re-load, and fire again from horseback. Ya'll learn to use a sabre on a horse, riding at full gallop. After that, how to use that same horse as a weapon to smash into an enemy cavalryman, or crush an infantryman under its hooves."

Ian and Billy became very close, while they trained. By getting to know Billy, Ian learned to understand a classic non-commissioned officer, his concern for his men's well being, his quiet efficiency and professionalism. He realized why these non-commissioned officers were so important to the cohesion and success of a military unit, why they deserved his respect. In turn, Billy was captivated by this young spirited highlander, whose intellect and style made him a born soldier, and whose natural leadership stood out as a beacon.

They were drenched in sweat, had just finished an unusually strenuous training session with the heavy German sabres Billy had scrounged from somewhere. Billy asked Ian to come sit by him on a log next to their makeshift training arena. He said, "Lad, ya've worn me out."

Ian said, "Splendid, my good friend, now we'll go have a drink, what say you? I'll stand you to the largest darkest mug of beer we can find."

"No, Ian, listen to me. I mean ya've worn me out, for sure. I've given ya all the learnin' I can. Ya'll be a fine soldier, and ya have the makings of a fine officer. Yer ready, my lad, as ready as I can make ya."

Ian sat a moment with his head down, then looked at Billy, "I know, Billy. I've known for some time. I could feel it inside. What you've given me, the gift you've given me, I can never repay. You've done Angus proud. Some day I will find a way to pay you back."

"No need, boyo, my pleasure and my honour. I'm a warrior, Ian, and we're a special breed, yer da, Angus, and me. Now yer to be one of us. Ya have a ways to go to become a good officer, but, by God, ya now have the fighting skills to back it up. Use them well.

"I've one piece of advice for ya, lad." Ian listened, intently. "When the enemy is at ya. Never hold back. Go for the kill, and never stop attackin'. Drive yer enemy into the ground and stomp on his neck. Don't try to wound, and for Christ's sake, don't think too much on it. Just kill the bastard, before he kills you. Rip his heart out, Ian, worry about it later. Do that for me, boyo, and it'll be payment enough."

Ian nodded.

Billy said, "Right. Enough of this sentimental shite, Ian, we need to talk about another thing. Ya'll not be getting off the hook that easy, bucko. It's time ya told me what the devil's goin' on here, and don't say nothin', or I'll run this here old German sabre right up yer arse."

Ian was guarded. He'd never told anyone of his thirst for revenge or about the incident.

"Ya haven't been down all the roads I have, Ian old son, and this here paddy can smell out a bad situation as fast as I can spot a new man in a line of old soldiers. Angus told me there was somethin' in the wind. Yer planning somethin' violent-like, now what is it?"

Ian wasn't really surprised. He knew Billy was perceptive and streetwise enough to fill in the gaps between the information Angus must have told him and what he saw and heard around Eton and Windsor.

He waited to reply, gathering his thoughts, "I must ask you to trust me, Billy. I'll tell you a little, but I can't tell you all of it. Truth of it is, I need to have a serious talk with some of my fellow classmates. You see last year they hurt my brother, Peter. They hurt him bad, Billy; he'll never be the same. They must pay for that. Before I go any further in my life I need to do this thing. It is my sacred duty. Do you understand?"

Billy smiled, "Course I do. Say no more, lad. But you'll not be doin' it alone. Get me? I'll have none of that. We'll visit these boyos together. I'll have it no other way."

Ian was elated, relieved. He'd never have asked for Billy's help, of course, but the odds of his success alone against all five of them were slim, even with his new skills. He was glad and said so, "My debt to you keeps growing. Soon I'll have to give you my firstborn."

"Jesus save us, not that," was Billy's reply. "Never you mind, boyo, it would be me great pleasure."

Ian told Billy his rather simplistic plan. Billy made several improvements on it. They agreed that it was time to act.

Chapter 13

"What are you doing here?" This seemed to be the question of the day. All four of Fairbain's minions arrived separately in the cellar where they had taken Peter and Ian that frightful night over a year ago. It was the same dirt floor room where Fairbain had victimized, often sodomized, so many other young Eton students.

Ian forged a note to Dame Vallencey indicating one of her relatives was ill in the north of England. She packed an overnight trunk and left the house.

Billy visited each of Fairbain's four cronies, delivering a cryptic printed message, signed with Fairbain's initials: *Come to the cellar room tonight at midnight. Be alone. Tell no one. We have trouble. – RF.*

Dame Vallencey left Fairbain in charge of the house, but Billy saw to it that he also received a note. His read: *Unless you want bad trouble, come alone to Lupton's Tower tonight at midnight – and wait for me. Don't leave or you will be extremely sorry.* Fairbain was not to be part of this portion of their plan. They wanted him elsewhere when they struck. Lupton's Tower was within the college grounds, across the School Yard, past the statue of the school's founder, King Henry VI, and, most importantly, well away from the boarding house.

The note annoyed Fairbain, but as Ian had suspected, he was unable to resist its impertinence. Fairbain left the house at half eleven, and headed for the college. Half an hour later, the first two of Fairbain's minions arrived simultaneously at the room, showing surprise that they had both received the same note. The third appeared shortly after, and finally the last one, Smyth-Foster, Ian's chubby former fag master.

The room was dark. There was some light from flickering candles, making eerie shadows quiver about the walls. They waited in awkward silence for Fairbain to show, feet shuffling, a bit worried about the reason for such a peculiar meeting. After ten minutes Smyth-Foster suggested leaving, "Not like Roger. Something gone wrong. We'll get a message to him or see him tomorrow, then we can meet him here tomorrow night, if we must have all this secrecy."

They were all agreeing, when a voice from the back in the deep shadows…quietly said, "What's yer hurry, boyos? Lost without yer fat friend?"

They were startled by the voice and by the bold reference to Fairbain's weight. Smyth-Foster recovered quickly, "I know that voice. You're the messenger that brought the note from Fairbain. Who the hell are you?"

The darkness was oppressive, like the stale, musky stillness of an empty crypt.

"You there…who are you, I say?"

Nervous shuffling followed, his words still ringing in the stillness. Their feet scraped the dirt floor, too loud in the awful stillness.

"Answer me. This is private property. We'll have the law on you."

More silence, then a higher-pitched squeal as another of them found his voice, "We'll report you."

Ian and Billy left the shadows, looking black as thunder, the more ominous as the flickering light bounced off their faces. If a mouse stirred, it would have sounded like the roar of a passing train. The four boys found an old uneasy memory as they stared at Ian, into the coldest eyes they ever saw. The oppressive quiet lasted for nearly a minute, while they tried to compose themselves.

Smyth-Foster recovered, "Carlyle, that is you, isn't it? See here, Carlyle, what's going on? Where's Fairbain? Who is that creature with you? What's the meaning of this?"

Another said, "Yes, Carlyle, I mean to say, what kind of game you playing at?"

Another edged cautiously toward the door, said, "If it's a fight you're looking for, Carlyle, you arrogant bastard, there's four of us and only two of you."

In a soft tone, Ian said, "Well, actually, Fairbain chose not to attend this little gathering, and you're quite wrong about the odds." Ian moved like a cat between the four of them and the door.

"You see it's the four of you against one...that would be me. My friend here is to see to it you don't leave."

Billy moved quickly to the door behind Ian, cutting off their escape route. He took a comfortable stance, crossing his arms, and smiling. They looked bewildered and uncomfortable.

By this time, Smyth-Foster, a coward by nature, was edging away from the others. Beginning to visibly shake, he said, "Come on, Carlyle, you know me, didn't I treat you right when you were my fag? I swear I wanted nothing to do with that business with your brother. I told them so. I got them to leave you alone, didn't I?"

Ian knew better. He said, "Did you know that my brother, Peter, never recovered from that little encounter? By the way, he sends his condolences."

"Condolences. For what?" one of them replied, bravado in his voice.

"Why for your accident, of course," Ian said.

The brave one said, "What accident?" There was contempt in his tone.

Ian said, "The one you're about to have."

His whole body tightened. He thought of Peter's empty eyes, causing his big sleeping cat to waken, tense, then spring. With the speed and grace of the leopard, Ian was across the room and at them. No talk. No negotiation. Pure bundled violence, pent up for over a year, exploded in controlled unrelenting rage.

He met them with a swift merciless onslaught. They were too horrified by the wild viciousness of the attack to defend themselves. Ian took them, one at a time, went through them like a deadly sickle, using the skills Billy had taught him to smash each in turn to the floor.

This was no gentleman's fight. There were no rules. They tried to come after him as a group, but Ian was too quick.

Ian hurt them badly, and kept on hurting them as he turned from one to another, kicking, punching, pounding, scratching, picking their bodies off the floor to smash them down again, until they whimpered for mercy, lying in pain in their own blood and urine.

No words were spoken, all of it lasting but a few minutes. Ian was heaving from exertion, standing above them, fists clenched, bloody. He looked over his work, feeling no pride or arrogance, nothing, thinking only of that look of terror and helplessness on Peter's face.

Billy watched from the doorway, amused, admiring the very techniques he had taught Ian, and the excellence with which his student applied them. He studied the four would-be gentlemen strewn about the floor, assessed the damage clinically.

One would never be handsome again, with a smashed nose, broken twisted jaw, one ear nearly torn off. His left foot was at an odd angle with his leg.

The second was holding his hand to his face. Billy could see huge gaps where teeth had once been. Half of his tongue hung precariously out of his open, bleeding mouth, bitten through by his own teeth.

The third was not likely to use his left arm soon again, perhaps never with a full range of motion. A bone protruded several inches from his forearm. His face was bleeding, both eyes would blacken, a large chunk of hair and scalp was missing from the front of his head.

Smyth-Foster was most badly handled. His face was ruined like the others, broken jaw, nose, blackening eyes, teeth missing. By the angle his head drooped, it was likely his collarbone was also broken. His right arm was bent at an odd angle, and his left hand was over his crotch. He was moaning and crying like a child, rolling about on the floor. Billy had seen Ian's well-placed blow, suspected the man's testicles had been driven up into his groin. Billy winced slightly at the thought of the pain.

Ian interrupted his musings, "Billy, let's finish it. Line them up and do what has to be done. I'll get the horse and cart."

Chapter 14

The Reverend Francis Hodgson, Provost, head of Eton College, appointed by the Queen, and a strong creature of habit, always rose well ahead of his academic colleagues or the students. He enjoyed walking from his quarters to a small pastry shop to purchase a rather large, still hot, sticky bun. He bought precisely the same type bun at the exact same time every day. He would then walk briskly through the school's main entrance, across the yard, the Great Quadrangle, past the fine statue of Eton's founder, to his office, where he would carefully brew a pot of jasmine tea. He would munch contentedly on his bun, sip his tea, and use the time to think the heady thoughts of all the great men, in the company of whom he considered he might one day stand.

On this bracing April morning, with the barest touch of fog, his thoughts on the way to his office were interrupted by a lump of bright pink in the middle of the green, around King Henry's magnificent statue. He approached with his curiosity rapidly turning to shock.

There were four of them, all naked. They appeared to be bruised and bleeding, but Hodgson was cautious, had seen elaborate pranks before. He recognized them as senior boys, knew only Smyth-Foster by name, thought: *A weasel-like sort, looks like a damned pink rat.*

They were tied hand and foot, gagged, and the lot of them fastened by a heavy chain inside the fence around the statue. They looked badly abused. On closer inspection, the Reverend could see that their faces were flushed red, no doubt from embarrassment. Numerous brown and blackened bruises were surrounded by a profusion of dark dried blood, with a brighter red still running fresh in places. If this was theatre, it was damned fine theatre.

The oddest thing was a hand-printed placard, hanging from the fence saying in blood-red letters: *We are bullies, cowards, and homosexuals. We are guilty of buggering other young men, our fellow students, by force. We are sorry.* It then listed their names.

Those of the four who were conscious squirmed and pleaded feebly through their gags, unable to articulate a defence for the terrible accusation. Provost Hodgson recoiled in disgust, coughed, walked rapidly to his office, and closed his door. *I've seen this sort of thing too many times before. They want me to get excited, over-react. Likely aimed at just that. I'll go for help, and when I return, the quadrangle will be empty, then the whole bloody school will be laughing at me. Not today. Damned pranksters, they'll be for it if I ever find them. For now, I'll ignore this. Allow someone of lesser stature than myself to find them and sort this appalling thing out.*

Unfortunately, this was not a mere prank aimed at Hodgson. This time the blood was real. The students began to flock toward classes soon thereafter, pointing, talking, and laughing. The King's Scholars leaned out of their windows overlooking the School Yard. Word spread like an out-of-control fire. Oppidans streamed through the main entrance from their houses on nearby streets to gather about the statue, eyes wide. None seemed to think of untying the pathetically struggling group, whose faces were becoming redder as the crowd grew. In the gathering throng were many of Fairbain's previous victims. They saw, knew these were their assailants. They didn't laugh.

Fairbain, himself, was eventually among the onlookers. The night before he'd waited at the tower until he saw a horse and cart pulling through the entrance with two men on it, and a pinkish pile in the back. Not wishing to be caught on the school grounds at that early hour, and feeling foolish for having come at all, he slinked out a side gate and returned to the house. As he now looked on at his faithful followers and their hideous plight, he felt like every eye was watching him. Many were. Someone in the crowd shouted, "Well, Roger, old fella, shouldn't you be among these sterling chaps?"

Fairbain merely glared at his fellow students. He grew pale and looked sick, as though he knew he had called down the thunder, was about to be crushed. When he couldn't stand it anymore, he ran off the yard and out the main entrance, knocking students down as he crashed through, top hat falling off, coattails flying behind him.

Within the next few days the story was carried prominently in the *Eton Chronicle*, and later even appeared in the *London Times*, with the names of the four boys and an unusual amount of detail, from an "anonymous source."

After they were repaired in hospital sufficiently to do so, all four boys left Eton in utter disgrace. Their bodies were broken, and the humiliation would follow them, taunt them, throughout their lives.

Fairbain missed classes and meals. Dame Vallencey returned, utterly confused, and tried to talk to him. He refused to answer her knock, would not leave his room. Within a fortnight, a few students saw Fairbain's massive bulk skulking away from the college down the hill toward the train station. As he departed, they noticed he looked furtively over his shoulder every few seconds. He was carrying a small valise with a few things. Fairbain was going into hiding.

Chapter 15

It was three weeks since Fairbain left Eton. He was holed up in a dingy set of rooms in East London. At first he thought he detected a shadowy presence haunting his movements. After a few days it seemed to disappear, and he dismissed it.

His arrogance was allowing him a feeling of relative safety. Thus one evening, with head hunkered down in his coat collar, Roger Fairbain felt free to leave his lodging to find food, drink, perhaps a nice young girl, or boy. It was a mistake.

Billy left the shadows of a doorway across the street. As Fairbain turned a corner, Billy moved up quickly behind him. He placed a knife not too gently against Fairbain's ribs, whispered, "Now me friend, don't make a fuss, or I'll have to cut ya arse to throat, and if yer wonderin', I'd be pleased as punch to do just that…Come along now."

Billy was about one-third his size, but the thought never occurred to him to fight or run…something in the voice. He just obeyed, for the first time in his miserable life feeling tangible fear. Billy forced Fairbain along the street and down an alley. Darkness closed around them. Billy shoved Fairbain's heavy bulk through a door into an even darker place.

"You've made a gweat mistake. I...I have no money. I'm a poow student. Please." Fairbain was cowering as he snivelled, no longer the bully preying on the weak.

"Shut yer trap, boyo, and act like a man, even if ya ain't one," said Billy.

"What do you want? I've done nothing to you."

There was a great cavern of noiseless expectation, then, "Hello, Fairbain. Frightfully sorry for all this inconvenience, old boy." A chill ran through Roger Fairbain, as he recognized the new voice coming out of the darkness. He suspected that Ian Carlyle was responsible for his being sent on a fool's errand to Lupton's Tower that night, and for the beatings and humiliation of his four henchmen. Now he knew.

Sweat was pouring from Fairbain, as he turned toward the new voice. He started to back away, but the quiet Irish voice behind him said, "Easy, ya've got to pay the piper now, don't ya."

Fairbain said, "I know it was you, Cawlyle. I know you did it to them, and I'll have the law on you."

"No you won't, Roger. You'll do nothing." Ian walked out of the darkness. He was carrying two swords. The heavy sabre looked clumsy beside the graceful fencing foil.

As Ian handed him the foil, a glimmer of hope appeared in Fairbain's eyes. He knew he could beat this upstart, and began to relish the idea. *Why the nerve of this bastard. I'll teach him a lesson he won't soon forget.*

"Roger, I thought you'd appreciate a challenge, rather than me merely killing you outright. Mind you, this is a sharp, extremely heavy sabre, loaned to me by my Irish friend behind you. It's not for sport, or gentleman's duelling. It's just a killing instrument. What say you to that?"

In answer Fairbain carefully removed the protective tip from the foil. It was a killing tool, as well.

Ian looked amused.

The expected rebirth of arrogance appeared on Fairbain's face and in his tone. He said, "Since you've given me the chance, you bloody bastard, it's me that'll be doing the killing, en gawde." He snapped to the en garde fencing position instantly, sword out front in his right hand, left hand behind – arched high up. Fairbain assumed Ian would do likewise. He was wrong.

In a flash, Ian stepped in and swung the heavy sabre around and down sharply, using the semi-dull chopping edge to strike. He came to rest in the en garde position with sabre, but only after the thick blade had done its work. Fairbain was shocked by the speed and ferocity of the blow, as he felt the jarring contact on his foil blade. To add to his stunned disbelief, he saw that his foil was now lying on the floor, bent into an "L" shape, useless.

Fairbain's fear returned instantly, increasing in strength by the second. The kind of fear he had taken such relish in producing in no small number of students during his nocturnal sessions.

"You...you never gave me a chance," he cried, almost in tears.

"More chance than you gave my brother. At least you're not bound and helpless." With that Ian flicked the last extremely sharp eight inches of the sabre's blade at Fairbain's head. It took a second or two for Fairbain to feel the odd flowing liquid sensation and excruciating pain. He grabbed at his left ear, finding only a wet, sticky hole. Blood was gushing out of it. Fairbain began moaning, "Jesus, oh Jesus, my ear. What have you done?"

Ian said, "Do you recall listening to Peter's pleas with that ear, Fairbain? It was obvious to me the ear was useless, not working at all, because you merely laughed at his pleas. Now it's gone, and good riddance, what?"

Fairbain fell to his knees, "Jesus...please, have mewcy. I beg you." Holding the left side of his face with his left hand, he reached out to Ian with his right, groping forward. Another mistake.

Ian was unmoved, a stone, "Do you recall casually poking Peter in the chest with your foil? He was crying out in pain. You carved your initials while your henchmen held him. He was screaming? As I recall, you held that foil in your right hand."

Not realizing the significance of Ian's remark, Fairbain said, "I'm sowy, so sowy."

Ian reached up with his free hand and lightly touched the tiny scar below his left eye, felt the leopard brain take over completely. He stepped back, raised the sabre with lightning speed, said, "Not quite good enough, old chap."

The sabre came down solid and firm, all of Ian's strength behind it. The unsharpened lower part of the blade sliced crudely through the flesh and bone at the wrist. Fairbain's right hand tumbled to the floor with a grotesque thudding sound, and bounced only once. Fairbain screamed insanely, stared at the blood gushing from his blunt ragged wrist, and went into shocked silence.

Billy moved in. With the deftness of an expert, he applied a tourniquet above the wrist, then a tight bandage over and around it. He plugged the hole where the ear had been with a rag. He whispered to Fairbain, "We wouldn't want you dying from loss of blood, would we?" Billy stepped back, allowing Ian to finish.

Fairbain was whimpering, softly. Ian said in his thickest Scottish brogue, "Och, Roger, yer no much a man, are ye?"

No response. Ian said, "Well, buck up, there's only a wee bit more."

Ian flicked the sabre's point at Fairbain's chest, slicing open his shirtfront from cravat to where his gaudy silk vest was buttoned together. About six inches of his pasty white chest was exposed. A few more deft flicks and Ian carved the initials "PC" into Fairbain's huge fatty bleeding mass, a present for his brother. They were a bit larger and cruder than the initials Fairbain had carved in Peter's flesh, but they would do nicely.

Ian had practiced this carving technique for months as his own private exercise in learning to use the sabre. Billy didn't understand until now just what it meant to see Ian constantly trying to carve the alphabet into every tree in sight.

Fairbain didn't quite lose consciousness. He collapsed, muttering to himself and rolling back and forth on the floor. There was blood flowing through the rag stuck in the hole where his ear had been, and from his wrist, in spite of Billy's work.

Ian leaned down into Fairbain's good ear, "You know, Roger, I thought about cutting off that other offending appendage, as well. You know the one I mean, that sometimes erect, but constantly misplaced member you seem so proud of." Obviously Fairbain still retained some of his faculties. He instantly recoiled in horror, his left and only hand reflexively moving from his ear toward his crotch as he tensed into a ball.

Ian continued, "That would be too easy, Roger, my dear fellow. I've just made another decision. Killing you now would also be too easy. Peter and I will enjoy it this way a great deal more. You won't be much of a catch with the young lads you seem to prefer, looking the way you do, sort of lopsided, and stumpy. Aye, it will please us to think about your suffering each day for the rest of your life.

"Roger, I know you can hear me with the one ear you have left, or do I have to cut it off to get your attention? Can you hear me?" Fairbain bobbed his head vigorously, still in pain and shock.

"Good. You won't have the law on us, or tell anyone how this happened, will you? You're a cowardly little swine, by God, and you know I'd hunt you down and kill you...very, very slowly."

Ian let that sink in through the pain, "Then there's your ego and your freedom. You see before the four cowards were left on the green, they each wrote a confession implicating you as their leader in numerous misdeeds from sodomy to bestiality. I have those confessions tucked away. I doubt you'd want that made public, to add to your disgrace. Might even be a jail sentence in it for you."

Fairbain was an empty shell. Ian was gratified to see that same vacant stare in his eyes that he had seen in Peter, the edge of madness.

While Ian was explaining all this to Fairbain, the good 'doctor' Billy was at work again. He wrapped the tourniquet more tightly around Fairbain's right wrist to slow the bleeding further, put a bandage around his head to keep the rag in his ear hole, then stuffed another rag deep into Fairbain's mouth. They pulled Fairbain into the alley in plain view, then walked away.

Billy poked his head into a nearby tavern, the one Fairbain had been heading for to enjoy the evening. Billy shouted in his best imitation cockney accent, "Hey, there's an Irish paddy bastard in the alley screaming and making trouble. Called our beloved Queen a whore, he did. I stuffed a rag in his mouth, but he needs a lesson in manners. Who's with me?" Billy darted back out the door, and stepped aside quickly to where he would be hidden when the door swung outward. It took a second or two, then several patrons angrily charged out, fists clenched, flying right past Billy.

Billy smiled, slipped away from the tavern entrance unseen, and met Ian down the street. He looked at Ian as they walked, then pulled him up short with a grip on his arm. He said, softly, "Ian, my friend, remind me never to get you angry with me." Ian wasn't smiling.

Some, mostly those who had been Fairbain's victims, put it all together. They often made it a point to pleasantly greet Ian in passing in the coming months at school, and a few came to him simply saying things like, "Bravo, old chap, bravo." The incident on the green was generally forgotten, replaced by a hundred other school activities and local escapades. Fairbain was never heard from again, and Ian refused to discuss the subject with anyone at the college. The whole affair became an oddity in the folklore of Eton.

After a time, Billy quit his barman's job, said goodbye to Ian, and left for new horizons. He told Ian, "Ya know, I've never been to France, and any enemy of England is for sure a mate of mine." Ian laughed with his friend as they parted.

Ian left Eton in 1848.

Chapter 16

Soon after his return to Dunkairn, Ian and Angus rode far out into the fields and away from the curious. Angus methodically tested Ian's newly learned abilities. He was actually overjoyed at the results.

It was here that Angus told Ian for the first time that Peter had confided in him, and he knew all of what occurred at Eton. Ian had suspected as much, and told Angus the tale of his revenge and Billy's help.

Ian found to his joy that Peter had improved considerably. In the privacy of Peter's rooms, Ian told him in detail the extent of his revenge on their attackers. Peter smiled and nodded, taking in one more of Ian's tales of adventure, as he always had. When Ian tried to urge Peter to talk more about it, there was always a heavy hush. Peter's memories were still locked in the shadows in his mind, not ready yet for the light of day.

The art of persuasion had to begin cautiously with his father. Once the strong-minded Earl made up his mind, he was usually quite inflexible. Oddly, his mother was far easier to sway. She saw his passion, and knew in her heart that there was nothing she could do. In spite of her aversion to violence and misgivings about the military, she loved her son more. She accepted Ian's choice as inevitable.

When His Lordship stopped grumbling at the very mention of his son going in the military, Ian said, "Let me show you Father, please. Allow me to show you what I can do."

The Earl finally yielded, "All right, all right, if you must, you're driving me bloody mad. Let's see what you can do, but you'd better pray for a merciful God if you're wasting my time."

Angus laid out a course on a back paddock, and prepared Savage, Ian's favourite horse, for the exercise. Every activity at Dunkairn ceased. The family and their entire household were to attend this pivotal event.

Early next morning, the crowd gathered at the paddock. It was like a jousting match of old, even with a cheering section. Although there was an atmosphere of gaiety about it; his father's face was creased by a considerable frown. He didn't look happy. He looked determined not to be won over. Ian wore a waistcoat and white linen shirt, open at the neck, no hat, not a very military appearance. His father noticed this.. His frown intensified.

"Right," was all Ian said, as he swung easily onto Savage. Ian still had Billy's heavy German cavalry sabre, and had borrowed Angus' old Tower pistol, which held only one ball…no chance for error.

The course was set up with a series of straw-stuffed heads on top of poles set in a line fairly close together. The trick was to ride the line weaving in and out between the poles slicing heads along the way.

At the end was a straw-filled dummy, the size of a man standing upright. There was a circle of white paper pinned over the dummy's heart.

Ian began his run some distance away, at a walk, then a trot, then a controlled canter. He finally gave Savage his head, coming to a full gallop with sabre drawn and pointed forward at precisely the correct angle. He screamed like a wild man and bore down on his prey. He pierced the first head, pulled the sabre expertly free as he rode by, swung it striking the next head cleanly as he passed, weaving in and out of the heads, cutting right, then left rear, then right again, each as clean as the last, straw spewing from the heads behind him.

Having slashed the last head, Ian allowed the sabre to dangle from his wrist by the leather knot. He drew the heavy pistol from his belt with the same sword hand, closed on the dummy target, and, leaning forward, carefully placed a shot at the centre of the circle over its heart as he passed.

Ian drew back, replaced the sabre in its scabbard, swung about expertly on Savage's hindquarter, and rode full out to where his father was standing. He reined in inches from His Lordship, forcing him to involuntarily step back several paces. As he reined in, his right leg swung over the top of the horse's head, and he was flying off Savage's back. Ian landed on both feet at once, caught the reins to pull Savage next to him, and stood eye-to eye with his astounded father, in perfect control of himself and the animal.

Ian bowed calmly, drew the sabre, sweeping it before him with a flourish and salute, not even out of breath. He said, "At your service, M'Lord. Would Your Lordship wish to see it again?" His mother, Peter, and the entire household broke their astonished silence, clapping uproariously and shouting praises.

Ian had never seen a stunned look on his father's face before, but he was pleased to see it there now. His Lordship cleared his throat several times before speaking. Then said, "I am, ahh, I mean…"

Then he warmed to the subject, no longer able to hold back his pride, "By God, boy, by God. A splendid thing, aye, most splendid. There may be hope for you yet, boy, indeed there may. By God…by God." Then he turned abruptly, cleared his throat again, and walked away, strongly motioning with his head for Angus to walk with him. The family rushed to Ian patting his back, shaking hands.

When a distance away, His Lordship, in a low voice, said, "Angus, I never knew, never realized. What a lad, what? Where did he learn all that? I'll wager a sly Scotsman had no small part in this, you cagey scoundrel."

Angus said nothing, hid his smile, His Lordship continued, "Did you see the speed, Angus? Cut those damned heads, every one of them. Treated that horse like it was a part of him. Still managed to put one shot…one shot…on horseback no less, into the heart, by God."

Lord Dunkairn stopped, gently taking Angus MacLean by the arm, "Angus, I won't ask you how you managed this."

Angus replied, "I swear on my blessed mother's grave, sir, I didn't break my oath to Her Ladyship. I never taught these things to the lad, but I might have had a hand in seeing they were taught, if ye'll forgive me, M'Lord."

"Forgive you? Nothing of the sort. Angus, I'm most grateful to you. I truly am."

Angus said a prayer, thanking God and Billy Murphy.

While Ian was taking for granted the purchasing of a commission in the Guards, His Lordship was swiftly moving in another direction entirely. A few weeks later, after a sumptuous dinner, His Lordship clanked his glass for attention, and made a shocking announcement to a surprised audience, "I have rather spectacular news. I have succeeded, over many obstacles I might add, in getting Ian a special appointment as a gentleman cadet at the Royal Military Academy, Woolwich. Upon completion, he shall become an officer of Royal Artillery, or if scholastically high enough, he may choose the Royal Engineers."

Lady Dunkairn and Peter were overjoyed, applauding His Lordship heartily. "Richard," Lady Harriett said, "how on earth did you manage it?"

"Yes, well my dear, as it happens the Master-General of Ordnance at the moment is Fitzroy Henry James Somerset. Has great influence in choosing cadets. He was with me at Waterloo, you know, under the Iron Duke. You remember Fitz, my dear, lost an arm. Used to come by the odd weekend."

"Ah, yes," she put in, "a very quiet gentleman."

"Thought very highly of our lads. He's now Baron of Raglan. Owes me a favour or two. He was delighted to oblige."

Ian was thunderstruck. He swallowed hard, hiding his disappointment behind a weak smile. What could he do? His father had called in an important favour to gain this position, and it was a prestigious one at that, although he knew gunners and engineers were not in the habit of leading infantry troops to glory. Ian thanked him for this wonderful opportunity, swallowing hard, saying, "Sir, I shall try to make you proud."

When Angus heard the news, he was confused. That evening Angus approached Lord Dunkairn's study. The huge doors were ajar. He knocked, "Sir, a word."

"Of course, Angus."

Angus cleared his throat, "Yer Lordship, perhaps it's not my place, but we both know the lad wanted the Guards. He wanted our regiment...follow in your boots. He's disappointed, sir, but he won't show it."

His Lordship said, "If it's not your place, Angus, then whose? You're more than entitled to know why I want him at Woolwich, and I know he's disappointed."

Angus waited.

"Ian is an intelligent lad, far more than most, and I dare say far more than me. He wants to be a soldier, and he's earned that right, but I can't see him in the infantry, Angus, even our beloved Third Guards. He'd have scant military training and be around young officers with no battles under their belts. There's trouble coming, and I don't want my son wasted. I don't want him dead on some field for the glory of the regiment, even the Guards."

He continued, "What Ian has learned up to now is a superb effort, quite amazing, really, and most useful...but not enough. War isn't merely swordplay and fancy shooting, as you well know."

Angus nodded.

"There is no infantry training, Angus. It simply doesn't exist. Sandhurst is aimed at putting out pretty staff officers. The only substantial training I can offer my son to ensure his survival on the battlefield at the moment is Woolwich. He will there receive the best England has to offer."

Angus saw the logic, "I think I understand what ye have in mind, M'Lord, but, forgive me, I fear I still don't understand why ye don't just tell the lad."

His Lordship said, "I'm not certain he'd accept and respect these reasons now. It might drive him in another direction altogether. He is of age to go the way he wants, and he's headstrong. At the very least, promotion in the Royal Artillery, or the Engineers, is based on seniority, not whether your father has the funds to purchase. The lad will prove his own worth and earn his rank."

"And the Guards, M'Lord?"

"Aye, aye, of course, should he want a commission in the Guards later, I shall not stand in his way. What say you of my rather underhanded scheme?"

"Yer Lordship, I give ye my word to be as silent as the tomb."

"Good, Angus, I'll hold you to that."

Chapter 17

This was Ian's first uniform, and in spite of his disappointment, he was thrilled. "Peter, come look at this."

Armed with His Lordship's established accounts and sage advice, Ian had travelled to London. He quickly acquired a full set of uniforms for the gentleman cadet made up at Meyer and Mortimer Limited on Sackville Street. The informal dress consisted of a dark blue coatee with red collar and other facings, dark blue trousers with a wide red stripe, the lot set off by a white belt and white doeskin gloves. The dress uniform was more elaborate with a gold-trimmed coatee. He went to Locke and Company Hatters, Saint James Street, for the formal cadet shako and a dark blue gold-trimmed forage cap for informal wear. Finally, he was fitted for a pair of sturdy walking shoes and fine riding boots at Lobbs.

After his return from London, Ian posed in dress uniform before the huge mirror in the entrance hall at Dunkairn. When Peter came in to admire, Ian said, "Aye, it's not the Guards, but I could definitely become accustomed to this."

Peter, in his healing process, was by now smiling at Ian's enthusiasm. "Where are you off to, brother?" asked Peter. Ian's keenness was infectious.

"Oh, I must pack and be on the road to Woolwich in two days, Peter. These are my last times at Dunkairn for a while. I'll miss you."

Peter replied, "And I, you, dear brother."

Lady Harriett helped Ian pack his uniforms and personal comforts. He was not to have a servant with him at Woolwich. His father thought that best, and put Lady Harriett's protests aside with a simple, "May as well start him right. On his own, depending on no man, or servant. He'll need to learn that."

After long good-byes, resplendent as a new gentleman cadet, Ian mounted the carriage, waved, and was gone for a soldier.

The time at Woolwich flew. Ian adjusted rapidly to the rigorous military routine each day, the constant drilling, endless inspections. He found the artillery and engineering subjects fascinating, and excelled in military history. He immersed himself in his studies, constantly pestering fellow cadets to engage him in tabletop war games using blocks of wood for formations. Ian waged the ancient battles and wars until, if allowed a few modest changes in either numbers or materials of war, he could win fighting for either side.

"Come on, fellows, join me. I'm doing Waterloo. I'll be the bloody French. Any takers?" His reputation was for ruthlessly winning, regardless which side he chose. Often there was no one who wanted to have a go at him.

Ian was thrilled by this new world of learning. The complexities of the various military subjects were interesting and gratifying. He soon came to realize that had he gone into the Guards, most of these complexities would have remained hidden from him. He began to see his father's insistence on the Academy as something His Lordship had done _for_ him, not _to_ him.

by silken black hair, which, when free, hung below her waist. She never allowed it to hang free in public, of course.

Her skin was the colour of caramel, and as milky soft as the petals of the jasmine flower itself. She walked tall, erect, with grace and dignity. Her beauty was ageless, but one could guess she was in her thirties, perhaps ten years older than Ian.

They said she was from Ceylon, of a wild mix of Sinhalese, Portuguese, and Dutch. She spoke with the mere hint of an accent. That was part of her mystique. There was always an underlying tension about her, dangerous, the way a coiled sleeping cobra was dangerous. It would be folly to awaken that creature, and everyone knew it. In Jasmine's business, being thought dangerous was an advantage.

She worked as barmaid at the pub, but in reality managed it. Her presence gave the place style, like having foreign royalty amongst them, making her more mysterious and appealing. There was no problem or drunk she couldn't handle with ease. She made them all want to please her, fall over themselves to do so. Jasmine was gracious, gentle, and understanding, yet leather tough and iron-fisted with patrons who crossed the line.

Some said Jasmine sold her favours to wealthy men, but there was no proof of this, and none would dare speak of it, even behind her back. If she had money, she hardly showed it, living modestly in lodgings close by the pub. Jasmine earned a small salary for serving drinks, but gathered much more in gratuities from the customers. When she left for the night, she was always alone.

Ian, serving in his first assignment as a fresh Royal Engineer officer on staff at Horse Guards, was bored to a fair-thee-well. Over the interminable months of routine, it became his nightly habit to stop for several glasses of ale after his day's duty ended. He liked Jasmine; had from the first time he saw her serving drinks. She seemed to like him as well, and spent extra time talking to him while she served others.

From their conversations, Ian knew she was erudite in the arts, literature, even the classics, but he had no idea how that came about. Most women with a formal education were far more apt to be associated with wealth and the aristocracy, than serving drinks in a public house. Although his curiosity was piqued, he knew better than to ask, deciding merely to enjoy her companionship from across the counter.

They had long and interesting talks. He thought few others in the establishment appreciated her wit, charm, and intellect. They preferred to leer sheepishly at her stunning beauty. She was certainly not the typical staid, withdrawn, conservative lady Ian was used to conversing with in drawing rooms. Jasmine's presence was alive, assertive, confident, even commanding.

She began to save a special place for him at the end of the long mahogany counter, near the beer taps. That way they could converse while she poured the amber or dark brown liquid for other patrons. When Jasmine was not actually serving, she would linger across from Ian and they'd talk the hours away.

Ian's sexual attraction for Jasmine was kept inside. He suspected that any advances might cause her to think of him as she did the other leering patrons. He was often ashamed that invariably while conversing with her he was physically aroused, and his mind filled with heady lustful thoughts.

Jasmine, finding Ian's unpretentious honesty refreshing, was becoming increasingly more interested in this dashing young officer. She found his failure to see her interest one of his more charming qualities, along with his shallowly hidden attraction for her.

Chapter 19

On a particularly wintry evening, the tables in the Red Lion were empty, except for three Guards officers, in full dress uniforms, quietly sipping port at a back booth. A tall thin, handsome man in a black frock coat, cream-coloured brocade vest, starched shirt, and silk cravat was standing at Ian's usual place at the far end of the bar, talking animatedly to Jasmine.

There was a tough-looking giant of a man, with greasy dark hair and a shoddy coat standing obediently behind him, like a great hairy dog, waiting to do his master's bidding. He had scars all around his left eye, a bulbous nose and puffy lips. It made him look unusually sinister.

The tall thin man talking to Jasmine had dark shifty eyes, a long, angular face, and a strong chin. His hair was immaculately groomed. He wore a large diamond stickpin, an elaborate timepiece chain, and a gold pinkie ring with a huge diamond centre. The man exuded wealth, even if more than a trifle tawdry. From what limited experience Ian had since coming to London, he took the tall man for a scoundrel, perhaps someone from the criminal world hierarchy, but not a panderer. That low-life pimp look he often saw on the streets was just not there.

Ian stood several feet down the counter from the tall man. He heard him talking with a rather upper class accent. In a quiet voice the tall man said, "Jasmine, I don't particularly care why you left, but you're mine, you see. I've found you again, and you're mine. You're coming back with me, now, and that's the end of it."

Jasmine didn't look frightened. She replied in an equally relaxed tone, "No, Sidney, I'm not. I told you when I left. I'll not go back, and that, indeed, is the end of it. Now, I want you to leave, and, please, don't come back."

So his name is Sidney, Ian thought.

The tall thin man seemed to have had quite enough. His face noticeably reddened. His entire demeanour changed from smooth and polished to menacing and cruel. He pointed his finger into Jasmine's face, hissed, his accent reverting instantly to the gutters of London, "Bollocks that, you bitch, I'll have Herbie here play a tune on yer face. You'll change yer mind that quick."

Jasmine laughed, "Sidney, whatever happened to all your manners? That pathetic animal of yours doesn't scare me. Be a good boy, take your pet bulldog and move along."

The tough standing behind Sidney moved fast, came up to the counter between his master and Ian, slammed his fist down, and glared at Jasmine. She jumped, startled, a slight edge of concern showing for the first time in her face.

"Ya bloody fucking whore," the man spit out, "I'll soon change yer pretty smile." He looked quickly at Sidney, obviously waiting for orders.

Ian had enough of this, himself. The strong words toward Jasmine brought the leopard forth, in controlled anger. He'd been looking straight ahead, merely listening. Now he turned slowly toward them, stepped away from the counter. He ignored the tough, and addressed Sidney, politely, "Excuse me, sir, I do so hate to intrude, but I fear I must. You and your friend are incredibly rude. I really don't like rudeness, you know, it's so, well, common."

The giant tough turned about, facing Ian, leered down at the smaller man in the scarlet coatee. He looked mean, but said nothing, assuming his mere size would intimidate this little soldier boy. Ian was still looking at Sidney, ignoring the tough. Sidney's face was turning crimson, his eyes bulging in anger.

Jasmine pleaded, "Please, Ian, stay out of this." She was afraid of what might happen to her quiet, gentle friend.

Ian was standing on the balls of his feet now, made his voice light and thick with Scottish accent for his own amusement, "Och, Jasmine, I'd love to oblige, lass, but I cannot do that. I have a thirst upon me, and I'm feeling dry. This gentleman seems to be taking up all yer time. No worries, lass, I think both these creatures were about to leave."

Sidney spurted out, "Not bloody likely you fuckin' jock. I'll have you first. Herbie, pluck this here red peacock's feathers."

The tough is Herbie, thought Ian...*ridiculous names, Sidney and Herbie, sounds like a duet of songsters.* Ian found himself quite calm.

Herbie, hearing his master's orders, was setting himself for the attack, when Ian's left hand shot up, grabbing a large chunk of the tough's greasy black hair. He moved forward and abruptly slammed Herbie's face down on the bar top. There was a sickening crunch, as teeth shattered. Ian held him there by his hair, face down on the counter. A pool of blood spread under his head.

Sidney watched the blood pool expanding, saw Ian's eyes turn cold, and thought: *This fucker is crazy.* An instant chill swept over him.

Herbie moaned weakly from the bar top, gurgling into his own blood, but didn't move. Ian slowly lifted his head up by his hair. The fight was gone out of him. Ian used his right hand to twist Herbie's ear, as he said in a quiet voice, "I think you owe this lady an apology...Herbie...then I think it would best serve you and your master to leave this place and never, ever, come back. If I were you, I'd also be finding a new master. Sidney strikes me as a waste of skin."

Through the blood, Herbie's eyes showed disbelief and excruciating pain. He'd never been handled like this. He was frightened, spit out a lot of blood and a couple of teeth, then turned his head toward Jasmine, who was still recovering from the shock of Ian's brutally swift attack. He said in an odd voice, only able to move his lips slightly, "S-Sorry, miss, it was a mistake, right enough. Didn't mean anything by it, I didn't... sorry."

Ian snarled, "Not good enough." He slammed Herbie's face down on the counter even harder...this time distinctly hearing the nose break, then let go. The big man slid over the side of the counter and crumpled to the floor.

Ian's eyes moved to Sidney, who had been watching his bodyguard's destruction in rising disbelief. He looked distraught, fear-sweat popping out. He said, "I'm going, I'm going, damn you."

Ian leaned in close, now staring up into the handsome face. He said, "While you're about it, Sidney, take this piece of rubbish with you." Sidney half pulled, half yanked Herbie across the room and out the front door.

Ian turned and smiled at Jasmine. The door burst open again. Sidney was back inside, glaring in anger. He walked up to face Ian, said, "I'm leaving, you bastard, but I'll be back for this bloody tart when you're not around to protect her."

Ian reacted quickly, insulting the tall man even more by slapping him hard with his open right hand, like one would smack a child who had done something very naughty. He said, "No you won't…not ever."

Ian slapped him again, "Not ever…understand?"

Sidney was staggered and couldn't speak, nodded his head in assent. Ian grabbed his arm and physically turned him about toward the door. He whispered menacingly, "Get out…now, while you can still walk. Should I hear about you harassing this lady again, in any way, I'll find you, rip yer testicles off, make a haggis of them, and feed them to you. Is that clear?"

Without waiting for an answer, Ian reached down, grabbed the man's testicles with his free hand, dragging the taller, but screaming man through the door and out into the street before letting go. Herbie was waiting for his master, not about to face off with Ian again. The two men helped each other hobble away, mumbling to themselves, one holding his nose and mouth, the other holding his crotch and walking very oddly on his tiptoes.

Ian came back into the Red Lion. In his mind he told his leopard to go and lie down. Jasmine looked at him curiously, said, "You have always amused me, Ian. This time you amazed me. I've never seen you like that. You're always so quiet, so calm and collected. I'd have wagered they'd eat you alive."

Ian smiled, "Sometimes I get upset. Rudeness does that to me. Guess it's not good for me to get upset, but I doubt they'll bother you again."

"I doubt they'll bother anyone again," she laughed. "Let me stand you to a dram of our finest." Despite her concern and the uproar caused by the intruders, her voice was soft and sensuous. Ian was aroused again, in spite of himself.

Under the surface he was a bit frightened by his own actions, knew at least part of it was to impress Jasmine, thought: *Suppose it hadn't worked?* He feared he would actually begin shaking, make a bloody fool of himself. He asked for their best single malt whiskey, Langavulin, drank it down, then another. As he calmed, he reflected back to the time when he met Billy Murphy, the fight in the public house in Eton, and his clumsy attempt to help. He seemed to acquit himself better in this go-round, *Thank you Billy.*

The officers at the back table had watched the entire scene, surprised by the quick and aggressive actions of this young engineer officer. As they left the public house, they stopped by Ian, and one said, "Beg pardon, Lieutenant, my compliments on your handling of that most bizarre situation…somewhat crude, but most effective."

Ian said, graciously, "It seemed appropriate, since the gentlemen in question were being such a bother to the lady. My apologies if I disturbed you."

"On the contrary, my fine fellow, you made our evening. That was very entertaining, although it could have gone quite the opposite way. Might I inquire your name, sir?"

"Ian, Ian Carlyle, at your service, gentlemen. You're right though, I suppose I could have used more delicacy, and it was a bit of a risk. I was damned lucky."

Ian saw the tall bearskin caps with no white or red hackle, the scarlet coats with buttons in sets of three down the front. These were Scots Fusilier Guards officers. He inquired, "Might I ask your names, gentlemen?"

"Of course, I'm Strange Jocelyn, this is Harry Fletcher and Edward Neville."

Neville inquired, "Do I know you, sir? Have we met?"

"Quite possibly. We may have met at the Third Guards Club while I visited my father, Lord Dunkairn."

"Of course, Waterloo, he's a legend to the rest of us," Neville said.

Ian replied, "I'm not certain my father would have approved of this night's work."

Jocelyn said, "Quite so, but then parents rarely approve of our actions. Good to meet you, Carlyle."

"Likewise, may I stand you gentlemen to a drink?"

Fletcher said, "Afraid not right now, Carlyle, sorry, duty you know. Besides, it's we who should be buying you a drink. I think your father would be proud."

Neville added, "Perhaps next time, we're on duty at Saint James shortly."

"My pleasure, gentlemen, any time," was Ian's reply. *On duty at Saint James, well, that explains the full dress uniforms. There'll be plenty of time to buy drinks, gentlemen, for soon I shall be one of you, by God I shall.*

Fletcher said, "Interesting meeting you, Carlyle. We'll say goodnight." What Ian didn't realize at the time was that these officers would carry this rather juicy tale to the Guards mess. Dunkairn's son had now sparked a reputation among the Guards as a scrapper, and a bit reckless, before ever entering the regiment.

Ian saw it as his duty as a gentleman to never again mention the tall man, Sidney, to Jasmine. She didn't see fit to explain further, but his respect of her privacy endeared him to her all the more. Jasmine thought: *This is an unusual officer, and quite handsome. I think I must have him. I'm bored with being alone. Need someone. He'll be a great diversion. I'll toy with him awhile longer, but I will have him. It's merely a question of when.*

Chapter 20

It was spring. The winter had passed frostily into the distance. Jasmine was closing the pub. Ian was standing at his place at the bar. She said, "All right, gentlemen, you've had last call. Finish up, I'm tired, and I want to go home."

The few remaining customers cheerfully downed the last dregs. This included Ian, who had imbibed a wee bit more than his usual. Of course, he would never allow himself to appear drunk in public, so it was impossible to tell when he'd had too much.

"Ian, would you stay," Jasmine whispered, as the others drifted out.

He said, "Certainly," wondering why.

After the last customer left, Jasmine looked to see that the street was clear, then locked the door. She extinguished lamps about the pub, watching him with her eyes. She then sat at a small table near the heavy wood counter, beckoning Ian to join her. The only lamp left lit was on the table itself, and gave her delicate features an intense glow.

Jasmine was always a vision, though she dressed quite plainly. She usually wore one of her two simple wool dresses, tight at the waist, and flowing out modestly in the skirt, no doubt from one or two petticoats beneath. Jasmine protected the dress from soiling with a white cotton apron. She perpetually rolled up her sleeves while working, preferring not to wear white linen over-sleeves. The rolled up sleeves gave her a rakish air.

On this night, Jasmine's black hair was parted in the middle, pulled back severely into a tight bun, accenting her dark silk skin and wondrously pleasing brown eyes. There was a stray strand of hair which had worked its way free and hung teasingly over her right eye. The whole picture came together in dazzling beauty. Whenever Ian was near her, especially when she looked at him, he could feel the heat, sometimes so strong he could almost embrace it. With the lamplight flickering on her face, this was definitely one of those occasions.

She was hushed, inches away now, looking at Ian intently from across the table, as though trying to make a decision. Ian returned her gaze, waited for her to speak, curious.

She stood up, "Ian, come with me. No questions. Say not a word. Just come with me, now. Will you do that?" Extinguishing the lamp, not waiting for an answer, she took his hand, and led him out the back door, locking it behind her. She was almost pulling Ian around a corner, down a carriageway between two brick row houses to the door of a couch house in the rear of one of them.

She said, breathlessly, "This is where I live, Ian. No one is here. Come."

They went inside, Ian breathing heavily, looking about, asked, "Where are the coaches?"

"Shush. I told you not to talk. The family I rent from has no coaches. Not anymore. Made this into my own rooms. I was lucky to get it. Now shush."

Jasmine was excited, childlike, as she took Ian into her lodgings, then up the steep, winding staircase to her bedroom loft. She calmed, became slow and deliberate, as she stood before him and removed his forage cap and scarlet coatee.

Ian, still in a state of joyous wonder, protested, "Jasmine, do you know what you're doing?" He didn't want her to make a mistake she would regret later. Wild she might be, but this sort of thing was just not done. He was thinking, *perhaps she is ill, had too much to drink. Wouldn't want to take advantage.*

Jasmine gently stroked his cheek with her delicate fingers. Ian felt a massive tremor run through his whole body. He almost swooned, as she said. "Of course I do, Ian, I always know what I'm doing. I've known this was going to happen for some time now. You shouldn't worry. My virtue will remain intact as long as you remain discreet." She unhurriedly slipped his braces off his shoulders, and pulled his shirt over his head, stroking his chest, licking playfully at his nipples.

Ian had only been with a woman once in his life, on a night at Eton when some of his classmates had devised a plan to sneak out of Dame Vallencey's house and visit a brothel in Windsor. The experience had been only modestly gratifying. His fearful, rushed, frantic climax was over before he knew much of what he was feeling. Although it nevertheless felt rather spectacular, it was nothing compared to what was happening to his body now.

Ian reasoned through it as best he could. It finally came to him, *you're thinking too hard. This is madness – you fool. She brought you here. She is seducing you. Damn it. Too hell with propriety.*

Ian didn't know what to say, or do, so he said and did nothing, which was exactly what Jasmine wanted. She needed a man in her life again, but not a chatty one. She needed a lover. One she could use and train.

Jasmine stood before him, allowing him to watch as she removed her clothing, slowly, one piece at a time. Aside from her stockings, she was naked. She chose to leave them on, smiled at the thought, the feel of silk on her feet and legs aroused her.

She moved to her knees in front of him and removed his shoes. Then, kissing his stomach, she began unbuttoning his trousers. She pulled them down gently to his ankles along with his under drawers…then took them off.

Ian by this time was swaying, finding it most difficult to remain standing, but hardly difficult to remain erect. Jasmine steadied him with her hands on his buttocks. She continued to kiss his flat stomach, the sides of his thighs and legs, bringing one hand round to stroke his hard erection gently. She kissed him there, nibbling, while massaging his buttocks.

Ian felt it surging through him, like warm rushing water, as Jasmine nursed him higher. She applied just enough pressure and persuasion to keep him a tad shy of climaxing until she felt he could take it no more, was at the height of his pleasure. She willed him to let go, then told him to, and he did. The full force of it was enhanced, prolonged, by her continued massaging, allowing him to expend himself in her mouth. Ian felt he was falling, couldn't stop, no control, the leopard taking over as he rushed to a place he had never been before. It was pure joy, uncontrolled ecstasy.

Ian fell back onto the bed, Jasmine moving like a cat up his chest, kissing, massaging. She was face to face, looking at him deeply, intensely, then slowly smiling, as he calmed a bit and began to recover his senses, "God, I…I…"

"Yes, you…you…," she laughed, mockingly. "Ian, you are priceless. You look so shocked. Did you think perhaps I was a bloody virgin? Even after that disgusting episode with my friend Sidney?"

"Well no, but…I merely never expected, and with me, I mean you are so beautiful… You could have any man, anywhere."

"…But I chose you. This is not a love affair, Ian. It is more a friendly relationship in which we make love, for our mutual satisfaction. I simply need a man in my life, again, and not merely a companion to talk with. No, I need someone to satisfy my more basic needs, as well."

Jasmine allowed him to digest this, then continued, "I chose you because I think you can handle such an arrangement, without becoming befuddled in emotion, or proposing something stupid like marriage, which we both know could never happen in this here England."

Ian's eyes were wide in astonishment.

"Was I correct? Can you handle an affair of pure lust, sprinkled with the delights of friendship and intellectual stimulation? Think before you answer, Ian."

Ian was thinking, had been thinking. He asked, "And if I can't handle such an arrangement?"

"Then we'll remain friends and fine companions. I'll never mention this night again, nor will you."

Ian smiled and succumbed willingly, "Jasmine, I'd be a complete fool to reject such an amazing proposition, as outrageous as it is. I'd be honoured to be your lover, as I'm honoured to be your friend."

"Wonderful. You've made me very happy. I assume that what we just did made you very happy, as well," Jasmine asked, smiling with mischievous and shining eyes.

"My God, Jasmine, of course it did. I've never felt like that before. You are truly astonishing."

"Good. I've pleased you." She paused, "Now, my young warhorse, I'll teach you how to please me."

Ian was happy, delighted, energized, curious, excited, mesmerized, intrigued, caring, and most eager to learn, all at the same time.

It was an odd relationship in many ways. At first Ian knew next to nothing about her, and was resolved never to ask. For his part, Ian told her everything about himself, his dreams, fears of failure, demons, and terrors, including the incident with Peter. He was reluctant, to some extent ashamed, but he ultimately told her of his revenge. Jasmine was easy to talk to, listened, and cared. She had an abundance of compassion.

They were wonderful lovers, but it took time to reach a state of mutual joy and fulfilment. At first Ian was clumsy, too cautious, then too fast, too self-absorbed. Jasmine expected this, was patient, nurturing, ever the teacher.

She taught Ian the importance of making his lover feel warm, comfortable, secure in his arms, the importance of foreplay, how to excite using words, even the sound of his voice. She demonstrated, and he practiced the delicacy and variety of touch, the essence of contrast in massaging his lover – strong, then soft; fast, then slow; hands, then fingers, then lips, then tongue…but never the same.

Jasmine knew how fundamental it was to appeal to all the senses, not merely touch, but sight, smell, hearing, sound. Sometimes she would tie him to the four posters of her bed with silk scarves, then when he was helpless and excited, make love teasingly to him. Later, of course, when he had learned more, he would do the same to her, playing passionately with her bound body until she screamed in wild unbridled climaxes, over and over.

Ian knew he had mastered the art of love-making when he could enter her and bring her to a multiple orgasm, hold her in that state of ecstasy, then bring her back down gently, at his pleasure…and, of course, hers. He was eventually able to guide her to a climax with a touch or soft scrape of his fingernails at the right place, the soles of her feet, the back of the neck, her inner thighs, inside her upper arm, or even with mere words, while he looked into her eyes.

Ian thought no one in the pub was aware of their intimacy except themselves. In fact, very little went unnoticed. Most of the regular patrons suspected Ian was a rogue, and using Jasmine for his own pleasure. No one would have believed it was her idea.

Chapter 21

Ian spent his days at Horse Guards with endless military paperwork, and most nights with Jasmine. The days seemed to be getting longer and longer, with nothing to show for his toil but more paper. It was nearly two years of mundane staff duties before Ian could take it no longer. He told Jasmine he was leaving London for a time, and went home to Dunkairn Hall on furlough to see his father.

"Father, I'm glad to be an officer of Royal Engineers. It is a wondrous and prestigious thing, but it is not my dream, and I must follow my destiny as I see it. I want a commission in the Scots Fusiliers Guards, your old regiment."

His Lordship cleared his throat, turned quickly away. Ian thought sadly: *He thinks I'm still not worthy.*

His father turned back. To Ian's disbelief, the eyes of the Earl of Dunkairn were tearing. He said, "My boy, that would make me most happy, and most proud. You have proven yourself beyond my expectations."

Ian was elated. At last he had come to terms with his father. At last he felt he had gained the trust and approval he so desperately sought all his life.

"I'll need your help, Father," Ian said, "and not only with the purchase of a commission. I believe, as you do, that there's a war brewing in the East. If war comes with Russia, I want to go with the Guards, not the Engineers."

"Of course you do, my boy, of course. I'll do what I can."

Lord Dunkairn went to work at once. His efforts were rewarded. By August 1853, he was successful in acquiring for Ian a commission in the Scots Fusilier Guards as an ensign and lieutenant.[1] This was only possible due to the untimely death of a young officer when his carriage overturned, crushing him beneath its wheels.

Upon reporting with his new orders to Wellington Barracks, in his newly bought Guards' uniform, Ian was assigned to 2nd Company, 1st Battalion, Scots Fusilier Guards. He was finally a serving infantry officer in his father's regiment. To celebrate, he went straight off to the Red Lion and told Jasmine of his good fortune. Jocelyn, Fletcher, and Neville, who had become friends with Ian since the Sidney episode, were at the pub. He passed the night in rather robust drinking with his fellow Guards officers. This was followed by passionate lovemaking with Jasmine. She was pleased for him, and he now knew just how to please her.

---

[1] During this period, Guards officers only were privileged by the Crown to hold dual rank. They had a rank in their Guards regiment and a higher rank in the Army system, itself. This higher rank gave them an advantage in seniority within the Army, but was disliked by the less advantaged line regiment officers. The system was eventually abolished after the Crimean War. It meant that within the Scots Fusilier Guards, Ian Carlyle would function as an ensign, but was referred to by his higher Army rank of Lieutenant. When serving outside the Guards, as on a General's staff, he would function and be treated as a Lieutenant. His next promotion would be to Lieutenant and Captain, then to Captain and Lieutenant Colonel. In this book Guards officers will be referred to by their higher Army ranks, as would have been the custom in 1854. This may be a bit confusing, as company commanders, usually Captains in line regiments, will be referred to as Lieutenant Colonels.

Chapter 22

"Mister Carlyle, the enemy in this training exercise is our own 2nd Battalion. Number 2 Company is to move to this crossroads, here, and establish a picquet post to cover approaches to the main body behind us in camp around this hill, exactly here." The company commander, Captain and Lieutenant Colonel James Hunter-Blair, pointed to a crossroads on a map of the Chobham Training Area, Surrey, and the main Guards Brigade camp about a half mile behind it on and around a large hill. Hunter-Blair was thinking. *This Carlyle chap is supposed to be a good officer, Woolwich, and all that. Well, we'll see. Actually, there is something about him.*

Hunter-Blair, a rather tall, well set up man with good bones and a huge, thick moustache, was a fine officer, well respected among his peers, highly thought of by his men. *From what I've seen so far,* Ian thought, *the kind of leader Billy Murphy would have enjoyed serving under – hard, but fair.*

"Carlyle, are you listening?"

"Yes, sir, I was studying the map."

"Well, pay attention, by damn. On our left flank will be Number 1 Company, 1st Battalion, on picquet, as well, approximately one thousand yards down and positioned along this same east-west road. On our right is Number 3

Company's picquet, along this same road at the next crossroads, perhaps twelve hundred yards distant."

Ian nodded his understanding.

"Unfortunately, we will be somewhat under strength, and will be well and truly on our own. The field officer of the day is Colonel Walker. He'll be at the brigade camp, and make rounds of the picquet posts from there. Our orders are to hold this crossroads until we're flanked, then withdraw slowly, remaining engaged until we reach the brigade position. We are then to move to its rear and assume duties as a reserve. Are we clear, thus far, Lieutenant?"

"Yes, sir," Ian replied, thinking: *He doesn't know me yet. Thinks I'm a complete imbecile. Of course it's clear. I wonder what he's playing at. Why so much detail this far in advance, not his normal style, I'll wager.*

"Here's the immediate difficulty, Carlyle. One section of the company is to be detached as the personal escort to the Colonel of the Regiment, General His Royal Highness George, Duke of Cambridge." Lieutenant Colonel Hunter-Blair tried to look proud, concerned, and disappointed at the same time.

He failed, but continued, "I find it necessary to lead this escort detachment, personally. Too sensitive to allow anyone else. Other subalterns have no training, and you at least have time at Woolwich, even if you are rather new to the Guards." He looked directly into Ian's eyes, "Quite an honour and responsibility, for a new man. You'll lead the company, understand, Carlyle?"

"Yes, sir, I understand perfectly."

"I'll give you Colour Sergeant Skein, good man, experienced, and two other sergeants, as well as three full sections, two-thirds of the company, about sixty men. Should do you nicely. Doubt you'll even see the enemy."

"And the other officers and sergeants, sir?"

"Ahhh, well, I'll be taking them with me. Know you'll do us proud, lad, what with all that training you've had. I'll be watching you."

Ian said, "Thank you for the opportunity, sir." Then he thought: *So that's his game. Well-played Colonel. If I'm successful, you get the credit. Should I mess my copybook, you'll be able to cast sufficient blame, stay clear of any flying feces. After all, you were told I had "training."*

Colour Sergeant Archibald Skein was tall, on the heavy side, with a rather fat, ratty face, wide punched-in nose, thick shaggy side-whiskers, and a clean chin. Skein was like far too many non-commissioned officers Ian had encountered in his relatively few years in the military. He was wise in the ways of soldiering, and how to avoid unpleasant duties, but thought little of his men, except as it allowed him to feed his ravenous thirst for power over them. He excelled at manipulating officers, particularly young new ones. He would talk behind their backs with undisguised disgust, saying, "Ink not dry on their damned bought commissions, lots of pedigree, no brains to speak of, sod 'em all."

In Skein's eyes Hunter-Blair was a figurehead, his personal puppet when it came to running the company. Skein was a rock-hard disciplinarian, used to getting his own way, having more or less a free reign. In his arrogance, he was unable to understand that Hunter-Blair was merely allowing him the latitude to do his job as senior company sergeant.

Ian had been with Number 2 Company only a few weeks before they moved to Chobham for training. He saw Colour Sergeant Skein handling the men only once or twice, but had his measure. Angus' advice and Billy's training came back to him in a rush. This was an old-school sergeant, thoroughly impressed with himself, but not with officers. He knew he'd have to take hold and thrash him about a bit to get his attention, respect, and fear, if necessary.

After his talk with Hunter-Blair, Ian returned to Number 2 Company camp and found Skein holding formation, screaming at the top of his lungs at a cowering, frail-looking private.

Ian said, lightly, "Colour Sergeant Skein, excuse me a moment. Might I have a word with you…over here."

"Sir." Skein, obviously annoyed at being interrupted, walked the several paces to where Ian stood with his back to the men. Skein was forced to circle around in order to face the officer, as was proper. He saluted and remained at attention.

Ian returned the salute, but did not say stand at ease. He said, "We've been ordered up, Colour Sergeant. Tomorrow morning we're to take three sections on an exercise. We'll take the first three. The Captain will take the fourth section as escort to the Colonel of the Regiment. It'll be you and me and two other sergeants; you pick them, make them good men."

"Humph, now ain't that just dandy," Skein grunted.

Ian stared hard at Skein, for several seconds, then said, "Is there something you wanted to say, Colour Sergeant?"

Skein blinked, surprised at the directness and confidence of this new officer. He said, "No, sir, er, they'll be ready at dawn, sir. Ye can count on that."

"Good, Colour Sergeant, full canteens and one day's ration, salt pork and biscuits."

"Sir." Skein expected a degree of new officer reluctance or fear of first contact with senior non-commissioned officers, but there was none of that. *Something in those cold eyes,* he thought. *Careful of this here officer, Skein my lad. He's not yer usual green sprout, all thumbs and two left feet. This one bears watching.*

The next morning Skein had the men turned out smartly, brasses shined, uniforms clean, standing in two ranks, in open order. They told off at sixty-three in all, with Skein and two other sergeants included. As Ian walked up, Skein snapped to attention, saluted smartly, "All present or accounted for, sir. Every man a full canteen and one day's ration, caps and blank cartridges issued."

"Very good, Colour Sergeant. I'll inspect the men now." Ian adjusted the bearskin cap straight on his head.

Skein said, "Won't be necessary, sir. Just inspected them m'self, sir. They're right as rain."

Ian turned his head very slowly and deliberately to look at Skein again with instantly cold eyes. He said precisely, "I'll inspect the men *now*, Colour Sergeant. You will follow me. Clear?"

"Yes, sir," said Skein, taken off-guard again. This veiled rebuke was not lost on the men in the company. Some even smiled, guardedly.

Ian walked the line of the front rank, stood before each man, asked his name, and a few other questions. He focused his full attention on them, listened to their answers, memorizing, analyzing the overall experience level.

Skein followed at his heels, notebook in hand, looking very much the nanny, but with an underlying viciousness. Ian could see this was quite disconcerting to the troops when Skein stared them down. *Not necessarily a bad thing. He certainly has their attention,* Ian thought, *we'll see.*

As Ian faced each man, he took his musket, examined it for rust, inspected the percussion nipple to ensure it was clear, tested the hammer, then sprang the rammer lightly by lifting it a few inches out of the muzzle and letting it fall back. This made certain the barrel was clean by the ringing sound the rammer made when it hit bottom. He said nothing about the weapons as he moved. Skein was thinking as he watched: *Why's he spending so much time with these devils? He'd best learn these bastards is scum, to a man.*

When Ian came to the private Skein had been admonishing when he first approached the formation the previous day, he asked, "Your name?"

"Private Swann, sir." Ian suspected from his accent that he was about as Scottish as East London.

"How old are you, Swann?"

"Seventeen, sir."

"How long in the Fusiliers?"

"Six months, sir."

Ian took Swann's weapon. It glistened, not a speck of dirt, lint or rust. Ian asked, "When did you clean this musket last, Swann?"

"I clean it once a day, sir. Cleaned it late last night, sir."

"Good work, Swann. Did the colour sergeant instruct you?"

Swann hesitated, "Uh, no, sir. It were 'Gregor' and 'Fergie,' sir, I mean MacGregor and Fergusson." From the corner of his eye Ian noticed Skein flinch and scowl. His lips snarled at Swann. Ian had already passed both these men, but made a mental note of their names, and moved on to the next soldier.

Completing the front rank, Ian walked behind it, examined bayonets and cartridge boxes. He asked each man how many percussion caps and blank cartridges they had been issued, if they had rations, and checked for full canteens. He followed the same meticulous procedure with the rear rank.

When he finished, he asked Skein to step off to the side with him. "Colour Sergeant, did you say you'd inspected these men?"

"Yes, sir." Skein smiled, expecting a compliment.

"Then, Colour Sergeant, we have a problem."

"Don't understand, sir. Something wrong?"

"Yes, Skein, there is something wrong. Some of these weapons are dirty, and some are plain faulty. With a few possible exceptions, I wouldn't trust any of them to fire true or consistently."

"Sir, I take exception to..."

"Shut your damn mouth, Skein. I don't recall asking your opinion. Is it your habit to talk back to your officers?"

"No, sir, beggin yer pardon, sir," Skein involuntarily came to attention.

"Good. You will have the men clean their weapons again before we depart. You will personally check them, and correct any problems. Do we have an understanding?"

"Sir," replied Skein.

Ian said, "Right. There's another problem. Half these men didn't know how many caps they have or cartridges they were issued. That's unacceptable, Colour Sergeant. I want them to know and be able to shout out clearly the number remaining at all times."

"Yes, sir, but..."

"Not 'but,' Colour Sergeant, the proper reply to an officer is, 'Yes, sir.'" Ian waited...

"Yes, sir."

"Lastly, issue the men two more packages of blank cartridges and extra caps to put in their pockets before we leave. I've already told the ordnance sergeant to expect you."

"Yes, sir."

"We leave in one hour. Think you can manage that, Colour Sergeant?"

"Yes, sir, of course, sir. I'll see that it's done, sir, and see that those men who've offended ye are punished, sir. If ye'll give me the names, I'll…"

Ian interrupted, "Skein, none of these men have offended me. Only you have offended me. This was you're fault, not theirs. Your responsibility. You simply haven't trained them right, or inspected them properly. Also, Skein, as long as these men are assigned to me, you'll not punish them without my approval. Clear?"

"Yes, sir."

Ian walked away, calling back, "One hour."

Chapter 23

They arrived at their picquet position on schedule. Skein began to form the three sections on line in two ranks facing north, centring on the crossroads.

Ian stopped him, and said in a low, but intense voice, "Colour Sergeant, in the future you'll not deploy the men until you know how I want them deployed."

"Sir."

"Now, deploy the men with all sections facing north, but not in one line. I want number one section in line just south of the crossroads, straddling it. Number two section southeast of the crossroads, but in the woods further back, in echelon. I want the third section well back behind the first, hidden in reserve. You are to build low hasty works, well concealed, and ensure that all the men are hidden from view from the likely approach of an enemy. That would be from the North, Colour Sergeant."

"Sir, you're splitting up the sections? That isn't wise, sir. We've never done that before."

"Skein, damn you, man, I will not have you question my orders. Place a file on each flank, and rotate files forward as sentry posts, one file from each section, three sentry posts.

They're to give warning if troops approach, then withdraw beyond our positions, understand, beyond them. Then return to their stations from the rear, while remaining concealed from the advancing enemy. I'll give you the exact locations where I want them presently. See to it."

"Yes, sir," Skein said, but thought: *Go ahead, ye bastard, this'll likely do ye in better than if I'd planned it.*

Ian began observing the position. The north-south road cut his position in half. There was an open field to their front on the right of the north-south road. Beyond that field was a dense treeline at the edge of a thickly wooded area. On the left side of the north-south road, to their front were low trees, scrub, and swamp, giving much less cover for an advancing force than the thick woods beyond the open field on their right.

Ian had the left sentries placed 200 yards out in this swampy terrain, with orders to stay hidden, low to the ground. The centre sentries were on the north-south road, about 250 yards out. The right sentries were to cover the wood line on the far side of the open field to their right front, again about 200 yards out. The crossroads, itself, contained sufficient foliage to conceal low works by blending them in with the trees and scrub.

Ian had the sergeants set the men to building defence works with available fallen trees and bushes in front of the three section positions. These were high enough to allow a kneeling man to fire over the top, but long enough to allow the section to line up behind them in one continuous rank, rather than two ranks, thus doubling the frontal length of the section. Ian hoped this would give the impression to an attacker that there were at least twice as many men. The two sections being side by side, but in echelon, with one section forward and the other back, furthered this illusion.

The hastily thrown together works completed, more for concealment than solid protection, Ian used what time he had left to practice all three sections in the volley firing drills, and firing by section by rank. He alternated men from the front and rear ranks in the single line behind the works, so that if he fired by rank, muskets throughout the length of the line would be firing. Every other man was from the rear rank. This was again to support the illusion of more men.

It was several hours later, when not one, but two companies of the 2nd Battalion "enemy" appeared, marching by fours toward them straight down the north-south road. Ian could see them clearly, knew his picquet was outnumbered more than two to one. His men, even in a single line, could be easily outflanked by a force double its size. *I'll have to be very careful,* he thought.

Ian first heard scattered popping, as the skirmishers advanced ahead of the main body, exchanging shots with Ian's two-man sentry posts. Each post followed orders and fell back in measured segments, fighting as file-mates, firing alternately as they moved.

Ian was actually impressed by their spirit and zeal. They made their way around the crossroads and came back in the position from the rear, staying concealed, as they were told. They reported that the two attacking companies were moving into the dense woods on their right front, beyond the open field, as Ian suspected they would. Their commander had not wanted to get mired down in the swamp to the left of the road. They were moving forward slowly, skirmishers in advance, by the book.

Ian also suspected that when they came into the open field, having deployed into a two-company front, they would cross the field in a simple frontal attack, thinking they'd force the small picquet to withdraw by sheer weight of numbers. Such a tactic wasn't very imaginative, but it was the accepted

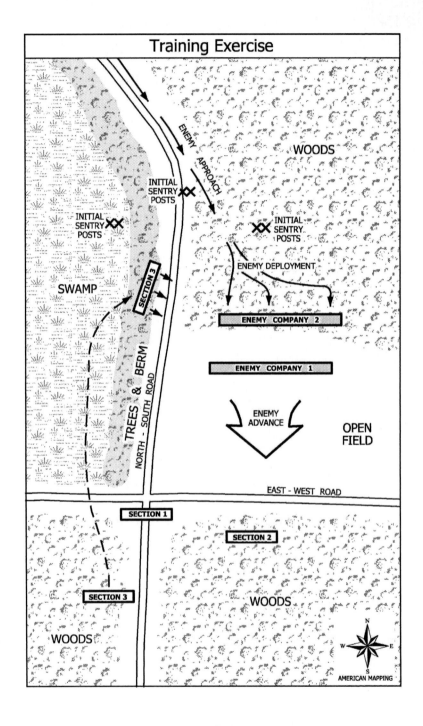

Training Exercise

doctrine, and presented Ian with an idea. *Hell, it's two companies; they'll be fronted on line moving through dense woods. We'll only have to take on the first company in the open field until they bring the second company up next to the first. If I move fast, I may be able to hit them in the arse before that happens. This may be an opportunity.*

By now their skirmishers could be seen appearing along the treeline, 200 yards away. Ian's front two sections were still hidden behind their low works. The third section was lying flat behind their works to the rear, completely out of sight, ready to move as needed.

Ian ordered, "All sections, load and prime." Each man tore open a blank cartridge, poured the powder within down the barrel, then stuffed the paper on top and rammed it home to tamp the loose powder in place of an actual musket ball.

The 'enemy' skirmish line advanced into the open, cautiously, knowing someone was out there, somewhere. Behind the skirmishers the first company broke out from the wood, spilled into the open field in a ragged line, reforming rapidly in the open, dressing their ranks, anxious for contact. Ian's works were still unseen, even by the advancing skirmishers, his men holding quiet and steady behind them.

Ian said, "Sergeants, we will open the ball. Commence firing by volley, by section. On my command..."

Ian shouted, "Number 1 and 2 Sections, present, FIRE!" The volley crashed out in perfect unison. The "enemy" was surprised, in spite of their anticipation, by the abrupt ferocity of the volley, and the apparent length of the line in front of them. Both the skirmishers and advancing company faltered upon seeing the muzzle blasts spread out in two long lines behind works, even without the effect of live ammunition. The 'enemy' skirmishers commenced an orderly withdrawal around both sides of the advancing lead company, unmasking its front.

An officer came into the open field behind his company. He looked extremely young, even from that distance. They halted and fired a ragged volley. Ian barked, "Sergeants, continue firing by rank. Skein, you're in charge here, keep the bastards busy."

Skein replied, briskly, "Sir."

There were quick short commands and volleys were on their way, with loud singular crashes. Ian thought: *Good volleys, lads. Now just keep that up. They'll trade volleys trying to figure out who we are and how many. Hopefully they'll hold the second company in the woods for a time before deploying it on line with the first in the open. That's what I'd do.*

As he thought through it, he moved back quickly to the third section, 20 more men hidden on their bellies in reserve. There was no sergeant with this section, all the other NCOs being with Hunter-Blair on escort duty. Ian asked, "Who's the best man here?" Two or three muffled voices said, "MacGregor, sir." Ian recalled the name as one of the men who had helped Swann, the recruit, with his musket.

He hissed, "MacGregor, here, quickly." No one moved, "Now, damn it."

"Sir."

Private Sean MacGregor crawled forward, briskly now. He was a giant of a man. When Ian had stood before him at inspection, he was at least a head taller, and wider at the shoulders. MacGregor had a narrow waist, brown hair, and a ruggedly handsome clean-shaven face, with penetrating almost black eyes.

MacGregor, 'Gregor' to his mates, was born near Fort William, in the highlands north of Glasgow. He was the eldest of six children, having three brothers and two sisters. His parents were simple farmers, who scrapped out a living to feed the large family. Sean decided to leave home early, to give them one less to feed.

MacGregor came to London, where no 'legal' work could be found. He eventually joined the Scots Fusilier Guards, a few steps ahead of the constables, and was well suited to the life. He even managed to send a bit of money home from time to time, by depriving himself.

MacGregor had been made up to corporal twice and broken down both times. Ian wasn't aware of these particulars, but thought it might be something of the like. The big Scotsman was impressive. He looked like a non-commissioned officer.

Ian said, "MacGregor, you are now Acting Sergeant."

"Me, sir?"

"We don't have much time. Here's the plan. We're going to our left front, around the right of those lads out there from the 2nd Battalion. We'll move double-quick through that swamp, staying low, hidden by the trees and the rise in ground. We'll come up behind their right flank, then give them a taste of what for. What say ye to that, MacGregor? Are ye with me?"

MacGregor didn't answer immediately, not used to being asked such a question by an officer. Ian gave him a chance to ponder, wanting a steady man he could count on, not an empty-brained yes-sir type.

MacGregor saw immediately the simple beauty of the plan, a covered flank movement followed by a surprise assault on their rear. The manoeuvre was easy enough, but the act of doing it as a picquet company was dangerous and unconventional. It certainly wasn't what routine picquet duty was all about. As far as he understood, they were to defend, then fall back…give warning, but never attack. This plan was aggressive and outrageous, *and it might just work*, he thought.

MacGregor said, "I'm yer man, sir, indeed I am."

"Excellent. Move sharply, MacGregor. Carry on."

MacGregor turned to the section, spit out several orders. *He's done this before,* Ian thought.

MacGregor then did something Ian liked. He rapidly briefed the section on exactly what they were going to do, so every man knew what he was about. The section jumped at his commands. He had them moving in short order, but not out of fear. There was respect in their eyes, an eagerness.

Ian led the way, motioning to MacGregor, "Come, we're about to show those sods a thing or two."

They moved at the double-quick, 150 paces per minute, a slow bent run, under cover of bushes and scrub trees on their right. The swamp was wet, but not deep. They were soon looking at the flank, and then at the rear of the two companies moving toward their works.

We haven't been seen yet, he thought. At Ian's order, MacGregor set the men in a simple section front, standing in two ranks. They were hidden behind a small thicket.

The second attacking company was just approaching the edge of the wood line with Ian unseen at their right rear. Ian was not about to let them clear the woods and deploy both companies on line. He commanded, "Rear rank, present, FIRE!" A sharp volley went out. Without command, and as rapidly as possible, the rear rank began reloading.

Ian paused only briefly, then, "Front rank, present, FIRE! The volley was crisp and together.

Most of the eager rear rank had reloaded, and come to the ready position to prime. Ian then commanded, "Rear rank, present, FIRE!" Another thunderclap. The volleys continued as each rank reloaded.

The advancing companies were taken completely off-guard. Had Ian been using live ammunition, they would have paid heavily at this close range. The enemy was now receiving fire from two directions, front and right rear.

The volume of continuing fire seemed to the attackers to be overwhelming. The muzzle flashes and smoke bespoke a much larger force than their own. Rather than coming on line against their front, the rear company was forced to wheel right to face this new threat, a manoeuvre never meant to be effectively executed in thick woods.

The leading company was still engaged to their front. The sections under Skein were firing volleys from behind their works like the relentless beating of a giant drum. The surly, but experienced Skein was actually doing a splendid job. The young officer commanding the now stalled companies was confused and somewhat disoriented. The right wheel in the woods caused the second company to break up in some disorder. He soon found his position impossible.

He ordered his companies to withdraw. In doing so, they were barely able to hold their formation, and had to halt inside the woods to reorganize. All three of Ian's sections began cheering. Even Colour Sergeant Archibald Skein, although scowling, finally saw the method in Ian's plan, and its obvious success.

When they were disengaged, a truce was signalled. A lieutenant colonel, monitoring the training of the two 2nd Battalion companies, came forward. The captain who commanded the two companies, head lowered, was trailing behind.

The lieutenant colonel shook Ian's hand heartily, "Good show, young man, by Jove, brilliant show. Your battalion is made of most excellent stuff. Boxed us in to a fare-thee-well. Where is your commander? I should like to congratulate him myself. He certainly gave my captain here a right jolly towelling." The captain standing behind the colonel nodded to Ian, who returned the nod.

The captain saw fit to add in his own defence, and rather smugly, "We didn't expect to engage the entire 1st Battalion line so soon, Lieutenant. We expected to encounter a picquet post, and, frankly, we would have dispatched them straight away. Your numbers were just too much for us."

"Thank you, sir," Ian addressed the lieutenant colonel, ignoring the captain, "but I'm afraid the battalion commander is elsewhere. I commanded these men, sir."

"You, sir, a junior officer commanding a whole battalion, how very odd."

"Not a battalion, sir. We are but three sections of a company, about sixty men in all." Ian then turned to the captain, who had become pasty, and added, gently, "My apologies, Captain, but we're just what you expected to 'dispatch,' as you put it. We are, in fact, a company-sized picquet post, under strength by about twenty men. The entire 1st Battalion is well behind us, hopefully by now having established a strong defensive position."

The lieutenant colonel was incredulous, "Sixty men? A picquet you say? My nearly two hundred were attacked and thrashed by sixty men? Why I'd have sworn…"

Ian replied, "I'm afraid so, sir." MacGregor was standing within hearing, hardly containing himself, as were the rest of Number 3 section. He was thinking, *now here's a story to tell the boys around the campfires.*

After digesting the truth of it, the lieutenant colonel laughed, heartily, congratulating Ian on his tactics, initiative, and the resolve of his men, "By gad, you're a dangerous man, Lieutenant, for an outnumbered picquet post, attacking was a risky move, but damned audacious. Splendid work, what say you, Captain?"

The captain said blandly, "Yes, sir, splendid." He didn't seem quite so taken with Ian's audacity.

The lieutenant colonel was smiling, "I shall see that this engagement and you in particular, are mentioned to your superiors. What's your name, lad?"

"Carlyle, sir, Lieutenant Ian Carlyle, but if you please, sir, it was Number 2 Company, 1st Battalion, who fought this engagement. The credit is theirs."

"Of course, Carlyle, as it should be. Again, my compliments to you and your men, fine work."

Ian saluted, turned about, and walked back to number three section. As he passed MacGregor, he winked, "Bring the men along, Acting Sergeant MacGregor."

At the crossroads, to Skein's amazement, Ian thanked him, "Good work, Colour Sergeant, good work indeed."

Ian then had him form the other two sections so that all three were together, and said, "Guardsmen, you've done excellent work today. You should be proud of yourselves."

He ordered Skein to march them back to camp. Ian noticed their step seemed lighter, more determined. When they talked about it afterward in the tents in the field, in the barracks and public houses, and they did talk about it, they could not recall many young officers the likes of this Lieutenant Carlyle.

Chapter 24

Private Broderick Swann came from simple roots, an orphan of the East London streets. He was seventeen, had been a thief most of his young life. He was a bit too clumsy for a master pickpocket, and a bit too conspicuous for much else. The criminal underworld merely adopted him as its own, and said no more about it.

He was built small, unusually thin, and bony. His mates called him "Little Twig," or "Skeleton." His light blond spiky hair, large beakish nose, and narrow face added to his diminutive stick-like appearance, which always seemed in contrast with itself. When you looked at Private Swann, you had the feeling he should have been tall, then his whole façade would have somehow come together. No matter how hard he tried to clean or brush his uniform, he always seemed to look like a small bundle of ill-fitting red rags with a great black bearskin cap sitting on top.

Swann always wanted to strike out on his own in the world. When he joined the Fusilier Guards, he had never before been a stone's throw from East London. The adjustment wasn't easy, particularly in a Scottish regiment. Colour Sergeant Skein was a hard Scotsman. He hated the English and took particular joy in singling out the smaller, weaker ones who came into his sights. He seemed to know precisely

Swann's failings. Punishment was severe, and in many cases not undeserved. Swann was improving, but slowly.

He was in Number 3 Section, with Sean MacGregor and Alexander Fergusson, two of the more experienced privates in the battalion. Swann thought MacGregor might well have been a sergeant except for his fists. Fergusson was the oldest man in the company, a wise veteran campaigner, respected by all. Having no liking for Skein, both helped Swann learn the odd ways of soldiering, keeping him away from even more serious folly.

Swann was with the section earlier in the day, when the new officer led them to victory against their friendly enemies in 2nd Battalion. Later, around the cookfires, he was feeling very good about their triumph. He told his mates, "That'll do for those 2nd Battalion sods. Serves 'em right, the bastards."

As Swann walked swiftly toward the officers' tents, he felt very uncomfortable. He had been ordered by Skein to go to the officers' mess, find Mister Carlyle, and tell him Lieutenant Colonel Hunter-Blair wished to see him as soon as possible. Swann found the officers' mess soon enough, set up as it was in a giant marquee tent, sides rolled up due to the heat, with a large number of officers under the tent top enjoying tea and sherry, discussing the morning's training.

He hoped to unobtrusively locate Mister Carlyle, deliver the message from Lieutenant Colonel Hunter-Blair, and be on his way. As he tried to slip past a group of officers standing just inside the tent, one of the officers turned abruptly and faced him, "You there, private, what brings you here?"

Swann snapped his best salute at the officer, preparing to ask where he might find Mister Carlyle. In the process, his right arm brushed against a tall captain, as he was bringing a glass of sherry unsteadily to his lips. The contents of the glass splashed wildly, staining his scarlet dress coat and three-inch-wide white cross belt.

The captain was furious. He shouted, "You clumsy clod. I'll teach you to respect your officers." He then commenced to berate the young cringing soldier for nearly a full minute. The abuse was so strong it set Swann off balance, and he dropped to one knee.

He cried, "Sir, I-I beg yer pardon, sir. It w-won't happen again, sir. Very sorry, sir."

"Nonsense, you're either the clumsiest man alive, or you did that on purpose. Either way, you deserve a good thrashing." The other officers standing about were stunned. They watched the spectacle, not their business.

The captain was just gaining momentum. He looked menacingly at Swann, and continued to berate him. Swann managed to get to his feet and snap to attention to take his dressing down like a soldier.

There were a few other ranks on a work detail, standing a short distance from the officers' mess tent. Having heard the loud commotion, they stood watching the incident unfold through the open sides of the tent. It certainly appeared the officer was about to strike the soldier, and they knew they could say or do damned all about it. Among them was Private Alexander Fergusson, who was rapidly becoming steaming mad.

Fergusson had been in the Fusiliers since he was a lad, beginning as a bandsman. He was of ordinary height and weight, with ordinary blue eyes. His washed out brown hair was cut so short it hardly showed under his cap. His most distinguishing feature was that he had no distinguishing features, which suited him nicely.

Any time Fergusson thought his skills were getting him noticed or placing him in line for promotion, he would purposely get very drunk or in a fight. This had been highly successful thus far in keeping him a simple private, with occasional fits of extra duty or time in the guardhouse.

Now he watched as Swann, who didn't know how to use ash to shine his brass, was being severely and publicly dressed down for a perceived infraction that should have been resolved with a healthy rebuke and on your way. If the officer actually struck Swann, Fergusson wasn't certain he could hold back. He and MacGregor had taken young Swann under their protection when he first arrived, and he considered the youngster his ward, almost like a son. He also knew, as an old soldier, the consequences of any action or interference on his part. He would be well done for.

The captain was still shouting. Swann, at rigid attention, looked terrified, eyes wide and wild. Fergusson was about to step forward into the officers' mess tent, when a figure stepped between the enraged captain and Swann. It was the new officer who had put that bastard Skein in his place, then so ably led their company in defeating those 2nd Battalion sods. He was thinking, *bless ye sir, ye've likely saved me from a flogging, as well as the boy from a beating.*

Ian was one of the officers relaxing in the mess tent, drinking his own glass of sherry, talking about the day's training. He came to the mess thinking he might locate Lieutenant Colonel Hunter-Blair to report the morning's action. He saw the commotion near the tent entrance, and approached the growing circle of officers. There was a tall officer, highly agitated, admonishing a young private in a very loud, slurred voice. He asked an officer next to him, "What's all this, then?"

"Well old boy, the private spilled the good captain's sherry all over him. He's been shouting at the poor lad since, and there doesn't appear to be an end to it. I thought he was going to pummel the lad, may yet, by gad. Court martial offence if he does."

Ian recognized young Swann just as the red-faced officer was raising his voice even louder, and raising a riding crop at the same time. Without hesitation, Ian stepped between. He said, "I beg your pardon, sir. If you'll forgive me."

The captain was shocked, "Excuse me, Lieutenant, and what the bloody hell are you about?"

"My name is Carlyle, sir, Number 2 Company," Ian said in measured tones. "At the moment, this is my man you're shouting at. I submit, with due respect, that should he deserve such admonishment, it would be the decision of the battalion commander and his own company commander, not yours."

"The bloody cheek...you damned insubordinate pup. I'll have none of this." The officer speaking was Captain Malcolm Vane, 5th Company, 1st Battalion. He was a tall, handsome officer, with thick dark brown hair, and square-shoulders. He looked immaculate in his splendidly tailored scarlet uniform, except, of course, for the sherry stains. If there was a physical flaw, it was that he had a haughty droopiness about his eyelids, giving him a somewhat vacant, superior look, as though totally indifferent to whomever he was speaking to and his surroundings.

Although Vane was, in fact, arrogant and condescending to those not considered by him as equals, of the proper class, he was otherwise intelligent, witty, and had a reputation as a highly competent officer. On this day, however, he had taken a bit too many glasses of the most excellent officers' mess sherry.

He said to Ian, "Get out of my way." He then made the mistake of taking hold of Ian's arm in an attempt to push him aside to get at the lad again. Ian, from pure reflex, with startling speed, put the heel of his right hand flat into Vane's face, one of Billy's favourite moves.

Vane was knocked off his feet, into a table, landed on his backside, with a frozen look of wide-eyed astonishment. His nose began to sprout blood. He grabbed his bent facial appendage, mumbling nasally, "My God, you've broken my nose."

Ian was about to say something, but another voice interrupted him. Stephenson, the regimental major, pushed his way through the gawking officers, said, "Vane, you damned bloody fool."

He turned, "Mess Sergeant, take the staff outside."

As the soldiers filed out, Stephenson turned to Vane and said, "On your feet, Vane, I can't recall ever seeing a more unofficer-like exhibition in a Guards mess, or anywhere else."

Vane stood unsteadily and stared at Stephenson, tried to stem the flow of blood from his nose with a large reddening handkerchief, said, "But he broke my nose."

"Humph," was Stephenson's retort, "and I'm told you chastised a soldier in front of the entire mess for spilling sherry on your uniform, and even threatened to strike him."

There was a pause for Vane to reply.

When he failed to do so, Stephenson said, "From what I can see, it's quite true. Damn good you didn't hit him or you'd be on charges. Utterly disgraceful, and for messing your damned uniform. Then to top it all, you laid your hands on a junior officer, who was, as I see it, trying to prevent you from making an even worse fool of yourself. I'm only glad the colonel didn't witness your disgusting conduct."

The major looked around the room at the taciturn assembly of officers, "And as for you, gentlemen, I didn't see any of you stepping in to stop Vane. This disgraceful episode will not be discussed outside the mess or the regiment. The sooner forgotten, the better – understood?" There were nods around the tent, heads hanging. They understood.

"Now, for God's sake, Vane, go get tended to and pull yourself together." The humiliated Vane turned a brighter red, which to some degree matched the blood on his face. He looked to be in some pain as he replied simply, "Sir." He unsteadily spun on his heels and walked briskly away. His left hand was clenching his blood-soaked handkerchief to his face, while his right hand, in a fist, punched his leg.

Swann, who had been much relieved by the interruption, was still mightily afraid. He continued to stand at attention while the major was speaking.

Now the major turned to him. "Name private?"

"Swann, sir."

"Swann, why are you in the officers' mess?"

"I come to deliver a message to Mister Carlyle, sir," he said, nodding toward Ian.

Stephenson said, "Well, get on with it."

"Yes, sir. Er, Mister Carlyle, sir, Lieutenant Colonel Hunter-Blair wants to see you at your earliest convenience, sir."

Ian nodded, "Thank you, Swann."

Stephenson said, "Swann, you will forget this incident happened. Is that clear?"

"Yes, sir."

The major said, "You're dismissed, Swann. Return to camp."

The major turned toward Ian, "Carlyle, is it?"

"Yes, sir. I apologize for all the trouble, sir."

"You should, Mister Carlyle. You struck a superior officer, whatever the cause, and you'll not get away quite that easy."

The major lowered his voice, "You will report to your company commander and tell him I have awarded you seven days extra duty as picquet officer."

"Yes, sir."

"You're dismissed." He turned to the officers crowding around, "As for the rest of you, get back to whatever you were doing. This incident did not happen." Ian left the mess quickly, and returned to camp. The other officers drifted back into their own conversations and card games with, of course, something new to talk about.

"Really, Carlyle," Hunter-Blair said, somewhat amused by the whole episode, "damned good thing the colonel wasn't present. Major Stephenson handled it exactly right. I'm certain the commanding officer will find out what happened and approve of his actions...but not officially, of course. This way it will go no further."

He continued, "On the other hand, Carlyle, I suspect you've made an enemy in Vane. Better watch your step. His father's got a handle, a Baronet, or some such. In any event, he has a relationship with His Royal Highness, the Duke of Cambridge."

"I'll be cautious, sir," Ian replied.

"You were right to put a stop to Vane's unseemly behaviour, but you must know you were absolutely wrong in the way you went about it. You confronted, verging on insubordination, a superior officer, then knocked him down, even if there was provocation. Damned well could have ruined a promising career – yours. I heard about your actions this morning, unorthodox, but highly successful. Well done, Carlyle. Knew you could do. Now I know I can count on you, and I shall. We'll put this little episode behind us...after you've done your picquet officer duties. So good of you to volunteer."

It was not only Hunter-Blair who heard of that morning's success on the training field and the confrontation in the mess. The stories spread quickly throughout the small world of the Guards Brigade. Everyone knew in short order. Among the officers, there was a fresh, grudging respect for the young officer of engineers, recently come to the Guards.

The non-commissioned officers and other ranks were also aware that there was a new officer on parade, and an unusual one at that. His competence had been proven, and the incident of saving Swann from further embarrassment and possibly a beating became the talk of the camp.

The way Swann told it, "Mister Carlyle's a bloody good bloke. You should have seen him belt that bastard Vane. Busted his nose right proper, put him down on his bloody arse." Fergusson, of course, was able to confirm what Swann described, and no one disputed Fergusson's word.

The talk continued when the Guards Brigade returned to Wellington Barracks after they completed their training exercises. By then it was common knowledge that Vane's nose was in a bad way. It was not broken, but his sinuses and nasal passages were damaged. Vane was continually dripping from the nose as though he had a permanent cold. He was forced to constantly sniffle, and dab it or blow it with his handkerchief. The doctors could not seem to do anything for it. It was most unbecoming to a dashing officer of Guards.

Vane was left seething with rage and humiliation. He was conscious of other captains' wry smiles, junior officers, non-commissioned officers, and even rankers laughing at him. He now had an abiding dislike of that upstart lieutenant he had seen so briefly through a red haze. On the other hand, without realizing it, Ian had recruited three loyal subordinates in MacGregor, Fergusson, and Swann.

Ian never actually told Jasmine the story. She heard it from Guards officers who were calling it the 'sherry stain incident.' She laughed, and said to Ian, "You're fast becoming notorious, my love, getting a reputation in the regiment." She found the whole affair highly entertaining, "I must take care being seen talking to you, I have a reputation of my own to uphold you know."

Ian looked at her hard, said coldly, "I do not find this whole affair amusing." There was a long pause, then his face broke into a huge grin.

They both laughed.

Chapter 25

In December 1853, through the financial assistance of his father, and well ahead of the customary waiting period for promotion in the Guards, Ian purchased the rank of lieutenant and captain, for the modest sum of 2,000 pounds. This quick jump in rank was allowed, considering his Royal Military Academy attendance and his time in the Royal Engineers.

Unfortunately, the notoriety caused by the early promotion brought to the surface his engineer training. He was soon back in a staff position at the Horse Guards, almost the exact posting he had happily left as a Royal Engineer. Lieutenant Colonel Hunter-Blair was extremely sorry to lose him as a company officer. Ian could not and would not complain: *My time will come. At least I'm in the Guards.*

When the time for war with Russia did come, Ian watched the Guards Brigade march away. His staff assignment at Horse Guards was considered a priority posting. Ian was not to be allowed to go east with his battalion. *I've got to do something. This can't happen without me. They can't go without me.*

Ian's father was in London attending the House of Lords. They met at the Third Guards Club for lunch. Over roast beef and a good claret, Ian said, "Father, I must go. This is a real war. It's my chance to make my way in the Guards. If I'm forced by circumstance to stay behind while my regiment goes to fight on foreign soil, I'll be shamed, mortified. Surely a soldier like yourself can understand that."

"Aye, lad, I understand too well, but your mother won't." When the meal ended, His Lordship lit a cigar, stared at his glass of Taylor Fladgate tawny port, and said, "Let me call up some favours. You might make good volunteering for staff duty in the East. At least it would get you there, then, of course, you're on your own."

"That would be most kind of you, Father."

"Mark me, you young devil, if you breathe a word of my part in this to your mother, I'll see to it ye serve the rest of your career on recruiting duty in the Orkney Islands, understand me, boy?"

"Yes sir, I do," Ian said, smiling gratefully.

The deed was as good as done. Lord Dunkairn's influence was considerable. Orders were cut within the week for Captain Carlyle to proceed by way of Malta to join the personal staff of Lord Raglan, his father's long-time friend, who was commanding the Army of the East. Ian was officially an extra aide-de-camp and liaison officer to the 1st Division, the Duke of Cambridge commanding, which, to his joy, included the Guards Brigade.

Ian booked passage on a steamer bound for Malta, leaving Plymouth in a few weeks. That night he visited Jasmine to say farewell, before returning to Dunkairn. She knew it was coming. Ian's destiny was to be a warrior. As she saw it, she had merely borrowed a piece of time from that destiny, and knew their being together was but temporary. Ian knew it also, but it didn't make parting easier. By now they were spectacular lovers, and, although neither was in love, they had built an intense friendship.

Jasmine didn't go to work, the first night she'd missed in five years. When Ian arrived at her lodgings, she was waiting in her very best dress, prim and beautiful, as always. She said, "You're taking me out to dine, a proper dinner."

Ian said, "Why the very thing."

They ate a sumptuous meal at a tavern they liked, with a fine bottle of Burgundy. Afterward, he looked at her in the candlelight across the table. She slipped her shoe off and ran her stocking-encased foot up the side of his leg. He could feel the silk, feel her toes playfully teasing him awake, erect, making him recall their first night together, when she'd removed all but her stockings to make love. That was now a tradition in their lovemaking.

Ian had a wonderful idea; one he knew would make her smile. He said, "Do you remember our first night? What you said?"

"Yes, of course I do, every word, why?"

Ian looked into her eyes for a lingering moment, then said forcefully, as she had said to him long ago, "Jasmine, come with me. No questions. Say not a word. Just come with me…now." He threw several shillings on the table, grabbed her hand, and led her out. She giggled, barely had time to slip her shoe back on.

Ian's movements were now polished, practiced, but tonight they were special, very special. He guided her into the bedroom, lit two small candles while she waited, then kissed her lightly on her lips, her eyes, her neck. Ian was still in uniform. He knew he aroused her, dressed as well as naked, just as she did him. He was determined she should nurture and savour every morsel of her own excitement.

He ran one hand up and down her back, and with the other gently freed her hair. It fell long and straight, shining in the soft candlelight. It smelled delicious, like fresh flowers in the fields. He loved the lush silky feel of it. He brushed it with his fingers, then grabbed it at the back of her neck, strongly, but not painfully, pulling. She inhaled, sharply, her excitement spiking higher. He brought her face to his and kissed her lips long and slow, building in intensity, his tongue playing inside her mouth, manipulating her gradual arousal from the kiss alone, an overture to the symphony of their passion.

Ian felt his manhood swell and pressed it against her. She had taught him, "Making love, Ian, isn't just about you. It's about your partner. If you understand that, you'll know more than most men in this world."

He would touch her and use his arousal to bring her to heightened sensations when she felt it, felt the heat. They said nothing at first. They spoke with their senses, each one at high intensity. Then they made whispered love-talk to each other. In their vehemence, they reached new heights of excitement and ecstasy as the night wore on.

Afterward, he laid with her, in her. They were both feeling aftershocks, enjoying the sensations. When he eventually pulled out of her, he held her tightly. They lay next to one another and slept, deeply, both thinking of the wondrous physical joy they brought to each other.

There would be no sad goodbyes for them. Each knew the strength of their sexual attraction and their deep, deep affection. She was glad for Ian that he'd found the path to his own destiny again, yet under the surface, she worried for his safety. Their fate was to meet again. Whatever path each would take, they were certain that they'd make love again.

Chapter 26

Ian's mother was distraught. The ever-supportive Peter was cheerful. Lord Dunkairn asked Ian to join him in his study. Angus MacLean was there, smiling broadly. His father said, "Ian, lad, you'll be needing a servant in your new posting. Have you thought on that?"

"I have, sir, but haven't found a soldier suitable as yet..."

His father interrupted, "Well, he's no longer a soldier, mind, being retired. Since he was a sergeant and couldn't be your servant while on active service, that's just as well...but I can vouch there's none better than our own Angus MacLean. That is if you'll have him to tend your needs in the field."

Ian was flabbergasted, "But, sir, I...You'd allow him to leave, allow me to take him away from Dunkairn Hall...from you?" a pause, "Sir, you astound me." He searched for the right words to express his pleasure and gratitude at the suggestion, "Father, I'm honoured. Of course I'll have him...but, Angus, what of you? The hardships of campaigning? Is this to your liking? Will you have me?"

Angus said, "Aye, lad, that it is, and that I will. It'll be like old times, like as if I was back in uniform again, where I belong."

His Lordship said, "Splendid. Settled then. I'll also give you Savage and any other horse you wish, take your pick. Now, let's have a glass of something special to seal the deed and send you both off on your new adventures."

Peter walked into the library to join them in their farewell toast. He looked bright and happy for his brother, some of the old Peter coming into his eyes again after so long.

His Lordship went to a small locked walnut cabinet, brought out a squat, brown bottle, and poured four glasses of his fine old Drambuie liqueur. This was a bottle the Earl was never, ever, known to share. He toasted, "To the glorious events you'll be a part of."

He turned to Angus, "Your oath, Angus, you'll take care of this young Turk. He's not a real soldier yet."

Angus was solemn, "Ye have my word, M'Lord. I'll never leave his side."

Later, when they were alone, His Lordship said to his old friend, "Angus, I am trusting you with my youngest son. I'd trust no one else. There'll come a time, as you know, when his search for glory will end. When he'll know the truth, find what it really is…he'll need you then."

Angus replied, "Aye, M'Lord, aye."

Chapter 27

"M'Lord, Captain Ian Carlyle, reporting for duty as liaison with 1st Division," Ian said on entering the room and coming to a rigid attention.

Lord Raglan was relaxing in his makeshift office in Constantinople. He had been travelling back and forth between there and Scutari, where the army was marshalling, a short boat ride across the Bosphorus. He was a bit tired, but energized by his mission.

Ian was surprised at Lord Raglan's appearance. As a friend of his father, His Lordship always came to Dunkairn Hall in civilian attire. Ian expected that in uniform he would be a resplendent figure, tall and imposing. Now he looked upon an older man, with grey hair, and a somewhat unimposing countenance. He wore a plain frock coat, white vest, no rank showing. On his desk was a plain blue forage cap with a gold leaf headband. Without the cap, he could well have been a civilian. The sleeve of his missing right arm was pinned unceremoniously to the right breast of his coat. He was a bit frazzled and worn around the edges, not at all the look Ian had anticipated for the commander of the British Army of the East.

On the other hand, Lord Raglan's eyes were strong and penetrating, and his demeanour every inch the gentleman. He greeted Ian warmly, "Yes, of course, Dunkairn's boy. I remember you, lad. Sit down…sit down. Your father and I, well, we share many memories." He unconsciously touched his empty sleeve.

Lord Raglan pulled his chair close to the one Ian sat himself in, said, "I used to watch you playing soldier when you were a tot. Knew then I'd see you on active service. Your father denied it, called it youthful fantasizing, but I knew. Nothing else for it. In the blood."

"Yes, M'Lord, I remember well."

Raglan looked the boy over slowly and carefully, "Liaison with 1st Division…those are, of course, your orders, lad, and we shall make use of you in that capacity, as well."

"As well, M'Lord?"

"I received a letter recently from your father. Asked for no special treatment in your regard, but reminded me that you're a graduate from Woolwich, and have a fine mind. I'll use that mind, Ian. It would be a damned waste to have you a mere galloper, delivering the odd message. No, I'll use you for far more than that, if you have no objections?"

"Of course not, M'Lord, I'd be honoured. All my skills are at your service."

Raglan said, "My staff family is literally my family. I have four personal aides. They are either nephews, great nephews, or related by marriage, all good lads, mind you, one even in your own regiment, Captain Nigel Kingscote. Know him?"

"No, M'Lord, but I've heard the name."

"Well, all fine lads, but none have your training, and they are family. Tell me more what they think I want to hear than what I should hear. I'll count on you to tell me what's what, even if I don't want to hear it. Can you do that, lad?"

"Of course, M'Lord, you may rely on me."

"Of this I'm certain. You are your father's son."

Raglan reflected a moment, said, "It is my desire that you serve in your liaison duties. I'll also inform The Duke of Cambridge and my staff that we are to make best use of your training at Woolwich for other staff assignments, as need arises."

Raglan pierced Ian with his eyes, "Ian, as I trusted your father with my life more than once, so shall I trust you. This is an order. You tell me, Captain Carlyle, what I need to know."

"M'Lord," was Ian's reply. He left Lord Raglan's office, thinking, *I truly like this quiet unassuming gentleman. On my oath, I'll give him my loyalty, even as I would my own father.*

Chapter 28

The unrelenting sun baked the Crimean earth, and brought Ian out of his drifting thoughts, back to the dusty plain, back to the very real prospect that he might lose his beloved Angus. British soldiers marched toward their destiny, and Ian rode wildly back through the line of march toward where Piccard reported his Angus had fallen. Ian dismounted even before Packey came to a halt, and ran to where Angus lay, small and frail in the arms of the young musician.

He shouted, "He only needs a bit of water. Give him water, for God's sake. He just needs water." But he knew better, saw the tinged lips, blackened skin, vomit on the ground, on his old teacher's dusty brown coat front.

The lad looked up, "Been trying to help him, sir. Nothing I could do. Keeps calling for a 'wee bairn,' sir. Must be his child. Maybe he'd be thinking I'm him."

Ian composed himself, felt the excruciating pain surge over him, stabbing his heart. "Best you let me have him, lad. I know who he's calling for." Ian had hated being called "the wee bairn" by Angus. Now it tore him apart.

The boy drifted away, joined the march. Both Packey and Savage stood nearby, motionless, their great heads hung down, like sombre mourners at a dear friend's funeral. Ian sat on the ground, cradling Angus in his arms. He tried to give him water and comfort, protect him from the merciless heat.

"Angus, I'm here now."

Ian sat with his friend for a long time. The army passed by with occasional curious glances at the young officer holding his old grizzled comrade, weeping.

Angus opened his eyes only once. He said, "Och, Ian lad, it's good you've come. I didn't want to leave without saying goodbye. Ye'll have to take care of yerself now, lad. Tell yer father…tell His Lordship I'm sorry, so sorry." Then he closed his eyes for the last time, no more suffering, he found peace.

At some point later, after Angus was still, Ian spotted a straggler trying to catch up to the column. He was from the Royal Sappers and Miners, and carried a shovel.

"Soldier, I need your assistance, if you will." The sapper saw the young Guards captain tenderly holding the old man.

"At your service, sir, how can I help?"

"I'll need to borrow your shovel for a time."

The sapper realized instantly what was needed, but would have none of this officer digging. He asked Ian to stay with his friend, while he dug a shallow grave in the hard earth nearby.

Ian gently placed Angus in the grave, laid a blanket over him, while Savage, Packey, and the sapper stood by. The sapper slowly filled in the dirt as Ian watched, and said his unspoken goodbyes. *What will I tell Father? What will I do without him?*

Chapter 29

As Ian rode to catch the columns, he heard scattered shots from up ahead. *Skirmishers firing, and that sounds like cannon.* When he finally came to the Bulganak River, more like a stream, he saw the army making camp on its banks. Stragglers were still drifting in steadily. He passed them as he rode.

They'd be coming into the camps for hours. It was impossible to believe, but the army had only marched ten miles from the landing point since morning. This was a long sad day for Ian, and a long gruelling day for the exhausted army. Ian rode down to the water, above the camp, first allowing the horses to drink, then drinking himself. He filled his empty canteen with the fresh running water.

Ian found the small circle of tents around the fire where his friends were gathered. They could see in Ian's face what had happened, and left him alone to his grief, ready to help if asked. He was glad for their quiet companionship.

It took several hours to write the letter to his father. The saddest letter he ever wrote. Later in the evening, Ian joined his comrades to sit by the campfire. Slowly, as good friends will, they drew him out of his sadness and into their discussions. Life went on.

As the night cooled, and the fire crackled, Ian asked his friends, "This afternoon as I rode here I heard firing. I thought the ball was beginning, but all's quiet now. What happened?"

Curzon answered, "When we approached the stream, we saw Cossacks on that ridge beyond. His Lordship sent Lord Cardigan with two regiments of the 'Light' to drive them off. They did just that, but found Russian cavalry on another ridge beyond."

Nolan took up the tale with a sarcastic tone, "Lord Raglan, for some unfathomable reason, ordered the Light Brigade to withdraw. It was hard to watch, Ian. Their skirmishers traded a few shots, then the artillery on both sides traded a few more, and that was the end of it."

Curzon turned on Nolan, "Lord Raglan was absolutely correct to withdraw the cavalry, Lewis. You didn't see what we saw. There were numbers behind those ridges, Russian infantry, and many more cavalry. Cardigan was outnumbered several times."

"Humph," was all Nolan replied.

Curzon said, "His Lordship and the Frenchies are meeting tonight at that burned out post-house over there to decide our next move." He realized immediately that his referral to the 'Frenchies' may have been ill-chosen, and apologized, "Frightfully sorry, Antoine, no offence."

Piccard said, "None taken, Captain, after all, we are 'Frenchies,' are we not?" They all laughed.

Piccard continued, "One can only hope they can come together with a plan."

"Let's drink to that, gentlemen," said Lewis Nolan, as he produced an untouched bottle of port and passed it to Piccard.

Major Capecci said, "Amazing, splendid. Lewis, how do you manage it?"

"Magic, Major, pure English magic." They drank the bottle dry, went to their tents, and slept. All, that is, except Ian, who sat looking out over the hundreds of bivouac fires, blinking like so many stars. *I miss you already, Angus. Rest well, old friend.*

Chapter 30

"Rise up, Ian, my boy, it's a glorious new day, and we're but five miles from the Alma River," it was Major Antonio Capecci's voice through a cloud of sleep. "I've been assured there are Russians there, waiting to be thrashed by your noble English army and their splendid French and Turkish allies."

"And I suppose this noble army on this glorious day couldn't wait until I sip a cup of something strong and hot," Ian replied, crawling out of his tent, scratching his head vigorously with both hands.

He half-staggered over to a set of sticks tied together as a tripod, with a tin pan of water balanced on top. He splashed it's ice-cold freshness on his face, shook his head like a big cat, and welcomed the morning with his face toward the sky…then, with a painful jolt, he remembered Angus, squeezing his eyes tightly shut to stop the tears.

The major brought him back, "Captain, you have little faith in your superior officer, a major of the Bersaglieri. Already brewed, Ian. Tea – strong and hot. Until we can find you a suitable replacement for MacLean, poor fellow, you shall share my servants. Your tea awaits."

Ian thought: *No one will ever replace Angus. Never.*

"You really are most kind," Ian said softly, remembering, looking down, watching the drops of cold water fall from his hair splattering the dusty ground in tiny explosions. He tightened inside, recovered his composure, looked up, cleared his throat, and said, with just the right touch of ironic insincerity, "...but, if that is truly to be, my dear Major, I should prefer coffee in the mornings." They both laughed. There was a war happening, and it was most definitely time to move on.

The day, 20 September 1854, commenced as a clear brilliant morning, with a cool breeze blowing from the sea. The camps awoke with renewed briskness, coffee brewing on small fires, men eating a cold breakfast of hard crackers and jam. The soldiers began to form for the march.

The troops marched off in fine fettle, refreshed by sleep, their blood rushing, knowing that this day would bring contact with the enemy. Without Angus' help, it was more difficult for Ian to get sorted out, but he managed, barely.

Lord Raglan and his staff moved south along the Eupatoria-Sevastopol road, in the same formation as the day before. Two divisions in front, the right division tying to the French forces on their right. Two divisions followed them, with the 4th Division in reserve, the civilians, cattle and supply train to their rear. Artillery equipments were spread amongst the infantry, and the Light Brigade guarded the advance and flanks.

Ian rode with Major Capecci and Lewis Nolan several hundred yards ahead of Lord Raglan's entourage. At 11 o'clock, they observed a treeline, which hid the Alma River in front of them. There was a small village ahead on the near bank. Around the village were fields, gardens, and vineyards. The land south beyond the river rose gradually toward two prominent pieces of higher ground.

Ian swept these 'hills' with his telescope. All along the heights across the river the Russian army stood waiting. Russian guns straddled the road, which cut through the heights. The two hills were natural defensive positions. The hill to the right bristled with Russian infantry and more guns. Oddly, there also appeared to be some sort of tower surrounded by what looked like gaily dressed civilians.

To the left of the road was the higher and larger of the hills, named on Ian's map, 'Kourgane,' although he suspected that merely meant 'hill.' Below the crest of this hill was what appeared to be a strongly fortified redoubt. Ian counted a dozen guns, supported by infantry. There were more guns and infantry farther to the left, around the eastern side of 'Kourgane Hill,' and another smaller redoubt, obviously protecting the Russian right flank. To their more immediate front were the village and the river.

The major suggested, "Their deployment on those heights has power, Ian. Those massive blocks of Russian infantry seem well placed, in depth."

Ian studied the village more closely. He had been told the inhabitants were peasants descending from a mixture of Greeks, Goths, Mongols, Venetians, Tartars, and Russians. They were goat herders, sheepherders, or farmers. The roads were dirt and the bridges wood. The village contained fifty . or sixty one-story, shoddy-looking whitewashed houses with crude red-tiled roofs. Willows and cypresses surrounded the houses. Outside the villages were fields containing stacks of hay. Low stone walls divided the fields.

"I copied a map in my notebook from one I found lying on Lord Raglan's desk," Ian added. "The village in front of us is called Bourliouk. Not very large, but damned well suited to hide Russian riflemen. They'll cut us to pieces from behind those walls. Very dicey."

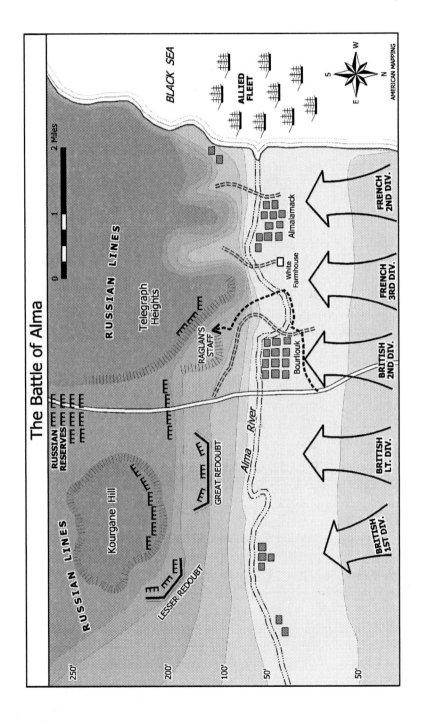

The Battle of Alma

Nolan said, "Pray to the god of war that His Lordship knows what he's about, uses his cavalry to hit their flank, draw them away, before committing infantry to the slaughter."

Major Capecci searched the heights thoughtfully through his own telescope, "I think not, Lewis, for many reasons. I fear Lord Raglan must hammer this one out frontally, but your absolutely right. It'll be expensive, damned expensive."

Nolan offered in sheer frustration, "But Major, surely you aren't suggesting that a brigade of cavalry merely sit on its arse, watch this battle, and do nothing."

Major Capecci calmly continued, "I'm not suggesting anything, Lewis, merely commenting on the lay of the land and the defences we face. I doubt Raglan will commit his cavalry. We've both heard Curzon speak of the strong possibility of thousands of Russian cavalry and Cossacks somewhere either to our left flank or perhaps in our rear. With that unknown I doubt Lord Raglan will commit his cavalry to an assault."

The major continued to sweep his telescope across the heights, "What's your opinion, Carlyle, you're the terrain and fortifications man?"

"Hardly that, sir, but I think you're correct, with all due respect to the prowess of your splendid cavalry, Lewis. Frontal assault it'll be, without cavalry support."

Nolan was outraged, as usual, "Gentlemen, we must use the cavalry to turn their right flank while the infantry go in frontally. The risk is worth it, by God. A whole cavalry brigade, sitting on its arse. A damned disgrace."

Major Capecci replied, "Lewis, you seem to feel most strongly. Good thing you don't have to make those decisions?" Ian laughed, and Nolan merely grunted.

Chapter 31

Around one o'clock the advance was sounded, and both armies moved forward over a rise in ground above the River Alma. The British moved slowly by divisions, double columns on the centre, with the green-clad Rifles as skirmishers a good distance in front.

Lord Raglan with his staff moved south along the post road. His Lordship was conspicuous by his ordinary appearance, plain dark blue frock coat, white shirt, and black cravat. He walked his horse, Shadrack, remaining nearly abreast of his lead divisions. Oddly, the number in his staff had tripled, "Where did all these officers come from?" asked the major.

"They're every damned staff officer we have, down to the lowest acting assistant quartermaster," Nolan said, "wanting to get a better view of the battle, tell their grandchildren they were here, fought alongside the great Lord Raglan. A bloody huge lark for most of them."

"Ah, I understand," said the major. "Let's see how many are still here after the first 'dance' in this ball."

Ian was about to comment on the major's observation when there was a distant clap. A strange whizzing sound was heard as a round shot passed very close. It hit behind them, skipped, then bounded along the ground. Ian could actually see the lethal ball rolling. Pounding crashes around them followed the first shot, as balls struck the ground, and there were more of the terrifying whizzing sounds of incoming shots passing close by. The enlarged 'staff' rapidly disappeared in every direction. As the cannon balls came in, they scattered, caps flying off, spooked horses dancing in circles, some riders thrown, others caught on scared runaway mounts, all to the amusement of the infantry line close by.

They seemed to be the focus of the enemy fire. Ian jerked in his saddle, just managing to maintain control of Packey. *Jesus. Well it's no bloody wonder. His Lordship's staff is the largest group of horsemen around, and the farthest forward. They're firing round shot thus far, but that won't last. Must get myself together.*

Ian's stomach was tightening, fear creeping in. He regained composure, ashamed of his skittishness. He saw Raglan's immediate staff returning, minus the "extras." Raglan, of course, never slowed or faltered, continued to gently walk Shadrack forward, smiling at the staff's disarray.

Ian dismounted and walked Packey behind His Lordship. Lord Raglan summoned gallopers, ordered, "The Light and 2nd Divisions will deploy on line and lie down. Advise the other division commanders to remain in column until they might see fit to deploy, or receive further orders."

With a resounding thud, a shot landed almost at Lord Raglan's feet.

Raglan turned to General Airey, unperturbed, "General, I don't have faith in this plan. I genuinely wonder how long it will take our French allies to seize those heights on the right. I'll not commit our men a step further until they've arrived there. Damned Frenchies."

Airey nodded agreement, "Aye, M'Lord."

Lord Raglan's entourage remained a major target for Russian artillery fire. Shrapnel-filled shells exploded overhead, round shot pounded into the ground, then skimmed along its deadly trail. Ian thought, *Raglan's movements so close to the infantry line may bolster the men, but it also makes them excellent collateral targets. Hmmm. I wonder how much they appreciate that.*

The French crossed the river, which appeared to be only knee-deep in most places. British artillery batteries hammered Russian positions, but the range was excessive. Congreve rockets were fired. In spite of their fierce fiery tales and swirling white smoke trails, they were ineffectual, except perhaps to rattle their own gunners and at least confuse the enemy.

Ian joined Major Capecci and Nolan, both watching the spectacle through telescopes. He said to the major, "What progress the French, sir?"

The major said, "Crossed the river. Under severe musket and cannon fire from above. They reorganized admirably on the far side, advanced up the heights, took casualties. Looks like many fell. Can't see too much from here."

Nolan added, "Appears the Russian skirmishers are falling back. Their main body of infantry hasn't fired yet."

Curzon joined them, said, "Wait till their skirmishers pass to the rear, unmask their front. The Frenchies will be for it then, poor bastards."

"Leicester," the Sardinian major asked, "how long do you think Raglan will keep these men in the open, under fire and not moving?"

"No idea, really, Major, but I assure you not a minute longer than necessary."

There was a massive rumbling musket volley from across the valley beyond the river on the right. "There," said Nolan, "the Russians are looking down their throats. Their whole front is firing at the Frenchies now." It was not pretty, the muzzle blasts could be seen along the line, and the ground in front of the Russians was soon covered in smoke. Nonetheless, the French lead elements kept a steady advance up the heights, into that shroud-covered deadly haze.

"Look," shouted Nolan, "you can gauge their advance by the line of Zouaves emerging from the smoke...see the red baggy pants, white turbans."

"Yes, I see," said the major. "Magnificent. They may be rascals, but they fight like demons, truly magnificent."

Their admiration of the French progress was interrupted when Lord Raglan mounted and began moving off, round shot landing close by. Calmly, he turned to his staff, and said, "Let us move along across the division front, gentlemen."

There was a different sound. Not like any other. A tremendous thwacking sound. Ian saw a horse not twenty feet away almost cut in half, its rider unhurt, but collapsed and shaken on the ground next to his dead animal. Another thwack! A second horse's head disintegrated in a shower of blood, pieces of rider and horse disappearing in all directions.

Ian was speechless, stomach turning over and over, panic rapidly growing. Then he looked at Lord Raglan, heard him say calmly to Airey as they moved their horses at a walk toward the village of Bourliouk, "Shadrack seems unusually nervous today, Airey, don't you think? Makes it difficult to use my glass, what?" He referred to his specially mounted telescope with the rifle stock attached, needed due to his missing arm.

His Lordship calmed Shadrack with quiet words as he rubbed his neck, "May need you to interpret what's happening from time to time, Airey, sorry to bother."

Airey replied, "Of course, sir. I should be honoured." The effect on Ian of this casual conversation amidst exploding shells was instantaneous. He blinked, calmed, steadied Packey.

"I expected by this time to hear from Marshal St. Arnaud that those heights were his," Raglan said to Airey, then whispered to the skittish Shadrack, "Easy, my boy. Nothing to worry about. Easy."

Airey took his meaning and dispatched one of the staff officers to find out. He rode off quickly toward the French on their right. Shortly after his departure, Lieutenant Piccard pointed at a highly agitated French officer approaching at the gallop. Piccard knew Prince Napoleon, who led the division of French troops closest to the British. He also knew his entire staff quite well. This was not one of the Prince's aides. Rather, he was coming from the French general headquarters. Piccard intercepted the overwrought officer by placing his horse between him and Lord Raglan.

"Le quel est?" Piccard asked.

"Nous sommes massacres," the rider shouted at Piccard. Raglan heard this, and interrupted with questions in French to the animated officer, who seemed to genuinely think the French attacking force was being massacred. Lord Raglan gave him assurances that the British would be moving very soon. The officer was abruptly dismissed and sent on his way.

Lord Raglan said to General Airey, "I give little credence to an officer that excitable, a Frenchman at that. Very unprofessional, what? However, gentlemen, we have heard nothing from the French who are fighting on that high ground to our right. We'll remain here being shot at no longer. Airey, write this down and give the order: The infantry will advance. I will have the 2nd Division deploy on line to the right of the Light Division, the both advancing accordingly, as we discussed. The 1st Division will form to the rear of and supporting the Light Division in the advance. The 3rd Division will allow itself to conform to the right of the 4th Division, as a further reserve." Ian calculated that the British soldiers had at this point been lying under musket and artillery fire for nearly two hours.

Airey scribbled madly, then handed barely legible orders to the various staff gallopers to deliver to the division commanders. They rode off, their task soon completed.

The divisions were on their feet, aligning themselves and advancing to their front. The 1st Division deploying into line, shifted left, moved forward, and came abreast of the Light Division on their right, to extend the first long line to three divisions. The 3rd Division remained in column, and dropped back to align itself with the 4th Division, in reserve.

The cavalry had no further orders. Lewis Nolan was furious, but contained himself, as he rode up to His Lordship and General Airey. He reported, "M'Lord, the division commanders have been informed." Then to his immediate superior, Airey, he said, "Sir, orders for the cavalry brigade?" Lord Raglan looked at Nolan quizzically. Airey was astonished at such a bold question from a junior officer.

Airey answered him with some irritation, "No, Nolan, not at this time."

Nolan didn't move.

"You're dismissed, Captain Nolan," Airey added in a harsher tone.

Chapter 32

Lord Raglan turned to his staff, "Let us cross to the far side, gentlemen." By now he was well forward, nearly up with the skirmish line of the 2nd Division. He led the staff at a trot toward the right of the village of Bourliouk.

They passed haystacks, a hundred yards away, some of them burning. Enemy musket fire was coming from beyond these stacks. Raglan shouted, "There, gentlemen. The road leading down to the river. We'll take that ford." He swung Shadrack expertly onto the dirt road. The wooden bridge across the Alma was to their left. Many village houses had begun to burn. The fire was spreading, set by the Russians to slow them. Smoke obscured the road ahead. They were not yet taking small arms fire.

Ian looked to his left beyond the village, could see through the smoke and haze that the Light Division, with no village or other major obstacles to their front, was already crossing the river under intense fire, some even crossing on the bridge, itself.

Ian's attention was jerked back to his own immediate danger. He heard for the first time the new and unique sound of musket balls being fired directly at him, a soft buzzing as they passed very close…searching him out. In a perverse way this was a relief from the impersonal, vicious, unseen, and indirect artillery fire.

As they moved along, Ian almost trampled a green-uniformed rifleman, who had taken cover in a shallow ditch by the road. Ian shouted to the rifleman, "Can we cross up ahead?"

In a North Country accent, the man replied, "No, sir, and ya'd be a damned fool to try. They're like bloody flies around there."

"Thank you," Ian said. Lord Raglan was riding straight into those "flies." He urged Packey ahead of the staff group, shouting, "M'Lord, we can't go this way. Dangerous, sir. Please follow me." Raglan did so, without question, and the rest of the staff as well.

Ian had no idea where he was going, but knew there was a good chance it was a better crossing than where they were headed. He led them right along the river toward the French line of attack until he saw a crossing where the banks appeared friendly. He was immensely thankful to discover that the rifleman had been right; the firing from enemy skirmishers was far more intense where they just left. He probably saved Lord Raglan's life, and his own.

The near bank where they crossed was only two feet high, but the far bank looked much higher…and at least a hundred miles away to Ian's eye. Although taking the initiative in the crossing occupied his thoughts, Ian could still feel the sickening fear rising.

They began receiving musket fire from Russian skirmishers hidden beyond the opposite bank. Two staff officers were shot from their saddles, splashing into the churning water. Artillery fire was focusing on them from the heights above. Ian held back, looking up and left, beyond the village. He caught a glimpse in the distance of the Light Division reorganizing to move up the slope toward the great redoubt on the hill.

The others, including Lord Raglan, were crossing ahead of him. *Time to go.* Ian spurred Packey, who leaped into the water. The horse no sooner gained purchase on the river bottom, when the water exploded in front. Ian felt the horse buckle, heard him grunt in agony, saw the blood, a huge wound in Packey's shoulder and chest, wide open, white of bone, glistening. The valiant horse went down struggling, and Ian was slammed underwater. He scrambled and jerked himself free of the stirrups, while swallowing muddy water and sputtering.

Packey righted himself, unsteadily, snorting wildly, then disappeared down the river at a terrified gallop. Ian was still half underwater, choking, gagging, arms flailing, as he tried to right himself, grabbing blindly for the horse that was no longer there.

The staff kept on moving, anxious to get out of the river bed and away from the rigorous fire pouring down on them. They fought their horses up onto the opposite bank, onto flat ground, and away, Raglan pressing forward in the lead.

Ian's head came out of the water, eyes wide, watching them disappear up the slope. A round shot landed inches from him, erupting in a huge spout of water, slamming him back under again. He came up a second time, involuntarily gasping, vomiting water from his lungs. He couldn't think, stark terror gripping his soul. There was a blinding flash! His eyes went dark...ears deaf. His whole body was smashed back under the churning river for a third time, the shell peppering white-hot sizzling shrapnel on the water all around and above him.

Ian was still conscious, but dazed. He was bleeding from nose and ears. This time he reacted from pure horror, stayed low in the knee-deep water, choking as he frantically made his way to the inviting shelter of the far bank.

There he found a welcome deep notch and crawled thankfully into it, curling up. He held himself in a tight ball, trembling uncontrollably. Exposed scraggly roots above the notch hung down sufficiently to hide him from view, gave him the illusion of protection. He pulled them frantically around him.

Ian's eyes wouldn't focus. He couldn't stop shaking. He wasn't wounded. It had been the concussion. He knew he should get up, find Packey, join His Lordship, do his duty, but couldn't move. Ian was content to remain there, relatively safe, for what seemed like hours, but was only minutes.

His focus slowly returned. He stared in wonder at the sand inches from his face, crumbling off the river bank, crumbling without anything causing it, save the trembling of the earth and his own pathetic quivering.

Chapter 33

The war, the nightmare, appeared to have passed him by for the moment, although the sounds were again beginning to penetrate through his temporary deafness. He tried to move, found it just possible, felt a hand on his shoulder, felt instant relief. *I'm saved.*

Ian turned his head to see his savoir and found himself staring into the open, unseeing eyes of the upper half of Lieutenant Antoine Piccard, floating in the muddy water. He was grinning pleasantly, the way he did when they sat around the fire. Grotesquely, his hand was still on Ian's shoulder, caught in the hanging roots. Ian began to scream, loudly at first, then silently, inside his brain, scrambling, clawing his way deeper into the notch, burying his head in the sand, his eyes, ears, and mouth filling with it.

Later, he stopped screaming, but his body wouldn't allow him the escape of unconsciousness. He could feel the hand on his shoulder, feel the water around him, taste the sand, frozen. Then he heard the artillery fire coming closer. He heard noises all around him, horses, water splashing, men shouting, wheels creaking, breaking.

I've got to get out of here. Have to run. Have to go home. Now. Please, God, let me move.

With a massive effort of will he rose up from the water, crawled, twisted, slithered up the bank to get to level ground, to run, to run anywhere away from this hell…

He stood shakily on the bank, turned to run, and smashed into an artillery officer, staring incredulously at him, "Carlyle, isn't it? I know you. Raglan's staff. It is you, ain't it? Thank God, man. I'm Captain Turner, 2nd Division. Where the bloody hell is Lord Raglan? Called us up at the double, but his galloper was killed. Can't find him, damn it. Bloody Russians up there looking right down on us."

Ian pointed feebly to where he'd seen Raglan climb the rise, while choking sand, unable to speak.

Turner saw where he pointed, said, "He can't be up there, that's in front of our own troops for Christ's sake. I could only get two guns across this damned river. Lost a wheel horse already to round shot. Very messy. Losing gunner-drivers now. Rest of my gunners are on their way, but God knows when they'll catch up."

Turner saw the soaked uniform, drenched in Packey's, Piccard's, and his own blood. He shouted, "You all right, man? What in hell's wrong with you, Carlyle? Are you wounded? Where's your damned horse?"

On colliding with Turner, Ian was shocked back to reality. While Turner was ranting, it gave him time. Ian was calming. He took a long breath, went deep inside himself, deeper than ever before, found the leopard's cave, pulled the beast to the surface, with all the inner resources he had, felt at last some control returning…He spoke to the leopard – "Where in hell were you when I needed you?"

Turner said, "What? What did you say?" Ian realized he had spoken the words out loud.

They were now receiving both shot and shell with increasing intensity, many enemy guns switching to canister rounds, firing their small clusters of round shot like giant shotguns, with devastating effect. The buzzing of musket balls screamed in Ian's ears. He felt the stinging texture of fear and terror still there under the surface, tasted the dryness, but he could also feel the beast rising, taking back control.

Looking around, he saw the two guns limbered up, poised, bodies of gunner-drivers lying about, floating on the red-stained water. He saw a gunner-driver slump in his saddle on a wheel horse and slide to the ground, saw another lifted from his seat on a caisson, his chest exploding in a burst of bright red, as lead balls tore through it.

Ian snapped awake, shook his head to clear it, "I'm fine, Turner, just fine. I was thrown. My horse is gone. I'm fine now. Give me a horse. Raglan is up there. That's where he was headed, and that's where he'll be. He needs us. Give me a horse."

Turner looked at him in amazement, then said, "Right you are, Carlyle."

He turned to a young mounted orderly, demanded, "Give this officer your horse, Johnson." The orderly dismounted, handed Ian the reins, then jumped up onto a gun carriage.

Turner bellowed to his battery, "Follow this officer."

Ian was in the saddle, galloping along the road, soon found himself among French soldiers from Prince Napoleon's Division moving forward just before the road veered left and under the heights above, which were bristling with Russian guns.

He was searching above, searching for...*Yes. There it is. Raglan's flag. He's far up. Maybe 70 – 80 yards, on a flat place below the crest. Close to the Russians. Too close. That's no place for the army commander. Well, if he wants guns up, by God, he'll get guns up.*

Ian never slowed the horse's pace, pulled way ahead of the two horse-drawn 9-pounders. He turned back in the saddle to Turner, and pointed up off the road to his right toward Raglan's flag. Turner moved his head back and forth, in recognition of Lord Raglan's audacity, and the difficulties such a climb would entail. Without further hesitation, he ordered the guns to follow Ian up the hill.

The only thing saving them was that the Russians were firing their muskets high, over their heads, and likely couldn't depress their cannon low enough to be effective. *That's fine with me,* Ian thought.

Ian reached the small plateau. Raglan and the staff were still mounted. He was amazed by what he saw. There was a sort of ridge of land above them on Telegraph Heights, which hid their position from the enemy's view. From this place, they were high enough to observe the Russian positions. Lord Raglan's eye for terrain had not failed him. Guns at this position could enfilade the entire Russian flank and rear – artillery, infantry, and reserves.

Ian's engineer's eye examined the panorama quickly. He saw 18 or so Russian guns straddling the post road. The larger redoubt was beyond that, lower than where they were. The smaller redoubt was out of view. Not far behind the large redoubt was the reverse slope of the Kourgane, and plainly visible, the Russian reserves. *It's the bloody prize,* thought Ian.

Ian looked down across the battlefield at their advancing troops; saw that almost all the British infantry had crossed the river. There was confusion, lines breaking up, officers and sergeants reforming them in battalion front, as they made it across the river, sometimes placing men in ranks as they were hauled out of the water. Now those still delayed at the river were beginning to move up the gradual heights toward the larger redoubt, the first lines far ahead were already there.

General Airey, who was at Lord Raglan's side, shouted at the artillerymen, "The Light Division was able to take the redoubt, but Russians are counterattacking. Light Division is being forced to retire. Look there," he pointed, "the 1st Division is coming up from the river. They will go through the Light Division and attempt to retake the redoubt. The Russian guns straddling the post road and in the redoubt will wreak havoc with their counterattack. You know your duty."

Lord Raglan said to no one in particular, "Look how well the Guards and Highlanders advance. Thank God the guns are here at last." Through his telescope Ian recognized his own Fusilier Guards advancing almost to the redoubt.

Although Turner had succeeded in bringing two of the battery's six guns on the plateau, several of his gunners were killed or wounded at the riverbed. Turner shouted to the assembled staff officers, "Gentlemen, if you want these guns in action, you'll have to lend a hand."

General Strangeways, the overall artillery commander, his staff, Ian, Nolan, and a few other officers with artillery training immediately assumed the gun detachment positions and began loading. The guns were trained on the enemy cannon straddling the post road, still firing with great effect.

Turner's arm came down. The first 9-pounder boomed, heaving several feet to the rear on its carriage, round shot falling short. He adjusted. Another blast, and the second shot went through a Russian covered cart used to carry artillery ammunition, killing two horses. Turner commenced firing both guns as fast as they could be reloaded.

This was enough for the Russian gunners. Their commander saw that they were taken completely in their flank, and ordered the artillery to limber up. Although the enemy retired in good order south along the post road, the two British 9-pounders inflicted great losses as they went, firing on the reserves as the retiring gun carriages met with them on the road.

A staff officer reported, "M'Lord, two more guns from Turner's Battery are here, and a complement of gunners have arrived." Lord Raglan saw the new guns being readied for action, and trained on the redoubt. He said with satisfaction, "Excellent. Keep up the pressure. It's working, by God."

Adams' Infantry Brigade, called up on His Lordship's orders, was in place above, around, and below the heights occupied by Turner's Battery and Raglan's staff, allowing them some relative safety. The firing continued in earnest. Now all the guns trained upon the main redoubt, and proper gunners manned them.

With the arrival of replacement gunners, Ian was free to observe the battlefield before him. His beloved Scots Fusilier Guards advanced on the redoubt up the gradual hill at a fairly rapid pace.

Elements of the Light Division had streamed back from the redoubt, forced to retire after having taken it earlier. In their withdrawal, they swept through the advancing Scots Fusilier Guards ranks. The Fusiliers were delayed to realign their companies, then pressed forward up the heights.

Ian watched as the Fusilier Guards came closer to the redoubt. The Scotsmen were in a precarious position, with masses of Russian infantry closing on either flank. They were obliged to refuse their line against the oncoming Russians by pulling back both flanks.

They were seen to retire a short distance, halt, then rally on their colour party. They were now in more or less an inverted or upside-down "V" formation with the colour party at the apex. They held their ground tenaciously, as the other two Guards regiments and Highlanders came up the slope from the river.

The Russian guns were withdrawing from the redoubt, and the Scots Fusilier Guards were holding, when Ian saw three heavy masses of Russian infantry, over 5,000 men, advancing at a slow walk down the hill and over the top of the redoubt, moving directly at the Scotsmen.

It was an apprehensive moment, but the rest of the 1st Division came up. They appeared to slow as they moved up the steeper portion of the hill in front of the redoubt. A staff officer near Raglan exclaimed, "Look you, the Guards are going to retire."

Ian knew this would never happen, as did Lord Raglan, who said with confidence, "No such thing, they'll carry the battery." His Lordship paused, then confidently said, "I think it's time for us to join them."

The four remaining comrades, Ian, the major, Nolan, and Curzon, rode together behind His Lordship, descending across the valley, in the direction of the greater redoubt, horses at a walk.

Lord Raglan turned to his military secretary, Colonel Steele, "I should like the names of those men in the Fusilier Guards colour party. Brave lads all, by God. Get me their names, Steele, when this is over."

"Certainly, M'Lord," he turned to Ian, "Take care of that, Carlyle, won't you?"

"Of course, sir, consider it done."

As the staff party crossed the post road, the Guards Brigade, all three regiments now on line, with reformed elements of the Light Division, advanced within 60 yards of the Russian columns. In his glass Ian actually saw the flat Russian faces, bushy side-whiskers and moustaches, greenish collars, mustard-like greatcoats, under black high helmets.

The Highland Brigade was brought up and around, approaching the Russians on their right flank. With resounding crashes, the Guards and Highlanders fired shattering volleys into the enemy from two directions. The Russians staggered under the blows.

The thunderous British volleys killed or wounded nearly every man in the first two front ranks of the approaching Russian columns. These were their seasoned veterans. The British fire destroyed their ability to respond effectively.

Ian and his comrades stared, transfixed, as the Russian column first faltered, reeling back from the jolting impact, and then halted. They fired a raggedly weak volley in return, turned, and began to retire from the field, still in some semblance of order.

This was an instant signal. No further commands were needed. The Guards lowered their bayonets almost as one. With a tremendous roar, they charged in, around, and through the redoubt, unstoppable, bayoneting the enemy as they cheered their way forward. As the Russians withdrew from the redoubt, the Highlanders fired volley after volley into their flanks, speeding them on their way, those who were not cut down by the withering fire.

The 2nd Division was advancing on the British right, capturing a Russian gun, herding the enemy before them. The Royal Artillery, with guns now well placed at various locations on bits of high ground, harassed the retreating Russians. The French on the far right were equally successful in driving the enemy from the heights before them.

The Russians retreated, losing formation as the pressure increased. The field behind them was littered with discarded muskets, accoutrements, greatcoats, blankets, and helmets. Many of the Russians broke formation and ran for their lives from the fast approaching infantry and the deadly British artillery.

On the ridges just beyond the Kourgane and Telegraph Heights, the allied pursuit paused, lost momentum. Then, as Lord Raglan's party drew closer, from every corner of the battlefield, a crescendo of cheers arose from the victors, picked up by the wounded lying about, their blood still running into the brown hard earth as they shouted.

The British soldiers were exhausted and parched, with little or no water for most of the day, but nothing deterred their jubilation. Officers, non-commissioned officers, and rankers congratulated each other, shook hands, slapped fellow warriors on the back, with more than the occasional tear. They spoke brightly of the battle and, more to the point, of surviving it.

Lord Raglan rode the line to the loud and excited cheers of his soldiers. Ian and the others were not far behind. As they rode through the Guards Brigade, Ian called out to many of his friends, and they called back: "Most glad to see you, Pakenham."…"A grand day, Carlyle, a grand day."… "Neville, I saw you. The Guards fought like tigers today. You were glorious."…"Aye, Carlyle, that we were, I'll be bound. I'm happy to see you, my friend, but I must tell you, Buckley lost an arm, poor sod."…"Lord Ennismore's badly put down, as well…pity, damned fine fellows."…And on he rode.

Chapter 34

Lord Raglan and his staff halted among the cheering soldiers. His Lordship wanted to share the spirit of a fight that had been won.

Ian looked pensively at his friend, the major, and said quietly, "We were lucky, Antonio."

"Yes, I fear more luck than skill. Are you all right, Ian? You seemed a bit out of sorts when you returned with the guns."

"I'm fine now." He couldn't bring himself to confide in anyone about his frightful brush with the terror of battle, and his disgraceful actions. "I lost Packey, though, as we crossed the river."

"A shame, lad, I know how much you love your horses."

"I fear the worst. He was hit square on, then ran away…Antonio, I learned something about myself today. A humbling experience I'd not like to repeat, but I believe I'll be fine now."

The major patted the neck of his own horse, reached into his past, his personal baptism under fire, said, "War has a way of teaching us about ourselves, I'll say that for it, and not always what we want to learn."

They were both silent for a long time, then pulled ahead to join the staff crowded around their commander. Lord Raglan stopped by his old friend, Sir Colin Campbell, commanding the Highlanders. Sir Colin was on foot, his mount having been shot out from under him. His Lordship leaned down from Shadrack and they shook hands heartily. Sir Colin said, "By Jove, M'Lord, not the first battlefield we've won together."

"No, my friend, it's not. Your Highlanders fought magnificently today."

"Aye, that they did. Thank ye M'Lord." He hesitated, "Might I beg a privilege of yer Lordship, sir."

"What is it, Colin? Today, you've earned just about any favour you might ask."

"I'd like permission to shed this cocked hat, and wear instead the Scottish bonnet, in honour of these courageous men."

Lord Raglan said nothing, nodded his affirmation, warmly, and rode on. Sir Colin immediately flung his white plumed hat into the air, and snatched up the colourful-feathered bonnet of a recently fallen officer. The noisy cheers and piercing war cries of the Highlanders around him showed their delight.

Lord Cardigan's Light Cavalry Brigade arrived at the farthest left flank of the British infantry line. These cavalrymen were fresh and impatient, not having taken part in the battle.

The infantry advance had halted all along the line. On their own initiative, elements of the light cavalry eagerly pursued the Russians and took some prisoners. The Russians continued their rapid retirement. Lord Raglan sent Ian and other staff officers to curtail the cavalry's zeal on those further heights, not much over a half-mile from the site of the battle. It required repeated orders to recall the reluctant troopers, who, in disgust, released their prisoners.

Some time later, the staff waited impatiently for orders for further pursuit, which they knew would be coming. They saw Lord Raglan meeting not far away with Marshal St Arnaud, both on horseback. It looked like a tense meeting, an important one. General Airey, Lieutenant Colonel Steele, and his aide, Curzon, were there with Lord Raglan. It was an odd grouping, British staff officers in their white plumed cocked hats, the grand marshal and his staff in kepis and bright French uniforms, and in their centre, the quietly unassuming Raglan in his plain blue frock coat.

"We must pursue," said Nolan to no one in particular. "We've a cavalry brigade which hasn't crossed a sword, and two infantry divisions never engaged. The Frenchies have at least an equal number of reasonably fresh troops to stick in."

Ian voiced the thoughts of the entire staff, "I agree, Lewis. The Turks weren't engaged either."

Nolan burst out, "By God, we can get them, gentlemen. End this thing, now. Probably push them right into Sevastopol, and take it as well. We'll go…we'll have to keep going."

"Let us hope they make the right decision," Capecci said, solemnly.

After what seemed like far too long a time, Curzon rode back from the fateful meeting of the generals to join their little band. His frustration showed. He began, "His Lordship wanted the French to pursue. He offered our cavalry, and some artillery, but said our infantry had suffered much, and could not advance without severely weakening the British force."

Nolan shouted, "What…but…"

"Allow me to finish, sir," Curzon interrupted. "Lord Raglan made it clear that he was in favour of pursuit, but the Marshal said he could send no infantry, something about their knapsacks being left on the north river bank when they moved across to attack. He also claimed their artillery ammunition was exhausted."

Curzon paused. The others looked at him blankly, in disbelief. He continued, "Marshal St Arnaud obviously felt that his forces and ours did enough for now, and it was time to rest and re-supply. After the Marshal left, His Lordship announced that we would be remiss to pursue the enemy without the French, citing our relatively smaller numbers, the superior numbers of Russian reserves, the exhaustion of so many of our troops, and the possibility of Russian cavalry showing up on our flank and rear."

Even the usually outspoken Nolan was speechless. They wanted to agree with their commander, wanted to see his logic, but were disappointed, frustrated, and concerned about the decision. In the end they were assigned to pass the order to the division commanders to stand down, and did so.

Chapter 35

At five o'clock, Lord Raglan, accompanied by Major Capecci, Curzon, and Ian, rode down from the Kouganie and back across the river. The village remained ablaze in many places, a shroud of smoke lying low to the ground. Wounded were huddling beneath the walls of burned-out houses. The thick smoke was acrid, almost putrid.

His staff may have had misgivings over their Commander-in-Chief's decision not to pursue, but it was difficult for any of them to remain troubled when they observed his compassion for the wounded. He paused frequently, dismounted, and spent time among them, showing tenderness to those suffering, and thanking as many as he could touch for their sacrifices.

Captain Nigel Kingscote, one of His Lordship's inner circle by marriage, and a member of Ian's own regiment, rode up to Ian and Curzon. He said to Curzon, as he watched his commander, "I say, Curzon, the strain is showing on him. I'm worried for his health. He badly needs rest."

Curzon said, "I agree. I understand his tent is ready. Shall someone suggest he move there?"

"You can suggest it, old man," Kingscote said, "but I fear he won't leave here for some time."

Kingscote, who was extremely close to His Lordship and his family, was right. It was past seven when Lord Raglan finally rode across the field to his quarters. He dined there around nine, a small piece of fresh meat, found by his cook, two small potatoes, and fresh greens.

His rest after the meal was interrupted, "Come in, gentlemen, come in. Forgive me for not rising. What have you to report?" Lord Raglan was lying on his small bed. Colonel Steele was sitting at a table, reviewing reports.

It was Ian and Captain Curzon who entered the small tent, standing awkwardly inside the entrance flap. "I'd offer you a seat, gentlemen, but these accommodations are a bit spartan."

Curzon said hurriedly, "No, M'Lord, we're fine, I'd not have disturbed you, but you did ask for casualty reports as soon as received."

"Of course, Captain Curzon, of course."

Ian reported, "M'Lord, these are very preliminary numbers, but thus far I make it slightly over 350 soldiers dead." He bowed his head.

"And wounded?"

"A bit over 1600 wounded or missing, M'Lord. I've also been informed that Marshal St Arnaud is again very ill, and seems to be getting worse."

Colonel Steele asked, "Officers, Curzon?"

Curzon responded quickly, "We count thus far 20 officers dead, sir, no wounded or missing numbers yet."

Curzon and Ian stared straight ahead, Steele looked at the ground, and His Lordship slowly came to a full sitting position on the edge of the bed. A long several seconds passed in silence, then Lord Raglan said, "Well, yes then. Thank you, gentlemen. Steele, when the exact returns come in from the regiments tomorrow morning, I want to see every one of them."

He continued, "Gentlemen, please take your leave and rest for tomorrow. My thanks for your good staff work this day. You were a great help to me."

Steele said, "Of course, M'Lord."

His Lordship asked, "Carlyle, would you be so kind as to remain for a moment?" The others left the tent.

Lord Raglan looked sad and subdued, eyes almost watering, said, "First, my boy, I know you've asked to be returned to your regiment, but I can't spare you at this time. Perhaps later."

Ian said, "Aye, M'Lord, wherever you need me."

"Carlyle, I want your honest views. Have you been about the camp?"

"Yes, M'Lord, I just returned. That's how we arrived at the early numbers we reported." He handed Raglan a piece of paper, "M'Lord, here are the names of the guardsmen in the Scots Fusiliers' colour party."

"Thank you. I'll see they're recognized. Now, give me a feel for it, Carlyle. I must know what we can still do. I saw the wounded. High spirits, but so many. The men, Carlyle, how do they fare to you?"

"Aye, M'Lord, they could do with a night's rest, well enough, but the spirit, M'Lord, the spirit is excellent. They won today. They feel it running through them, sweet, like having a good woman, pardon my frankness, Your Lordship. They're ready to do it again."

Lord Raglan's face brightened for the first time. "I see. You'd stand by that appraisal, would you, Ian?"

"Aye, M'Lord, and there's more. It's the talk around the fires, other ranks as well as officers. It came out of today's battle, and brought a sparkle to the eye of the lowest guardsman, highlander, or line regiment private."

"And that would be?" asked Raglan, curious.

"The muskets, M'Lord. So many of our men are now armed with the 'rifle' musket, the Minié, and its conical bullet. Far more accurate than the Russian smoothbore muskets. Like throwing rocks in comparison. It was noticed all along the line, M'Lord. Our volleys were cutting them down as we moved forward long before their fire began affecting us."

Raglan digested this for several moments, then said, "Good, Ian, splendid. You are a fine officer, my boy. Make your father proud. Get some rest. I'll need you strong tomorrow."

"Aye, M'Lord," Ian said, and left the tent. He'd expected the rejection of his request, but felt a wrenching inside him at hearing His Lordship's other words. *Proud? Proud indeed. He should have seen this fine officer grovelling beneath that sandy bank, sopping wet, terrified, and shaking like a schoolboy about to receive a caning. Damn the artillery, damn the fear. Can't allow that to happen again. I was lucky no one saw my disgrace this time, not even Captain Turner, but I must stay on my guard, keep the leopard closer. I must.*

Chapter 36

Wood is getting very scarce, indeed, Ian thought, as he used a stick to stir the burning roots. The small trees and brushwood were gone now, used up. Their servants were digging up roots as best they could to provide firewood. Ian's stirring caused more flame to catch parts not yet scorched. It was a month after the battle at the Alma, the evening of 24 October 1854. The nights had become quite brisk.

Ian, Major Capecci, Nolan, and Curzon were assigned a small outbuilding at Lord Raglan's chosen headquarters at a farm on the plateau before Sevastopol. For the first time since landing, they had an actual roof over their heads. Their servants organized the necessary duties to take care of their officers. With them pitching in, it wasn't necessary for Ian to immediately replace Angus. The siege was progressing, but at a glacial pace. British and French artillery had finally begun shelling Sevastopol a week before.

The staff work was becoming routine. Ian spent his days scouting, surveying, and drawing maps. He also used up considerable time touring the camps to report on morale and general fitness, as Lord Raglan expected of him.

"They seem to be keeping you quite busy these days, Ian, you're never about until evening," Nolan said, as he lit a longish clay pipe.

"The redoubts, Lewis, haven't you been informed? I'm the official, most exalted, 'Grand Keeper of Redoubts,'" Ian retorted, with a broad grin.

Nolan and the others seated around the small fire chuckled. Nolan asked, "What, pray tell, does that mean?"

Ian gave him a deliberate look of superiority, said, "Well, my old sod, some of us, from the Guards mind you, have skills beyond mere mortals. Officers such as yourself, a mere clerk, just wouldn't understand the complexities of the more responsible staff of the English army in the East." More laughter was heard.

Nolan mocked a scowl at the reference to his rather substantial duties as aide to General Airey, the Quartermaster of the Army, who was also the Chief of Staff. They were constantly jabbing each other about one thing or another, anything that came to mind, with no mercy. It relieved boredom.

"Fuck off, Ian," replied Nolan. He really wasn't offended.

Ian retorted, "Right, but that activity would be more in your line, I should think. Rumours abound of a certain Hussar paymaster's wife. I've also heard that what modest skills you possess had to do with gambling and flitting away your precious time and coin in a frantic search for a brothel in Balaklava. Could any of these things be so, old chap?"

Nolan laughed, "At least I haven't totally ruined my right hand from too much of the nasty with myself, fella."

"Curb yer tongue, Lewis," a smiling Curzon inserted. "You know not of what you speak. Why Ian here has been given a critical mission. Hardly time for such invigorating, yet frivolous self-abuse. I can testify that His Lordship is quite dependent upon The Honourable Ian Carlyle's daily reports. Couldn't sleep soundly without them. Do enlighten these heathens, Ian."

"So I shall, Leicester, my dear fellow. Glad someone appreciates the subtleties of my assignment."

There were friendly groans from Capecci and Nolan. Ian continued, unaffected by their derision, "Yes, well my friends, I protect our fair port of Balaklava. His Lordship will have me out bright and early most mornings, observing progress on the defences, and the fitness of our mighty Turkish allies who serve the guns within them. I inspect all the redoubts along the causeway, observing keenly as I go, to report humbly my findings to His Lordship by each day's end. Thus, he can sleep in comfort, knowing the army is safe, and we are well protected by the gallant Turk."

More chuckling around the fire. Not many believed the Turkish troops were much good, although rumour was they had beaten the Russians at a place called Oltenitza, and had more or less caused the Russians to scurry home.

"An awesome responsibility," said Major Capecci, "fit for the second son of an Earl, I should think." Again they laughed, but each felt a bit jealous. Ian, at least, was doing something other than the never-ending paper passing, orders and reports.

Although Ian jested about it with his fellow officers, he was perfectly content with his current duties. His tours of the redoubts became routine, but not unpleasant. He visited the various Royal Artillery gunners who had been sent to explain the British guns to the Turkish gun detachments at each of the four manned redoubts, the outer ring of defences of the important supply port at Balaklava.

It became his habit to rise a few hours before the sun, saddle Savage, and exercise him in the breaking dawn light. Transitioning between a fast trot and a canter, and occasionally a gallop, Ian would take Savage across the plateau on the road to Balaklava, down onto the plain of South Valley, through the camps of the Heavy and Light Cavalry Brigades, then east across the valley floor. At the far end, he'd ride to the village of Kamara, nestled among the hills not far below Number 1 Redoubt, the eastern-most defensive position. This was a several mile journey, exhilarating for both man and horse.

There was a house there, which had been an inn of sorts, about the only thing that this small village had to offer before their arrival. The owner, an old Greek, was told to clear out, but quietly refused to do so. It was his regimen for twenty years to rise before dawn each day to bake bread and pastry. He was not about to change that, come war or pestilence. With fewer and fewer customers, he was more than willing to make Ian a cup of thick strong coffee each morning, served with warm fresh-baked bread and a spicy jam, as long as Ian did not report him.

It was Ian's time alone with his thoughts. Ian would sit in the enclosed courtyard behind the decrepit old inn at a tiny table beside the kitchen door. There, he could enjoy the smells of cooking, daydream about romantic interludes with Jasmine, glorious deeds he might yet do, or ancient battles fought in places not unlike this one.

It was the following morning, and he was sitting comfortably at the inn by four o'clock. Ian was unable to sleep. He couldn't drag his thoughts away from Angus, Piccard, and his unseen disgrace at the riverbank. In the pre-dawn fog, the air was cool and crisp. The fresh coffee smell was coming through the open kitchen door.

Ian bit into his bread and jam. He felt so alert these brisk mornings, so alive. He sipped his coffee contentedly, stared at the slowly lightening sky.

The brew was extra strong. Ian would remember its taste for the rest of his life.

Chapter 37

The old Greek burst out of his kitchen, screaming. There was the crack of a musket fired from inside. A gaping hole appeared in the old man's chest where a large round ball exited out the front. Out of pure reflex, Ian fell to the ground under his table. There was laughter within the kitchen and loud voices in Russian…several voices. Thankfully, no one came out to inspect the results of their musketry. They knew the old man was dead.

Ian stayed buried nose down in the dirt under the table, frozen, mind racing forward like a riderless horse at full gallop. Savage was tied not far away within the courtyard, but hidden by bushes. Ian heard the snorting and rustling of saddled horses from the street in front. If any of the mounted Russians came around to the courtyard, they would certainly see him over the low wall.

He reviewed his options: *How the bloody hell did they get past the Turkish sentries in the old chapel east of the village? Probably killed them. A patrol, like the ones reported further north. Audacious bastards, but too many to take on alone. Get mounted, quietly; get past them and up to the redoubt.*

Ian silently made his way along the ground to Savage, reached up and untied him, pulled himself awkwardly into the saddle, keeping as low a profile as he could. He steered

Savage slowly out of the courtyard, not daring to breathe. He made his way down a back alley until he was able to circle and come out at the small town centre where several roads met, a few houses distant from the Greek's home.

The redoubt was almost a mile from the village out a long finger of land. He had to pass back by the Greek's house to get there. The hazy dawn was becoming day, as he nosed Savage into the main dirt street of the village, body low along the horse's neck, looking carefully in the direction of the house.

What's this then? Ian expected to see half a dozen empty horses at most, held by perhaps one rider. He was shocked to find the entire intersection filled with Cossacks. Then he heard the unmistakable creek and clank of moving artillery equipment. *Fuck all...this is no patrol.* Hundreds of Russians were milling about between him and the redoubt, between him and safety. He was trapped.

More horsemen appeared in the street, 50 feet away. These were Russian army officers talking excitedly. They wore long greyish overcoats in the chilly morning. *Perhaps the redoubt was not aware,* Ian thought, *still too dark and foggy. Even the gunshot might not have carried that far. If they knew, they'd open fire.*

Ian heard other sounds not far off, the crunch of marching feet, could feel the urgency behind the movements, felt his fear rising, but with it, the leopard came to him. *This is a major attack,* he thought. *They're moving into position. I'm right in the middle of it. Must get to the redoubt. But how? Haven't a chance of bullying my way through. Think. Angus taught us to think...now think.*

A plan formed. He smiled, roguishly, as he took his forage cap off. He carried in his kit a black India-rubber rain cap cover, which he slipped over his cap, thinking, sardonically: *The cap band's Scottish dicing might be a bit too obvious, there being few Scottish regiments in the Russian army.* He was wearing his dark cloak, which easily covered the British uniform, especially in this light.

Ian moved, but not recklessly, his luck holding. It was still a shadowy dawn, with fog hanging horse high. There was confusion in the street, as cannon were hauled into view. Soldiers scurried from their path. Ian used this diversion. He sat ramrod straight in his saddle, and rode into the street, aiming deliberately through the middle of the mounted enemy officers. He nodded to a few, said one of the few words he could recall in Russian, "Da, da," which he was certain meant, yes.

It's working, by damn. One officer even smiled and spoke casually to him in Russian. He smiled back, no idea what the officer was saying. With every step, he expected exposure, a shout, followed by shots and his inglorious death.

He passed the officers and continued toward the Cossacks in front of the former inn, feeling an icy chill up his spine, wondering how many eyes were following him suspiciously. The Cossacks saw him leave the officer group and assumed he was one of them. A few saluted, as he neared. Ian returned their salutes with a vague wave.

After passing the Cossacks, he moved Savage into a slow trot, heading first down the dirt road, then up toward the finger of land leading to the redoubt. It seemed so very far away in the fog and blackness.

He reached the finger and turned left, toward the redoubt, shifting Savage into a canter. It was at this moment he heard the shout he had feared, obviously directed at him, but no shots. *They must be frantic about one of their foolhardy officers moving ahead of their line, alerting the enemy of their presence.*

Chapter 38

As Ian hoped, things were moving too fast for the Russians to react. He gave Savage his head. Still no shots came.

Savage made for the redoubt, up the long sloping finger. The mile seemed to take forever. It was after five o'clock, and becoming lighter. As he approached the fortification, the ground becoming steeper, he made out a man wearing the short blue jacket, and the round cloth red and blue forage cap of the Royal Artillery. The gunner was standing on the parapet, legs wide apart, frantically waving at Ian.

As Ian came closer, he recognized the man as Gunner Tinsley, a short, bulky, black-bearded artilleryman he had spoken to on past inspections. Obviously, something or someone had alerted the redoubt, because Tinsley was screaming, "Sir, get the bloody hell out the way, so's we can fire."

Ian realized his folly, veered Savage sharply to the left, ducking along his neck. The brilliant orange flash from the cannon's mouth blinded him. He thought his head had split open. His ears rang from the deafening discharge no more than forty feet in front of him. Ian thought as he tried to recover from the blast…*if that didn't kill me, nothing will.*

It wasn't Ian's time yet, and his mind began to clear. He shook his head, vigorously, and found he could still actually see and hear. Savage was magnificent. The blast caused him to jump, and stumble, but he kept moving forward and Ian stayed in his saddle.

The Turkish gunners within the redoubt began earnestly responding to the Russian threat. Ian found the road around the south side of the redoubt, which had been used to bring in guns, ammunition, and supplies. He rode through a line of Turkish infantry, then entered the position from the rear. In the redoubt were hundreds of Turkish soldiers dressed in blue frock coats and red fezzes, some in shirtsleeves, preparing for the inevitable attack. The Turkish gun detachments were firing the redoubt's three 12-pounders at a fairly rapid pace, directed by their own officers and sergeants. Enemy counter-battery fire had begun, but they hadn't yet found the range.

"Tinsley, who's in command here?" Ian shouted, as he dismounted and tied Savage loosely to the wheel of a nearby supply wagon.

"Same as always, sir, them Turkish officers somewhere's over there. Don't speak the King's English much. Haven't seen them command much either. These here are militia, mostly from Tunisia, not regular Turkish soldiers. They calls themselves, Esnan. Their sergeants seem to run just about everything. The two of us, we're supposed to be here to help them...explain the guns, nothing more."

"Where's the other gunner?"

"Lucky sod, sir, he's down in Balaklava getting supplies. Went down last night."

"Tinsley, how'd you know they were coming? You couldn't have seen them that far below through this bloody fog."

Tinsley said, "Well, sir, two of our wayward Turkish comrades, infantry types, was getting a bit of the old in and out in the village last night. They was awakened by the Rooshians, and ran for it. Got here just ahead of you, sir, and warned us."

Ian laughed, but turned serious again, quickly, "We've had this discussion before, Tinsley, but now it's critical. Will these men fight?"

"Yes, sir, for a time. They're not cowards, sir, and that's a certain fact, but they's no fools either."

"What do you mean? Speak plain."

"They'll stay, right enough, sir, as long as they's officers stay, and as long as they feels they'll be supported and can win. It all depends on them officers and sergeants, some damned good, some bloody fucking awful."

While they talked, the redoubt's guns, served by their Turkish gunners, were hammering away steadily at the enemy batteries, and at their infantry masses forming up in the village and beyond the causeway north of the redoubt. The fog was clearing. The Russian efforts to assemble were now in view through the cannon smoke, but they were taking time.

Chapter 39

The roar of the redoubt's guns firing one after another was deafening within the fortification. Russian solid shot was smacking into the redoubt walls now, but without much effect. Now and then, an odd one landed short and skipped in over the low front wall, smashing everything in its path.

The redoubt's 12-pounders were answering effectively, their gunners working smartly. Guns barked and rolled back, the acrid smell of gunpowder cut the air. It filled Ian's nostrils. Billowing smoke obscured his view.

Minutes passed interminably, as more Turks were wounded or died in their positions. The Turks returned fire against an ever-increasing number of Russian guns. Enemy howitzers began lobbing in shells, which exploded overhead and rained fragments of death down on the redoubt.

Ian felt the fear creeping in. *Damned artillery.* The leopard had actually been by his side since the ride through the village. The big cat was keeping him calm. Ian found himself shouting over the cacophony, but in an unexpectedly natural-sounding voice, "Actually, Tinsley, the Turks' artillery practice appears most admirable. Did you have anything to do with that?"

Tinsley was pleased, "A bit, sir, a bit. Some's damned good. I train 'em good on our guns, I do." Ian knew that the gunners sent out to these redoubts were not the very best the Royal Artillery had to offer, but this one had real promise.

Ian merely watched the action. Trading shot and shell with the enemy played for the better part of two hours. The volume of Russian fire escalated steadily.

In the end it was impossible. There were over thirty Russian guns pummelling the redoubt from commanding positions, with only the three 12-pounders to return fire in two directions. Large bodies of Russian infantry were moving on them from over the causeway and from Kamara below. Many of the Turks in the redoubt were either wounded or lying dead.

They're putting up one hell of a fight, Ian thought, somewhat surprised they'd held this long, and were still steady. Ian expected to see British infantry moving in support by now. He had only seen Cardigan's Light Brigade move toward them with a few Royal Horse Artillery equipments. They came forward, then withdrew.

It was after seven o'clock. Tinsley beckoned to Ian to join him kneeling behind the forward wall. He pointed at what Ian estimated as thousands of Russian infantrymen approaching in massed columns from the causeway, their skirmishers heavy out in front, firing as they came. Ian looked about him, could feel the uneasiness building among the Turks.

Ian thought the grand plan was to reinforce the redoubts if they were attacked. So, where was the promised support? Where were the British and French?

Ian said to Tinsley, "Turks have been holding for far too long."

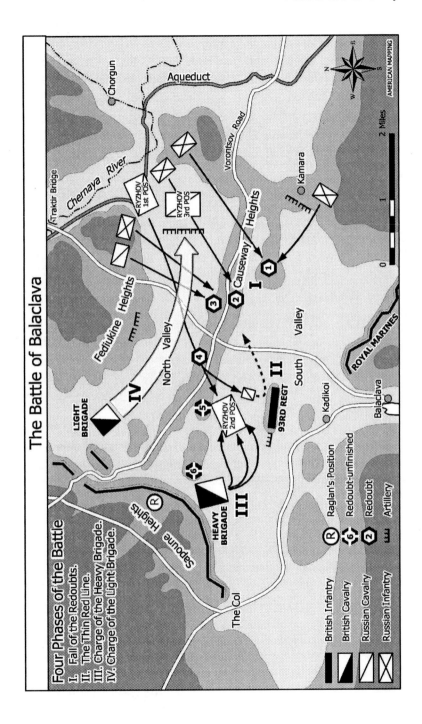

The Battle of Balaclava

Four Phases of the Battle
I. Fall of the Redoubts.
II. The Thin Red Line.
III. Charge of the Heavy Brigade.
IV. Charge of the Light Brigade.

British Infantry
British Cavalry
Russian Cavalry
Russian Infantry

AMERICAN MAPPING

Tinsley nodded, solemnly. Turkish soldiers with terror on their faces were nervously beginning to flit about, looking for encouragement and guidance from their officers and sergeants, who had no answers, had nothing to give. Uneasiness turned to panic as some of the Turkish infantry from the forward rifle pits stumbled into the redoubt, firing at the Russians behind them as they came. Ian could feel the alarm building inside himself as well, but this time it was different.

There was Tinsley, a simple artilleryman. He wasn't even a non-commissioned officer, but Ian watched him giving advice to the Turkish gunners, setting an example by moving decisively where most needed, helping lay the guns. He was standing upright, exposed, while shot and shrapnel rained down, reapers of death, searching for prey.

A Turkish soldier standing next to Tinsley was hit in the chest by a round shot, his body exploded, limbs flying, dissolving in a spray of blood. Chunks of torn flesh covered Tinsley. The shot went on to hit, rip apart, and kill three men who were unlucky enough to be standing behind the first Turk blown apart by the large round ball.

Tinsley never flinched. He calmly used his coat sleeve to clear the gore from his face, then dragged a Turk attempting to flee the carnage back to his gun, shouting, "Get you back there, ya heathen bastard. Fight, damn ya."

Ian moved back from the front wall and was crouching near the wheel of a battery wagon while he watched Tinsley. He awoke as if from a dream, galvanized into action by some hidden force. He knew he could do no less than this courageous gunner. *No time for fear. Work to do.*

It wasn't their mission, but he and Tinsley tried to rally the Turks with words they couldn't understand, and didn't want to hear. There were blank looks, a tough Turkish sergeant pleading with Tinsley, "*Where is English? We cannot stop* them alone. Too many…too many." The Turkish sergeant was crying, not from fear, from frustration, exasperation.

The Russian infantry column kept coming, only a few hundred yards away now. The first Turkish gunner jumped the low parapet at the rear of the redoubt, running toward the British positions across the valley, opening the floodgates. These men had held against terrible odds, more than anyone had the right to ask. By this time, nearly half their original number lay dead or dying.

The Turkish survivors who had been serving the guns and acting as protecting infantry began streaming southwest down the heights onto the floor of South Valley, toward Balaklava. Even now, not all of them fled. A courageous infantry detachment, held steady by their young Turkish officer, was still firing at the oncoming Russian horde. They had already charged the leading Russian skirmishers once from their rifle pits with bayonets. They had been overwhelmed and forced back into the redoubt, still firing.

Some of the Turks who fled into the valley, those with good leaders, turned about along the way to fire a volley at the Russians. They would then withdraw further, reload as they moved, turn and fire again, slowing Russian pursuit. Others, leaderless, just ran.

"There's nothing for it, sir," Tinsley shouted over the din. "These lads have had it, and they're not going to do the work that has to be done."

He looked at the three big guns, held up three long heavy spikes, looking like large six-inch carpenter's nails, and a heavy hammer he'd found in the battery wagon. He said, "Sir, I'll be buggered if I'll give over these guns to them Roossian bastards."

"Right you are, Tinsley, let's get it done then."

They raced to the first gun, already deserted by the Turks. Ian held a spike over the gun's vent, while Tinsley tried to pound it in. A shell exploded near the ground, the other side of the gun, and knocked them both down. Tinsley screamed above the pandemonium surrounding them, "I've lost the bloody spikes, sir." He was scrambling on the ground, looking.

"Forget it, come with me."

Ian ran to the gun's limber, rummaged about, and came out with a gunner's gimlet, used for boring out plugs or other obstructions in the vent of the gun. Tinsley smiled at the officer's knowledge.

Ian intended to put the gimlet halfway into the vent and use the hammer to bend it slightly. This would cause it to fit into the vent more tightly than usual. He'd then hammer it all the way in. There was no head on the end of the gimlet, but Ian knew that the screw at the gimlet's tip would be hanging into the breech. He and Tinsley could use the gun's rammer down the barrel to bend the gimlet. They ran again to the first gun.

They stopped and ducked by the base of the gun, chests heaving slightly, but something was very wrong…

There was an eerie quiet. The Turks were nearly gone, except for the stalwart detachment and their young officer. They were waiting with fixed bayonets. The only other Turks in the redoubt were lying about in grotesque poses, some still moving.

Tinsley looked at the guns in frustration. Both of them knew it was too late to spike them…time had run out. The Russian artillery was silent. Ian knew that meant their infantry was dangerously close and they had lifted their fire.

Ian thought: *We failed…they'll soon be using them against our own men.*

He shouted, "Tinsley, we're too late. We need to be going."

They heard the Russian drums beating a steady rhythm of impending doom, could almost feel the ground shake, as the Russian column steadily advanced, skirmishers nearly at the parapets. Their front being wider than the redoubt, they would soon envelop it.

Gunner Tinsley replied, with sadness in his voice, "Right ya are, sir."

Ian was glad to see Savage still tied not far away, unhurt. Savage saw, smelled, felt the swirl of death and slaughter, but waited patiently for Ian to need him.

Tinsley said, "Look there, sir."

Ian looked where Tinsley was pointing, saw the Turkish officer and about forty of his men, bayonets fixed, charging over the redoubt's front parapet. Ian and Tinsley watched in shocked amazement. The odds against these gallant Turks must have been over a thousand to one. Their young captain was first up on the berm, showing magnificent courage. He looked back at his men, and was immediately cut to ribbons by Russian musket balls.

This was a grotesque signal to his soldiers. They saw their leader die, and screamed as one man, charging forward with the bayonet...disappeared over the edge. That was the last Ian or Tinsley saw of them.

It was time. It was past time. The gunner said, "If we're done, sir, may I suggest we get the bloody hell out of this horrible little place?"

"That strikes me as a splendid idea. Tinsley, would you feel at all uncomfortable sharing my mount?"

Tinsley looked at Ian, startled, until he realized the humour in Ian's voice and saw the twinkle in his eye. He smiled wickedly, and they both made for Savage, Ian leaping on first. Locking an arm with the gunner, he twirled Savage around, swinging Tinsley up onto the back of the saddle. Savage sprang away, and made for the rear of the now deserted redoubt.

Chapter 40

They both saw them at the same time, Ian reining in Savage with some difficulty. Two eager Russians were standing at the rear of the redoubt, their bayonets pointing at the two men on the horse, an easy capture, and an officer too...what luck.

Ian shouted over his shoulder to Tinsley, "Shall we?"

Tinsley replied, "At yer pleasure, sir." Tinsley was a trained gunner-driver. He knew horses well. They could feel and hear the buzzing of tiny round balls passing mere inches from their heads. Skirmishers, having climbed the redoubt's front glacis, were firing at them from behind.

Ian patted Savage's neck, "Let's go lad, show 'em what you've got." He touched a spur into Savage's flanks, almost gently. Savage jumped forward, Ian veering him left away from the Russian bayonets, straight toward the low rear parapet.

The leap over was a stretch carrying two men, even for a huge and excellent jumper like Savage. The Russians stared in disbelief as the magnificent animal and its two crouched riders sailed cleanly over the parapet, then galloped down the steep opposite slope. Savage's hooves found purchase on the ground, and he was away, head back, nostrils flaring.

It was a spirited ride onto the valley floor, overtaking their Turkish allies, some fleeing for their lives, others standing to fight. Ian saw Lord Lucan, the overall cavalry commander, rather calmly riding back toward the cavalry camp, saw the Turks from the other three redoubts along the causeway pouring down into the valley, running for their lives. Cossacks appeared, riding fast, catching some of the less lucky Turks. They cut them down mercilessly.

Ian also recognized Lord John Blunt, of Lord Lucan's staff, who spoke the Turkish language, trying to stem and redirect the rush of Turkish troops gushing past him toward Balaklava. The valley was a mass of confusion.

Ian leaned back and turned his head, shouting, "What's your full name, Tinsley? You've done fine work today, and I'll see it gets mentioned."

The gunner leaned forward, into Ian's ear, said, "Thank you, sir, it's Gunner Alfred Tinsley, W Battery. My battery is…" There was a sickening thunk, a crunching sound. Ian now knew that sound well…a musket ball burying itself deep in flesh, crushing bone on its way.

Ian felt Tinsley slip slowly from the saddle. Pulling Savage up, he jumped to the ground, and ran to the fallen gunner. Tinsley was face down. The back of the gunner's blue shell jacket was stained dark with blood. The blackish-red pool was rapidly growing larger, already mixing with the dust and sand of the valley floor.

The gallant Gunner Tinsley was hit square in the back by the musket ball. He died still on the horse, without finishing his reply to Ian's question. Ian turned him gently over on his back, saw the face, so calm and noble in death, as it had been in life. He thought as he climbed back in the saddle: *So this is 'glory.' Where was their support?* He knew the answer. Ian knew in his heart that there was no support, that there was never any intention of supporting the Turks. They were merely sacrificed to delay the attack. They'd been expendable, but by damn they'd cost the enemy dearly.

As he turned away, Ian thought: *You were a fine soldier, Alfred Tinsley, and deserved better than to die on this dusty plain...glory be damned.*

Chapter 41

Ian reluctantly left the fallen gunner, remounted, heard his name being called, "Ho, Carlyle."

Captain Kingscote from Raglan's staff approached at a gallop, reined in expertly, and said, "Ian, good to see you. Just delivered a message from His Lordship to Sir Colin Campbell. He's on that knoll over there with the 93rd," pointing west toward a rise in the ground north of Balaklava.

"The orders I brought told him to hold, whatever the cost," Kingscote continued. "I have still to deliver a similar message to the Marines on Mount Hiblak. I say, be a good chap and help me out."

"I'll do what I can, Nigel. What is it?"

"You can see the Russians up along the causeway. Sir Colin is trying to gather as many men as he can at his position to protect the port. He's certain there'll be an attack across the valley. I can't help him gather them up. Must get to those Marines."

"Where are the reinforcements to be found?"

Kingscote replied, "There are certainly men at the hospitals and on work details. They'll need someone to lead them out to his position. Can you organize that?"

"Of course, Nigel. I'll go now."

As Kingscote rode off, he shouted, "Good man. Go to Balaklava. See what you can do. Thanks awfully, Ian."

Ian didn't quite agree with Kingscote's advice. The Russians were already on the causeway. The most logical place to start looking for troops who might get there in time to be of help was the small town of Kadikoi, not Balaklava. Kadikoi was less than a mile from Campbell's knoll position, while Balaklava was several miles further. There was a sizable hospital at Kadikoi. He rode fast, pushing Savage, passing the 93rd position. He saw that some of the Turks who had fled the redoubts were being reorganized at the knoll.

Ian found his task much easier than expected. At the army hospital, a nervous captain named Inglis was standing before a mixed formation of troops. He had gathered some green-clad riflemen, around 50 convalescing guardsmen, a few 93rd Highlanders who were on supply details, and 30 or so assorted line infantry with minor wounds.

When Ian introduced himself, Inglis said, "I'm waiting for directions, Captain. I have the men, I merely don't know where to take them."

Ian said, "I know where you're to go. I'll guide you."

Captain Inglis formed them quickly, and they marched off. Ian led them on the road from Kadikoi, past Battery Number 4, and on up to the 93rd Highlanders position.

Ian climbed the side of the knoll to where the 93rd were drawn up in two ranks facing north toward the valley and the causeway ridges beyond. He dismounted and found Colonel Ainsley, who commanded the 93rd, standing with General Sir Colin Campbell. Both were arduously studying the causeway. Sir Colin was wearing a plain blue staff officer's frock coat, but sported the conspicuous highland bonnet he had adopted at the Alma.

Ian saluted both, faced Sir Colin, the senior officer present, and reported, "Carlyle, sir, Lord Raglan's staff, I have with me Captain Inglis. He's brought you over a hundred fighting men."

Sir Colin said, "Excellent, we can use them. Carlyle, have Inglis report to Lieutenant Colonel Devaney commanding our battalion of detachments. He'll place them to the rear of the 93rd, until we sort this mess out a bit."

Ian gave Inglis his orders, then looked over the position. The knoll was well situated in the direct path of any attempt to capture Balaklava. On the forward slope, the 93rd waited patiently in line of battle. On the reverse slope was Devaney's ad hoc battalion, and on the flanks what appeared now to be two battalions of Turkish militia, including the reformed Esnan remnants from the abandoned causeway redoubts.

A field artillery battery returned from the causeway, and was being placed on the left flank below the 93rd Highlanders, in prepared positions. Like all field batteries in the army, they had four 9-pounder guns, two 24-pounder howitzers, and a Congreve rocket carriage of questionable usefulness. The battery's efficient gunners were wasting no time bringing their six field guns to bear on the causeway, and the now Russian-occupied redoubts.

Ian scanned the causeway with his telescope. This was by his estimate not far under 2000 yards distant, an extreme range for the battery's guns, but it could be done.

With a crash, a round shot fired from the causeway heights landed in front of the 93rd line, bounding over the heads of the Highlanders, but dangerously close. This proved Ian's appraisal of the ability of good gunners to reach out that far effectively.

More tremendous crashes followed, round shot, then shrapnel shells exploding above. One Highlander was left with a shattered foot from a round shot, and another's knee became a mass of blood and bone, hit by a shell fragment. A supply cart disintegrated into tiny deadly splinters.

Sir Colin ordered the field battery to commence counter battery fire on the causeway guns, while Colonel Ainsley drew the 93rd back to the reverse slope of the knoll under cover of the crest. Although this was a dignified, quite proper manoeuvre, to limit exposure of the troops, some of the Turkish infantry seemed to use the artillery fire and the movement of the 93rd slightly to their rear as an excuse. A number of Turks began drifting back toward the port city and the inviting harbour. The rest of the Turkish militia stood their ground.

Ian moved down the side of the knoll to the rear of the artillery battery, whose gunners were taking the causeway batteries under fire. He noted that their guns were at the extreme lowest elevation for maximum range.

Ian quietly introduced himself to the battery commander, a cocky little captain of artillery, "Excuse me, sir, I'm Carlyle, Lord Raglan's staff, would you mind terribly if I observed from here? I won't be a bother, I assure you."

The artillery captain was a young man, Ian's age, short of stature, handsome, well turned out in his flashy blue field artillery uniform, forage cap worn straight and well over his piercing eyes. Ian saw with admiration that he remained perfectly calm, reserved, and cold as ice. The captain said, "Not a bother at all, Carlyle, glad to have you. I'm Barker, W Battery."

Ian was surprised. "W Battery, indeed, sir. I had the honour of making the acquaintance of one of yours not long ago, Gunner Tinsley, Alfred Tinsley."

"Tinsley, of course, a bit of a pain in the arse in garrison, mind you, but a damned fine man in a scrap. Wish I had more of his sort. He was at Number 1 up there. I hope to God he got out in time. Looked like his Turks left in rather a hurry."

Ian said, "He barely managed to get out of the redoubt, but before he withdrew he acquitted himself valiantly. It was his courage that aided in keeping the Turks at their posts until they were being overwhelmed. There was no support. The casualties were appalling."

Barker replied somewhat defensively, "Support…yes, well, we were there. Went up as soon as we saw what was what, but too little too late. Damned Ruskies were all over those positions. Like bloody ants they were. We couldn't return fire effectively and were fast running out of ammunition. Had to retire…orders. Would have liked to have stayed the course, though. Left those poor Johnny Turks hanging there with their coat-tails in the breeze, and that's the God's truth. What of Tinsley?"

"Tinsley was the last man to leave that redoubt, with the Russians coming over the front," Ian explained.

Barker brightened, "Capital. Good show Tinsley. Where is he now?"

"Killed…musket ball in the spine. Lies out there on the valley floor. His last words were to mention the battery. He was proud. Died a warrior."

Barker looked directly at Ian, studying him through the sadness in his eyes, said softly, "Damned shame, Carlyle, but how do you know all this?"

Ian saw no need to play up his role in the affair, and said simply, "I was there, saw it all. I should be honoured to render a report of his courageous actions if it would mean gaining him recognition for his bravery. I'd also like to see to his body after this affair is concluded."

"Your report would be most appreciated, Carlyle, and I'll see it's placed in the right hands, with my endorsement. I'll also see a copy finds its way back to his two children. They're with their grandmother back home. Wife drew the lottery to come along with the regiment. She was here, but died of cholera while we were at Varna."

Ian thought of Angus, who went the same way on their first march.

Barker said, "They were on the regimental strength. Official marriage, fortunately. We'll see to the children, take care of them." Ian was pleased that this officer knew so much about one of his men, and that Tinsley's wife had been on the official rolls. It gave the feeling Tinsley was valued as a soldier and as a man, as it should be, and that his children would be provided for in some fashion.

Barker continued, "Although I also appreciate your concern for his body, we'll find him and see to it. We're a rather close family, the artillery, just as are you Guards. I'll see that he is cared for properly." Ian nodded his acceptance.

Barker was still studying Ian. From his knowledge of the details, quiet demeanour, and limited response, Barker suspected that he had more to do with the fight at the redoubt than he was willing to take credit for. Barker liked this Fusilier officer, not the usual sort he'd met.

Ian changed the subject, "I see your position is a bit masked by the knoll on your right." Ian had observed that although W Battery had an excellent view to fire on the causeway, and to their immediate front, the knoll blocked their firing to their right front.

Barker looked perplexed, "Yes, damn all, I've mentioned it to Sir Colin. Told him I can't support him on his front from here. Requested permission to move forward. He didn't seem too concerned, and I've no orders to shift my position."

Barker was scanning across the valley, spoke to no one in particular, "Looks clear to me right now. Appears Scarlett might be moving the 'Heavies' toward us. We could use their support."

Ian left him to his work, and moved back up the side of the knoll where he could see a full view of the causeway to his front, W Battery to his left and down the hill, and Sir Colin's infantry on his right on the reverse slope. It was by now around nine a.m. It had been an exceedingly long morning.

What Ian saw next gave him deep concern. Several hundred Russian horsemen were crossing the causeway between Numbers 3 and 4 Redoubts, moving slowly, steadily south, generally toward them.

Shortly thereafter, a much larger body of Russian cavalry crossed the causeway on the left side of Redoubt Number 4, moving extremely slowly, cautiously, south into the valley.

To Ian's left front, General Scarlett's Heavy Cavalry Brigade was definitely moving south, in column, strung out one regiment after another. They came toward the knoll from the cavalry camp, less than a half-mile away.

The British cavalry were close enough that by telescope Ian recognized Scarlett's two leading regiments as the 6th Inniskilling Dragoons, red coats, sun reflecting off brass plumeless helmets, and the Scots Greys on their magnificent grey horses.

Scarlett seemed oblivious to the main body of Russian cavalry moving into the valley more or less behind him. The Russians, however, were well within range of W Battery, and were being effectively shelled by Barker's guns and howitzers.

Ian calculated from where he stood close to the crest of the knoll that the larger body of cavalry was within Barker's view, but only Sir Colin, and the troops on the knoll itself, could see the smaller cavalry formation, now heading directly toward them.

Chapter 42

Sir Colin was standing with Lieutenant Colonel Devaney. They were intently watching the smaller Russian cavalry formation, while Barker was busy targeting the advancing main body. As the main body moved carefully closer, Barker began firing shot and shell into their advancing ranks in earnest with his 9-pounders. He also began to reach out to them with shell from his two 24-pounder howitzers. Deafening ear-ringing crashes came from all six cannon. They lurched back as they fired, blue-uniformed gunners expertly working their well-practiced gun drill.

Ian shouted toward W Battery, hands cupped to focus his words, "Barker, on your right front, beyond your view, several hundred enemy cavalry bearing down on your position. By their line of direction, they'll be within a few hundred yards before you'll see them."

Barker looked, but could see nothing. He responded, "Does Sir Colin see them?"

"Aye, he's poised and ready, but I think staying hidden until they're closer."

Barker said, "Right, Carlyle, thanks. Keep me appraised if you can. We'll be ready. Meantime, we'll keep well employed directly to our front."

The 400 Russians, who moved from a trot to a fast trot, were crossing in front of the knoll at an angle, still over a thousand yards out, by Ian's reckoning. Colonel Ainsley had by this time brought the 93rd from the reverse slope in line, two deep, forward of the crest of the knoll, in perfect order, Devaney's thrown-together battalion to the right of the line. The men were kneeling low and remained out of sight from the front. Two additional companies of the 93rd arrived to further lengthen the line.

Ian moved closer to where Sir Colin was talking to Devaney. He heard Devaney ask, "Shall we form square to receive cavalry, Sir Colin?"

"No, Devaney, we shall not."

"But, sir, we are very vulnerable in line."

"Colonel Devaney, a short lesson on the Minie´ rifle musket. It is sighted for 900 yards, accurate at about 600, give or take. Those Russians are advancing across open ground. They're used to having their way, not taking casualties till they're within 200 yards. They are certainly not expecting to be hit hard at the range my Highlanders will slam into them."

Sir Colin looked up at the sky, thought a moment, then said, "I'll not waste three-fourths of my rifle muskets by placing them on the sides and back of a square. Aye, we'll remain in line, I'll be bound, and the devil take the bastards."

Colonel Devaney's head was lowered, and he appeared to be studying his horse's mane intently. He knew it wasn't good to rile this high-strung Scotsman.

Sir Colin continued, "In line two deep, every rifle musket we have will rain terror down on those poor cavalrymen. When it begins, it won't last long. They'll break, and we'll have won the day."

"Yes, sir, I understand, sir. In line, two deep, and I'll say no more about it." Sir Colin said, "Aye." Ian could swear he saw him wink at the Colonel.

As though to bring the point home, Sir Colin spurred his horse, moved deliberately in front of his Highlanders, shouted, "There's no retreat from here, lads. Ye must die where ye stand."

This was a timely admonishment, because the Russian batteries on the causeway had increased their artillery fire from across the valley.

Round shot came in, destroying bodies, throwing them back like rag dolls. Shells were exploding overhead, raining fragments of death on the 93rd. Nothing unnerved the Scots. Not a soldier moved. The kneeling ranks were steady, bayonets leaning forward, determination on every face. Ian's Scottish pride swelled as the Highlanders stoically watched the approaching horsemen looming larger as they closed.

Shrapnel shells were exploding over W Battery, not far down the hill from where Ian stood. The fear of the creek bed had returned, but more controlled this time, each time. Ian was gaining strength over his fears, his faithful leopard close by.

W Battery gunners died at their places, some quietly falling, some torn to ribbons in an unrecognizable bundle of bright red, with white pieces of leg bone or skull protruding grotesquely. Spattered blood and pieces of flesh landed on scalding hot cannon barrels, sizzling like grease poured into a hot pan. The odour rose up the side of the knoll to where Ian stood, filling his head with the smell of fried meat. Behind them, battery horses were being hit, wild fear in their eyes, thrashing violently in their harnesses, gunner-drivers struggling to hold them steady or cut fallen horses from their traces.

Closer. Closer. The Turks on the flanks were also holding, waiting.

As Ian had suspected, the Russian cavalry line approaching the knoll was long enough that its right would crash into W Battery when it hit, but it would only be in W Battery's view for the last several hundred yards. Their fast trot was covering ground rapidly, and there was no artillery fire to slow them down…yet.

Nine hundred yards. Closer. The Turks fired a ragged volley, totally ineffectual at that range. To their credit, most remained steadfast, reloading.

Eight hundred yards. The 400 Russians moved into a canter, then slowly up to a full gallop, eating up the ground, faster and faster. Ian thought it a bit early, and showed their nervous eagerness.

Ian shouted down to Barker, "Barker, they're closing fast. When they come into your view, I think they'll be in canister range."

Barker replied, "Right you are, Carlyle." He alerted his gunners to expect them, ordered the howitzers to continue shelling the causeway, and had his four 9-pounder guns traversed to their farthest right in anticipation. He commanded, "Case shot."

The gunners had been waiting. They ran to the limbers, brought forward and loaded the case shot, many of them amused at what was about to happen. Case shot rounds, known as canister, were filled with lead balls, causing a cannon to become more or less a giant fowling piece, spreading a pattern of death and destruction before it up to 300 yards out. The gunners knew what ruin this could bring to charging cavalry…horses and men.

Now the detached Russian squadrons were about six hundred yards out. Sir Colin's Highlanders rose and fired a smashing volley. The effect on moving horses at this range was more psychological than otherwise. Although no Russians were actually seen to fall, Ian knew that horses could sometimes take half-a-dozen hits in non-vital spots before being disabled, and wounded men would hang on for dear life, because they knew if they fell they would be trampled to death.

The Highlanders felt the strain after firing their first volley at the oncoming Russians. They didn't want to stay and wait. They wanted to charge across the hundreds of yards, bayonets bristling, jab at the horses, cut at the horsemen, gut them close in.

As they finished reloading, bayonets pointing again toward the enemy at the ready, they leaned forward in anticipation, kilts flaring out. Sir Colin saw it, felt it, and bellowed, "Ninety-third, ninety-third...damn all that eagerness." They instantly calmed, the shoulders of the front rank men visibly relaxing from their forward leaning position.

The Russian supporting artillery along the causeway lifted their fire, as the Russian cavalry closed. The field in front became still, except for the clatter of horse equipment, the familiar clank and rattle of sabres and lances, the thunderous beating of hooves, champing of bits, the breathing snorts of the large animals as they pressed down, ever nearer. Ian knew he had to keep the leopard close by, close to the surface. No one to attack now, but needed it to conquer the gnawing, growing fear...the desire to do the sensible thing – get the hell out of there.

Ian watched through his telescope. The Russians were now at a fast gallop, sabres drawn, Cossack lances forward and down, hooves flying, kicking up giant clods of earth, nostrils flaring, horseflesh ruthlessly pounding toward them. The Highlanders, unperturbed, calmly faced the onrushing horsemen, eyes fixed, bayonets still thirsty for blood.

Four hundred yards...then a second roaring volley came from the Highlanders, their Minie´ rifle muskets now within easy range, taking their toll. This was a butcher's bill written in Russian blood. The volley had a shattering effect. Riders and horses fell. The back ranks colliding with the tumbling, faltering front rank. Sir Colin's men were reloading, but the spirit was ripped from the charge by the well-aimed volley at less than 400 yards. Bayonets would not be necessary. Their speed began decreasing.

Ian called out, "Barker, watch your right front."

Three hundred yards! Captain Barker was now able to see the edge of the right flank of the galloping Russian squadrons, as it was unmasked before his already aimed guns. They were still far out, not enough of them visible. Ian moved down to the battery and stood with Barker. Barker shouted, "Wait for it, lads. Wait for it." He willed them to wait for the command.

"FIRE!" Four rounds were fired in quick succession from the 9-pounders. Brilliant orange flashes. Ian was shocked at the ferociousness of the discharges and the vicious path of destruction they cut. The ground was kicked up all the way to the target in a widening spread, as the small lead balls rolled out.

The ground was bathed in yellowish smoke and dust from the sawdust-packed case shot. Ian lifted his telescope to his eye just after the series of blasts. As the smoke cleared, he saw the portion of the oncoming Russians right where the rounds had been aimed. The Russian line was still coming on, the front rank now covered in yellow dust.

The slaughter was dreadful. Horses and men hit by the deadly balls, wounded Russians clinging to their bleeding and torn mounts, shreds of flesh, gaping holes in bodies and horses. A few were wrenched from their saddles, hanging off, but not falling. Most of those hit were carried on with the momentum of the relentless charge. *Jesus. I never knew. Couldn't have known. Never knew the raw killing power, the horrible shredding of horse and human flesh. This isn't 'glory.' This is carnage.*

Oddly, the old fear was gone, replaced by a numb feeling, a dullness, impersonal, a hardness he had only felt once before

– when he saw what was happening to poor Peter that fateful night at Eton. He was changing again. The idealistic, glory-seeking young man was fast disappearing, replaced by one who saw the horrors, fought the fear, and toughened himself to it all – conquering his own demons of terror in his own way. He was becoming a new creature, for good or ill, a seasoned veteran.

As the horsemen came galloping down, they again disappeared from Barker's view. The battery was unable to fire a second round of case shot, but they had done their damage.

Ian moved quickly back up the knoll. The Russians were at two hundred yards, but before Sir Colin could again bring his men to 'Present,' the leader of the Russians veered the long line of cavalry to the left. It appeared at first that he was attempting to flank them. The Turkish militia on the right flank began collapsing to their rear. Ian saw Sir Colin pointing at the Russian leader, shouting to his adjutant, "That man understands his business."

Captain Ross, the Grenadier Company commander on the right flank of the 93rd also knew his business. He could see the possibility of the Russians swinging around their right. Without orders, he took immediate action by right wheeling his men forward to face and follow the Russian horsemen as they passed his front. He managed to get off one valuable, rock-hard volley into the flank of the Russians, cutting the outside riders to shreds. The effect was instantaneous.

"That tore it, laddies," bellowed Captain Ross to his jubilant men. The Russian cavalry leader swung what remained of his men harder left, in a wide circle heading them back across the valley toward the causeway, spent, and, by this time, disorganized. As they retired, the Royal Marine batteries on Mount Hiblak poured shell after shell at them, causing much severe damage.

Chapter 43

Ian turned his attention to events rapidly building to a crescendo of violence at his left front. In this arena, Scarlett's Heavy Brigade had finally noticed the large Russian cavalry mass crossing into South Valley behind them. His lead regiments turned to meet their enemy, closing at a gradually increasing pace on the massive Russian formation, which outnumbered the 'Heavies' two to one.

Then the Russians did a very unusual thing. They halted, appearing to stare at the British cavalry moving toward them.

Scarlett and his "heavies" missed Alma, Ian thought. *They're fresh troopers, just barely landed from the ships. Time to get sweating. I'd say, past time. He likely has orders to support Sir Colin. What better way than to attack. Scarlett's no fool. He knows the odds.*

When the lead elements of the Heavy Brigade, advancing up the grade of the valley floor, were within 30 or 40 yards of the Russians, Scarlett's trumpeter sounded the charge. They smashed head to head with the front of the Russian formation, the red-coated English cavalrymen merging and disappearing amid a sea of grey Russian overcoats.

General Scarlett's other squadrons of heavy cavalry, who had not been on line in time to advance with his initial assault, began smashing into the Russian formation on both its flanks. The Russians had already been pounded severely by W Battery's guns and the Royal Marine guns on the heights. The viciousness of the assaults by the squadrons of the Heavy Brigade, which hit one after the other, disorganized and demoralized the Russians even more. This deadly combination of artillery fire and hard-hitting cavalry forced the gradual withdrawal of the entire enemy main body of cavalry back across the causeway.

So far, this was an expensive and inglorious day for the Russian cavalry. The 93rd threw their bonnets in the air, cheering victory. The Heavy Brigade troopers joined their cheers. The Battalion of Detachments, from Kadikoi, and even the Turks who had stayed, did the same. They had stopped them. The engagement involving the attack on the 93rd knoll had lasted about eight minutes, and the clash between the Heavy Brigade and the main Russian cavalry not much longer.

The battle was over for Ian. He mounted Savage, reported to Sir Colin that he was returning to Lord Raglan, and rode slowly to Kadikoi. He found a picquet line with several horses of the 4th Dragoon Guards tied off. These Irishmen were happy to provide Savage with more water, hay, and even a few oats to top off the gallant horse's well-earned repast. Later, as the morning passed, serious firing was heard from the North Valley.

Ian asked a dragoon sergeant, "What do you make of that firing?"

"Well, sir, sounds to me that some poor sod's getting the worst of it." Indeed it did. There were the unmistakable sounds of a major engagement beyond the causeway ridges. Ian could see smoke rising from the east end of the North Valley. Judging by the repeated crashing of heavy cannon, Russian artillery was playing havoc with someone.

Having seen to Savage's welfare, Ian felt he could take leave to satisfy the inner man. The Royal Irish cavalrymen obliged by steering him to a house that had been converted into an officers' mess for the medical staff at the hospital. A surgeon was leaving just as Ian arrived. He told Ian, "There's no one about now; they're all pretty busy after today's doings. Feel free to help yourself to whatever fare there is. There's a servant inside will take care of you."

"How very kind of you, sir," Ian said, tying Savage to a post. He relieved his horse of everything but his halter, said, "You take a long rest, boy, you deserve it."

Ian entered the one-room house, found it empty except for a few tables and chairs, and an old tired Tartar. He ordered coffee, then put his head on his folded arms. His last thoughts were of Jasmine, her touch, and her sweet sensual smell; Angus' sly smile; and Tinsley bleeding on the valley floor. He was fast asleep before the coffee arrived.

Chapter 44

A hand was shaking him gently. Ian raised his head. It was several hours later; the sun had gone down, the coffee cold in its cup, the small room still empty, except for the smiling Sardinian major standing by his chair.

"Antonio, what brings you here?" Ian asked.

"On the way to Balaklava to check on supplies for General Airey, Ian. Saw Savage tied out front. Thought we'd lost you, old friend. Couldn't have that, could we?"

"I'm fine, Antonio. I've been with Sir Colin Campbell most of the day. What time is it?"

"A bit after dark, my boy, around eight o'clock."

Ian was highly upset, "Good God. What will His Lordship think? Must get back and report for duty. I may be in some trouble, am I?"

"Not at all, lad," Antonio laughed. "Kingscote came back and told Lord Raglan where you were and what you were trying to do for Sir Colin, to get him more men. His Lordship heartily approved."

"How is everyone, Antonio, did we all make it?"

"I've bad news, Ian. Lewis Nolan is gone." Capecci paused.

Ian sucked in air. There was silence. Ian remembered vividly that first day of landing, and his friend Lewis sitting so calm and elegant on his horse above where Ian was pinned. He remembered the quiet times around the fire, when Lewis produced the unending supply of port from God knew where. Tears swelled as he asked, "How?"

"Died the way he'd have chosen, I should think. Shrapnel cut him down in the middle of a glorious, although rather senseless cavalry charge."

Ian looked at the cup of cold coffee still resting on the table from hours before. After a time he asked, "He was with General Scarlett in his attack on the Russian cavalry? I watched it all, you know."

"No, it was afterward, with the Light Brigade. North Valley. There was some confusion. His Lordship was unable to get the infantry up. Saw the Russians carrying off our guns from the redoubts on the causeway. He ordered Lucan to stop them. The Heavies were still shaken from their engagement in the South Valley. Light Brigade was ordered forward with the Heavies in support."

"How did Lewis become involved?"

"Lewis delivered Lord Raglan's order to protect the guns to Lord Lucan. After doing so, he remained with the cavalry to make the advance with them."

Ian mused, sadly, "Now that must have been a sight to behold. No love lost there."

The major continued, "For some reason, for the life of me I shall never know why, Cardigan led the Light Brigade into the entire Russian army. Not at the causeway to stop the Russians from carting off the English guns, but right into a bloody gauntlet. Straight up North Valley, Russian infantry and artillery firing down on their flanks from both sides, and directly at a mass of Russian artillery and cavalry at the end of the valley."

"Why, Antonio, why in God's name would he do that?"

"I don't know. Perhaps incredible stupidity? Who can guess. It was sheer folly...glorious, magnificent, but utter folly. Murderous, by God. Had Nolan survived, he'd have been livid. They say he tried to stop Cardigan, was doing so when he was killed. Cardigan denies it. Everyone blaming everyone else. A right cock-up, as you English say. We'll never know the truth of it."

Ian continued to study the stale cold coffee. "We're slowly losing our friends, Antonio, first Piccard, now Nolan."

"Yes, my friend, we must all be more careful."

Chapter 45

"M'Lord, I worry for our flank," Airey said. "Inkerman Ridge or Mountain…that's what the men are calling it. There are four or five hidden approaches, deep, low areas, through which the Russians could funnel an army almost unseen.

"De Lacy Evans has responsibility, of course. Good man, one of our very best. I only wonder if that's enough."

It was early evening, 25 October 1854. The nights had become very chilly. Winter was almost on them. Lord Raglan, General Airey, his Chief of Staff, and General Sir John Burgoyne, the army's chief engineer, were examining maps of the British positions around Sevastopol and Balaklava. They had been caught out by the attack that morning, and didn't want a repeat.

Sir John agreed, "Airey's concerns are well founded, M'Lord. Deep fissures and ravines, covered with boulders, blackthorn thickets, and stubby oaks. In the ravines, it is especially difficult to see very far. Large troop formations could move within easy musket range without our knowing."

Airey added, "It keeps me awake nights, M'Lord."

Lord Raglan looked at his two chief advisors, "I share your worries about the flank, Airey, but we must remember why we're here, what? I need to know more about the flanks, much more, before I divert men from digging trenches. We need to move the siege forward. After all, that's our mission; isn't it, Airey, to take Sevastopol?"

Airey was emphatic, "Yes, M'Lord, I understand, but I have grave concerns, very grave indeed. Were we ever to lose the port, well, what then?"

"Get me more information, Airey, then we'll see."

Ian was curious and somewhat uneasy. He'd only just returned from Kadakoi. It was not usual being summoned by General Airey, personally, and this late.

Ian reported, "Sir, you asked to see me?"

"Come in, Carlyle. Sit down."

Airey signed a few more returns at his desk in the old farmhouse. "I've something for you, Carlyle. His Lordship asked for you. Trusts you, lad."

Carlyle had learned to worry when such conversations began this way with a superior officer, "I appreciate his confidence, sir."

"It's delicate, Carlyle, most delicate. I want you to do a major reconnaissance, but without a fuss, discretely, if you get my meaning."

"Perfectly, sir."

"We need to know about our right flank, the area here on the map, surrounding this Home Ridge place, the 2nd Division area, you see?" he pointed at a map on his table.

"We are most concerned, Carlyle. What little information we have points to their testing us on our eastern flank, as they did today before Balaklava. We must be prepared. Take a day or two if you need. Discretion, mind, mustn't ruffle the feathers of our generals. You know the way His Lordship works."

"Aye, sir. Of course, sir. You don't want General De Lacy Evans, General Brown, or the Duke of Cambridge to know of this mission, in that they might take offence."

"You are indeed as sharp as His Lordship has said of you, lad. Carry on, and good luck."

Savage was saddled in no time. To avoid getting lost in the ink-black night, Ian headed Savage east along the Sapoune Heights until he found the metalled Vorontsov Road, then northwest to the Duke of Cambridge's 1st Division camp, near the intersection with Post Road. *The way to avoid ruffling feathers is not to bother the division commanders at all*, thought Ian, as he rode.

Chapter 46

Ian located the Guards Brigade officers' mess tent, said hello to a few old friends, and then asked, "I say, Bayly, I'd like to get some action in before this damned war is over. Any chance I might tag along on a picquet or a patrol tonight?"

"Ah, Carlyle, happy to see you're well and looking fit. Not much chance of this mess being over soon, old fellow, but I can understand your boredom with all that dreadful paper pushing you do, day after day." This produced a chuckle from the other officers present. They all knew he was on staff, some resented it, some envied, others just thought it humorous.

An officer chimed in, "You'd have to ask the Field Officer of the Day about the picquet, Carlyle, but there could be another way if you've the stomach."

"Another way?" Ian asked.

The officer continued, "As I recall, you're a fair hand with a musket. If you really want to see what's what out there in the never-never, you should tie yourself to Captain Goodlake and his merry men. They're all Guards Brigade, mind, and all fine shots with our new Minie´. They roam the whole bloody area every night looking for mischief, and usually find it."

Bayly, a stout jolly officer who loved his drink, said, "Splendid idea, Carlyle, if you really must bugger about out there. I'd say stay right here, and I'll stand you to a large glass of port."

"Another time, old man, but thanks." Ian left the tent thinking: *Just the thing, and I'll be able to see an old friend, as well.*

Captain Gerald Goodlake, Coldstream Guards, was an exceptional officer, and well known as a huntsman. Ian knew him at Eton. He occasionally came home with Ian and Peter on holiday to Dunkairn Hall. He would hunt with their father. Although young, the same age as Ian, he really had a keen reputation for marksmanship. Their families had been friends for years.

Goodlake was tall and thin. He had hair and eyebrows the colour of black coal, set against pale pink skin, and surrounding a beakish nose. He sported a huge drooping black moustache and long side-whiskers. When Ian found him, he was sitting at a table by his tent, meticulously and lovingly cleaning a rifle. Ian could smell the cleaning oil as he approached.

Goodlake was wearing a tattered grey private's greatcoat, with a black sword belt worn over it loosely on a gaunt frame, topped by an odd brown small-brimmed civilian hunting cap. He wore no snappy officer's boots, but sturdy ankle-length laced boots, with his frayed trousers rolled up above them.

Only he could have pulled off this eccentric combination with panache. He looked like he was about to go on a hunt, and cleaning his rifle was his last sacred duty before doing so. He was smiling at Ian, "Ian, damned if it isn't you. Knew you were out here. Damned glad you're still here...so to speak."

"So am I, Gerald, it's a fine day to still be 'here,' the alternative being quite unacceptable." He sat, unasked, in a camp chair opposite Goodlake, and made himself comfortable. Goodlake poured him a scalding coffee in a tin cup.

Ian accepted it and sipped.

Goodlake asked, "So, Ian, to what do I owe the pleasure of this unexpected visit? Surely not to catch up on old stories."

Ian said, "You recall the time I lied to my father about who shot that sheep in the old farmer's pasture near Dunkairn Hall?"

Goodlake came right to the point, "I do, and I said I owed you a debt. You've come to collect. I'll be bound. So, who do you want me to shoot, one of those very fat, very senior officers you're now courting?"

Ian brightened at his friend's no-nonsense retort, and sick humour, "Christ no, Gerald, I just want you to keep dispatching Russians…but with me by your side, at least for the next 24 hours."

Goodlake laughed, then turned serious, "Ian, what's stirring in that overworked brain of yours? You saying you'd like to go on patrol with me?"

"That's the truth of it, Gerald." Ian looked dead into Goodlake's eyes. "I need to take a close look at our flank, the whole area around 'Mount Inkerman' as I think you call it…on the quiet."

Goodlake hesitated, said, "On the quiet, is it? Not to upset any general officer's fragile egos, aye?"

Not surprised at the accuracy of the guess, Ian said, "Perhaps, can you help me?"

"Of course. Not to mention I know from personal observation that you are a fine shot. I'll get you a rifle musket; you'll do even better. Spend a day with my lads, you'll learn more than you ever wanted to know."

"I'm grateful," Ian replied, sipping the harsh coffee.

"Must hurry, though, we're leaving in a few minutes. Be gone tonight and most of tomorrow. Won't be like Eton. Hard going. Suit you?"

"At your service, Gerald. You lead, and I'll follow."

Goodlake found Ian a new-looking .702-inch Minie´ rifle musket, and a filled cartridge box. He hung the box over Ian's shoulder and stuffed caps into the small leather pouch sewed onto the front of the cartridge box cross strap. Goodlake then introduced him to "his lads."

There were no more than thirty of them, no other officers were present, older-looking privates, and an abundance of sergeants and corporals. The only qualifications for Goodlake's little band were to be a guardsman, and a marksman. Rank was not an issue. The Coldstream, Grenadier, and Scots Fusilier Guards each initially provided an officer, and ten men. Although the numbers grew some with their successes, the casualties were high, and they were now back where they started.

It was nearly impossible to tell which regiment they came from, bearded in threadbare greatcoats, filthy cloth forage caps or field service caps, and rolled up trousers. These were the same clothes they had worn since landing, and had seen service on too many long patrols. Each carried a cartridge box, bayonet, canteen, and white cloth haversack, containing cold rations. Ian noticed that their shabby appearances were in sharp contrast to their sparkling clean rifle muskets.

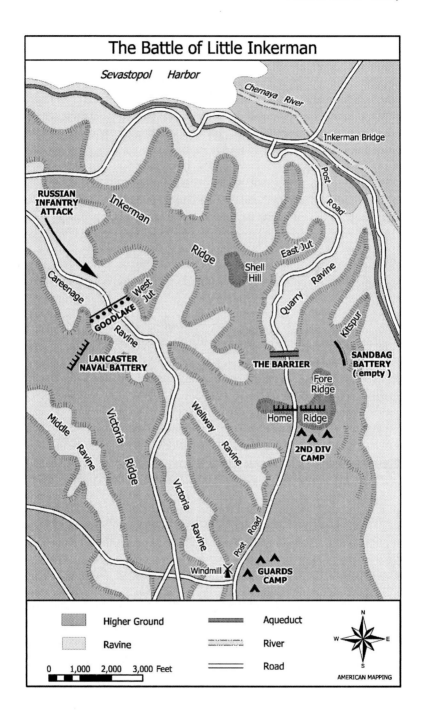

The Battle of Little Inkerman

Sevastopol Harbor

Chernaya River

Inkerman Bridge

Post Road

RUSSIAN INFANTRY ATTACK

Inkerman Ridge

Shell Hill

East Jut

Quarry Ravine

Careenage

West Jut

GOODLAKE

Kitspur

LANCASTER NAVAL BATTERY

Ravine

THE BARRIER

SANDBAG BATTERY (empty)

Fore Ridge

Middle Ravine

Victoria Ridge

Wellway Ravine

Home Ridge

2ND DIV CAMP

Victoria Ravine

Post Road

Windmill

GUARDS CAMP

| | Higher Ground | | Aqueduct |
| | Ravine | | River |

0   1,000   2,000   3,000 Feet

Road

N W E S

AMERICAN MAPPING

Before departure, the men made certain they were prepared, nothing rattling or clanking; not even a half canteen of water sloshing about to alert an enemy. The rifles were loaded and on half cock, to prevent an accidental discharge, which might give them away. They were divided into sections of three or four. For sharp-shooting purposes, they could divide again into two-man teams or fight as individuals. Ian walked with Goodlake, as they set off northwest at a blistering pace.

From the camp they moved into the Victoria Ravine, which spilled into the larger Careenage Ravine leading straight into Sevastopol. They were on the left flank of Home Ridge and the 2nd Division defences, within one of those hidden approaches General Airey was worried about.

Before they were too far from camp where they would have to be much quieter, Goodlake explained their mission to Ian, "At first we worked in two- or three-man groups against artillery positions, crawling within range, prepared to remain all night and day waiting for targets. We shot gunners and officers, at six- to eight-hundred yards, while they were feeling cozy and secure.

"We performed, if I do say so, as good, if not better than the Rifles. We were thus in demand, and worked all around the flank positions, not merely in our own Guards area. Now I'd say we've evolved into a large, deadly fighting patrol, targeting or capturing any enemy we see. We patrol throughout the flank and rear of the army, in and out of ravines, moving constantly. A few days ago we captured a high-ranking Russian officer. He'd wandered off to have a piss. Should have seen his surprise."

They reached the intersection of Victoria, Wellway, and the larger Careenage Ravines. Goodlake raised his right hand high above his head. The response was instantaneous, every guardsman freezing in place, listening intently, until the advance was given by another simple hand signal. Ian was impressed.

In the stillness, Ian was startled by a scraping noise above him, "What was that?"

Goodlake whispered, "Not to worry, Ian, above us on the right are two-man sentry posts of the 41st Regiment, 2nd Division. Above on the left are Light Division sentries and picquets on Victoria Ridge, 7th Fusiliers closest, I believe. Also up there somewhere is a Lancaster gun battery looking along Victoria Ridge and down this ravine toward Sevastopol, a formidable equipment."

They moved forward again into the eerie dark expanse, high ground on both sides. "Is this a road we're moving along?" Ian hissed to a sergeant next to him.

"Aye, sir, but more a track than a road. Travels the base of this here large ravine we're headed into, ends in Sevastopol. The captain thinks they'll come out of the city this way, hoping to catch us snoozing. It'll either be their all-out attack or a feint of some kind. If they was to get through us, and kept going back the way we come, they'd bloody well end up in the rear of the whole damned army, sir."

Jesus, Ian thought, *what a cock-up that would be.*

They went a short distance beyond to where a shallow trench was dug from one side of the ravine to the other, Goodlake explained, "This trench is our last defence position if the bastards come at us this way. We'll hold here or die trying. My men all understand this."

Ian asked, "Are there no cavalry out in our front?"

Goodlake answered, in disgust, "Cavalry? This close to the enemy? Not bloody likely."

They were under a large looming hill on the right, Goodlake pointed, "That's called the West Jut, for lack of a better name. At night we use it as a landmark. We'll set up base a quarter mile beyond this trench, then send section patrols up, down, and across the ravine, all night. If they see an enemy or even hear one, they're free to fire at will, and kill as many as possible. It's really quite simple and most effective. Some nights we move almost into Sevastopol."

Ian went out with Goodlake and his sergeant, Ashton, on several short patrols throughout the night, and into the dawn. Although there was sporadic firing from other patrols, they made no contact with the Russians.

With each patrol the things taught him by Billy Murphy came back with increased clarity. Good lessons about moving quietly, flank and rear security, seeing at night, using your ears rather than eyes to detect an enemy.

At dawn Ian was tired, but content. This was work more to his liking, and, at least in this sector, security was impressive.

He asked Goodlake what his opinion was of security in other 2nd Division sectors he patrolled.

Goodlake was direct, "Actually, not that good. If it were my show, I'd do with a bit more cavalry further out front for very early warning. Some picquet commanders are more timid than others; don't place their sentries out far enough to give timely alert. We can't be everywhere, every night. On the whole, security is rather shabby."

Chapter 47

It was midday. After their stand-to at dawn, they advanced several hundred more yards and began day patrols. Those not on patrol were strung across the ravine in a thin skirmish line to relax and wait their turn to go out.

The men were finishing their rations close to one o'clock when the first shots were heard. This was not unusual if a patrol made contact, but the firing gained in intensity for a time until it was apparent there was an attack in the area of Shell Hill and Home Ridge, to their right and rear, on the plateau above.

"If they're attacking up there," Goodlake said to Ian, "they might try here shortly. There are caves a half mile or so ahead in the sides of the ravine, Ian. We usually don't check them by day, too dicey, but with all this shooting, I'd like to see what damned pests are lurking about. Not to worry, old chap, taking my sergeant with me for a little walk. Be back in no time."

He and Sergeant Ashton moved off cautiously, while Ian waited with the other men. Twenty or so were on the skirmish line across the ravine, and on hearing firing instinctively established security in all directions.

The firing from the rear and above escalated. Ian looked at his timepiece. *After two o'clock. Gerald's gone a long time. Hmmm. I seem to be the senior officer present at the moment. I hope he isn't taking a nap in those bloody caves.*

A slight tremor came up from the ground before they heard or saw anything. It was real and unmistakable. Men moving fast…a great many men. The skirmish line was by now alert, patrols coming back in at a run to take their places in line. Their sergeants extended the skirmish line up on both banks of the ravine. Rifles were trained toward Sevastopol. *Where was Goodlake?*

It wasn't long. Closer, the sounds came. Around a bend in the ravine…*there – Russians.* Moving rapidly forward, toward the sound of the guns in the distance behind and above them, at least a battalion, spread across the ravine floor. Three companies forward and one in the rear, in two ranks. This was their normal formation for advancing in close country, not knowing who was waiting for them. The odds were formidable; Ian guessed they were outgunned thirty-to-one.

The Guardsmen, without orders, began firing as targets appeared. The weight of the massive enemy numbers, and their relentless speed caused the line of guardsmen to slowly begin moving back along the ravine floor. They withdrew in good skirmish order, firing as they stepped backward. Then they were at the shallow trench line.

Ian could see the Russian uniforms, black caps with red bands. *They look like sailors. Damn, where is Goodlake?*

The senior sergeant looked at him, questioningly. Ian understood, mustered his confidence, and said, "Sergeant, we'll go no further. Hold here. Send someone back to warn the camps."

The sergeant was instantly in motion, commanding the line of men, "Halt where ye are, and take what cover ye can. Fire at will. Pick yer targets, lads. Captain says we hold right here."

The sergeant turned to a corporal next to him, as the firing from the guardsmen continued taking effect on the advancing Russians, "You there. Back you go. Take one man, give them boys warning back there, tell 'em what you see, then return." The corporal and a second man began running back along the ravine toward the camps.

There was supporting fire now from above the ravine on both sides as the sentries of 1st and 2nd Divisions joined the fray firing down at the oncoming Russian column. The sergeant shouted, "Mark your targets, lads, make them hurt…officers first," he looked at Ian. "No offence, sir."

"Look there." A corporal pointed excitedly at the left side of the ravine about halfway up, "Two men, sir, the Captain and Sergeant Ashton, I'd know the Captain's hunting cap anywhere. They're trying to get back to us. Walking quiet as ye please, right through those Rooshians. What'll we do, sir?"

Ian thought quickly. Russians around Goodlake would surely take notice of them soon. He turned to the senior sergeant, "Pass the word down the line, shift fire to the right, except the leftmost section. Tell the men on the left to cut down anyone trying to stop your officer and his sergeant."

"Aye, sir." The sergeant went to carry out his orders. Ian climbed onto a boulder, in plain view of the Russians. He felt the buzzing whisper of musket balls passing close, heard a thud as one hit the boulder, a chinking sound as another chipped away rock.

By now it was apparent the Russians were onto Goodlake. Ian waved his arms, motioning him to run for it back to their line across the ravine. Goodlake saw him, understood. He and Sergeant Ashton began moving faster along the side of the ravine. As they slipped ahead of the now halted Russian infantry, a few enemy skirmishers took aim at them. The left section cut the Russians down before they could fire.

Ian hadn't fired the rifle musket Goodlake had given him yet. He looked down at it, still standing like a bloody fool atop the boulder. The sergeant shouted as politely as he dared, "Get the fuck down, sir, er, beggin' yer pardon, sir, but it's too damned hot up there."

Ian felt a tug at his cloak, knew it was a musket ball tearing through. He jumped unceremoniously down from the boulder, looked out across the deadly space to their front, trying to track Goodlake's progress. He saw them, saw a Russian skirmisher only a few yards away stand and bring his weapon to shoulder, directing it toward his friend, Gerald. The fourth section was still reloading.

Without thinking, Ian slammed the rifle into his shoulder, cocked, aimed, breathed in, all at once, then a gentle even squeeze on the trigger. The rifle cracked and recoiled into his shoulder. A large red hole appeared in the forehead of the Russian, a startled look on his face. He fell like a sack to the ground. Ian had killed his first man in battle. He felt nothing. There was no time.

The corporal next to him said, "Fine shooting, sir." Ian took a breath, looking down at his rifle again. When he looked back at Goodlake and Ashton, he knew with an awful certainty they weren't going to make it. They were past the enemy skirmishers, but were too far, fifty yards or more. The Russians were recovering fast, some faster than others, more bullets ricocheting off rocks near them. Russians, maybe ten of them, were running forward of their own skirmish line to intercept. It wasn't the whole skirmish line, but enough to do the job.

Ian turned to the sergeant, "Bloody hell. They're not going to make it."

Ian dropped his rifle, drew his sword, shouted, "Sergeant, give me the left section."

"Aye, sir. You lot…there and there, at the Captain's orders."

Ian directed the section, "Fix bayonets."

The line of guardsmen were stunned, *who was this crazy bastard officer?* They could see the Russian numbers, enemy soldiers crawling across and along both sides of the ravine, like so many ants, they froze for a second. Ian feared he wouldn't get out there in time. He barked, "Now. Damn you."

With relief he heard the sergeant scream, "You heard the officer, what the hell are ye waiting for, an invite from the Queen? This ain't Saint James Park, get cracking, fix them bayonets."

Ian heard successive metal snapping, as the bayonets were fixed to the ends of rifles along the left, and even intermittently elsewhere along the line. He leaped among the guardsmen, raised his sword in the air, shouted, "Section, follow me."

He leapt forward with a scream which came from somewhere deep, felt the beast running alongside. It was his childhood nightmare, but this was real. *Will they follow?* There was a moment of awful silence. Then he heard the cheer from behind, felt the movement of the left section and a few others along the line, bayonets lowered, charging at the Russians attempting to intercept Goodlake and Ashton.

The Russians were closing fast. Ian led the guardsmen, sword swinging in circles over his head, "Forward, laddies, kill the bastards." They were among them too quickly for the Russian skirmishers to react. Ian saw their eyes widen in disbelief, saw fear as the bayonet points bore down on them, saw them turn and run, some dropping their weapons.

He passed Goodlake and Ashton, as he ran toward the main Russian line. He shouted at Goodlake, "Move, Gerald, move yer bloody arse, before we're all done for."

Ian headed straight for the group of Russians who were now fleeing away. The guardsmen who were with Ian had their blood up. They caught Russians as they fled, hacked them badly, bayonets and rifle butts killing as many as they caught. The rest of the Russian skirmish line couldn't fire without hitting their own. They were confused, as their own men ran straight at them in panic.

Ian confronted a determined Russian he thought was a sergeant or corporal. The man tried to thrust forward with his bayonet, grotesque fear on his face. Ian stepped aside, the bayonet missed, Ian's sabre sliced across the man's belly with such force and momentum that the last eight inches of highly sharpened blade sliced through layers of clothing and split his stomach wide open. As he fell, screaming, his intestines spilled onto the ground.

Ian didn't have time to analyze the situation. *Have to take advantage of the confusion. Must get these men back to the trench line...before the Russians can react. If they open on us at this range, we'll be dead for certain.*

Ian found the sergeant, who shouted, "They're running, sir, by damn, they're running."

"Bollocks that Sergeant, in another few seconds they'll unmask their line, and we'll pay the very devil. The Captain's safe. Get these men the bloody hell out of here. Right now."

The sergeant caught on at once, ordered, "Fall back. Double-quick. Move yer arses, or ye'll be feeling a musket ball up them." The guardsmen began moving back, quickly, to the cover of the shallow trench.

Chapter 48

Goodlake and Ashton barrelled into the guardsmen's position, hatless, exhausted, but smiling broadly, just a few steps ahead of Ian and the others. The guardsmen cheered, and they drew slaps on the back.

When he could again speak, Goodlake looked at Ian, "Thanks, old man. Guess I owe you another, this time a bloody great one. You're quite the hero, Ian."

"Hero, my aching arse, I was so damned scared I couldn't breathe." Ian wheezed breathlessly. "Damn me, I'm not even sure what made me do that…but your men, Gerald, your men are superb. They cut those devils apart like we were a thousand strong, by God."

Ian looked at the ground. "When I saw you weren't going to make it, I thought it best we charge, surprise and all that, hope you don't mind me assuming command."

"You must be joking, Ian. Not many would've stayed with these odds, and none I know would've decided that a dozen odd men should charge ten times their number."

Ian bowed his head, embarrassed.

Goodlake said, "Well, Sergeant Ashton, tell the boys we're staying. We'll hold here until we're relieved or reinforced.

Can't let these bastards through. They'll go right up 2nd Division's bum."

"Yes, sir." Ashton, still a bit out of breath, gave the orders.

The Russian skirmishers fell back behind their regiment in reserve. Their infantry line first retired, then made several attempts to outflank the sharpshooters. They failed, and with each try they paid dearly to Goodlake's sharpshooters. The Russians were using ordinary muskets, firing lead balls, accurate at 150-200 yards at best, against Goodlake's more accurate rifle muskets, firing conical bullets accurate at 1,000 yards in the hands of his marksmen. The Russians could load and fire barely one round per minute, to the better-trained guardsmen's two to three. Every Russian assault was met by a fusillade of fire, cutting down first officers, then sergeants, then soldiers. Leaderless, each attack died an ignominious death.

The sharpshooters were low on ammunition, but made every shot worth a dozen. Cannon and small arms' fire was still severe on the plateau above, and especially toward Home Ridge.

Ian was standing off to the side of the ravine, somewhat useless now that Goodlake was back. A green-clad Rifle officer approached him, "Captain, are you in command?"

Ian forcibly calmed his voice, "No, that would be Captain Goodlake. Come with me." Ian brought the officer to Goodlake.

"Goodlake, I'm Markham. I have a detachment of Rifles with me. If you haven't dispatched all the Russians, my men would like a chance to join your little bash."

"Our pleasure, Markham, by all means."

The fight continued in the ravine for as long as the major battle continued up on the plateau. Wounded guardsmen and riflemen remained on the firing line. If they couldn't fire, they loaded and passed rifles to those who could.

Goodlake said over the din, "A bullet through the heart is the only way you can conquer such soldiers as these."

"I believe that," was Ian's reply.

Markham and his riflemen fought side by side with the guardsmen, as the day wore on.

When the fighting finally slackened around Home Ridge, soldiers were freed up and men from the 30th and 41st Regiments slid down into the ravine to support the guardsmen, and bring fresh ammunition. Eventually it was too much for the Russians to their front.

They retired in good order, their skirmishers following as a rear guard. Guardsmen, riflemen, and soldiers of the line followed them at fixed bayonets, killing or taking prisoners of the slower ones. When the Russians were out of infantry range, the Lancaster guns on Victoria Ridge gave them parting gifts of death.

After returning to camp, and after a celebration at the Guards Mess, Ian made ready to return to headquarters. In parting, he said to his boyhood friend, "My thanks, Gerald, a most interesting day."

Goodlake said, "On your way, Ian, I can't afford having you hanging about my men. They've become too fond of you."

As Ian rode away, he shouted, "They're fine men, Gerald, take care of them. Good luck, God speed."

Chapter 49

"M'Lord, Carlyle is back with a report," Airey said, as he entered Lord Raglan's office the following morning. Ian was at his side.

Lord Raglan looked up from his desk, "I've just spoken to Kingscote, who told me what you've been up to with your Guards. You know, my boy, when Airey sent you out there, we didn't expect you to start your own war." He and Airey laughed.

"Sorry, sir, but I believe the Russians might want to take full credit for that little piece of the work, except, of course, we did send them home a bit dishevelled."

Lord Raglan said, "Now what of your mission, Carlyle, after today perhaps we can rest easy, what?"

"No, M'Lord, I would be derelict if I reported our flank is secure."

Raglan's eyes narrowed, "Give us your report."

"M'Lord, General Airey wanted to know the weaknesses of our flank defences, quietly. During the attack today I was with Captain Goodlake and his sharpshooters. I saw the Careenage Ravine, and questioned Goodlake about the other areas of the flank he operated in, which covers them all. I have observations and recommendations."

Raglan nodded.

"M'Lord, it isn't the men, as you know. They fight courageously, but we waste them. The first problem is a strong need for fortified positions all along the perimeter, and there are basically none. The division commanders can't build them because they're sending large numbers for daily trench duty in the siege lines, either digging, covering parties for the diggers, or supply details. After these men are pulled away, there are barely enough left to cover the many hidden approaches, let alone build positions…and they're exhausted."

Raglan wrinkled his brow, "Go on."

"M'Lord, there is also a need for an earlier warning system. Better than can be provided by infantry picquets and sentries. I would recommend cavalry videttes well in advance, patrolling the ravines and fissures continuously. That's my report, M'Lord. I consider our flank weak."

Lord Raglan thought a moment, and said, "Thank you, lad, I'll take your report into consideration. Now I have news for you. It seems like everyone is concerned on your behalf. They want me to consider transferring you back to your regiment. First it was Major Capecci, then Colonel Steele…my own secretary. Today it's General Airey, and I've just received a letter from your father."

"My father, M'Lord?" He was shocked, but secretly pleased.

"Not asking directly, my boy, but certainly suggesting that you might serve us better as a regimental officer. I've turned down your prior requests, as I strongly dislike losing your engineering skills. However, after your conduct in the field today, I'm equally sure you'll make a splendid company officer. I've reconsidered. Here are your orders, Captain

Carlyle. Report to Colonel Walker tomorrow morning for duty with 1st Battalion, Scots Fusilier Guards."

Ian was elated – at last, his real destiny. He said, "Thank you, M'Lord, you won't be disappointed."

It was evening. Ian went to his quarters, saw his comrades at their fire, and told them the news. They were pleased, although Curzon thought he was a bit crazy for leaving a "soft" staff position. Ian thanked the major and the rest for their friendship and support. He also made arrangements with the major's groom to care for Savage, temporarily, until he was settled in at the regiment.

The next morning before dawn he gathered his kit and found a ride on a cart to the Guards camp near the old windmill on Vorontsov Road.

Chapter 50

"Captain Ian Carlyle reporting for duty." Ian handed his written orders to Captain Hugh Drummond, the Adjutant. He actually didn't know the battalion adjutant very well. Drummond's tent was next to the larger tent of Colonel Edward Walker, Battalion Major, and commanding the Fusilier Guards in the field. Ian stood between Drummond's bed and a tiny desk, which served as the adjutant's office.

"Carlyle, ah yes, on the staff of His Lordship. You must have blotted your copybook rather badly to be reassigned back to the regiment?"

"Not at all, Drummond, at my request, actually. Been trying to get away from staff duty since I arrived in the East months ago. Finally succeeded."

Drummond laughed, "Well, I wish ye luck. It ain't a dinner party. You've been assigned to 2nd Company. Your record shows you were in that company before."

"Aye, that I was. Is Hunter-Blair still commanding?"

"No," Drummond said, casually, "he's been promoted, Captain Percy commands. Good man. He has only one officer, other than you, fella named Vane, his second officer. Seems a decent chap."

There was a moment's pause as Ian digested this bit of rather startling news: *Hmm. My old chum. I wonder if his nose still runs freely.* He was sad to hear Hunter-Blair was no longer commanding, had looked forward to serving under him again.

It was obvious Ian knew the name. Drummond asked, "You know Vane?"

"We've met. Does he still sniffle rather often?"

Drummond thought he recognized Ian's name. He now recalled the stories of Carlyle's altercation with Vane at the officers' mess at Chobham…the 'sherry stain incident.' He had also heard about Carlyle's reported escapades in London as a Royal Engineer, drinking, womanizing, even a pub brawl had been talked about around the mess. Carlyle had achieved quite a reputation among the officers as a loner and a bit of a rascal.

Drummond said, "No, he seems to have gotten over those annoying sniffles, but I suspect he hasn't forgotten how they came about."

"No, I suspect not," Ian said dryly.

Drummond offered, "I say, old fellow, that was you, wasn't it? A bit awkward I'd say. Never realized. After all it wasn't an official story, blind eye and all that. Want me to speak to Colonel Walker. I could ask you be assigned elsewhere?"

"No. Thanks Drummond, but I'll play the cards dealt me. Afraid I've only met Vane, shall we say, socially. What sort of officer is he?"

Drummond replied, "Rather a good one, I'd say. Bit of a martinet, but then so is Percy. Both strong on discipline. There's no doubting his courage. Vane led his section from the front…all the way up that blasted hill at Alma. Found three bullet holes in his bearskin and two more in his coat.

His men don't like him much, but Percy and Colonel Walker think he's tops."

"That would seem all the more reason I should take the assignment given me."

"I suppose, Carlyle, but I'd watch my step. He does have a reputation as a right bastard when he wants to be."

Ian nodded, lifted the flap and left.

Ian made his way through the Guards camp to the 2nd Company officers' row and found Captain the Honourable Seymour Percy, completing ration requisitions at a table outside his tent. Percy would later become by birthright the 4th Earl of Portarlington. He was a short, compact man, reaching baldness, with a rather large moustache, which drooped an inch or so at both ends. The moustache and what hair was left were bright red.

Percy looked up as Ian approached, "Carlyle, upon my word. One never knows one's luck, what? From Lord Raglan, himself, to me. I'm humbled." The dripping sarcasm in Percy's voice was inescapable.

Ian stopped, came to attention, and saluted his senior officer, "Captain Ian Carlyle reporting for duty, sir."

"I know. Heard yesterday," Percy scowled at Ian. "I've been waiting for a damned second subaltern for weeks, and they send me you. A bloody staff officer rumoured to be a damned upstart, insolent bastard at that. You know I've been warned about you. Is it true, Carlyle? Are you the insolent bastard you've been portrayed?"

Ian was not surprised or put off balance by this aggressive rebuke, "Not that I'm aware, sir, opinions might differ, depending upon whom you ask."

Ian had been introduced to Percy only once, and had never seen service with him. Ian surmised that Percy's warnings came from either Captain Vane or Colour Sergeant Skein, if he was still with the company.

Ian was right. The previous night Percy had separately spoken to Vane and Sergeant Skein, still the senior sergeant with the company. Each had different reasons and came to Percy at different times, after hearing that Ian was to be posted to their company. Sergeant Skein described him as an unorthodox officer who tended to disobey orders, and go beyond his authority, a 'loose cannon.' Vane told Percy that Ian had struck him, but he had chosen not to pursue the matter, for the good of the regiment, of course.

Now Percy was thinking about what he had been told. There was something about this officer he found appealing, perhaps even honest and charming, but he was as yet unconvinced that his most senior company officer and sergeant were both wrong.

Percy said, "Stand easy, Carlyle."

Ian, relaxing somewhat, said, "Permission to speak frankly, sir?"

Percy nodded.

"Sir, I've been trying to get a battalion posting since I arrived from England, to get out from under the staff. Now I have one. I'll serve as your subaltern happily, and serve you well. You'll not have any trouble from me."

"I dare say you might at that. If not, you'll find yourself in more of a pickle than you can handle. Is that clear?"

"Perfectly, sir. If you doubt my credentials, you may inquire to Hunter-Blair, who had this company before you."

"That won't be necessary. Far as I'm concerned, it's settled. Run your men hard, Carlyle, do your duty, obey orders, and we'll get along. Fact is I damned well need you. The company is down to 60 odd rank and file, more to the cholera than fighting."

He allowed that to register, continued, "Our two subdivisions have two sections currently about twelve to fifteen men each. When separated by subdivisions, Vane will command the right, and you'll command the left. When we're detached by sections, I'll naturally command the 1st Section; Captain Vane, as senior subaltern, will command the 4th Section, and you, the 2nd Section. We're the only officers. You remember a Colour Sergeant Skein?"

Ian said, "Aye, sir, that I do."

"He doesn't seem to have much affection for you, Carlyle, but he's still the covering sergeant. When detached by sections, he'll run the 3rd Section, until we get another subaltern. As a company, Skein rules the men the way I like, with a strong grip. You'd do well to follow his lead in matters of discipline."

"Aye, sir, I'll bear that in mind," replied Ian, hardly able to hide his disgust with Skein's kind of sergeant.

"One more thing, Carlyle, I know you and Vane have had your, shall we say, disagreements." Percy's face turned serious, "I won't tolerate it, not for a moment. You two will get on. You will do your jobs, by God, or I'll bloody well break the both of you."

Percy stood, "Dismissed, Carlyle."

Ian saluted and was about to turn and leave.

"Use that tent," Percy said, pointing to a small bell tent down the row, "should be empty except for odd bits of furniture. Belonged to Lieutenant Lord Giles, damned fine man. You'll have the devil's own time filling his shoes. Caught the cholera. Invalided home, lucky bugger. Your servants can pitch tents nearby."

Ian said, "Don't have any, sir."

Percy looked puzzled, "None. How odd."

In the tent Ian found a bed, linen, and some blankets, apparently left by the former occupant. He settled his meagre belongings, and went to have a look around.

Lieutenant and Captain Malcolm Vane was seated in front of his tent having tea.

"Carlyle, my word…sniff…what a surprise."

Ian said, "Rubbish, Vane, I know you spoke 'lovingly' about me to Percy already. Do try not to be too much of a hypocrite." He knew he couldn't go too far, Vane being the same rank, but having seniority.

Vane's face reddened, he stood abruptly, but held himself back, recalling a pointed lecture from Percy about their getting along.

Vane calmed himself with an effort. Ian said, "Vane, I don't like you, and I'm sure it's mutual, but we don't have to like each other. Merely do our duty…for the sake of the men, if for no other reason."

"Surely you don't mean these scum we lead," Vane said wrinkling his nose. "Let's not go too far. Carlyle, you keep your nose clean," he laughed at his own irony, then continued, "and when this is all over…sniff…we'll settle our little differences. Agreed?"

"Agreed, Vane, very sensible. It'll be my earnest pleasure to oblige. I am at your service anytime you wish, after this is over."

Later, on the company street, Colour Sergeant Skein seemed distressed to see him, "Er, welcome back to the company, sir."

"Thank you, Colour Sergeant," Ian replied, and with more than a touch of sarcasm, added, "I'm pleased you're well, but you look a bit pale."

"Fit as a fiddle, sir." The sarcasm was lost on Skein, who continued, "Small tiff with the camp fever, sir, but I be fine now."

"I'll need a list of the entire company, and particularly the 2nd Section. Get that for me, won't you, Skein, right away, off you go."

"Sir," Skein said. He was thinking: *He ain't changed none. Still an uppity bastard officer, what doesn't know his place. Off you go, indeed. I'll see to him. Missed him last time, but I won't this time.*

Ian was pleased to see on the roster of his 2nd Section that the corporal was MacGregor, and that Fergusson was among its soldiers. He looked for Swann's name and, unfortunately, found it in 3rd Section, under Skein. At least he wasn't under Vane, who might have recognized the lad as having been the ultimate cause of his long-suffering nose problems.

Ian saw another familiar face, "Corporal MacGregor, I see you've come up in the world."

"Aye, sir, ye were a bad influence, right enough."

"Well, I'm back. In fact I'm your section officer."

MacGregor said, "I'll tell the boys, sir, och, they'll be that pleased to have ye back."

"I see Swann is in Skein's section. He still giving the lad a bad time?"

MacGregor looked sad, "Worse, sir, without Fergie and me to sort of take care of him. Skein gives the poor wee lad the devil's own hell. Skein punishes him constantly. He's seen to it the boy was flogged twice. Gives him every rotten duty, never allows him to rest. The lad be ill, but ain't allowed to attend sick call."

It was the next day before Ian found Swann, in shirtsleeves, digging a latrine ditch outside the camp. He hardly recognized him. He was even thinner than before, very pale, uniform in tatters, and filthy. Ian called to him, "Swann. Come here."

Swann ran to him, bounced to attention, saluted, "Sir."

Ian returned the salute, "How are you doing, Swann?"

"Fit, sir, fit and ready." *The lad doesn't look it,* Ian thought.

Swann continued, "Begging yer pardon, sir, but it's good to see you back, if I may say so."

"Good to be back, Swann, carry on with your duties."

"Yes, sir." He saluted, spun about smartly, and returned to his digging. Ian could see lines of dried blood across his back, staining through his undershirt.

This was impossible. Ian knew the company spent much time on detached duties, thus Swann was in Skein's direct clutches too often. That same day he asked Percy if they ever transferred guardsmen between sections at an officer's request. The captain was adamant, "Carlyle, we officers can't be trading soldiers about willy-nilly. I leave those suggestions to the non-commissioned officers. They know best. You stay out of it, Carlyle."

This was the reaction Ian had half expected. He must get the lad out from under that right bastard Skein, but he had to do it more cleverly. He did a bit of quiet inquiry regarding Percy, recalled Percy's comment about it being odd he had no servants.

Two days later he approached Percy, again, "Sir, I lost my soldier servant to the cholera before Alma. Been without one since then, damned inconvenient. I'm desperate, sir, haven't had clean linen for weeks."

Percy, who had also lost an excellent servant, but to a stray Russian musket ball, was in sympathy, "Of course, Carlyle, find someone, not a corporal or sergeant, and I'll see that you get him."

Swann became Ian's servant later the same day. He was no Angus, but he was eager and most willing to learn. Percy suspected he'd been had, no fool he, but said not a word. Actually he found it quite amusing, and resourceful on Ian's part, the way he got around his first refusal. Skein was furious, but could do nothing save swallow it. Swann was now immune from him, officer's man.

What Ian had done did not go without notice in either his section or the company in general. The men had grown fond of the young London pickpocket.

Chapter 51

Ian woke to the sound of firing just before six. He opened his tent flap and looked outside, seeing nothing but thick fog. Others were poking heads out of tents, barely awake. Muster played to call the entire Guards camp to arms. Ian gathered his sword, Colt pistol, frock coat, cloak and forage cap. He carried a canteen, but left the haversack in his tent, choosing instead to stuff bits of dried beef and a few hard biscuits in a cloth bag in his pocket.

Ian watched as the company formed in close order, two ranks, at shoulder arms, Percy in front. The armourer sergeant was already there, ensuring in the dark that each man had the standard fifty cartridges, with the necessary number of percussion caps. The company moved quickly to their place in the battalion line, Ian behind the centre of the company. Swann ran up to join him, adjusting his equipment as he came. In the last few short days he hadn't had time to learn his duties as a proper soldier servant.

The battalion was short a few companies on parade. The 1st company was still on duty as a covering party in the trenches. The 3rd and 4th companies had some of their number on guard or working parties.

As soon as formed, Colonel Walker gave Captain Drummond their marching orders. Drummond ordered the battalion into fours, then marched them away, north, toward the sound of the guns. The Duke of Cambridge, commanding 1st Division, and General Bentinck, commanding the Guards Brigade, led the column. The Highland Brigade was absent on detached duty in defence of Balaklava.

The Grenadier Guards marched first in the column; the Scots Fusilier Guards marched behind them. The Coldstream Guards, just off picquet duty, were delayed in forming. It was after half seven when the Guards regiments arrived at Home Ridge to reinforce the 2nd Division, which was already heavily engaged.

Home Ridge contained a low wall hastily built and little improved since the Russian probing attack ten days before. On its far right, facing north, the ridge extended forward making the letter "L." This forward extension, the short leg of the letter, was called Fore Ridge. In direct front of Home Ridge and down the slope on the post road was a low stone wall called the Barrier, at the upper head of the large Quarry Ravine.

Down the slope to the right front of Fore Ridge, and about 400 yards to the right of the Barrier was a partially completed battery position, christened the Sandbag Battery. It was meant initially to accommodate two field guns. In front of this position was a finger of land jutting out with ravines on both sides, called the Kitspur. Along the left side of the Kitspur was Saint Clements Ravine.

The 2nd Division had been building the Sandbag Battery, when time permitted, because they were worried about the Kitspur and the Saint Clements Ravine being used as covered approaches by attacking Russians. Aside from the incomplete Sandbag Battery, the Barrier, Home and Fore Ridges, there were no substantial fortifications along this part of the eastern flank defences.

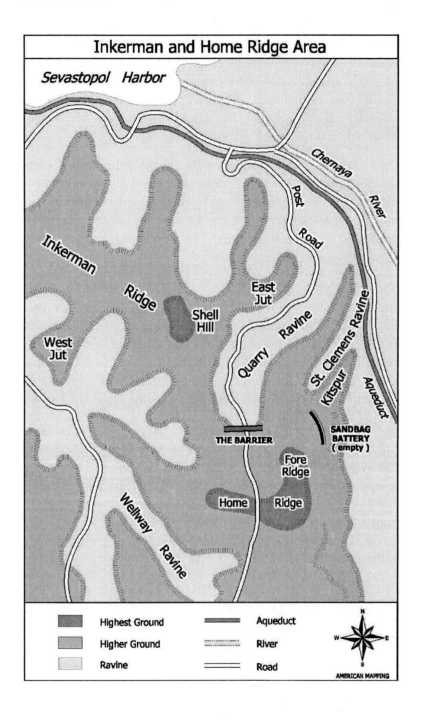

Inkerman and Home Ridge Area

Sevastopol Harbor

Chernaya River

Post Road

Inkerman Ridge

East Jut

Shell Hill

West Jut

Quarry Ravine

St. Clemens Ravine

Kitspur

Aqueduct

THE BARRIER

SANDBAG BATTERY (empty)

Fore Ridge

Home Ridge

Wellway Ravine

Highest Ground		Aqueduct	
Higher Ground		River	
Ravine		Road	

AMERICAN MAPPING

Ian's battalion passed through the 2nd Division camp, behind Home Ridge on the post road. By then they were taking occasional shellfire coming over the ridgeline ahead without much effect. They reached the crest of Home Ridge, and formed a column of companies. Ian's 2nd Company, in the absence of 1st Company, was leading the battalion. They moved across onto Fore Ridge. The battalion began receiving more effective enemy shot and shell from high ground known as Shell Hill not far away to their left.

This was another first time for Ian, marching behind the company, advancing steadily. He was on foot, unable to dodge or move about, as he had on horseback. He waited for the crash of shells, the thud of solid shots hitting the ground. Fear came back, with a vengeance. Although the November morning air was cold, Ian was soon soaked through with sweat.

A shell exploded above him to his right. Ian involuntarily flinched and ducked, his brain screaming at him to find cover, hide. He saw the bodies of two guardsmen being delicately marched over, as they lay torn apart on the ground. Ian forced himself to calm. *No hiding this time. Stand tall, advance with the company. Where's my leopard? Ah.... there you are...I can feel you. Good. Stay with me, stay with me.*

Ian's battalion formed to the left of the Grenadiers among the cannon on Home and Fore Ridges. They were ordered to advance behind a wing of the 95th Regiment. They moved down the slope toward the left side of the Kitspur, while the Grenadiers moved down next to them on the right directly toward Sandbag Battery.

There were Russians firing at them from inside the Sandbag Battery, much closer than Ian had expected. Off to his right, he saw the Grenadiers break into a charge, and drive the Russians out of the battery, back down the right side of the Kitspur. The Russians reformed and made a series of counterattacks against the Grenadiers, who ebbed back and forth, jockeying for position to hold the battery, taking and retaking it.

Ian's battalion, which had halted, was now moving rapidly forward. He'd heard no orders in the din, he merely moved with his company, their bayonets level, just short of a charge. They were still in the lead of the battalion's column of companies. Percy was out in front, sword drawn, urging them on. Ian was at the centre rear of the company, shouting along with the other subalterns and sergeants, "Steady men, keep your dress, dress is left – Steady."

The sergeant next to him said, "Sir, look ahead." They were moving toward the left side of the Kitspur. Ian could see a Russian column slowly advancing out of Saint Clements Ravine, also to the left of the Kitspur. Colonel Walker saw the oncoming threat, ordered them to form battalion by the flank, on the march. The Scotsmen did so with perfect precision, coming on line two deep to face the emerging Russians.

The regiment halted. The Duke of Cambridge had a few of what seemed like harsh words with Colonel Walker, who was then apparently ordered to oblique the battalion right and form to the immediate left of the Grenadiers line, extending it. Ian thought: *Not a good choice of movement. What the devil is the Duke thinking? The Russians will flank us on our left when they come out of the ravine. We need to face them, head on.*

Russian skirmishers were steadily advancing, emerging from the ravine. As though reading Ian's mind, General Bentinck saw the tactical error, and ordered the Scots Fusilier Guards back to the left again. They swept through the enemy skirmishers and reached the head of Saint Clements Ravine with the bulk of the oncoming Russians a mere fifty yards away. The battalion halted, Walker commanded, "Baa...talion, pree...sent, fire!" There was a thunderous volley, with telling effect at that close range. It broke the back of the advance, the Russians collapsing back down the ravine in some disorder.

Colonel Walker did not give the command to charge after them, in fact, by then he had received orders to the contrary, but Percy and other captains, in their enthusiasm, commanded "Charge." The Fusilier Guards stoically drove the hapless Russians in shocked disarray further down the ravine, until they were halted by Colonel Walker's shouts, and repeated bugle calls.

The 2nd Company moved back up to the top of the ravine. The Fusilier Guards formed battalion, creating a defensive line along the edge of the spur, facing into Saint Clements Ravine.

Colour Sergeant Skein ran up to Ian, "Sir, where's Captain Percy?" There was a quick, frenzied search for their captain, to no avail. *Probably dead or wounded down in the ravine,* Ian thought. *With this fog and dense brushwood, he could be wandering about almost anywhere. Nothing for it.*

Ian approached Vane, "The Captain's gone missing. You're in command of the company, Vane."

Vane digested the news only momentarily, then said, "Right. We'll hold this line until ordered otherwise. Skein, have the men make breastworks from this brushwood. Carlyle, I'll take the right of our company line. You take the left."

Ian was impressed with the way Vane was taking charge. He replied, "Yes, sir," moving to the left as he spoke.

Ian looked over at the battery position, saw that for some unknown reason the Grenadiers had moved up the slope of Fore Ridge behind the battery, leaving it empty. As he watched, he heard the increase in firing, the shouts in Russian. He saw Russian infantrymen swarm into the unmanned battery, using it as cover to fire volleys at the Grenadiers up the slope.

Colonel Walker rode up to the company, "Where's Percy?"

Vane replied, "Missing, sir, I've taken command."

"Vane, take your company and drive those bastards out of that battery." As they were speaking, sporadic firing was coming their way from the battery, itself. Two men fell, one with a wide-open chest, dead, the other with a hideous wound in the knee. He was screaming.

Colonel Walker continued, "No idea why the Grenadiers moved up that slope, but we can't have the Russians on our right flank. Have at them, sir, have at them."

There was a loud thud! Colonel Walker's horse reared, snorted, a gaping wound in his side. The horse rolled sidewise, and the colonel rose up, skilfully extracting himself from the saddle, just as the dead horse came crashing down. Walker stumbled, unseated himself, stood up tall, the dead horse beneath him.

Vane commanded his company to face by the rear rank, toward the battery, only 40 or 50 yards away. Without hesitation, he commanded, "Company, pree...sent, fire!" The roaring volley took its effect on the Russians scattered outside and on the berm of the battery.

Vane ran out in front of the company. Their bayonets were already fixed. Loudly and precisely, he commanded, "Forward, march." Swann was marching in ranks by this time, his bayonet forward, rifle looking bigger than he was, a serious look on his face. Vane shouted, "Double March." They increased their pace.

The company rushed forward, soldiers fell, the dress of the line started to decay, as they closed the distance. Vane was well in the lead, sword upright in front of him, showing magnificent leadership. Ian tried to locate Colour Sergeant Skein.

He saw Skein well back among the onrushing Scotsmen, and dropping back further. Skein was unusually slow in following the company, yet didn't appear to be wounded. *He should be with Vane in the forefront.* Ian recalled something Murphy had told him, "The worst tyrants sometimes turned into devout cowards when struck by uncontrolled violence."

Ian dropped back quickly. Swann followed his officer. Skein stumbled. At Ian's direction, he and Swann each grabbed an arm, lifted, and guided the sluggish sergeant forward between them. Ian said quietly, "There you go Colour Sergeant, try to keep up, won't you." Skein glared at him in fear and hatred, humiliated even more by Swann's being there.

Skein said, "It's the damned dysentery, sir, slows me down." He quickly jerked free, increased his pace, moving forward, passing other guardsmen, shame and hatred conquering fear.

Twenty yards from the battery, Vane commanded, "Charge." The company raced forward, climbing up the embankment of the battery position. They'd lost their formation, now. Their blood up, they paid scant attention to dress.

Ian drew his sword, as he climbed. He saw Skein top the battery wall ahead, and stop for a moment on the berm. He raised his rifle, and with the butt prodded a private near him, propelling him forward. He shouted threateningly at the privates around him, pointing his rifle at them.

Ian caught up to him, gave him an icy look, straight into his eyes. The last thing Skein saw was that cold animal stare. His head exploded in a ball of bright red blood, bone and brain matter, much of which landed on Swann, as he also reached the top. Skein's body flopped over the berm, bouncing down to the battery floor like a child's toy sand bag.

The momentum of the charging guardsmen eliminated any chance of using the berm as a platform for firing down into the battery. The guardsmen were forced to jump into it as soon as they reached the top. It was at least eight feet deep.

Swann, his tunic covered in the sergeant's blood and brains, never missed a step. He leapt into the battery and stabbed a half-fallen Russian twice with his bayonet. Ian followed, jumping and sliding down into the battery position behind his section. Ian was thinking of Skein: *Not sorry to see that piece of horse dung gone. I wonder if the killing shot came from front or rear.*

Ian immediately knew why this was a bad position for infantry, why the Grenadiers moved up the slope and out of the protected position. The eight-foot parapet had no fire step, making it impossible for infantry to fire over the top. The cut embrasures for the missing cannon would only allow a few rifles to fire through at once. If the enemy held the top of the parapet, they could fire murderously down into the battery, a slaughter. Judging from the bodies strewn about, this had occurred once or twice.

Without its artillery pieces, the battery was utterly useless. Ian couldn't figure out why this worthless piece of ground was being fought over so viciously.

Ian pushed through to the front of his section, led his men by example. He had been excited as they charged. All fear was forgotten now in the confusion and exhilaration of the conflict. The beast was with him. His mind was consumed with but two thoughts, killing and survival...*Do the first... and guarantee the second.*

Vane's assault had succeeded. Colonel Walker, now on foot, was leading the remaining Fusiliers in a charge around the battery at the fleeing Russians.

The attack drove them off the Kitspur, but they reorganized in the dead ground below and were soon counterattacking. Ian was at one of the embrasures, peering out carefully. He saw Colonel Walker still on his feet, although wounded twice already. He led his men in driving the Russians back down the ravine a second time.

Ian watched in shock as the adjutant, Captain Drummond, walked into a hail of musket balls. They tore him apart, his body jerking in several directions at once, as each lead ball found its mark. In the same volley, Colonel Walker was wounded a third time. This ball pierced his jaw, and he was forced to turn over command to Lieutenant Colonel Charles Seymour.

Ian stared at the scene of carnage, unable to take his eyes away, until Swann tugged at his sleeve, "Sir, beggin' yer pardon, Captain Vane's looking for you."

Ian snapped out of his trance and headed over to Vane. Vane said, "Carlyle, we'll remain here. Do what we can to support and cover the rest of the battalion."

No sooner had he said this, when the Russians counterattacked yet again. This time they were more determined. They drove Colonel Seymour and the entire battalion of Scots Fusilier Guards back. The 2nd Company reluctantly withdrew from the battery, halting to fire continuing volleys into the flank of the Russian assault. As the Russians came into the battery, the Grenadier Guards from up the slope, with heavier numbers, attacked the Russian flank, driving them again out of the battery and back down the spur.

As this attack by the Grenadiers was taking place, the battalion of Coldstream Guards arrived and formed line on their right. The Guards brigade was once again intact. The Coldstream Guards were on the right. With a space between, the Grenadier Guards were in the middle, then another larger space, and the Scots Fusilier Guards on the left. The Guards Brigade overlooked the Kitspur and Saint Clements Ravine. This was a formidable red line of the Queen's very best. The Russian counterattacks were thwarted for the time being.

Chapter 52

General Bentinck fell. The Duke of Cambridge assumed direct command of the Guards Brigade. He attempted to use recently arrived reinforcements to fill a dangerous gap between the Sandbag Battery and the Barrier, several hundred yards to the left of the battery, itself. There was heavy fighting along this line, especially around the post road, where Russians were surging out of Quarry Ravine.

At about 8:30 a.m., Ian saw a significant part of Cathcart's 4th Division attack into the valley to the right and below the Kitspur and Guards Brigade line. Vane's company was again on the right of the Fusilier Guards.

A wing of the 95th Regiment came up on the battalion's left, and a wing of the 20th Regiment, which was part of Cathcart's division, came up on the right, between the Grenadier and Fusilier Guards. Seeing Cathcart's attack down in the valley, the 20th charged down the Kitspur in a futile gesture to assist their comrades. This began a critical and unfortunate chain of events. Seeing the 20th charge to the right, the 95th on the left charged down Saint Clements Ravine.

The Scots Fusilier Guards were swept with them, Vane's company included, heading over and down the left side of the spur. The Russians went tumbling down in front of them, dropping knapsacks, weapons, and equipment as they ran. The British soldiers began shouting and cheering at what they thought was a grand victory.

The 2nd Company advanced well down the ravine, into the undulating ground, thick underbrush and scrub. They managed to remain together, but found themselves alone. In the fog they lost track of the rest of their own battalion on their left, and there was no one to be seen on their right.

In spite of his dislike for Ian, Captain Vane couldn't resist shouting, "Well, Carlyle, this is a victory we can all be proud of. Indeed we can."

Ian was not so certain. He was nervous at losing the company to their immediate left as they raced down into the ravine. Ian could also see nothing but dense fog on his right. He could hear steadily increasing musket fire from the Sandbag Battery above them. He asked, "Sir, request permission to send men to our flanks and back up the ravine to see what's what, find the battalion."

"Right you are, Carlyle, better safe than sorry, but I tell you this is a victory. They've run, by God, the bastards have run away."

"Yes, sir." Ian turned and called, "MacGregor, take two men back up the ravine and find out what all that shooting is about. Send two men and find the battalion on our left, and two more to locate the 20th on our right. Move smartly now, at the double."

MacGregor had the three parties moving in a flash. They were gone only a short time. Fergusson, who had gone to the left, reported no joy in finding the battalion. The party going right had equally bad luck.

They were truly on their own. Vane was now beginning to show nervous signs.

MacGregor came running back down the ravine, breathless. He reported to Vane, "Sir, the bastards have come in from the left, big numbers, took the battery again, they're crawling all over up there, sir. We're cut off."

Vane heard, but as he started to react, a mass of Russian infantry appeared out of the fog twenty yards ahead of them, halted, and fired a volley. Vane was hit twice, in the leg and stomach. He went down hard, knocked unconscious. Two other guardsmen were killed outright. Only a few men recovered quickly enough to return fire.

The company was in trouble. Ian, realizing he was now in command, barked, "Form company, quickly." The corporals were already forcing men into ranks, before the Russians had time to reload for a second volley.

"Company, fire by rank, rear rank, present…Fire!" Ian's commands brought a sharp volley, which tore into the Russians. "Front rank, present…Fire!" This one took a toll. Ian had paused a second or two between the volleys. He knew that after the casualties from the first volley had fallen out of the way, the volley from the front rank would strike new targets, making the fire much more deadly at this close range.

The two crashing volleys from the aimed rifle muskets caused the Russian line to evaporate. It disappeared back into the fog. There were only the two dead in Ian's company, both sergeants. Vane was holding on, stomach wound bleeding badly, barely conscious.

Ian pointed to the Russians on the ground nearby, turning to a corporal, "Make a stretcher from two Russian greatcoats. Find ones tied to their packs if you can, it'll be faster. Use their muskets for poles. Be quick now, and careful."

The corporal asked, "The Russian wounded, sir?"

"Leave them. Let their own surgeons worry about them."

Ian needed to get his company moving. He called to his one remaining sergeant, wounded in the arm, losing blood, but still on his feet, "Sergeant, come here. You too, Corporal MacGregor." They hurried over.

Ian whispered so that only they could hear, "Now listen. I'll brook no arguments. MacGregor is the new acting covering sergeant. Do you hear me?" The wounded sergeant knew MacGregor and respected him as a soldier and natural leader, knew he couldn't continue with his wound. He nodded agreement.

"MacGregor, get this company organized, fast. I want it moving in three minutes." They were ready in two, with Vane on a makeshift stretcher.

The new acting covering sergeant approached Ian, "We're low on ammunition. Where we going, sir?"

"I don't exactly know, MacGregor, but we sure as hell aren't staying here. You were up the ravine. Can we get back that way?"

"No chance, sir, unless we want to fight the whole bloody Rooshian army."

"Damn," he said, then recalled the maps he'd studied at headquarters. "We'll go down the ravine, carefully, use the fog for cover. This'll be tricky, MacGregor. Get the sergeant and the other corporals, fast, and quietly."

When they were gathered, Ian said, "This is what we'll do. Distribute the remaining ammunition so that each man has an equal portion. Non-commissioned officers each keep ten rounds; distribute the rest of yours among the men. I need to know the average amount per man."

He let them digest that, continued, "We'll form a loose moving square, one section in front with two men ahead as skirmishers, another section in rear watching our backs. The other sections will be in column, and provide flankers, but not too far out."

"Aye, sir," replied MacGregor, "protect ourselves all round." The others nodded their understanding.

"Right," said Ian. "We'll move down the ravine until we reach an aqueduct, turn right, go along beside it. As I recall there's roads leading up from this valley back onto the high ground. We'll find one and take it to our lines, tuck in there for a bit, then find the battalion. Any questions?"

One corporal asked, "Sir, begging yer pardon, sir, but if the odd bastard pops up from nowhere, do we run, shoot, or go at 'em with the bayonet?"

"Use your good sense, but we're not running. Shooting gives away our position. I'd say the bayonet as first choice, but if that's not useful, kill the bastard any way you have to, understood?" Heads bobbed.

"Go back and tell each man what we're going to do. In the fog it's better if each of them knows the plan."

Chapter 53

They began moving a few minutes later. Each man carried seventeen cartridges in his box. They moved only a hundred yards when several Russian infantrymen appeared off to their right, forming randomly to fire. They were too far away for the bayonet. The corporal covering the right gave his section the order to fire. The quick volley saved them. The Russians disintegrated back into the brush in disorder.

They kept moving slowly, cautiously, until they reached the canal-like aqueduct and turned right as planned. They could hear heavy troop movements beyond the aqueduct, but could see nothing through the fog. They moved another hundred yards, hearing the definite sounds of troops moving up the slope on their right, as well as moving about to their left across the waterway.

One of the advanced guardsmen appeared from the fog at a run, and whispered, "Sir, there's about a hundred of the bastards dead ahead. Don't think we can go round them, they's too many, sir."

"Damn." Ian went forward for a look. He could make out a mass of Russians stopped by an access point to the aqueduct filling canteens. In the fog, it was impossible to gauge how many or how deep the formation went. They could attack, or take a chance at getting around by striking away from the aqueduct, circling, then coming back. Both of these were bad options in Ian's eyes.

It was too soon to try moving up onto the plateau. Ian chose a third alternative. He returned to the company, where MacGregor whispered, "What do you think, sir?"

"I think we must wait here awhile to see what develops. Order the men to ground, wait, and stay perfectly quiet. If we're lucky, the formation ahead will move on. I left two men watching the Russians. Send Fergusson up there with them, and send two men from each section out a distance in all directions as advance skirmishers."

They could hear constant firing of muskets and duelling cannon up above toward Home Ridge and Shell Hill beyond. They could also distinctly make out the sound of soldiers milling about ahead of them, and voices talking in Russian. They waited long strained minutes without moving. They heard the sound of a larger cannon, firing from the direction of Home Ridge.

Ian knew Lord Raglan planned to reinforce any attack on Home Ridge with French troops. He thought if they could stay hidden long enough, perhaps they could work their way back up to the Kitspur, and the French would be there in force. In the end, the decision was made for him.

MacGregor whispered, "Sir, Fergusson's back. Says they's even more of them now, many hundreds, two, three battalions. They're getting ready to move, he says, and straight at us." Ian checked on Vane, who was only just holding his own, drifting in and out of consciousness.

The fog was lifting, and they would soon be in plain view. He said, "Tell the men we're moving. We can't go forward, so it's back the way we came, and quietly. Just reverse the order of march. Keep it simple."

They started moving back the way they'd come, as quickly as they could without making too much noise. Ian went forward to take the lead, Swann a permanent fixture at his side. MacGregor took the column.

They came to the Saint Clements Ravine, where they had started their trek, but there was intense firing still coming from up on the Kitspur above them. Ian chose to keep going straight, bypass the ravine, hoping to find that the post road south through Quarry Ravine was now clear. It wasn't.

Chapter 54

The pain in Ian's back was sharp and unexpected. Something heavy struck him squarely, as he rounded a large bush. He fell, dazed and confused, heard sounds of scuffling, saw Swann standing over him, fighting like a man crazed. Swann bayoneted one Russian, and clubbed another to death with his rifle butt. Fergusson made short work of two more who came out of nowhere. Ian struggled unsteadily to his feet, shook off the pain, peered ahead.

Coming out of the gradually lifting fog forty or fifty yards away was a formation of unsuspecting Russians with their muskets held casually at various angles. It was obvious these first four were a Russian advance party, just as Ian, Fergusson and Swann were theirs. His own company, MacGregor leading, was only yards behind him, moving up fast. Ian knew it was too late for guile, too late for manoeuvring, too late to hide and let them pass. It was time to stop thinking and act.

"MacGregor, bring them up," Ian shouted. "Guardsmen... Charge! Give 'em the bayonet, laddies. Follow me."

The men were already edgy. The forced quiet, the marching back and forth, and the long wait had been hard on them. The command to charge was a welcome release from the tension. Without hesitation, they rushed forward, screaming as they advanced.

The Russians were caught out. They must have thought their world had come to an end hearing the shrill highland war cries as the Scotsmen slammed into them, bayonets, rifle butts and musket balls.

MacGregor took on the first Russian he met, a sergeant of some kind. He stabbed him full in the chest, the bayonet going deep, up to the muzzle. He fired to dislodge it. The Russian's chest exploded from the contact wound and his mustard-coloured greatcoat burst into flames around the ragged hole.

Ian cut his way through the mass of Russians, slashing back and forth with his sword, feeling the blade smash into flesh and bone under the layers of clothing. He was enraged, had become the beast, the leopard, chopping left, then right, until he reached their commander. He was determined to cut off the head of this Russian bear.

Ian was alone among the enemy soldiers, separated from his own men, even from his self-appointed bodyguard, Swann. The Russian officer was stunned, thought he was safe surrounded by his own men. He was visibly shaken, as he stared into the animal eyes of this obviously insane British officer.

He might have been trying to offer Ian his sword; if so, the gesture was entirely too late. Ian lifted his sabre high in both hands, cutting down and across with all his strength. He caught the officer at the base of the neck, not much clothing in the way there. The blade cleaved six or eight inches deep into flesh. His head flopped to one side, a surprised look on his face, eyes glazing over in death. The Russian officer dropped hard to his knees, then fell forward, as Ian tried to pull the sabre out and clear of his falling body.

Now enraged Russians pounced on Ian. He was forced to the ground, lost his sabre, and felt rifle butts and kicks, as he began losing consciousness. He felt a white heat across his back, then a sharp pain deep in his left leg. Ian tried to get his pistol free of its holster, but it was useless. *I shall die here,* he thought. *It isn't so bad after all. At least it wasn't that damned artillery.*

The weight on his back began to feel lighter. He didn't understand, unless he was dead already, or they thought he was and were leaving him. Then there was hardly any weight at all.

He lifted his head cautiously, and saw the white leggings, leather jambieres, and red baggy pants of a diminutive French Zouave standing over him. He looked higher and saw other Zouaves fighting savagely.

The man above him pulled the last Russian off and threw him toward a huge Zouave nearby. This giant picked up the Russian's head by the hair and severed it cleanly with a long knife he was wielding in his hand like a sword.

The giant Zouave had lost his turban and fez, was dark-skinned, completely hairless, and swarthy looking. He held up the head like a trophy, smiling through his few front teeth as though he had just been given a sweet and was savouring it before popping it in his mouth.

Ian looked thankfully up at the small Zouave standing over him, said, "Merci, monsieur, merci."

The Zouave said, "Merci, is it then. Well, I'll be damned. Of all the ungrateful Scottish prigs. Here I save yer scrawny hide, and all ya can do is take me for a crapaud, a bloody frog."

There was disbelief as Ian realized it was an Irish voice, then whose voice it was, "Jesus, Billy? Is that you? Bloody hell."

Billy Murphy laughed, head full back, "Of course it is, boyo, the very same, and don't be blaspheming our Lord's name, or you'll be going to that bloody hell, for sure." Ian was astonished, speechless.

Billy said, "I watched this little fight from up on the slope, as the fog cleared, but didn't realize it was you. My whole regiment, 2nd Zouaves, be right up there 50 or so yards. Giving you a hand was the least we could do for our grand allies."

Ian could not yet comprehend. He sat up, gathering his strength, said, "But the Zouaves, Billy? You really joined the French. I never believed you would."

"Well, these lads are not exactly French, many are Algerians, that's where they're from, and the Frenchies who joined them are a different breed. They fight like the devil himself, and have the mischief of the rogue in them. Besides, Ian my boy, the English were not too keen on taking this wayward paddy back into their fond embrace. Had to get in this fracas somehow, didn't I? The Frenchies offered me sergeant, so I took it."

Ian was recovering, tried to stand, shakily, pain shooting up his left leg. He said, appreciatively, "I saw how they fight. Who's the big hairless one?"

"He's my friend, Ahmed, Ahmed ben Abbas. Doesn't speak a word of English. He was a leader in his tribe, now he watches me back, well and truly."

Ian was gingerly on his feet. He looked himself over, finding it difficult to believe he was still alive. He found countless bruises, felt what appeared to be a long deep cut across his back, but the worst was a serious triangular puncture hole, completely through his left leg below the thigh. Realization crept in...so did the pain. He collapsed.

Billy knelt down and applied a hasty tourniquet above and a tight bandage over the entrance and exit holes using a strip of dirty white cloth torn from his turban. Ian stood up carefully, found he could put pressure on the leg, but limped considerably when he tried to walk. The initial shock was wearing off fast.

Ian leaned on Billy as he looked around at the carnage. They had been met by at least three companies of Russians, over 200 of them. Enemy bodies were strewn about on the ground, killed or wounded by Ian's men and the fierce Zouaves. There were few prisoners, and they were in the hands of Billy's men, being treated rather badly.

MacGregor was gathering the company together, watching Ian's strange reunion with Billy. Ian called him over, "Acting Sergeant MacGregor, this is an old friend, Billy Murphy." MacGregor and Billy nodded to one another, two professionals, no words needed.

Ian asked guardedly, almost afraid to hear the answer, "How is the company?"

MacGregor said, "Seven dead, two more seriously wounded, and then there's Captain Vane. Many others with not so serious wounds. All in all, sir, we did much better than we had any right to expect."

"Right then, have the men drink water and rest before we try to find the battalion."

MacGregor added, "Never thought I'd be happy to see the Froggies, meaning no disrespect to yer friend, here, or these well meaning giants with him."

Billy said, "I'd be Irish, Sergeant, and these here boyos don't speak English, but thanks for noticing we lent a hand." There was no viciousness in either man's comments, only a gentle playfulness between warriors.

MacGregor saluted, said, "I'll sort out the company, sir. You take care of that leg. Good to meet ye Murphy."

Ian returned the salute, almost falling when he let go of Billy to do so. Billy said, "The same," then turned to Ian, "Well, lad, er, sir, I see ya've found yer calling. I watched ya fight. Very impressive. Must have had a good teacher."

"That I did, Billy, that I did. That calling, that quest of mine to be a soldier, has often been a nightmare of late, but I guess I'm content enough. When this wee fight is over, my friend, I'll find your camp, and we'll slip away somewhere for a long chat."

"You do that, sir. I'll bring the whiskey, and I'll be looking forward to it." Billy thought: *Ian, boyo, it's not the same now. I know in yer heart you'd like it to be, but it's not. Yer an officer, and by the look a passable one. I hope in the end yer dream lives up to yer expectations, but our time is past.*

The men were relaxing, even though the fight still raged beyond them. They were literally within the French line along the Quarry Ravine and safe. Ian had gotten them through with relatively few casualties. The company had found a new leader, in fact, two new leaders, since they also accepted MacGregor as their covering sergeant, and were glad for it.

Ian was given an improvised crutch, fashioned by some of the men from a sturdy branch with a fork for his armpit, given to him by a corporal. They knew he wouldn't accept being taken by stretcher.

The small company made its way up the eastern edge of Quarry Ravine, with Vane and the two other wounded on crude stretchers, Ian limping noticeably.

Ian ordered MacGregor, "Send a section back to bury our dead properly after things die down."

"Aye, sir, that I will," was MacGregor's reply.

They avoided the Barrier itself, at the ravine's head, where there was still fierce fighting. They made their way around it and back to Home Ridge. They found their colours, surrounded by the exhausted remains of the Guards Brigade, less than a third of those initially engaged.

The men were re-formed and issued ammunition, 50 rounds each. The fighting wasn't over. Without being told, MacGregor put the men at once to cleaning their rifles, while he had canteens gathered for a water run. Ian had the corporals sort out the more seriously wounded, sending them for aid. He declined to go himself.

As they reorganized, the Russians overwhelmed the Barrier, a few hundred yards to their front and below Home Ridge. The Russians then attacked the ridge, again and again. This was an error. They were blasted by canister from protected positions, and continuous volley fire by the British and French defenders behind the low stone wall.

For the rest of the morning, the defenders drove off attacks from the front and left flank, while receiving shot and shell from Russian guns stretching from West Jut, across Shell Hill, to East Jut. They returned fire with two 18-pounders, which were manhandled up onto the ridge.

By 11 o'clock, more guns and more troops had arrived, both French and British, including the French reserves. The Russians slowly withdrew. The British were too exhausted, the French too cautious to pursue them. The fight, which actually took place over four square kilometres of terrain, lasted about six hours. The allies had held.

The Scots Fusilier Guards marched back to their camp in the south, fewer by far than when they left it. There were 19 officers and 372 other ranks engaged in the battle. Of these, nine officers, and 170 rankers were killed, wounded, or missing.

Ian first made certain the battalion surgeon, Surgeon-Major Bostock, who was slightly wounded himself, had cared properly for his wounded at the marquee tents set up as a battalion hospital. Vane, still unconscious, and the other seriously wounded guardsmen were carted off to the hospital in Kadikoi. Others were treated and returned either as "light duty" or "fit for duty."

Bostock took one look at Ian on his rickety crutch, blood soaking his left trouser leg, and ordered him to hospital, as well. When the surgeon-major had gone, Ian allowed the wounds to be cleaned and dressed, but refused to be hospitalized. He returned to duty.

Chapter 55

The light was dancing on a canvas ceiling. Ian was soaked in sweat, light-headed, disoriented, and waking from a nightmare. Bad smells assailed him: blood, decay, stale linen, old straw, and a thousand others. He slowly realized the flickering light was a lamp, held close to his face by Swann, who was smiling down at him. "Sir, we thought you were gone, fer sure."

"My leg, my...leg?"

"Yer all there, sir, all yer parts is there. I wouldn't let 'em do it."

There was pain in his left leg, and across his back, but he was decidedly relieved.

"How long have I been here?"

"You collapsed, sir, about three weeks ago on parade, day after the big fight. Yer leg began turning green, pus and all. Bad fever. Surgeon-Major Bostock thought you was right done in.

"Surgeon sent me along with ya, told me to take care of ya good. Ya come awake once, tossing about in a raging fever, then was out again, till just now."

"Where am I?" He'd heard the horror stories about the hospital at Scutari.

Swann said, "They tried to send ya to Turkey, sir, but me and some of yer friends from the headquarters made 'em keep you here. Yer in an officers' ward at Castle Hospital above the harbour."

"I've been here for weeks?"

Swann nodded, "Yes, sir."

"I don't remember a damned thing."

"I been cleaning yer wounds couple times a day, sir. Wouldn't allow anyone to tend ya, not while I was about, Surgeon-Major Bostock's orders, as well. Surgeons here giving ya first-class attention. They's pretty much afraid of you around here after all those headquarters blokes made such a to-do. They kept saying Lord Raglan, hisself, were coming to visit you."

Ian smiled, weakly, "I owe you much, lad."

"No, sir, my duty." Swann was showing signs of bursting into tears, "Yer the first person ever showed me kindness, except for Gregor and Fergie, and I'll never forget that, sir. It's I what owes you, sir." Ian said no more. He couldn't have a grown guardsman tearing about the place; it was unseemly. Ian was damned proud of this lad. *Och, Angus, if you could only see yer replacement. He's no bigger than a stick, but a fine soldier and a worthy follower to take care of your own wee bairn. You'd have liked him, Angus.* Ian drifted into a quieter sleep.

When he awoke, a chubby, unkempt young orderly corporal with a great wound scar on the side of his face was standing over the bed. Swann was next to him. Ian said, "I'm feeling better, Corporal, but I know I'm weak. I can hardly lift my head. Swann said I was doing fine now that the fever's broken. How am I, really?"

The corporal became very business-like, said with conviction, but in a tender voice that didn't match his rough appearance, "Surgeon-Major Smith says the same thing, sir. He doesn't believe it, but you're doing fine. The bayonet wound below your thigh was clean through. Never touched a bone, or a blood vessel…just infected."

Ian asked, "Tell me more. I want to know everything, and what's your name, Corporal?"

The corporal's voice was very educated, he said, "My name's Appleton, sir, they call me 'Apple.' There was a good bit of gangrene setting in when you arrived, sir. Caused the fever you're just now shaking off. We've stopped the gangrene, controlled the infection, and the entry and exiting wounds are beginning to heal. The surgeons are amazed, and there's been a lot of them hovering about. Seems you rate special treatment."

Ian said, "I've no idea why."

Appleton continued, "The cut along your lower back might be a mite painful, but is superficial. A welt, no more. It'll heal itself, I'll wager. With the fever gone, you'll mend just fine, but it'll take weeks, perhaps months."

Ian asked, deliberately, "When I recover, will I be whole?"

"Well, sir, the surgeon seems most hopeful. Said he'd never seen such a clean recovery from gangrene. Somebody is watching over you, sir, or you're the luckiest officer I ever saw. The surgeon said, begging your pardon, sir, you might have, how did he put it, 'a slight, rather distinguished limp to show off to your legion of admirers,' uh….sir."

Ian laughed, for the first time, and pain shot through him.

Since the officer was laughing, or trying to, the corporal took a liberty. He said, "Speaking of admirers, sir, and special treatment, we know all about you. Your man can talk of nothing else, to anyone who'll listen. Why to hear him tell it, sir, you as much as won the battle at Inkerman Ridge alone. Tell me, sir, did you really cut a hundred Russians to pieces with your sabre?"

Ian laughed again; the pain came again, "Hardly a hundred," he said, with a twinkle in his eye, "more like seventy-five or so." They both laughed.

Ian looked about him, said, "Frankly, Appleton, I've heard some pretty bad stories about this place, and the hospitals over in Scutari, but it appears to me the care here is first rate."

Swann answered for the corporal, "Sir, the fact is, this here ward is a fine place, thanks mostly to Apple's work. The rest of this hospital is in bad straights."

Ian was listening. Swann continued, "That Scutari place be worse. I've talked to those what's come back from across the water, what few makes it back. It's a bloody shame, sir, it is. No surgeons visiting them, dressings filthy, lying on bits of straw, screaming for a bit of water, just dying, wearing the same clothing and linen they landed in months ago. They's women nurses just arrived over there, I'm told. Maybe they can help."

Ian thought: *Women...how odd.*

Appleton added, "We try, sir, with what we have. We try here, and I'm sure they're trying over there, but there's so many shortages – surgeons, orderlies, medical supplies, equipment, even medicines themselves. We do our best."

Ian said, "I'm sure you do, Corporal." Swann began talking again, but Ian was already soundly sleeping.

Chapter 56

Indeed, with time, attentive surgeons, and the help of Swann and Appleton, Ian's wounds mended. It was near the end of December, 1854. Ian was seated in a camp chair Swann "found" for him and had placed by the bed. He was intently reading the *Times*, only six weeks old, when a familiar and welcome voice said, "Ian, my lad, how are you?" It was Major Capecci, in all his elegant grandeur.

"I am splendid, Major, and you?"

"I'm fine. I hear you'll be fit soon."

Ian said, "So they tell me."

"That is most good news, and I shall carry it back to your friends."

Ian said, "Speaking of news, Antonio, tell me everything. All I get up here is what's in the *Times*, and what newly arriving casualties tell me, which isn't much."

Antonio said, "The siege is going badly. It's the winter. Too damned cold in the trenches, and we're running short of everything."

"Why, there's certainly enough supply ships in the harbour. I've bloody well seen them."

The major answered, "We've got stores down at Balaklava, but no horses or wagons to get them the eight miles to the soldiers in the camps. The road is so damned muddy nothing moves on it. Driving Lord Raglan and General Airey to distraction."

Ian asked anxiously, "What about the men?"

Antonio's voice saddened, "The men are exhausted from trench duty. They're on half rations, freezing cold, and dying of exposure or disease. The cholera's still after us. We lose more every day."

Ian was thoughtful, "I must get back…Antonio, when are you to return?"

"I'm only in Balaklava a few days, why?"

Ian was growing more anxious, "If I can persuade the surgeon to release me early, into your care, and if I can find a horse around here, could I return with you?"

"Of course, my boy, I'd be happy for the company, and proud to have the slayer of a hundred Russians, with his sabre no less, to protect me. Why I'll feel as safe as a baby in its cradle."

"Damn," Ian said, "where did you hear that?"

"Why, Ian, my boy, your heroics are the talk of the officers' messes. Seems they heard it first from some officers returning from right here. Surely you're not telling me it's a falsehood, surely not," Antonio laughed, heartily.

"Bollocks," was Ian's only reply.

Chapter 57

MacGregor, now with an intense beard and long hair, said, "This here zigzag trench we're about to go up, sir, and many others of the like, allow us to move forward from parallel trench to parallel trench without getting killed, long as ye stay low and keep yer arse down, pardon the expression, sir."

"I understand, Colour Sergeant." MacGregor seemed to have forgotten his officer was an engineer, rather well versed in trenches and siege warfare.

"We have an assigned sector of trench in the most forward parallel," MacGregor continued, "I've strung a series of two-man sentry posts out front, backed up by two men every several yards along the trench itself. The boys out front are posted and alert. The men are bloody cold, sir, but they'll do for now."

Ian said, "Where's Captain Vane?" Vane had returned after his own wounds healed, and was now commanding the company.

"Sir, ye didn't really think ye'd see him out here, did ye?" MacGregor replied with no little sarcasm in his voice.

Ian snapped, "Colour Sergeant MacGregor, just answer my damned question, if you please."

"Sir." MacGregor snapped-to and replied, crisply, realizing he'd overstepped his bounds. Carlyle would brook no disrespect from the ranks to an officer, any officer.

MacGregor took a different approach, said, "Sir, begging yer pardon, but yer fresh back and this here is a whole new world. It's yer first time out here in the trenches. Company's been out every other night for the past several weeks, ten hours a time. We're either a covering party or put to work digging the bloody trenches we're to freeze in the next night."

Ian was listening intently to his sergeant.

"We saw Captain Vane once, on the first night, sir, stayed about an hour, then went back to camp to his warm fire and cozy hut, beggin yer pardon, sir. After that, we saw him perhaps twice more. Both times he made rounds of the sentry posts, because he had to as Picquet Officer. Came out, asked if everything was correct, then hurried back. Said he had other more pressing duties. Now that yer here as his second officer, being junior and all that, I'd be surprised to see him at all...sir."

Ian nodded, chose not to respond immediately, "Sorry, sir, but that's the way of it."

Ian thought about this bit of news, finally said simply, "Let's have a look at the men, Colour Sergeant." He deliberately chose not to make an issue of MacGregor's surly attitude, wanting to wait, see, and hear more.

Ian stooped down, made his way behind MacGregor, knee deep in slush, slime, and snow. They worked their way through the connecting trench at a crouch, moving toward the advanced parallel trench within a thousand yards of Sevastopol's defences. As they moved along, stirring the muck, Ian could smell the decaying filth that accumulated in the trench bottom. They were in the British sector of responsibility, on the right of the Allied line. As he walked, Ian found himself favouring his leg a bit.

Actually the wound was healing quite well, except that the January cold and wet seemed to bring on some rheumatism...and it was cold. Just now there was a foot of snow on the ground.

Chapter 58

No matter how many times he'd been warned, Ian was ill prepared for what he saw when he cleared the connecting trench and moved into the much wider main trench, which formed a "T" with the zigzag leading up to it.

The men were lounging about along the trench, one man up on the fire step every eight to ten yards, his mate resting below. Many of these soldiers had fought next to him at Inkerman, but as he passed among them, he hardly recognized anyone, either by name or that they were members of the elite Scots Fusilier Guards.

Ian's frock coat was a bit shabby after months of service, and certainly his cloak was a wreck. The only new item he wore was a field service cap given him by Nigel Kingscote upon his arrival back from hospital. However, his worn and threadbare garments were nothing compared to these guardsmen.

Due to the scarcity of water, they were authorized to grow beards, and they were growing thick, long, and ungroomed. Their once bright scarlet coatees were faded and torn, with visible patches of every kind. Some cut their high collars off for more freedom. Many cut the swallowtails off to make patches of at least a similar colour for the upper coat. It mattered little, because the coats had faded, turning many an odd brown-purple colour.

Trousers were patched, mud-caked, and badly frayed at the bottoms, some with open holes worn through the knees. Ankle boots were in tatters, wrapped in bits of cloth, or strips torn from haversacks, tied with rope just to hold them together. Their wool stockings were either in bits showing above the boots or non-existent.

There were still a few bearskin caps visible. One odd-looking bearskin had been cut open and pulled down well over the ears. The men wore a variety of other homemade headgear, some from pieces of blanket; they ranged from turbans to haversacks pulled down. Others had hand-knit wool caps or stockings over their heads, cutting a hole for their faces. There were forage caps and field service caps, and a very few sealskin caps worn by the newer draft recruits.

Among some of the new recruits he also saw sealskin coats, but most of the company wore their shabby greatcoats over their tunics, wrapped in as many blankets as they possessed. A few had lost their greatcoats and wore only blankets with holes cut in the top for their heads or wrapped around their necks and tucked into belts. The seriously unlucky ones had lost both their blankets and greatcoats. These were merely standing along the trench, shivering in their discoloured coatees around meagre fires glowing from holes dug into the trench side. There was barely enough wood in the trenches to keep the tiny fires alive.

They even found a useful purpose for discarded news journals sent from home or bought or stolen locally, but not as fuel for the fires, as Ian might have suspected. They stuffed the paper as a layer of insulation down their trousers, inside their coats.

For gloves, they wore mittens made from woollen stockings, or wrapped blanket wool around their hands, tied with string. A resourceful few, the company quartermaster having no doubt overlooked them, even cut open the top of their bearskin caps and were using them as muffs to warm their hands.

Ian's initial impression was that they were drugged or drunk. They looked filthy, vermin-ridden, and were staring into empty space, leaning against the trench walls, weaving slightly, or sitting in the filth at the bottom, not caring. Their scraggly beards were surrounded by long hair poking unceremoniously out of whatever head covering they wore.

Ian was struck by their stone-like, stoicism. They weren't joking or grumbling. There was none of the expected soldierly banter as he passed through the trench.

Ian's nostrils cringed at the putrid stench of filth and decay. He saw, with sadness, their sunken hollow eyes, the grey pallor of their skin, chapped and cut lips. Their blank stares reminded him of Peter's look after the incident at Eton. There was no light in their eyes. The deplorable conditions were sapping them of their energy, their dignity, their pride. They looked like stooped old men, twice – three times their age.

There was only one item of equipment that was spotless and bright. Ian had seen it with Goodlake's lads, and he saw it again now. In the hands of each soldier was his Minie' rifle musket, clean, ready and fit for killing. Ian credited this, without asking, to the vigilance of MacGregor. *No matter how hard the system beats men like these down, they will still rise up fighting, given the right incentive,* Ian thought.

There was a flash of hatred, which coursed through Ian like a lightening bolt; the leopard, surfacing again, had to be pushed back in its place. *How could we allow this to happen to our Guards, our best, the ones who would stand and fight to the last, or attack and prevail against any odds? Why weren't these men held back as a strong hammer to strike the decisive blow when needed? Why was the strength of such professional soldiers sapped and squandered digging trenches or manning them day-in and day-out? Shame on them, and as fine a man as you are, Lord Raglan, shame on you. They deserve better. We'll never see the like again of the magnificent 3000-strong Guards Brigade I watched marching away from London last February.*

Ian turned to the colour sergeant, snapped, "MacGregor, get me the sergeants and corporals."

"Sir, the other two sergeants are back in camp with their duties, and we have only one corporal, that'd be Fergusson."

"Get him over here, then."

Ian motioned the two to follow him down the zigzag out of hearing of the other men. He hissed, "What the bloody hell's going on here? These men are a disgrace."

MacGregor came back defensively, saying, "We've made do with what we've been given, sir, but you're right, these men are bloody well done in. Och, they've been on half rations for weeks, they haven't bathed or even been out of those uniforms, if you can call them that, since we landed months ago. There's precious little water for drinking, let alone washing or shaving. It's rained almost every day it hasn't snowed, and the temperature's dropping fast. That's a deadly combination, sir." He paused, "…but there's worse to know."

"Carry on, MacGregor, I may as well know it all." By his concerned rather than angry tone, both men realized Ian wasn't looking to blame them, more to find out the facts.

"Pity of it, sir, is the wet."

"What do you mean?" asked Ian.

"Ye see, sir, the men can never get dry. They could stand most anything, cold, short rations, no clothing, no water, if they knew there was a warm fire waiting for them back in camp. Then they could dry their wet clothing down to the skin, warm themselves, boil water for coffee, and cook a hot meal, even if the rations be short."

Ian was puzzled, "I understand why they can't have large cooking fires out here, in the trenches, but why in God's name can't they do so in camp?"

Fergusson picked up where MacGregor stopped, "Beggin' yer pardon, sir, it's the wood, or I should say the lack of it. All we got is tiny trees, bloody scrub brush, and the like. Not enough, sir, not by far. All used up. Wood details range farther and farther out for the odd twig to make even a small fire among too many men. We dig up roots, and even they're fast disappearing."

Ian remembered that the wood was getting to be a problem at times even before he was wounded. He said nothing, listening solemnly.

MacGregor added, "They can never, ever, get dry, sir. Can ye think, sir, what that does to a man's spirit? They do their day's duties, wet, stand piquet duty, chilled and soaked through, fired on and maybe killed or wounded. If they make it through the day, they come off-guard only to be set to digging for hours more, still soaked through. Afterward, in the few hours they're allowed to rest, the poor beggars crawl under wet canvas, onto wet ground and sleep in wet clothing rolled in wet greatcoats and wet blankets."

MacGregor was warming to his subject, the first chance he'd had to vent his pent-up frustration. Ian let him continue.

"After too little sleep, they wake up still wet through, and have to slog out in the mud and snow to do it all over again. Is it no wonder, sir, we're carting them off dead or deathly ill, day after day…and so few return. We haven't lost a man to the Ruskies in weeks, but our numbers are less each morning."

After thinking for a time, Ian said, "I see, Colour Sergeant, perhaps I see too clearly. Thank you, gentlemen, for your honesty. MacGregor, I saw a few men out there without a greatcoat or blanket. I brought three blankets out with me, thanks to your advice and Private Swann's initiative. See that my blankets get to those men, will you?"

Fergusson looked at the officer quizzically, "What'll you use, sir?" Then more sarcastically, "....or perhaps ye'll not be joining us out here tonight."

"I'll manage, Fergusson. I've a heavy cloak, and I've put it to this use before. See to it. You're dismissed. If you need me, I'll be in that wee tiny hole you call an officer's hut."

Ian gained an understanding he wasn't certain he wanted. He went to the officer's hut, cut in the side of the zigzag trench a short distance from the parallel trench. It was a room about five by six feet, but only five feet high, so the officer had to remain crouched down or seated while inside. The room contained a small rope bed, a bread crate for a stool, and one small candle. There were planks over the roof, covered in sandbags and loose dirt.

Ian smiled to himself. How ingenious...unless the officer was a dwarf, he was forced into a most unbecoming posture. *Diabolical and cunning these guardsmen*, he mused, *Billy told me about this sort of thing.*

Ian went in the hut and sat on the crate. By the flickering candle, using the bed as a table, he completed the journal entry in his guard report, leaving out the men's condition. He was certain the command knew of it. That fight he would save for another time, but that time must be soon, very soon ... these men were dying.

Ian was then able to take a minute to reflect on the stark difference a few days could make. It was 11 January 1855. He had reported back to the battalion from hospital the day before. His company was already out on trench duty.

He found to his delight that his baggage had finally been brought to shore, having travelled back and forth to England at least once in the meantime. It was waiting for him in camp, in the small bell tent assigned him. He had not been able to locate Captain Vane, his company commander, and presumed he was in the trenches. Thus he had MacGregor escort him forward.

When he found that Vane commanded the company, it did not strike him as necessarily bad news. On the credit side, Vane had acquitted himself admirably at Inkerman, and had the foresight to promote MacGregor to permanent colour sergeant, and Fergusson to corporal, two excellent men.

In the first encounter Ian had with Vane at Chobham, he had been unnecessarily cruel toward Swann, but a large part of it could have been the drink he had consumed. There was still no excuse for it, but Ian recalled Vane's bravery before he was wounded. Ian thought: *He certainly is no coward. Damned cold...wish I'd brought more blankets. The company is in very bad shape. I can't do anything tonight, but by Christ I'll do something tomorrow.*

In his confined hut in the trenches Ian examined the most recent morning report. Counting Vane and himself, the 2nd Company list told off as 2 officers, 3 sergeants, 1 corporal, and only 33 men present for duty. This number was half their strength from when he left in November, when they were already at half strength. They were covering a piece of trench needing 60 to 100 men, and a reserve. To make it worse, of the 33, only 21 were veterans from Alma. The other 12 were inexperienced recruits from recent drafts.

These drafts, coming in from England to be exposed to the raw, biting Crimean winds, extreme cold, snow, sleet, and rain, simply died, some within days of their arrival. As MacGregor pointed out to him, the company was losing men daily from exposure, frostbite, foot rot, dysentery, diarrhoea, jaundice, and cholera. No replacements were filling these gaps.

Chapter 59

The morning after Ian's first exposure to trench life, he led the bedraggled detachment back to their wet miserable existence in camp. Ian knew he was required to report his return to the regiment to his now company commander, although he wasn't looking forward to it.

He found Vane in his dry hut, which he'd fashioned for himself, using guardsmen for labour. The sides were stone and mud, a few feet high, and the roof a mixed affair of old planks, scrub brush and mud. Inside, comfortably laid out, were camp chairs, a table with a portable desk on top, an elaborate bed, and a wood stove. Vane's baggage had also caught up with him, and he was well set up.

When Ian entered the quarters, Vane was wearing a warm smoking jacket, enjoying a long clay pipe, reading a *Times* newspaper sent from home. An entirely too fresh-looking frock coat hung from a peg with a fine woollen cloak next to it. Ian thought he saw a warm quilt lining showing beneath the cloak, felt his own discomforting chill.

The leg was not taking the cold that well after a long night in the trenches. He was also plagued with the bitterly fresh memory of the men shivering the previous night with no fires and scant clothing.

Vane greeted him, "Carlyle, glad to see you. Back with the company, excellent. Heard you arrived. Sorry we missed each other yesterday. Most excellent to have you back. Haven't been back from hospital too long myself."

Ian remained silent.

Vane was beaming, "Well, I certainly can use your help, old boy. I've two excellent bottles of claret, and I busted up my damned corkscrew. Not very good at that sort of thing. Just read that old Aberdeen's government is in for it, may not last long. Come join me. Do you mind, awfully?" he said, handing an uncorked bottle to Ian, presumably for him to magically open.

Ian looked at Vane in utter disbelief, held back his disgust, kept his anger controlled, saw that Vane was already tipsy.

Ian merely said, "Actually, Captain Vane, I do mind... awfully."

"Oh, come now, Carlyle, not still peeved are we? Listen, my good man, we've seen the elephant, by Jove, we've fought together. There should be a bond now between us. I heard you did fine work that day on Inkerman Ridge. Saved the damned company... and me, for all that. Fine work."

Ian didn't respond.

The conversation was becoming increasingly awkward for Vane. He tried again, "I say, you're not still ruffled about our first meeting? I ain't, by Christ, you saved my life. That changes us. Besides, all's forgiven...the nose works fine now. Surgeons fixed it in hospital. Fully recovered. Forgiven you, Carlyle, for my nose and all that. Now, you really must forgive me. Start fresh, what?"

Ian's eyes hardened, "Your conduct on that occasion was, and will remain, despicable, sir, but that's neither here nor there. Something you'll have to live with."

Vane took this as a great joke, laughing uproariously, as Ian continued, "You're the Captain of this company, Vane, and I'm your subaltern. Regardless of our differences, I shall continue to do what is my clear duty as your subordinate. I came in late yesterday. The company went for trench duty last night. I went as well, thinking I'd find you there to report. I didn't...find you...that is."

Vane frowned, tried to regain some control of the conversation, but found himself saying, defensively, "Yes, er, had pressing engagements last night, but damned glad you went, Carlyle. How are the men? I'm concerned about them."

Ian held his temper tighter, calmed the leopard, said, "They're not doing very well, sir. I'd say, for a certainty, they're not doing well at all."

Ian's accusatory tone made Vane uncomfortable, but he was also quite inebriated. He said, almost whining, "Carlyle, see here, what's a body to do? I'm exhausted. I've sent requisitions through the Adjutant General's Department, seen the Quartermaster, and pleaded with the battalion and brigade commanders for warm clothing and more food. They simply don't have them, ye hear, it ain't my fault."

Ian watched as Vane took a healthy swallow from his glass, and continued, "Did manage to get our time in the trenches reduced. Damned well did that, but still they will become ill and die off on me. Damned inconvenient of them, I must say, a bloody shame."

Ian was coming to a slow boil, but kept it contained...barely.

Vane continued to whine, "There's not a thing more I can do, Carlyle. You must realize that. After all, these men have had hardships before. They're strong, ain't they? Don't want to be seen coddling them, do we, old man? Certainly you see that, Carlyle?"

Ian didn't see it, not at all. He was already aware that the new Guards Brigade commander, Colonel Rokeby, was responsible for less trench time after his arrival, not Vane, yet this posturing prig was trying to take credit.

There was no excuse for his neglect, but Ian had sense enough not to show his full contempt by making more of the issue. He decided he was going to correct these wrongs, himself. This was about the men's welfare, not his personal disgust with Vane's poor leadership or pathetic social skills. As useless as Vane was, he didn't want his company commander working against him within the army system. He simply made his apologies and left Vane's hut, quickly, before he reacted badly.

Swann had unpacked his trunk and appropriated bits and pieces of furniture for Ian's tent. He was very skilled at 'appropriation.'

In the camp he saw what he expected to see. The officers had better tentage, warmer and better clothing, and certainly better food, purchased at extremely high prices in Balaklava, but they had the funds to afford it.

Ian had no illusions about his own officer status. He was of the upper class, a part of the aristocracy even, and a Guards officer, as well. In the Guards, many officers, in fact most, were from similar backgrounds.

He had no problem with officers faring better than the rank and file. That was the way of things in the military. Ordinarily he enjoyed his privileges, but with this status went the responsibilities of an officer to his men. They deserved to live in dignity, with the basic requirements in food, clothing, shelter, and general care that were due them. It was the duty of an officer to see to his men, and that was that. The overwhelming number of officers accepted that responsibility unflinchingly, doing what they could, whenever they could, for the men in their charge. *There has to be a way,* he thought, *I must find a way to do my duty to my men.*

Ian wrote a letter that night asking his father's assistance. He explained the dire condition of the soldiers. He also asked that some of the money he would eventually inherit be advanced to him, so that he might relieve the men's suffering in small ways.

Even as he wrote the words, Ian knew it would take weeks before he received a reply, and no guarantee his father would be willing to help. Either way, that would be too late. The men were dying every day. He needed solutions now.

He had two days before the next tour of trench duty for the company. In the meantime they were digging to reinforce artillery positions near the Guards camp. Ian saw the two critical problems he might be able to influence as warm clothing and wood for fires. He accepted these as his major challenges, in that order.

Chapter 60

The plan Ian devised started at first light the next day with a visit to Lord Raglan's headquarters on the heights, to see Antonio Capecci, and Leicester Curzon, and, of course, his beloved Savage. To get there he needed transportation of some kind.

Captain Drummond was invalided home to England after being severely wounded at Inkerman. Captain Robert James Lindsay, a most gallant officer and former company commander of the 1st Company, replaced him as adjutant. Ian and Lindsay had been friends since they trained together at Chobham. He was able to borrow Lindsay's extra horse, Caisson, for the day. Caisson was hardly the calibre of Savage. *Still,* thought Ian, *it's good to be riding again.*

Ian found Major Capecci and Captain Curzon warming by the fire outside their small hut. They offered him coffee and he gladly joined the circle. They talked of what adventures they'd had since they last met.

Ian slowly turned the conversation to his purpose, explaining his men's plight and the deplorable conditions under which they were persistently dying. They reminded him that all the soldiers, not just the Guards, were experiencing deprivations.

Ian was not deterred. He asked the favour he sought of Curzon, saying, "What I need, Leicester, is a requisition, signed by someone here at headquarters high enough on the quartermaster staff for the lower level clods at Balaklava Harbour to fill it, without question. I want you, my dear friend, to get it for me."

Curzon was incredulous, "Ian, surely you jest. What you're asking is not only illegal, but highly unseemly. It would be seen as stark favouritism to a former member of His Lordship's personal staff, which, I may say, is even now under disparagement from many quarters."

"Yes, it very likely would, if discovered," injected Major Capecci, "but it is also a damned fine and noble idea, as well as a grand adventure. What is it you actually hope to gain through this requisition, Ian?"

Ian said, "I can't hope to kit up the whole Guards Brigade, so I'm laying my guns lower, on my own company. I'll require sealskin coats and caps, woollen gloves, underclothing, and stockings, as well as ankle boots, all in various sizes."

Curzon, who was warming to the escapade, said, "Yes, somewhere in that mess at Balaklava these items are about. I saw the returns myself, even after the losses from the November storm. We have them…to be sure. Lord Raglan had all such items placed on priority for issue, but, as we all know, the problem is deeper. First, not sure they could be found in that nightmare jumble of stores, and, second, there's no transport from the harbour to the camps. Mud bath roads and damned few carts or horses."

Capecci didn't need convincing, he was in the plot from the start. He had already accepted his role in the conspiracy. He said, "At least one company of these poor chaps would be warm. That's something worth the risk, I'd say. So, Leicester, these items are there, somewhere."

"Aye," Curzon said, "likely some quartermaster sergeant has his fat arse sitting on bales of them and doesn't know it, but damn me if I know where to start looking."

Ian, skilfully drawing them in, added, "All I'll be doing is getting them to my men a bit early. I'll be sworn to secrecy. Should anyone ask, I'll say we sent out a sortie and stole them from the Russians, or some such nonsense."

Capecci asked, "You've no idea where they are, how will you find them, even if you have this requisition?"

"Some things are best left unsaid. If I can't find these items, the enterprise is off, and none the worse for it."

Capecci smiled, "Ah, what intrigue, this should be fun, what say you, Leicester?"

Curzon thought a bit. His forehead creased as he pondered, but he was emphatic when he finally said, "Right. We'll do it. For a company you say? So you'll need, what, 100 of each, and double that number of stockings, two pair per man?"

Ian looked at the ground, "No, gentlemen, as of this morning the company is less than thirty men, including officers."

A stunned quiet swept the group. If there were doubts, they disappeared. They looked with sadness at Ian. Curzon finally said, "We'll have something for you by end of day, Ian, trust us."

Ian thanked them, then walked alone over to the line of staff horses to talk to Savage. All the horses looked thinner, but he knew they were far better off attached to Lord Raglan's staff than were the cavalry mounts. Cardigan had gone home to England, and Lucan had told Lord Raglan that due to the lack of forage, his cavalry was ineffective. All those fine cavalry mounts were literally starving to death, daily. Ian's thoughts turned to his old friend. *It is perhaps as well that Nolan is no longer with us. He loved horses so.*

Savage was glad to see him. They spent some quiet moments together. Ian wished he had the time for a ride, but there was more work to do. He rubbed Savage's neck, kissed his forehead, and left.

Chapter 61

The first part of his plan was in play. He returned to camp and called MacGregor, Fergusson, and Swann to his tent. Closing the flap behind them, Ian said, "What I'm about to ask of you is voluntary. Captain Vane knows nothing about it, and won't until I'm ready to confide in him. I've a piece of work for you three. I'll not order you to do it. It must be done quickly and quietly, or it'll be a court martial for the lot of us, understand?"

They looked at each other, blankly, then all three smiled. MacGregor spoke for the others, "We're yer men, sir, who is it and what do you want done to him?"

"Nothing quite like that. The first part is the most difficult. I know for a fact that somewhere in stores at Balaklava Harbour there are sealskin coats, caps, boots, woollen underclothes, stockings, and gloves."

"Well, I'll be bugger all," said MacGregor, "and we're freezing our arses off in them trenches?"

"Exactly the point, Colour Sergeant. I aim to get enough warm clothing for all our men, but only if you three 'scoundrels' can find where they're stored in that chaos they call a supply system. You need to get to the town; I don't care how, and locate the goods we seek, quickly, tonight, in the dark, to be exact. Think you can do it?"

Fergusson replied in a harsh whisper, "If we can't, no one can, er, ah, sir, er, beggin yer pardon, sir. But I vouch we'll need a bit more help."

"What sort of help?" Ian asked, sceptically. MacGregor and Swann looked quizzically at Fergusson.

"Well, sir, that's a damned big place down there, and we're guardsmen, not quartermasters. If we want to save time and get this done, I'd say we ask for professional help, so to speak."

"How so?" asked Ian.

Fergusson said, "MacNab's yer man, sir, Elijah MacNab."

"Och, of course," MacGregor injected, "he was one of them thieving quartermasters before he came to us."

Ian asked, "You think we can trust this MacNab?"

Fergusson said, slyly, "For two reasons, sir," he raised one finger for emphasis, "he wants to be warm as much as any of us, and (raising the second finger) he's terrified of the good colour sergeant, here."

"Right," was Ian's reply, "fetch him yourselves and take him with you, if he's willing to go. Even if he agrees, though, tell him as little as possible of our purpose, and watch him close."

Swann asked, "Sir, when we finds these here goods, we steals them?"

"No. Find them first. I'll take care of the rest. We're going to 'appropriate' them, sort of legally."

MacGregor interjected, "Och, sir, ye sure ye don't want us to just steal the damned things?"

"And how, my fine Colour Sergeant, would you explain them afterward, when the provost are looking and our men are wearing them? That will also be a sizable load to haul over that long muddy road on your backs, undetected."

MacGregor said, "Aye, sir."

"Good, off with you. Remember, you have the rest of today and tonight. I want you back here by tomorrow morning, with good news."

In late afternoon a galloper arrived in the Guards camp with a sealed envelope specifically for Captain Ian Carlyle, from Major Antonio Capecci at headquarters. Captain Vane saw him arrive, but said nothing, thinking it personal. The envelope contained the requisition form for the desired items. The signature was a pleasant surprise. The note with it said: "We decided that you owe us each a bottle of the finest single malt whiskey, perhaps a well-aged Talisker from the Isle of Skye. We shall collect after this little war is over." It was signed, "Friends." The signature on the requisition in bold handwriting was General Richard Airey, Quartermaster-General, Army of the East.

Ian was elated.

The plan was progressing. It was time to see Vane. Ian entered Vane's hut with a smile on his face, and purposely showed deference to Vane's seniority as his company commander, "Sir, a word."

Vane was a bit taken back by this friendly approach. He said, "Yes, Carlyle, of course, come in."

"Sir, as you know, our men look ragged, even as compared to the other companies of the battalion."

"I told you, Carlyle, I've done all I can," Vane replied, expecting another unpleasant confrontation.

"I know, sir, but I've heard it said, since my return, that the cause may be some neglect on your part."

Vane was startled, "What! Who says that lie?" He was on his feet and highly agitated.

"Well, sir, it's actually common talk in the mess. I tried to dissuade the critics, it being a reflection on me as well, but…"

"Damn them for the rascals they are," Vane said, pounding his fist into his palm.

"Aye, sir, that they are, but I may have a way to tread on their lies, if you'll bear with me."

Vane said, "Tread on them, yes, a bit of scheming, what? Tell me, Carlyle."

"Well, sir, next time we're in the siege lines alone, I propose we send out patrols, small ones mind, for the purpose of securing clothing items from dead or captured Russians…say heavy coats, good boots, gloves, that sort of thing. Begin clothing our boys in them, quietly. These lies can't continue once they see our men dressed better than theirs, what?" he mimicked Vane.

Vane fell into Ian's trap, "Can't Carlyle, have no authorization for such patrols, we, I couldn't do that. If I were caught, there'd be bloody hell to pay."

"That's the beauty, sir, I'll be the one in the trenches, not you. You stay clear of them. I'll send the patrols out, and if I get brought up for it, you can deny all knowledge. I'll use my influence at Raglan's Headquarters to get myself out of the shit. If it works, the credit is yours, if not, the blame is mine. What say you?"

"Hmm. Well, if I don't know about it, it certainly can't be blamed on me, can it? And I don't know about it, Carlyle, since you were never here, were you?" He actually winked at Ian.

"No, sir. I was never here." Ian left the hut, without saying another word, but with a satisfied smile. The way was open for the next move.

Chapter 62

The following morning, an hour before dawn, his quartet of 'culprits' returned, hardly missed, but with mixed news. MacGregor reported, "Sir, we found the goods, all right, but not their exact location."

"What does that mean?" Ian asked.

Swann popped up, "Well, sir, MacNab here found an old, ah, friend, right off, who's a quartermaster sergeant, working for a senior officer on the wharf. He says he knows right where to lay his greedy little hands on them goods we need. Trouble is, the bastard wouldn't tell us."

MacGregor added, "He wants coin, sir, says he'll only tell for a price. Says he knows we'll sell these items for a tidy sum, and wants his bit up front."

"How much?"

"Started out wanting two hundred quid, a bloody fortune, just to tell where the stuff is, but Fergie here used a bit of personal persuasion, and got him down to half that."

Ian looked astonished, asked, "Well? Who's this sergeant, Fergusson?"

"I'll let MacNab tell ye, sir, it's his friend." This was the first time Ian had seen MacNab up close. He was seedy looking, small and compact, with a mixture of false subordination and wild cunning in his attitude and expression.

In a low wheezy voice, MacNab said, "Sir, I used to do a bit of business with this here sergeant. All legal and open, mind. He was a right enough sort then, and ye can't fault him for trying to make something for himself, for the risk ye know. He's no idea what our boys are going through out here, comfy as he is in his nice warm quarters."

"So you think he knows where the goods are, and he'll tell us if we get him money?"

MacNab replied, "Aye, sir, and if he doesn't, well I'll take care of that me self. Trust me, sir, he'll tell."

"I admire your confidence, MacNab. You'd better be right. So the question is, where in hell am I going to come up with a hundred quid? I've sent for funds, but if they come at all, it won't be for weeks."

MacGregor chimed in, "Beggin' yer pardon, sir, but we thought about that. Swann's yer man. He…"

Ian silenced him by raising the flat of his hand, said, "Excuse us a moment, MacNab, I need to talk to these gentlemen alone."

"Right ye are, sir." He moved a good distance away and stood looking at the ground.

Ian said softly, "I think I know where this is going, and I don't know if I like it. I also don't know if I trust this MacNab."

"Aye, sir," said MacGregor, "well, we figure Swann here can come up with that paltry sum quick as you can blink, if you'll give him the go."

"Yes, sir," said Swann, "that I can, sir."

Ian rolled his eyes, thinking about Swann's pickpocketing past, said out loud, "Jesus, what have I gotten myself into? Don't answer that. Swann, if I give you 'the go,' I want three things."

Ian told them off, "There'll be no physical harm to anyone…you will only victimize rich civilian sods, who can afford it…and you won't get caught. Do you understand me, Swann? On your life, by God. Do you understand?"

"Yes, sir, I understand," Swann replied.

Ian asked, "Where are we to meet this quartermaster sergeant, and when?"

Fergusson said, "Aye, that's the finger in the pudding, sir. He can't meet before tonight, eight o'clock, at a tavern in Balaklava, called the Bull's Dick. It's not far from the sick wharf, where they put the stricken lads on ships for the Bosphorus."

Ian thought a moment, said, "Bloody hell, that means the men will have to go out in the trenches again tonight and freeze. Well, nothing for it. Colour Sergeant MacGregor, you take the men into the trenches. Mind, not a word to anyone what we're about."

MacGregor looked concerned, "What about Vane, sir?"

"You mean Captain Vane, MacGregor? I doubt you'll see him tonight. If you do, tell him I've been called away to Lord Raglan's headquarters on special business."

"Aye, sir, that I will."

"Good…Swann, you will go into town now and do what you must. Meet Fergusson and me at seven, at the sick wharf. Now be on yer way, lad." Swann saluted, and rushed off.

When Swann had gone, MacGregor said, "Sir, if you'll pardon me, I don't trust that sod, MacNab, either. He's a guardsman, but I think money is more on his mind than his loyalty to the regiment."

"What do you think, Fergusson?" Ian said.

"I know he was my suggestion, but I've a queasy feeling about 'em, since we come back from talking with his friend, sir," was Fergusson's reply. "Something ain't right."

Ian said, "I share your concerns, but I think we have to trust him for the time being. No choice at this point."

Ian turned to MacGregor, "Sorry you can't come along, Colour Sergeant MacGregor, but I need you with the men, and to protect my arse in case someone's sniffing about looking for me."

MacGregor understood, and responded, "Aye, sir. What about MacNab?"

"Aye, MacNab. Fergusson, have you been inside this Bull's Dick place?"

"Aye, sir."

"How many doors are there?"

"Three, I saw, sir, the front, the rear, and a side entrance to an alley."

Ian gave orders fast and sure, "Fergusson, you head toward town now, but a ways along, lay by the road. When MacNab passes, stay with him. I want to know what he does and where he goes. Find out what you can and meet Swann and me at seven by the sick wharf."

"Aye, sir, that I will, but if ye don't mind my asking, what'll you be doing?"

Ian winked, "Why Fergusson, I'm an officer, I'll be doing officer-like things." MacGregor nodded, and Fergusson merely turned somewhat red.

Ian continued, now serious, "You just stay with MacNab, and report to me later."

Fergusson said, "Aye, sir," saluted and hurried off.

Ian talked to MacGregor a few minutes to give Fergusson time, then motioned MacNab to them, "Sorry about that, MacNab. I'm grateful for your help. The whole company will be grateful."

"My pleasure, sir, besides, some a them clothes'll be mine."

"MacNab, here's what I want you to do. Go in town, and keep an eye on this sergeant friend of yours until this evening. I will join you at eight at this tavern, what is it, the Bull's Dick...quaint name. Any questions?"

MacNab asked, "What about the money, sir, with all due respect?"

This question sent a chill up Ian's spine. He replied, "Not your concern. I'll take care of the money."

When MacNab left, Ian and MacGregor looked at one another. MacGregor said, "Be careful tonight, sir. Be damned careful of that bastard for sure."

"Aye, that I will."

MacGregor wished Ian good luck and went about the business of preparing the company for another cold night in the trenches. Ian left the camp on Lindsay's extra horse about an hour later. He had a lot of work to do. He took a separate route across country heading west toward the French camps.

Chapter 63

Ian whispered, harshly, "Swann, over here."

"That you, sir... Mister Carlyle, sir?" Swann arrived at the sick wharf shortly before seven in the evening. The wharf was crowded with medical orderlies, doctors, and sick or wounded soldiers. Swann was walking by several large stacks of boxes on the wharf when he heard his name called out.

"Aye, Swann, it's me. Over here, out of the moonlight. What have you brought?" Ian was standing between the stacks, unseen in the shadows, wearing his long dark cloak. Fergusson was a distance away, hidden, but watching to see Swann wasn't followed. When Swann approached his officer, he saw Ian's pistol drawn and cocked, but aimed at the ground.

"A hundred quid it is, sir, all yours and no one hurt, or for that matter, any the wiser…as yet."

Ian smiled at the young London pickpocket, said kindly, "I'll trust your word on that, Swann."

"You have it, sir. Is Fergie here?"

Fergusson spoke from the shadows. "Aye, never far away, Swannie, lad. Good work." The lad beamed at the compliment, since it came from an old hand like Fergusson, who'd seen more and gotten away with more than all the old soldiers in their company combined. This was work Swann understood. *I may not have been the greatest pickpocket in old Londontown, but I be well ahead of these here folks in this horrible little part of the world.*

Ian said, "Fergusson – your report."

"Sir." He moved in closer and almost popped to attention, "MacNab's been cozying up to this here sergeant all day, sir. Not unexpected, that, but right chummy they was. Talkin' all secret-like, och, and smiling as though they had some great surprise in store for someone. The fat bloke and MacNab also talked to some right nasty foreign types what hung about, and…"

"Fat bloke?" Swann cut in.

"Aye, laddie, this here sergeant's as big as a house. It sure looked to me like MacNab were part of their doings. I think this is a trap, sir, to rob ye of the hundred quid, then kill us all."

"Why us all?" Ian asked.

Fergusson replied, "MacNab knows if he only killed you, he'd be for it from MacGregor and the rest of us. No, he has to get rid of us all. Likely plans to go back to camp and do in MacGregor as well."

Ian saw his point, "Is the tavern crowded?"

"Aye, sir, that it is, mostly them foreign types and a few odd navvies hanging about. I say we lay-by, find MacNab and that there turd of a sergeant alone later, beat the location out of the fat bastard's hide, then steal the goods ourselves."

"No, there's a better way," Ian replied quietly, but forcefully.

Swann added his opinion, "Maybe we should forget it, sir. Maybe it's too risky."

"Can't do that, Swann. I can't just forget it. I saw the bodies of our men this morning…my men. Three of them in one night dead of exposure. I can't stand by and see any more die, it's too late for us to back away now, too important to the men out there, freezing. We'll take our chances. I've a trick or two up my sleeve, and maybe they won't even try anything in the tavern. Let's get it done."

Fergusson managed to say, "but sir…"

"I said we go now, Fergusson," Ian interrupted, "and there'll be no more talk. I will go in with Swann. You wait outside. Make sure if we have to run, the path is open."

Fergusson replied, reluctantly, "Aye, sir, it'll be open." He thought: *This damned pigheaded officer is going to put us all in it this night. He should listen to those what knows the streets.*

Chapter 64

Ian walked the three blocks to the tavern with a sense of dread. The streets, if you could dignify them with that title, were narrow, dark, and filthy with all types of refuse and garbage, human and otherwise. This was the dirtiest town he had ever seen, and the squalor did nothing to help his forebodings.

The hundred pounds were tucked safely in his vest pocket. The faithful Swann walked a few steps behind. He caught Swann's red hair in the moonlight. He looked very small and frail for the task they were about to perform. Fergusson wasn't alone in his concerns. Ian, too, felt this wasn't right; it smelled. As he walked, he summoned his leopard. *Here beside me old friend. I'll need you tonight.*

Ian walked straight into the Bull's Dick Tavern by the front door. He entered a large room, with a long crude counter for serving, and several tables on the dirt floor. The whole place was put together piecemeal, from ship's planking and other bits, likely left over after the severe mid-November storm.

The patrons looked like a rough lot made up of Maltese, Greeks, Turks, and some foreign sailors. No navvies, and no British soldiers or sailors were in sight this night, with two exceptions: the fattest quartermaster sergeant Ian had ever laid eyes on, and, of course, MacNab, who looked like a smiling, evil rodent. They were both seated at a table toward the rear, staring at him.

Ian started to walk to their table, but soon found his way blocked. A half-dozen foreign types rose from their tables. They moved into his path, each of them holding either a club or a long knife, menacingly. Others in the room stood up, and Ian saw that they were also well armed, and moving to surround them. The largest one before them said, "You stop, English."

The sergeant, his fat face beaded with sweat, pushed through the group and said in an East London accent, "You'd be Carlyle, I'd guess. I'm Sergeant Nathanial Tweed." He said this as though Ian should have recognized his importance.

Ian responded with more aplomb than he felt, "That would be *Captain* Carlyle, Tweed, and, actually, I failed to hear a 'sir' in there, Sergeant, or did I miss it?"

"I ain't about to 'sir' the likes of you, piss-ant. Yer a dead man, and yer pup as well," he gestured at Swann, who took a slight step backward.

Ian looked around him, actually winking at Swann as their eyes met. Ian said casually without facing Tweed, "Do I take it our business transaction is faltering? Perhaps you might explain?"

"I'll explain, all right. Ya see I'll be taking that there money you've been holding onto for me, then I'll be asking these fine gentlemen to get rid of the two of you in the 'arbour. That done, I might just gather up those items you've been looking for and sell them to yer precious Guards me self, using, of course, these fine gentlemen as middlemen."

He gestured with a sweep of his arm toward the gang of wharf rats surrounding him, asked, "Now how does that sound, piss-ant?"

"It's a bloody great plan, laddie," Ian shook his head, "but it won't work. Shame though, it's a great plan."

Tweed began to be concerned, looked quizzically at Ian, thought: *He should be shaking now, but he's not. He's having me on. He's bluffing, but them eyes is hard as stones.*

Tweed said, "Yer funny, you are. Empty yer pockets on the counter…now."

Ian didn't move. Swann, standing slightly behind him, began to shake. *Oh, shit, sir, what have ya got us into? We're dead for sure.*

After a long silence, Ian lifted his eyes up beyond Tweed and nodded slightly as though recognizing someone at the rear of the tavern. The stillness was immediately broken by a loud clear voice that came straight out of Dublin, "I don't think so, boyo."

Fat Sergeant Tweed was startled at the piercing voice coming from behind him. He had just time to turn and see the head of a small man in the back, smiling at him, as he put a small whistle to his lips.

There was a shrill screech from the whistle, then a louder crash! This was followed by two more crashes. All three doors burst open, and in rushed an impressive number of dark-skinned giants, not one under six feet. They were bareheaded and wore greatcoats to ward off the cold, but underneath there was no mistaking the red baggy pantaloons and white leggings of the Zouaves. Each was armed with a sword-like bayonet, and did not look happy. As they quickly surrounded the occupants of the large room, it settled into a deadly quiet.

A short time before, outside the tavern, the Zouaves had arrived, led by their bantam Irish sergeant and his huge, bald-headed friend, Ahmed. Fergusson saw them and immediately understood all. He remembered how friendly his captain and the Irishman had been that day in the ravines around Inkerman.

He said, "Good evening...Sergeant Murphy, as I recall. Out for a stroll, are we?"

Murphy replied with equal disinterest, "Thought I'd exercise me legs a bit before turning in. Wet me whistle in the process. It's good for the soul, I'm told."

Fergusson asked, "May I join you?"

"But of course," Billy replied. "Ya might even want to precede us a bit."

Fergusson didn't understand at first, then thought: *Captain Carlyle, you sly fox. Well, I'd better get inside and find that bastard, MacNab, and his fat friend, before they bugger out a there.*

Chapter 65

Inside the tavern, no one had been more shocked than Swann when the doors crashed in. He stood, mouth open, as afraid for his life from the Zouaves charging into the room as he was from the wharf scum they were facing. Then he saw Ian, calmly waiting for the toughs in the room to comprehend what was happening. It dawned on him that his captain had planned and orchestrated this entire affair.

Ian saw Fergusson grab MacNab by the collar and shove him out the broken back door. The rawness of the silence became deafening. Ian said, calmly, "Drop your weapons."

Ian waited. Nothing happened. He shouted, "Now!" The men in the room looked around at the gleaming blades in the hands of the fierce Zouaves. Then, slowly, one at a time, there was the sound of clubs, guns, and knives clattering to the plank floor.

Ian exhaled in relief, as Billy Murphy came up behind and said over his shoulder, "Ian, me lad, must I forever be getting ya out a trouble?"

"Looks that way, Billy."

"Ya owe me more than one drink now."

Ian looked at his friend and mentor, eyes flashing, "I've an idea, Billy, you tell your Zouaves this bar is theirs, and this miserable lot as well. They can take everything here, all the whiskey, ale, food, and all that's in their pockets. I doubt anyone will complain, it's likely stolen goods anyway. Take it, Billy, all except this worthless fat pig here. I'll take him myself." Ian knew the Zouaves lived to plunder the spoils of their victories, and this was right good plunder.

"Now that's a fine idea, lad, and my boys'll love it, that they will. We'll get right to it, and I won't forget the rest of what we talked about either. I'll be waiting for word."

Ian grabbed the fat shocked sergeant by his oversized blue tunic, and hauled him toward the front door, "I'll see you later, Billy, have a bit of fun."

Outside, Fergusson met them. He was alone. Ian asked, "Where's MacNab?"

Fergusson replied, a satisfied look on his face, "Well, sir, the bastard got clean away. Slipped right through my fingers, sir. Last I saw a couple of them Zouaves was chasing him toward the harbour. With all that water about, sir, might be he'll fall and drown himself. Och, one way or another, I doubt we'll see his face again."

Ian suspected MacNab was dead, but said, "You don't seem too upset about losing him."

"No, sir, fact is I think he went on French leave, if ye get my meaning, sir. Perhaps the bloody provost will get him. Tomorrow at parade, MacGregor will report him not being present for duty. That'll be the end of it, sir."

"I think that should just about do it, Fergusson. Sorry you lost him though. I had a few choice words for him myself."

Fergusson said, "Ye shouldn't worry, sir, I think he knew you, me, and the boys in the trenches were a fair bit disappointed in him, right enough. Sir, what'll we do with this tub of blubber?" The fat sergeant's eyes were bulging out of their sockets, as the full extent of his massive miscalculations struck home.

Ian, his eyes turning black cold, looked directly at the sergeant, said, "Listen, you bastard...listen." Ian pointed back at the door of the Bull's Dick with his thumb.

Distinct sounds of a major altercation could be heard from inside the tavern. Tables were breaking, bottles crashing. Slowly, one or two at a time, the patrons came flying or staggering out the door, beaten bloody by Billy's Algerians and Frenchmen. Ian said, quietly, to no one in particular, "This whale has two choices. He can take us to exactly where the items we're seeking are located, or I'll turn him over to those red-legged devils, with orders that he should be cut to pieces and fed to their dogs."

He let Tweed ponder on his choices. The sergeant became amazingly cooperative. He led them to a large fenced-in area farther down the wharf. It was filled with boxes, bales, and barrels of all kinds. Although it was after nine in the evening, there was a lamp lit in the small office. An officer and sergeant were on duty. Tweed pointed out to Ian the exact boxes and bales where the items he wanted could be found.

Ian said, "Fergusson, you and Swann get rid of this obscene creature, then report back to me here." Then under his breath, "Don't kill him, mind, but make certain he isn't going to give us any trouble later. Go back to the tavern, fast as you can. Find my friend Murphy...you know, the Zouave sergeant. Tell him I need him now, and lead him back here."

They left, dragging Tweed. Ian took a deep breath, and walked boldly into the quartermaster's shack. He approached the young slightly built ensign on duty and announced, "You there, Ensign, I'm Captain Malcolm Vane, 1st Battalion, Scots Fusilier Guards. I'm here on a rather special mission…hush, hush, and all that. I wonder if you might be able to help me?" (Ian amused himself by using Vane's name. *What would he say?*)

As expected, the surprised ensign jumped from his chair to a rigid attention, as did his rather portly sergeant. *Why do all quartermaster sergeants tend toward the bovine, perhaps it's all that luxury at their fingertips.*

The ensign replied, "Yes, sir, what can I do for you?"

"Your name?"

"Trowbridge, sir, Ensign Trowbridge."

"You may start by filling this requisition. I'm in a great hurry, lad…look lively."

The ensign glanced briefly at the requisition. His eyes widened. He handed it to his sergeant, who examined it sceptically. The sergeant then inquired, "Excuse me, sir, but what mission would that be?"

Ian appeared outraged. He said to the ensign, ignoring the sergeant, "Trowbridge, is it your habit to allow your subordinates to question a Guards officer on a mission direct from headquarters?"

The ensign was confused, "Uh, no, sir. The sergeant is only following orders, sir, to be accountable for all items within our control, especially these type items."

"I see, well, if you must know, I can tell you this much. A special detachment of French and English soldiers is going off to a place I'm not at liberty to discuss. They will need this clothing to survive, and General Lord Raglan, himself, wants them well-equipped."

The sergeant replied, "Yes, sir, but I'm afraid we have no such items."

"No such items. No such items. Don't play silly buggers with me, lad. I've been told otherwise. By God, if yer lying to me, I'll have yer guts for garters. I'm going out there in the yard right now, and have a look. You'd both better come with me." Ian walked out the door, leaving them no choice but to follow.

He walked directly to one of the bales pointed out by Tweed, praying the fat bastard was not lying. Pulling out his sword with a flourish, he cut the heavy manila ropes binding the bale, and slit the side. It burst open. For a moment nothing happened. Ian's heart sank, then ten or twenty un-issued, warm sealskin coats spilled out onto the ground. The ensign turned pale. The sergeant was looking down, fidgeting with the requisition.

Ian said slowly, "You lied to me, gentlemen, both of you." He played his high card, "Ensign, did you look closely at the signature on that requisition?"

"Uh, no sir." The ensign took it from the sergeant and looked. His face changed colour again, "By Jesus, Sergeant, this is signed by the Quartermaster-General of the army, General Airey himself."

Ian stared the visibly shaken ensign down, "I'm not sure what I'll do about this, Ensign, but I suspect your career is ended, and, Sergeant, och, I'd be taking those stripes off now, before you embarrass yourself by having them ripped off."

The ensign said, rather pathetically, "Sir, I'm dreadfully sorry about the confusion. I had no right to refuse you or try to hold up your request. We were told these items were to be held for requisitions from only the most senior officers, and we were to deny their existence, if asked. I didn't see the general's signature, really I didn't. Ever so sorry, sir, we'll get these items sorted out at once."

Then he seemed to regain some composure and a little spine, as he commanded, "Sergeant, fill this requisition immediately, and I'll be talking with you later."

Ian directed, "Stack the goods by the compound gate."

"Sir," was the sergeant's simple reply.

The sergeant was a good deal stronger than his overweight appearance made Ian believe. An hour passed, while the sergeant, often physically assisted by the ensign, staged the items.

When the work was finished, Ian said, "Trowbridge, I've given this some serious thought while you were about your business. Perhaps you were merely trying to do your duty. Perhaps we could overlook this incident…perhaps."

"I'd be most grateful, sir, most grateful," the ensign pleaded.

"We'll see. You certain all the items are there? I don't want one shoe or mitten missing."

"Of course, sir, of course. I checked them myself."

There was a rumbling and creaking coming up the road outside the small quartermaster compound. In perfect timing they heard the unique sound of wagons being pulled along the road.

If there had been any lingering doubts by the ensign or the sergeant about the legitimate and secret nature of the 'mission' with our gallant French allies, they were swept away when they saw two wagons approaching, pulled by oxen, each driven by a Zouave, accompanied by a guardsman. Swann was riding on one, Fergusson the other. Tweed was nowhere to be seen.

When the stores were loaded on the wagons, Ian turned again to the ensign, "The only reason I'm letting either of you off for your actions is the secrecy attached to this special joint effort with our allies. For doing this, though, I want your word, both of you, that this incident will never be mentioned, to anyone. You will merely file the requisition, buried under many others, and forget we were ever here. Are we completely clear on this, Ensign Trowbridge…Sergeant?"

The sergeant nodded briskly, said, "Sir." He, too, looked visibly relieved.

The ensign said, "Never here…sir. I understand. You were never here."

"Very well, I'll hold you to that." He mounted the first wagon with Swann, and they drove away toward the wharf. Fergusson and Swann only managed to suppress their laughter for a short block, then it burst forth. The Zouave drivers caught on and began laughing also.

Fergusson said, "Good show, sir, you'd make a grand thief."

Ian swallowed the backhanded compliment, said, "I see our fat sergeant has disappeared. I won't ask."

Fergusson looked at him, said, "Best not, sir, but he ain't dead."

Ian picked up Lindsay's horse from where he'd tied it at the wharf, and they made their way as swiftly as possible over the muddy road back to the Guards camp. It was a rough road, but the oxen helped. It was almost dawn when, after skirting the camp, itself, they stopped near the zigzag trench leading forward to their sector of the advance parallel trenches. It was as close as they could get without taking fire as the dawn came.

They remained hidden until the relieving company moved past them and forward, into the zigzag. Ian then sent Swann and Fergusson to bring the company quickly and quietly to the wagons.

This was done with proper haste, as daylight was fast approaching. The men of 2nd Company were surprised to see the wagons, driven by French Zouaves, but didn't question their good fortune. The bales and boxes were broken open, and the items distributed to them on the spot.

A few of the items left over were given to the grateful Zouave drivers for their help. Ian sent them on their way with a short note thanking Billy. As dawn arrived, the adventure was almost over.

Ian looked out at the grateful faces of his little band of guardsmen, now considerably warmer, and ready to march back to camp. The last thing he did was remind MacGregor that they needed to make the outside clothing dirty, and tell to their death the made-up stories of how each of them took these pieces from Russian dead, wounded, or prisoners.

MacGregor and Fergusson saw to it that each one of the men knew what Ian had done, and the enormous risks he'd taken himself and with his career…for them. As Ian looked into their eyes, he almost cried to see the quiet joy, the renewed sparkle that a bit of decency and warm clothing gave them. He felt good about what they had done this night.

Chapter 66

Captain Vane knew he'd been deceived, there being no way the entire company could have gotten the exact same clothing for each man from the Russians, in the same night. He asked around a bit, but each man had a separate, and most ingenious story as to how they had gone hunting while on patrol, and had seized the clothing from Russian bodies or prisoners they'd subsequently released to some vague, unknown provost, who happened to come by at just the right time.

No one could quite figure it out, including the other companies, their officers, or Lieutenant Colonel Seymour, commanding the battalion, but they did know that somehow Ian had been involved. When Ian was asked by his friend Robert Lindsay at the officers' mess table, he replied, blandly, "It does seem amazing, doesn't it, Robert? Why I am as flabbergasted as you are by the whole affair."

His reaction in the mess only added, grudgingly, to their respect for him and his reputation as an unorthodox, eccentric, but resourceful young officer. Ian didn't mind that reputation in the least, now that his friend Lindsay had made him aware of it. He found himself, in fact, rather proud of it.

Vane, for his part, basked in some of the glory for taking such good care of his men, masterminding the entire adventurous plot, carried out, of course, by that man, Carlyle. Since there seemed to be no repercussions, from any quarter, including the quartermaster department, Vane was quite content to let things be.

Something else mysterious occurred in camp over the next fortnight. Two or three wagons full of cut, dry firewood began showing up every few days at the 2nd Company camp. These were a Godsend, and the men were actually able to get dry after trench duty, boil water for coffee, and cook meals. Using his friendship with Lindsay to ensure equitable distribution, Ian shared this wood with the other companies and battalion headquarters.

Oddly, though, the wagons hauling the wood were pulled by oxen, in short supply in the British army, and driven by Algerian Zouaves, who professed, when challenged, to speak no English. They always smiled politely, gibbering away in their native tongue. Ian was seen to slip them a little something for their trouble, which he took from his own purse.

A few weeks later, Colonel Seymour called Ian and Lindsay to his tent, "Ah, Carlyle, I've spoken with Lindsay here, and he's flatly refused to discuss it as a matter of honour. I must ask you, Carlyle, do you happen to know anything about the wood arriving every week, apparently from the French camp?"

"Why yes, sir, I do," was Ian's reply, surprising both Lindsay and the colonel. "Actually, sir, I'm afraid I'm responsible. You see I was playing cards with a French officer a few weeks ago, and luck was with me. I fear I won a dreadful sum. The poor chap was beside himself, and unable to pay his debt. He pleaded with me to allow him to satisfy his obligation as a gentleman in some manner, or he'd be forever disgraced."

"Whole thing seems a bit odd, you ask me," Seymour injected.

"He's repaying it the best way he knows how. I'm afraid I agreed to it, sir, rather than allow a fellow officer to disgrace himself, even a Frenchman. It appears the wood was brought from France as cargo when the wood shortage became acute over in the French camp. A unique method of handling a wood shortage, isn't it, sir? Our own senior command has apparently not thought of it. I do hope I haven't caused an inconvenience, sir." Lindsay, who knew the entire true story, cleared his throat.

Seymour was no fool either. He didn't believe a word of it, and the remark criticizing the English senior command did not go unnoticed. The Colonel replied, with an amused tone in his own voice, "Inconvenience? I should think not. On the contrary, my boy, do keep it up."

He dismissed the two officers, mumbling, "Carry on, gentlemen, carry on. Cards indeed, my word, here's one for the senior officers to chew on." Ian and Lindsay left the colonel's tent. Lindsay turned to his friend and said, "Ian, should you ever need anything, anywhere, anytime, I'm your man. I mean that Ian, you may call on me as your friend."

"Thank you, Robert, likewise."

Chapter 67

It was early February. Wood was steadily arriving from Billy's Zouaves, but there was precious little food to cook on the fires. Ian had as yet not heard from his father, and there was little he could do to increase their food rations with what money he had of his own.

Vane listened to Ian's recommendation and promoted Fergusson to sergeant. All of the other sergeants, save MacGregor, were dead, in hospital, or invalided home. Although the men were warmer and drier, their time in the trenches was becoming more difficult. There were fewer and fewer men to secure the same assigned length of trench. The Russians, realizing the pathetic state the British were in, increased their sorties.

Vane's continual absence from the trenches became an embarrassment, even at battalion level. He was admonished to be with his company when they were there for duty, and began, reluctantly, spending nights with his men.

"How are the men, MacGregor?" Ian asked.

"Fine, sir, but it's damned hard to keep the sentries awake. 3rd Company had a man bayoneted in his sleep the other night."

Ian said, "Lets you or Fergusson or me, one of us, be out there on and off running the line of sentry posts left to right at all times. That might keep them on their toes."

MacGregor saw the tiredness in his officer, replied, "Being done, sir, Fergie's out there now. I'm up next. Perhaps ye might get some sleep, sir. Och, you're no good to us if ye keel over…sir."

Ian was about to respond with some sarcastic remark when a musket volley rang out! It was a full volley, close by, but not theirs. Dirt flew from the forward escarpment. A guardsman peering over the top grabbed his face, screaming, as he was projected onto the back wall of the trench. He was dead before he slid to the trench floor, a small hole at the bridge of his nose, a gapping hole in the back of his head, brains spilling, blood everywhere.

MacGregor was sorting out the men, as they ran out of their resting holes, slamming them up onto the fire step in their places along the trench. Ian ordered, "Independent fire, commence firing." A trickle of firing came from their men. With MacGregor and Ian shouting encouragement, within seconds the trickle became a somewhat respectable rolling volume of fire.

Half a dozen sentries came bounding and scrambling into the trench from their posts out front, Fergusson among them. They'd taken the brunt of the first Russian volley, and were missing two men. Three others were wounded. As soon as they jumped into the trench, even the wounded bounced back onto the forward parapet to return fire. This wasn't bravery or fortitude so much as self-preservation. The Russians were not taking prisoners.

Vane came scurrying up from the tiny officer's hut in the connecting trench, all tousled from awakening, adjusting his uniform, sword belt, equipment, pulling on his forage cap. He stood in the trench trying to see over the parapet. He was about to say something to Ian, when one of the men shouted, "Look out, sir."

Ian ducked from reflex, but Vane was not so quick. A large Russian leaped over the parapet into the trench, bayonet forward. His downward plunging thrust put his bayonet, muzzle deep in Vane's chest, and pinned him to the back wall of the trench. The Russian was clubbed to death quickly from the side, as he frantically tried to pull his weapon free. Vane was left hanging there like a fly specimen, the musket protruding straight out from his chest. There was a curiously surprised look on his death mask, the expression saying: *But, Carlyle, I was just standing here. I was just alive. What happened, old boy?*

More Russians were coming into the trench, killing his men. Ian's thoughts raged: *No. No. You bastards. No more of them.*

Ian didn't have time to draw his sword or pistol, he saw a Russian smashing down with the butt of his musket into the head of a man Ian had just been talking to, Private MacKay. Ian felt the beast emerge, felt the rage of madness for the first time, no thought of fleeing. He grabbed a shovel leaning against the trench wall, and held it in both hands, swinging it down with all his strength striking at the Russian who killed MacKay. The edge of the shovel sliced into his head, . splitting it open like a melon.

Ian stood, shovel across his chest, searching for a target, a victim, saw an enemy struggling with Sergeant Fergusson. Ian cried, "No, damn you."

The Russian's back was to Ian. He put the long handle of the shovel over the Russian's head, pulling it back under his chin hard with both hands, choking his life away as he hauled him off Fergusson. He heard the neck crack, a funny sound, then let go.

The blood lust was upon him now. No stopping it. He ranged about for another victim, and found two Russians heading straight at him, bayonets forward. He used the shovel like a giant claymore sword, swinging back and forth, knocking the bayonets aside, easily. He struck the one to his left in the head with the flat of the shovel, reared back and smashed his right elbow into the Russian to his right.

The one on the left was down…sinking in the ooze at the trench bottom. He concentrated on the one on his right, smashing his head over and over with the flat of the shovel until it was pulp. Ian swung around to finish the other lying on the trench floor. The terrified Russian's rifle was gone, hands up in front of his bloody head, obviously pleading for mercy.

Ian raised the shovel to full arms' length above his head, but was stopped from cleaving the man in two by strong hands holding his arms. He struggled to get free, continue his rampage. It was Fergusson and MacGregor holding his arms tightly, pulling him back.

Fergusson said, firmly, "Easy, sir, easy. It's over. Man's surrendering. He's done for. Ye have ta let him be, sir."

MacGregor asked, "Are you all right, sir? Yer covered in blood, sir. Are ye all right?"

Ian realized he was eagerly looking about for another target for his rage, his madness, but the trench was empty of live Russians, except for the one at his feet, surrendering. He slowly calmed himself, dropped the bloody shovel. Forcing the beast back down, he turned and saw Vane staring at him a few feet away, with that odd look still there. He looked down and saw that Vane's feet were a foot above the bottom of the trench. He was indeed dangling, skewered in place by the Russian bayonet.

Ian grabbed the musket and pulled the bayonet out of Vane's chest, watching, expressionless, as blood spurted from the unplugged hole, and Vane crumpled to the trench floor. MacGregor and others were trying to help him. Someone said, "Sir, you're in command of the company now. We're your men now, sir, and that's for certain."

He couldn't think, said, breathless, "Take care of Captain Vane."

He felt it coming, had to get out of there, felt himself losing control, what sanity left was slipping away. He pushed guardsmen from his path, stumbled down the zigzag to the officer's hut, dropped to his knees on the floor and began sobbing, uncontrollably. It wasn't the hot, sweaty fear of death or mutilation, as it had been at the Alma River, or other places along his journey to now. It was fear of a different kind. A cold, terrible fear that this war was making him lose his mind…making him an animal.

There was a horrible truth in this. An appalling recognition that he hadn't controlled the leopard this time. It had controlled him, demanding, powerful, all consuming. He was its toy, its victim. My God, he buried that shovel in the man's head, enjoyed the feel of it, the taste of it, and looked for more.

He would never again be able to see the leopard the same way. Either he could no longer control it, or, more likely, he'd never controlled it. Had it just been teasing him? Had he been deluding himself?

He knew the dreadful truth. *What amazing vanity is within man. The beast allowed me to think it a friend, when it was actually my worst enemy, something I must fight, constantly. It is so bloody clear now – so dreadfully, terribly clear.*

At last Ian had achieved his dream. He was a company commander in the Scots Fusilier Guards. He was leading men in battle. With the realization of his dream, it had indeed become a nightmare.

Chapter 68

They buried Captain Malcolm Vane with honours, just outside their camp, near the windmill. Captain Ian Carlyle was the new commander. On 20 February 1855, Colonel Rokeby, the Guards Brigade commander, announced that they were being relieved of trench duty altogether until they could bolster their numbers with guardsmen returning from convalescence or replacement drafts from England.

What was left of the Guards Brigade were moved to freshly built wood huts on the north side of Balaklava Harbour, where they set up housekeeping to await the arrival of more men. Their duties were light in comparison. They drilled, were called upon for various fatigue details, guarded their camp, and generally rested.

A week after arriving at the new camp, Ian received a note from Major Capecci:

My Dear Ian,

I have enclosed a card I recently received. This woman is reported to be knowledgeable in treating such ills as dysentery, jaundice, diarrhoea and even cholera, from which I know your men suffer daily. She is said to use natural remedies. More importantly, she may even be a source of extra food, although I expect you'll have to pay some for it.

Sir John Campbell, I think he knows your father, advised me that she has arrived at the harbour and set up somewhere along the wharf. She is building a permanent "hotel" not far from here. Sir John seems quite keen on her. Met her in the Islands or some such.

As your camp now lies overlooking the harbour, I thought you might inquire if she would be in a position to assist you with your men. If I can help, please allow me the honour of doing so.

YOS,

Antonio

Enclosed was a card, which read:

British Hotel

Mrs. Mary Seacole

(Late of Kingston, Jamaica)

Respectfully announces to her former kind friends, and to the Officers of the Army and Navy generally, that she has taken her passage in the screw-steamer 'Hollander,' to start from London on the 25th of January, intending on her arrival at Balaklava to establish a mess-table and comfortable quarters for sick and convalescent officers.

Ian wasn't quite certain what good this woman, who seemed to be looking to open an enterprise for officers and for profit, could do for his men, but she was close, and he was desperate. Late the following afternoon he mounted Savage, who had been brought down to the new camp, and rode to Balaklava. He arrived in town about seven o'clock, not quite dark yet, and asked around for this Mary Seacole.

An old sailor told him, "Many knows her around here. Some calls her Mother Seacole. Comes to the wharf sometimes, gives hot drinks to the wounded afor they're shipped to hospital."

"I heard she was a sutler of some kind," Ian replied with no little disdain in his tone.

"Well, she is, but she still spends time helping the wounded on the wharf. Them poor wretches needs it. Seen her one time give up her very own cloak to warm a chilled and dying soldier. Now mark me, in her store down there, she likes to turn a profit right enough, but she doesn't try to cheat us out of our last ha-pence." The old sailor gave Ian a look that would roast chestnuts, said no more, stalking away mumbling to himself something about "bloody officer bastard..."

Well, that went well, Ian thought, and rode on. It wasn't all that difficult to find what he was looking for. Along the wharf toward the harbour's entrance he came upon a rather large area stacked eight or ten feet high with huge boxes, baskets, barrels, and other containers of all sorts. Collectively these were arranged on three sides of a large open-front enclosure, covered in canvas.

It was getting darker, but Ian could see that the inside had counters made of planking supported by barrels, and well-stocked shelves of similar construction. There were three business areas: a store, an officers' mess of sorts, and a rankers' canteen. A kitchen serviced the mess and the canteen. The store stocked everything from writing materials and linens, to wild fowl, coffee, poultry, fresh eggs, bacon, tobacco, and cigars.

In the officers' mess there were English, French, and Turkish army and naval officers lounging about smoking pipes, talking gaily, and drinking beer, wine, and whiskey. Suspending the reality of the makeshift tented structure; it looked very much like the United Services Club of London.

The canteen was busy catering to soldiers and sailors from different regiments and ships. There wasn't the usual raucous gambling, drunkenness, or vulgar behaviour customary among other ranks in such places, yet everyone seemed to be having a grand time.

There were several Greeks and Turks serving guests in both the officers' mess and the rankers' canteen. At the counter in the store portion was a tall, thin man of at least fifty, in neat civilian attire, a white shirt, brown patterned cravat, brown vest and brown, Norfolk style, tweed jacket. He had a full, thick black growth of beard, topped by a small-brimmed black-felt hat. It was to this man to whom the employees paid deference. His orders were crisp, but not unkind, with a soft, yet demanding quality. He was obviously in charge.

Ian approached the civilian gentleman, asking, "Excuse me, sir, but where might I find a Mrs. Mary Seacole?"

The man was about to give him a don't-bother-me-I'm-busy answer, when he noticed Ian was a Guards officer. He replied, "Good evening, sir, I'm Thomas Day, one of the proprietors. Welcome. Afraid you've missed Mrs. Seacole until tomorrow, she sleeps aboard ship and is retired for the evening." Mr. Day had a soft, pleasant voice, and an easy manner.

Ian said, "That's a shame, sir. I can rarely find time to get down this far, and I'd like to explore some business with her." He shaded the truth only slightly by adding, "I was referred to her by Lord Raglan's headquarters."

"Ah, yes, His Lordship," Mr. Day raised an eyebrow, said, "Well, sir, I manage matters related to the accounting side of the business, and Mrs. Seacole manages merchandise. In what area was your business?"

"Actually, I am in need of victuals, and possibly Mrs. Seacole's services in the medical arena."

Day pondered, "I have a suggestion. My wife arranges much of Mrs. Seacole's affairs, and for that matter much of my own. Perhaps you might talk to her before you leave?"

"I'd be happy to do so, sir, especially if it'll save me another trip."

Day beckoned to a young man, a Turk, working behind another counter, "Omar, go fetch Mrs. Day, quickly now." The young man hurried out.

Mr. Day bowed slightly, excusing himself, and went to serve other customers.

Ian waited for a good ten minutes. There was a soft sensual voice behind him, "Sir, I'm Mrs. Day, may I assist you?" The most pleasant sexual sensations were aroused in Ian at the wondrous sound of it.

He spun around dumbfounded, to look into the gorgeous, sultry, and equally surprised eyes of Jasmine.

Chapter 69

They were both in shock, neither one able to speak. Ian was about to throw his arms around her. She saw this with horror, and brought him up short, raising a hand, the palm toward him, saying sharply and clearly, "Yes, sir...As I said, sir, I'm Mrs. Day...(*slowly*)...Mrs. Thomas Day...the wife of the owner here. The gentleman I believe you've been conversing with. How may I assist you?"

All Ian could manage was, "Uh, yes, uh, Mrs. Day, you know I completely forgot a prior engagement. I think it best I come back tomorrow and speak directly with Mrs. Seacole, if you don't mind."

Jasmine replied, with an almost physical show of relief, "Yes, well, whatever you think best. She'll be in around half ten."

Ian walked out, saying, "Good, I'll try to be here around half ten tomorrow. My thanks, Mrs. Day." He left and walked slowly to his horse with mixed feelings of joy, confusion, and curiosity.

Before he could mount Savage, a hand tugged at his coat. The young Turk who had gone to fetch Jasmine earlier was there. He said, "Soger not go. I am Omar. Work for Miss

Jasmine. She says you trust me. She says you come with me. Leave horse here, come with me – hurry – quick, quick."

Ian followed a few blocks up into the town away from the wharf area to a small Turkish eating establishment. Omar sat him at a table, said, "My brother, she own this place. You stay. Her come."

Ian ordered a cup of strong, sweet Turkish coffee, with great anticipation, curiosity growing. Thirty minutes later, Jasmine came in, wearing a cloak with a hood over her head, hiding her face. Omar followed her, but remained at the door talking excitedly to a man who could have been his twin. Jasmine was extremely nervous as she sat at the table, and grabbed his hand in both of hers.

She said, "Ian, thank you so much for your quick thinking. You're a true friend."

Ian smiled, "I'm also a true lover, Jasmine, who has not recovered from the shock. What in God's name is going on? You're married? Are you in some trouble? What are you doing here? Are you in some way being held against your will?"

Jasmine looked perplexed, said, "No. No. Not at all. Oh, you're so wrong."

Then she smiled warmly, said, "Your concern for me does our friendship and our love affair great honour, but, for the first time in my life, Ian, I feel pleasantly happy and most secure. You see I knew Thomas long before you and I met, long before I worked at the Red Lion. He came back into my life unexpectedly. I married him last year, a few months after you left."

Ian's mind reflected involuntarily on those wonderful nights in London. He had been examining his feelings about her being married while he waited, sipping his coffee, clearing his swimming head. He said, "I must admit I wondered why

I never heard from you, but when we were together, you never mentioned him."

Jasmine continued, "It was in the past. He and I lost touch. I thought I'd never see him again. I worked for him in Portsmouth, where he had a business supplying ships with stores and victuals. He wanted more from me than I could give at the time, and I felt, in good conscience, I had to leave his employ.

"After a few years on my own, some very hard years, like my time with Sidney and all that, I ended up at the Red Lion. Not long after you left, Thomas found me, much as Sidney had, but in this instance with a more joyous result."

Ian was listening, intently. Although she wanted a reaction, his face remained expressionless.

"He was very gentle, sincere, and persuasive. You had left. We both knew we were destined to be no more than friends and occasional lovers. When I thought of my situation and my future prospects at the Red Lion, I found myself far more amenable to his companionship in the long term."

Ian looked deep into her eyes, "Jasmine, do you love him?"

"I love him for the dear, sweet man he is. It isn't a passionate love, Ian, no fires within or explosions. Can you understand?"

"I think so."

"It has become, over time, a different sort of love. The kind of love that faces life's hurdles, and withstands them, blow for blow. A warm, sustaining feeling. I can look at him across a room and actually feel the intense warmth. I feel I must go to him immediately and touch his hand, or I'll burst. That sort of love, Ian, can you understand that?"

"I'm trying to understand."

"Perhaps some day you will."

They looked at each other tenderly and silently for a long time. He could see it in her eyes now. The intense warmth sparkling out of them, and he knew.

The warmth was contagious. He finally said, "Jasmine, I do understand, and I couldn't be happier for you. Now, you must tell me everything. How did you and your husband end up on the Balaklava wharf, selling goods to soldiers?"

Jasmine's fervour showed in her tone and her words, "Thomas is a business partner with Mrs. Mary Seacole, and also I think some kind of distant relative."

Ian said timidly, "I must tell you I've heard rather bad stories of the sutler's trade."

"As have we," Jasmine replied, determinedly, "but we are not that sort of sutler. We gain our business through support from Mrs. Seacole's numerous important connections within the army. Our merchandise comes from England and France, purchased wholesale at reasonable prices. Thomas and Mary are resolute that they will pass these prices with a modest profit on to our customers. So far it's working, with the exception of unrelenting and serious losses from theft while we remain on the wharf."

Ian said, "I do know Mary Seacole is well thought of by Sir John Campbell."

"That's true, Ian, and he's only one. There are several of your officers who know of her and support her efforts."

"I now command a company of men, my men," Ian said, "who have great needs, which the army, in its present state, is unable to provide. I was hoping that Mrs. Seacole could help."

Jasmine became intently interested, "Frankly, Ian, I'm certain Mary will help, if she can. What exactly do you require?"

"They're currently on half rations. I need food to keep them healthy. Right now they're too weak to fight off any diseases. They mostly suffer from dysentery, diarrhoea, and cholera. It's my understanding that Mrs. Seacole has had some success in treating these diseases with herbs or other natural remedies. The problem is that I have no funds. I've written my father asking, but haven't received a reply. They need help now, and there's no time to wait on the slowness of the post. I was hoping for a line of credit, or something."

Jasmine's shrewdness crept into her voice, "Mrs. Seacole has some skills, and I've an idea hatching. You must allow me to think on this overnight. Can you come tomorrow? I'll introduce you to Thomas, properly, and to Mrs. Seacole. You'll like her."

"If you think she can help, I'll be here every day." They kissed on parting, with the warmth of old friends, but neither could suppress the physical passion and intense sexual memories the kiss brought back.

Chapter 70

By half ten next morning, Ian was at the establishment. Thomas Day was there to greet him. Thomas said, "Well, good day Captain Carlyle. It is a pleasure to meet an old friend of my wife." Obviously, he and Jasmine had talked.

Ian said, "Likewise, Mr. Day. May I first extend my congratulations to you both on your marriage. I must say, sir, you've chosen a wonderful woman, my compliments."

"Please, do call me Thomas, and, if I may, I'll call you Ian."

Ian smiled broadly, "Of course."

Jasmine, who hadn't said a word, sighed visibly, with relief and joy.

Thomas quickly turned to business, "Mrs. Seacole should be here at any moment. Let's go in and have tea, or coffee, if you prefer. We can discuss your proposal as soon as Mary arrives. I, for one, am quite interested."

Ian had not the foggiest idea what he was talking about, since he had made no proposal, but he saw Jasmine wink at him, and played along, "Yes, that's fine, coffee, if you don't mind."

They were at the table sipping when Mary arrived, with a flourish, all bustle, wicker baskets, red ribbons flowing from her brimmed wide-awake hat, and all business. Ian was rather startled to be looking at a light-skinned Negro woman, at least in her fifties. He never would have suspected Mary Seacole was a Negress, a mulatto, and that old, although for the life of him, he couldn't figure out why he was surprised. She was, after all, from Jamaica, and they did call her 'mother' Seacole.

"Ah, a handsome young officer of Guards." Her voice was soft and refined, her diction would hold its own among the best of London society.

Jasmine was quick to introduce Ian, formally, "Mrs. Mary Seacole, may I present Captain The Honourable Ian David Carlyle, Scots Fusilier Guards...and Mary, be careful, I've known this charming man a few years. He will talk you out of all you own."

Ian burst into a bright smile, said, "Mrs. Seacole, a pleasure."

"I see. Well, you'd better call me Mary, if we're to be that close," she laughed.

Ian replied, "Mary it shall be, and I'm Ian. It's an honour to meet you, Mary. Your reputation certainly precedes you, and does you great credit. You seem to have many avid supporters among our most prestigious officers."

Mary beamed at the words of praise, "Oh, pish-posh, I've only done what I thought necessary, and, Jasmine, love, you're absolutely right about this one's charm. I must be careful when we talk business." Mary's tea was already made and waiting, served deferentially by two Turkish servants as she sat, placing her baskets and bundles down next to her chair. She accepted their attentiveness with the grace of an aristocrat.

Ian watched her as she moved and was served. Mary Seacole was indeed fifty, but was obviously much younger in spirit. She had black, tightly curled hair, with the barest hint of grey. It surrounded a gentle and pleasing face, smooth skin, and wide, kind eyes that captured you instantly. She had a full figure, with a portly frame.

Her only jewellery was a set of simple earrings. She wore a plain, but attractive, yellow dress, with petticoats beneath, to allow more freedom of movement than a crinoline, no doubt. A warm heavy brown cloak covered the whole ensemble. When she smiled, which Ian noticed was almost constantly, her face beamed radiantly, like the soft, gentle, glowing picture of every man's mother. With all her quiet wholesomeness, Ian suspected she possessed keen business acumen.

Mary said, "You know we have something in common, Ian…Scottish roots. I was born Mary Jane Grant. My father was Scottish."

Ian turned on that part of his brain that would forever be in Scotland, saying in his most charming brogue, "A course, Mary, och, I knew the moment I heard the wondrous soft lilt in yer voice. Ye can no forget that amazing sound. It bespoke the highlands to me at once."

"Oh, well," Mary said, "my, my, Jasmine, my goodness." That did it. Mary was a captive of this handsome young highlander. He could have most anything he wanted, and Jasmine, who had adroitly orchestrated the entire meeting, knew it, and was ecstatic.

They continued to converse in pleasant harmony. Jasmine waited, chose her time, and then suggested, "Mary, last night Ian proposed the most extraordinary business to me. I've already confided it, in part, to Thomas. It seems his men are camped north of the harbour, in sort of a rest status, with limited duties. They are just back from the trenches, but are still on half rations, weakened from months in those trenches, and have insufficient nourishment to bring back their strength. Need salt beef, biscuits, vegetables, fruits, and the like. Poor lads are suffering daily from camp diseases, including cholera. He hoped you might be able to bring some comfort there."

Mary said, "I see."

"Problem is, at the moment Ian has no funds."

"Hmmm, well, Ian, I'm afraid my medical services are highly overrated. I've some experience in the tropics with the odd epidemic, but my skills lie more in remedies that have come down through my family, rather than your traditional medicine. There's not much cost involved there. If your men could arrange to get here, I'd be happy to do what I can, but my business rather prevents me from travelling too far astray. The cost of raw food to feed a company of men is another matter, and more in Thomas' domain than mine."

Ian started to speak, but Jasmine interjected, "Yes, that's why I thought his proposal so mutually beneficial."

Jasmine looked hard at them both, then to Thomas said, "You complain constantly, both of you, of the thieving by our Greek and Turkish helpers, to say nothing of the wharf rats around here, and the loveable, but ruthlessly cunning Zouaves. 'Well,' says Ian last night, 'I have honest, disciplined guardsmen, the best soldiers in the English army. I could provide them to guard your goods until you have settled in your more permanent location, away from the wharf, or until our duties take us elsewhere.'"

She continued, "I'm assuming that what he'd want in return for this guard service would be food, and whatever help you could give his men, free of cost…based on the money we'd save without thievery taking place."

Jasmine, having finished, turned to Ian, whose mouth dropped partially open in awe and amazement, "Ian, I hope you don't mind my summing up your proposal. Did I forget anything?"

Ian, fascinated by Jasmine's intellect, and delighted by her brilliantly contrived solution to his problem, hesitated only the briefest moment before exclaiming, perhaps a bit too loudly, "Absolutely perfect, Jasmine."

Thomas, ever the businessman, asked, "How many men, Ian?" He was already calculating the cost of the food against the cost of losses through thievery that having guards on their goods would prevent. They were losing a massive amount each day.

"Let's call it fifty men," Ian exaggerated, "and we should only require the food until we are off half rations. I'd say no more than four to six weeks."

Mary was smiling again, "Well, Ian, you've convinced me, by heaven. What say you, Thomas, can we strike a bargain with this handsome officer?" She saw that this little plot was more Jasmine's mind at work than Ian's idea.

Thomas was still calculating, then rose from the table, his hand outstretched toward Ian, "Yes, by damn, I think we can." Ian shook hands first with Thomas, then with Mary, binding the deal.

Thomas sat down with Ian, and they talked through the details. Thomas said, "Our troubles are not during daylight. The few trusted servants, together with the roving provost patrols keep such activities down then. If you can give us two men, say from six in the evening to six in the morning, we have a bargain that will benefit us all."

Mary added, "As for the medical treatment, send me your major cases tomorrow, I'll also have a look at the guards for a while as they report for duty. We'll have your men in parade order before you know it. How does that suit?"

"Almost perfect, but there are a few cases I'd be hard pressed to have travel here. If I had a cart pick you up and return you, could you make a few visits to our camp?"

Mary said, "Of course, my boy." She looked at Jasmine, "I can deny him nothing. You must protect this old woman from giving him her entire wealth." They both laughed.

Jasmine said, "I told you so, Mary."

Ian blushed, "Then it's a bargain all round, and my thanks to all of you, especially you, Jasmine, for arranging this meeting and for so eloquently stating my proposal. It was a pleasure meeting you, Mary, Thomas, but I really must return to my duties."

Ian had a great deal to do now to make this work. He rode swiftly back to camp, summoned MacGregor and Fergusson, and explained the proposal. They were overjoyed.

MacGregor said, "Sir, you are the one, you are. The boys'll not mind at all, especially if they get more food and can visit the canteen in the process."

Ian said, "On their way back from guard detail, of course, Colour Sergeant – on their way back...right?"

"Right, sir, right as rain."

Fergusson said, "I'll send one of the lads to Mrs. Seacole first light tomorrow, with a cart. Bring her back here for a quick look at our two worst cases. They can't bloody-well move right now – one with dysentery, the other bad diarrhoea, possibly the cholera."

Ian was dead-on serious when he said, "Colour Sergeant, I'll count on you to tally off the men each day, set up the guard roster, and see it's kept. I'll need a copy. No interference with our battalion duties, understand, that's the only way this'll work, with no one suspecting. Not a word to anyone, hear? No one hears of this outside the company. If any of the guards on duty are sought after, send the curious buggers to me. I'll tell them I have the man on special detail. Any questions?"

"None, sir," MacGregor replied. They both saluted, and were off. The lads were more than willing. It was less than a week before they were on a routine schedule for guard and medical visits, as well as receiving food.

Swann "found" an old cart and a small, emaciated horse, no one seemed to claim. The cart transported the guard detail each day. It would come back to camp above the harbour with the cart full of the next day's supplemental rations. The sergeants would then quietly distribute them for cooking.

Mary and Thomas were most generous and the quantities were well over the needs of the company. Any extra rations were given to battalion hospital for the sick and wounded. They asked no questions.

Their luck held. No one seemed the wiser. The rank and file winked at one another, and there wasn't a man who wouldn't have marched into the gates of hell for Captain Ian David Carlyle.

Chapter 71

The bargain with the firm of Seacole and Day was only required for three or four more weeks, but ran as smooth as clockwork until then. It remained a well-kept secret, known only to Mary, Thomas, Jasmine, Ian, and the 2nd Company, 1st Battalion, Scots Fusilier Guards, who were exceedingly well fed.

By May 1855, many things changed. The men were taken off half rations, as supplies began arriving in bulk. The railway from Balaklava to the trenches on the heights before Sevastopol was completed, and supplies ran continuously to the troops. The 'British Hotel' as Mary Seacole envisioned it never quite materialized, but she and Day did manage some random huts inland on the heights near the camps. Eventually, Thomas, Jasmine, and Mary moved there with all their goods.

Replacements for the Guards Brigade began arriving in earnest. The Sardinian troops arrived, as well, allowing Major Antonio Capecci to take command of a battalion of his own Bersaglieri in the field.

Ian often visited Jasmine, Thomas, and Mary, in their new home. He also brought Lindsay and his friends from Lord Raglan's headquarters there for parties, catered by Mary. These parties were sponsored by funds he finally received from his father, unfortunately after they were no longer urgently needed.

For some weeks, Jasmine had been acting oddly. She avoided talking directly to Ian. He would catch her looking strangely at him from a distance. When he smiled at her, she'd quickly turn away.

He finally found her alone, except for the faithful Omar, shopping for small items at the market in Balaklava. He asked her, "Did I do something to offend you?"

She responded by pulling him behind a vendor's stall, and unexpectedly kissing him sensually on the lips, burying her tongue deep in his mouth for a long time. She said, "That's why, Ian, you bloody great fool. Because when I see you, I want to make love to you. I become instantly red in the face and exceedingly warm in other places."

She kissed him again, long and slow. He returned the kiss in kind, enjoying the surge of passion it evoked.

Jasmine said, "I think it shows to Thomas, but he is too kind to mention anything. I just can't allow that to keep happening. Forgive me, Ian. Please come with me...now."

She went back out into the street where Omar was patiently waiting. After speaking to him, they walked to his brother's café. There was a small bedroom in the rear, used occasionally by Omar's brother after late nights at the café. The loyal Omar stood guard at the door.

Jasmine and Ian made passionate love, with an intensity never before felt by either. Ian brought her skilfully to long sweet climaxes, weaving them together in a tapestry of sensual joy, as she had taught him.

When they lay naked, exhausted, Jasmine looked at him and said, "Ian, this can never happen again while I am married to Thomas. Do you understand?"

"I understand," was all Ian could say.

Jasmine dressed quickly, kissed him lightly on the lips, and hurried out of the café. Ian watched her walk away down the street with Omar at her side. He knew what he must do. It was a question of friendship and honour. He mounted Savage and rode back to camp. He never again returned to the home of Jasmine and Thomas Day.

Chapter 72

"Come in, Ian, sit down, please," Goodlake said in a quiet voice. Ian, having lifted the tent flap, was peering inside rather cautiously, surprised to see, through the cigar and pipe smoke, several officers already there. The last time he'd heard about Gerald Goodlake, his sharpshooters had been disbanded and he was supervising the hutting of troops in Balaklava. Ian ducked inside the crowded tent and sat with the others at a small table. There was a rather ominous looking map spread across it.

Goodlake said, "Captain Carlyle, I believe you know Lieutenant Colonel Kingscote, and you'll remember Captain Markham, of the Rifles. Gave us support in the ravine that time." As Goodlake spoke, Ian shook Kingscote's hand, then said, "Congratulations on your promotion, sir."

Kingscote replied, "Kind of you, Carlyle. Good to see you fit. We miss you at headquarters."

Ian and Markham exchanged nods of recognition.

Goodlake continued the introductions, "This is Lieutenant Guy Remy, French Liaison," Remy actually clicked his heels, "and this is Captain Barker, we borrowed him from W Battery."

Ian nodded to Remy, "I know Captain Barker, we met on a very hot hill near Kadakoi. Good to see you again."

"Let's get right to it," Goodlake interrupted, focusing on the crudely hand-drawn map across the table. "This is the best map I could find of the Left Attack, drawn up a week ago, based on a detailed reconnaissance. Look here," he pointed to the map, "this small dome-like hill northwest of our parallel trenches, beyond this cemetery...here."

They all found his reference. He continued, "You'll notice that this hill, called Little Mamelon, is in easy range of Russian artillery from Flagstaff Battery, farther northwest, and from Strand Battery, directly north."

"I thought we owned that hill," Barker said.

"We had the damned thing for a time. Russians have taken it back. They're in trenches and rifle pits, playing hell with our forward parallels every day, even killing French troops to our left across Picquet House Ravine. At night they're sending ugly little sorties against us. Orders are to get them off that hill."

There was quiet, then Ian spoke up, "Can't we merely shell the piss out of them?" There were nods from the assembled officers.

Kingscote injected, "Tried that. Didn't work. They hid down in their holes and jumped up after we stopped, apparently no effect at all. Headquarters wants them out of there with the bayonet."

Goodlake said, "Yes, but I thought we might try something a bit more sophisticated than a simple murderous frontal assault."

Silence again. Waiting. Each knowing they were to be the pointy end of this attack, somehow.

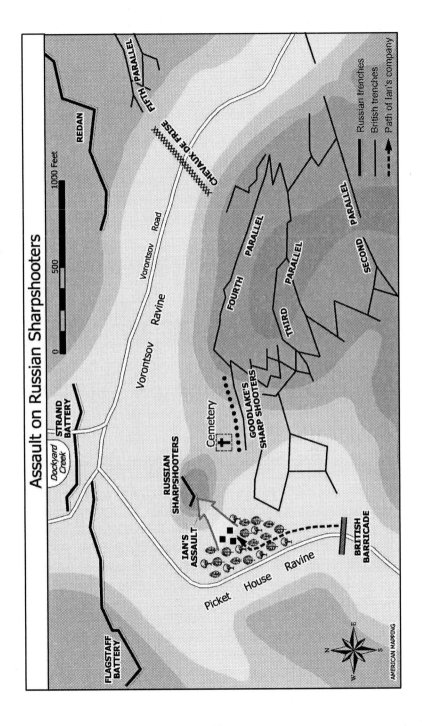

Assault on Russian Sharpshooters

"There's another finger stuck in the pudding," Goodlake said. "These aren't your ordinary Russians. We captured one last night. They're a special lot, drawn from all over, mostly Imperial Guard and Jaeger Regiments, we think about fifty men in all. Every one is a marksman with their copy of our Brunswick .70 inch rifle musket, and it seems like every one is a remorseless killer."

"Their Brunswick's not that accurate, Goodlake, only two grooves, and a great fat clumsy ribbed musket ball. Range about 300 yards, give or take. Are you saying they're as good as your lads, or mine?" asked Markham.

"Indeed not, but they seem to have developed a conical bullet of sorts for the rifle, increasing the range several hundred more yards. They've been hitting their targets regularly during the day, and some at healthy distances. At night their sorties are even more bother. We find sentries naked, with their throats cut, caught by surprise. This morning, we found a soldier from the 19th with his cock and balls cut off..."

Kingscote added, "Stuffed in his mouth, actually. Not pretty."

Goodlake allowed that bit of news to take effect, then continued, "These are right bastards, well enough, but their leader is the worst of the lot. A fella named Makarov, Major Vasilii Makarov, Pavlovski Guards Regiment, a very dangerous fellow indeed. Seems he enjoys patrolling himself. Orders and supervises the torture. Takes pleasure in watching the throat cutting, so says our talkative prisoner. He claims this Makarov fella flogged one of his own men to death, personally, all the while a huge smile on his face, if you can believe that."

Ian clearly saw what was coming. He said, "So I take it my company is going in to sort out this fellow and his crowd, while you gentlemen support us. Would that be accurate?"

"Spot on, Carlyle," Goodlake said. "You're my choosing, I'm afraid. Needed someone with the killer instinct, who wouldn't hesitate. Saw that in you at the ravine, old man. No offence, but you even showed it back at school, as I recall, that ugly bit of business with Fairbain and his minions."

"I'm so very pleased you remembered, Goodlake. I'm certain my men will be pleased, as well," said Ian sarcastically. There was laughter around the table, although no one else was privy to the Eton incident.

Kingscote asked, "How many men?"

Ian said, "This morning's report, up to eighty-six, sir, including the just arrived draft. All but 30 are brand new."

Goodlake said, "Now, Ian, not to worry. If we do this right, it'll be a walk in the park. This is the plan. First, I've been assured that for the next two nights there will be little or no moon. Carlyle, tonight, you'll send a small patrol generally north up Picquet House Ravine, which leads to the flank of the hill we want. They will establish the best route for you to travel with your company, then tomorrow night we all move."

They nodded.

"I'll bring sharpshooters into the 4th parallel trenches and move them as far forward toward the hill as I can before dawn," Goodlake continued.

He looked at Ian, said, "You'll take your company to a position as close to the flank of the hill as you can without being seen. Avoid the road in the ravine heading into Sevastopol. Stay within the heavy trees to the east of the road. Hide your men in the trees until near first light."

Markham looked at Goodlake, said, "I understood your sharpshooters were broken up, so I assume I'll be supporting Carlyle?"

"We were disbanded because I had only a dozen left. I've managed to get those lads back together for this tiny adventure, so it'll be both of us supporting Carlyle. If you can give me twenty of your best marksmen, with mine it should be enough."

"I'll give you my best, including myself," Markham said, modestly.

In rather good English, Captain Remy asked, "What happens at dawn?"

Goodlake smiled, "Ah, that's the simple beauty of it. At first light the Russians will be standing-to, as they routinely do. My lads and the Rifles will start aiming for head and chest shots to open the ball. We should be able to bring down a fair number, before they realize what's happening."

He looked at Carlyle, "You, Remy, and Barker should all hear this firing."

Goodlake turned to Barker, "You must wait thirty minutes from the start of the firing, no more, then have our batteries in the parallels play on that hill for all they're worth. Put yourself in a position where you can observe the hill, and order a halt to the shelling when you see Carlyle's men attacking."

He turned again to Ian, "You should be moving up that hill while Barker's guns are keeping them down in their holes. Carry a colour, Carlyle, so it can be seen."

Ian nodded again, but had already made a mental note to do just that.

Ian was more interested in the answer to his next question, "What about the Flagstaff Battery? By this map, we'll have our backs to them all the way up that damned hill. They can put round shot right up our bums."

Goodlake said, "That's where Lieutenant Remy and our gallant allies render assistance. Remy, you must also be in a position to observe the hill. I expect two things from you, Lieutenant. As soon as you hear Barker's guns or see Captain Carlyle break from the cover of the treeline, I would like your artillery to open hotly on Flagstaff Battery. At the same time, I'd like you to arrange an infantry demonstration toward the battery. Keep them busy, Remy, keep them off Carlyle's arse."

Remy quickly snapped to attention, said in a crisp voice, "You may consider it done, mes amis, consider it done."

Ian frowned, thought, *a bit eager, isn't he?*

Kingscote summed up, "The rest is routine, gentlemen. Hook in those trenches and rifle pits, Carlyle. Root them out, drive them off, or kill the bastards. The plan is from Goodlake, but the orders come directly from His Lordship. Tell your men that. It may give them heart."

Ian thought, *right, but neither His Lordship nor you, my dear Kingscote, will be going up that bloody fucking hill with us, will you?*

Goodlake looked at Kingscote with one eye cocked. He leaned over to Ian and said, quietly, "Bollocks all that 'heart' crap, Ian. You just remember my men'll be killing those bastards until we see you in their holes, then we'll be along to help root them out. Save some for us, won't you?"

Ian chose Sergeant Fergusson, his steady old soldier with good common sense. He'd borrowed Goodlake's map and showed him the approximate route he wanted him to take out and back.

Ian instructed Fergusson himself, with the map laid out and Colour Sergeant MacGregor by his side, "There's what looks like houses…here…and here…probably ruined or abandoned, in or near the trees at the foot of the hill. Might be a good place to hide the company and start the assault."

"Aye, sir, if the Rooshians ain't already there," Fergusson said.

"Right, that's your job, Sergeant Fergusson. I need to know a clear route in and out, so mark it in your mind. Pick five good men. Work your way to these houses or whatever they are; see what's what. If not there, find us another place to hide until dawn. Be back here, if possible, by midnight. You be careful."

"Aye, sir, piece a cake."

Chapter 73

Major Vasilii Makarov waited patiently. He was a tall, thin, strikingly handsome man, with black hair and a pencil moustache. He first started relishing pain in others as a child in Moscow. He was beaten daily by his aristocratic and sadistic father, and took his revenge by beating the odd peasant sometimes to death. By virtue of his family's status, he was, of course, above any punishment for such atrocities. He first realized that he particularly relished sadistic encounters with younger men, when he was sixteen.

Vasilii hated just about everyone, and thus, treated everyone with contempt, except his latest lover and slave, the ruggedly handsome Private Andre Bukov. Bukov was the ideal selection for Makarov's strange tastes. He was a devout sadomasochist, enjoyed torturing, being tortured, and worshipped Makarov as though he was a god.

This night Makarov was taking a special patrol out. Bukov pleaded to go with him.

"No," the major ordered, "you will stay outside in the trench, huddled like a dog, guarding my possessions."

Bukov replied, "Yes, master. Of course, master."

"Something is going to happen this night. I can feel it, smell it in the air, a coppery smell, like blood."

Each night since they had taken the hill he had set ambuscades at the likely approaches of the enemy, as well as sending out killing patrols. He knew they'd come at him from one of these approaches. It was a question of preparing and waiting. He had an uncanny feeling tonight was the night, and he knew exactly where they'd come at him.

"Are the men ready?" he whispered to the senior sergeant next to him.

"Yes, Major, ready," the sergeant replied, nervously. He feared this officer more than most.

Makarov said, "Remember, no guns. I want complete silence. Knives, not guns."

"Of course, Major, the men understand. They will do their duty for Mother Russia."

Stupid peasant pig, Makarov thought, but not unpleasant in appearance...perhaps later.

They were waiting, surrounding a small clearing containing the remains of a farmhouse with outbuildings. It was at the foot of the hill the English were calling Little Mamelon. The deserted farm was the most obvious point of departure for an assault on the flank of the hill.

There was no moon. It was soundless and dark. After several hours of waiting, Major Makarov heard the unmistakable sound of men trying unsuccessfully to move silently through a wood. He counted six men, as they emerged from cover and spread out across the clearing. Their leader moved toward the farmhouse.

Makarov commanded, "Now!"

There was a rush of movement from all sides of the clearing at once. He heard rustling, small groans, gurgling sounds, but no shots – then strained quiet.

"What time is it, Sergeant?" Ian said to MacGregor.

"Three in the morning, sir."

Ian and MacGregor were within their lines, at a barrier built across the dirt track along the bottom of Picquet House Ravine. Ian peered out toward Sevastopol into the thick black night, said, "At least headquarters was right about the moon. Where the hell are they?"

MacGregor said, "Och, sir, they's all right. There's been no firing, and ye know Fergie wouldn't go down without a fight. They're all good lads with him, sir. Give them time. They'll be fine."

As the sun rose, there was still no word. Ian finally reported to Goodlake, who reported to headquarters. By late afternoon it was decided, against Ian and Goodlake's protests, to go that night, with or without the information from Fergusson's patrol.

Chapter 74

Ian led his company into the inky blackness. Each man knew the plan and his part in it. Each man was examined to ensure nothing rattled or made a noise. MacGregor was in the rear, to see they didn't lose anyone. They moved quietly and carefully, staying well within the woods to the east of the north-south track, the high steep banks of the large ravine on both sides. It took them hours.

Ian saw the clearing through the trees ahead, at least three buildings, just visible. He sent three men to each side of the clearing, circling it, as Billy taught him, to flush out any waiting enemy. The two groups met at the far side, gave the all clear, and the lead section of the company followed Ian across the clearing. The other sections formed circular security as Ian instructed them.

There was no danger. Makarov had purposely withdrawn his men. They were hidden all along the crest of the hill, well above the clearing. They'd slaughter these arrogant English as they came running up the hill after seeing his handiwork. After that, he'd have his way with any of the bastards left alive.

Ian moved to the farmhouse, peered in cautiously; it was empty. One of the guardsmen who first circled the clearing came running from an outbuilding, face ashen, even in the dark. He whispered, "Sir, you'd better come."

Ian's insides went suddenly cold, a premonition. He approached the outbuilding, as a guardsman vomited off to the side.

Ian entered slowly, eyes focusing. He felt the horror like a punch in the stomach. Five naked, headless bodies were strewn around the floor of the one-room outbuilding in a crude circle, each stabbed numerous times, lying in their own blood. The heads were placed grotesquely in a smaller circle at the centre of the room; faces turned outward, mouths gaping open. Ian recognized each man by name. Fergusson was not with them.

MacGregor rushed in beside Ian, and came up short. They both looked up. Above the circle of heads, Fergusson was suspended from the ceiling by his ankles like a side of beef. He was naked with his hands tied behind, bleeding from various stab wounds and cuts over his torso, many several inches long. His blood ran down in heavy streams looking black in the darkness, smelling of death.

Fergusson had been beaten severely over his whole body by something large and heavy. He had died slowly, probably while Ian and MacGregor were waiting for him by the barrier on the road.

Fergusson's genitals had been torn off, jaggedly, and left on the ground beneath his naked body, in the centre of the grotesque circle of heads. They lay in the expanding pool of his blood. *There's no reason for this. It's senseless. Hideous. Unspeakable.*

Another guardsman vomited, running out the door, head bent. MacGregor, in a rage, bolted for the door. Ian knew he just wanted to kill something, knew because that's what he was feeling.

Ian shouted, "No! Not yet, MacGregor. That's just what whoever did this wants. We'll do this right." MacGregor calmed only slightly at Ian's words, but held himself in check.

After recovering some from the initial shock and pain, Ian had MacGregor set security around the clearing, then allowed the rest of the company to see the bodies of Fergusson and the others, all friends of theirs. The effect was substantial, and intended. They gently cut Fergusson down and laid the body out, their stony expressions barely concealing pure hatred. Ian wanted, needed, that hatred for tomorrow, but focused, not blind rage.

He reminded them of the plan for the morning, ordered the sergeants, "Get them hidden. Tomorrow we'll go on my signal, after the guns have given them a right good pounding, and not before. When it's over I don't care if there's one of those bastards alive. Understand?"

The sergeants nodded.

Ian thought: *They know we're coming. They'll be waiting.*

As the first rays of light appeared, the crackle of spaced gunfire began from above, mounting in tempo as the light increased. *There's Markham.* The men about Ian began to tense and stir.

He hissed, "Stay quiet – no movement." MacGregor and the other sergeants echoed his urgent words.

Precisely thirty minutes after the first shots were fired the Royal Artillery began shelling the hill with great energy. *Give it to them, Barker.* The hilltop was no more than a hundred yards above them, but the sides of the ravine were steep. The occasional round shot landed in the woods nearby, but did no damage to Ian's men.

Ian tensed – *all's well so far*. He told the sergeants to bring the men on line, two deep, bayonets fixed, at the edge of the wood. There was no movement yet from above them.

His men were all looking at him, waiting for his signal. Swann moved to his side. It was a comfort to see the lad smile up at him.

Ian waited a very long ten minutes while the shelling took effect, then stood and commanded, "Company rise…Charge Bayonet…Forward, march." They moved from the wood line, walking briskly up the hill, leaning into it, front rank with bayonets forward, rear rank at arms port.

They dressed centre on the regimental colour Ian had borrowed from Captain Lindsay, carried by a young ensign he had also borrowed from the adjutant. MacGregor was behind the line dressing the men, calling to the other sergeants to dress the line on the colour as they marched. Their line was perfect.

Ian didn't want a repeat of what happened when he lost his sword in the struggle below the Sandbag Battery, so he drew and cocked his Colt revolver, holding his sword in his right hand, and the pistol in his left. No shots had been fired at them yet, *why? I know they're there. What are they waiting for?*

The first round shot from behind them landed among his men, killing one guardsman outright. More Russian shots landed on the hillside from Flagstaff Battery, some finding their mark. Then shells began exploding overhead, again from the rear, and Ian saw men falling around him from the shrapnel.

Fear gripped him tightly, but he controlled it, kept walking forward, leading his men…anger replaced the fear. For good or bad, his leopard was again by his side.

Another shot landed from behind, from the Flagstaff Battery, wounding two men. He shouted out loud to no one, "Where the hell are the bloody French?"

More of his men were falling, more shells coming at them. Ian shouted for the double march, and the line began to move faster. It was too soon, but they had to get off that hill quickly, before he lost them all.

Heads and shoulders poked above the ground ahead. He saw the Russians taking aim, careful aim. There were muzzle flashes, as they fired at close range. The Russian marksmen began methodically murdering what men the artillery shot and shell were not.

There was nothing for it. No choice. They couldn't go to ground or back down the hill, it would be a worse slaughter. The distance left was too far, no choice...he rushed to the front and gave the final command, "Follow me, men. Charge!" His men began running and screaming.

He heard his colour sergeant's familiar voice, "Get in them holes, death to the Ruskies, kill them for Fergie and the others." MacGregor and Swann were by his side, had pulled up when the dressed line of men fell apart, as they ran faster in the charge. Swann's bayonet was already blooded, and as he ran, he gutted another Russian in the neck.

Ian's men fell around him, maybe half the company down. He kept moving...*No stopping now.* The young ensign waving the colour abruptly disappeared in a cloud of smoke and dust, as a shell exploded a few feet above his head. The colour was on the ground, shredded badly by the shell fragments. The ensign was unrecognizable.

Ian shouted, "The colour, Swann, get the colour," but Swann was already there, picking it up as he dropped his rifle musket. A Russian moved in for the kill, but Swann swiped his bayonet thrust aside, clubbing the Russian to the ground with the flagstaff. Without hesitation, Swann ran forward waving the colour and its bloody staff to rally what was left of the company. Swann jerked twice as bullets found him, staggered, but remained erect and moving forward.

The men saw the small wounded lad waving their flag. There was a cheer, and they ran harder. At last, they were in and among the rifle pits on top of the hill, shooting, cutting, smashing, killing.

The Russian artillery from the rear had ceased when Ian's men reached the hilltop, for fear of hitting their own men. Ian looked to his right across the cemetery toward the British trenches, saw green-jacketed riflemen and red-jacketed guardsmen running to join them, made out Goodlake and Markham leading them. Ian lost sight of Swann in the confusion. He prayed the courageous boy was safe.

Now his guardsmen were clubbing and bayoneting anyone in their way. The Russians, seeing these wild demons screaming at them, jumped from their holes, trying to flee down the hill toward their lines…it was too late. The guardsmen were too angry, and too fast, the bloody memory of Fergusson and the others fresh. Few of the enemy reached safety.

Ian could feel victory. They had taken the hill, even without French help, but at a terrible cost. His men were finishing the last of the defenders as he searched.

Ian was looking at a larger trench with a shelter dug into its side, a sign in front written in Russian. He was certain it said something like "commander." There was a torn canvas over the opening. He ran into the trench, felt someone close after him. He yanked open the canvas, heard the shot, and felt a jolt of searing pain in his right shoulder. His arm went limp. His sword dropped to the trench floor.

MacGregor pushed him roughly out of the way, raised his rifle musket, and shot the half-dressed Russian sergeant who had wounded his officer. From the shadows in the dugout came a tall, thin Russian officer aiming his pistol at MacGregor. Ian saw him, lifted the revolver in his left hand and fired. The bullet caught the officer squarely in the face, in the middle of his pencil moustache, leaving a strange expression; two mouths open in surprise, one on top of the other.

MacGregor stood by the door while Ian, right arm dangling at his side, went through the officer's papers. They were in Russian, but identified him as Major Vasilii Makarov, or at least that's who he was before he gained a new mouth. Ian was satisfied. He smiled at MacGregor, who said, "We've done fine work today, sir. Fergusson would've been proud."

Ian nodded, went past MacGregor, pulled the canvas flap back, and walked out into a gloriously bright morning. His shoulder ached, but the sun felt warm. He knew the wound wasn't serious. It didn't matter. He thought of the terrible price their moment of glory had cost.

The Russian private, Andre Bukov, had been waiting in the trench for hours, crouched like a dog, as his master had dictated. When his master returned from his patrol, he saw the blood on his uniform, knew it wasn't his. He saw the young sergeant follow Makarov into the dugout, assuming it was to make a report. Bukov waited in vain to be summoned inside so that he might please his master.

Bukov heard the attack, thought it was coming closer, but didn't believe it...this couldn't happen...not to his master. He was invincible.

Then he saw the British officer and his sergeant go in his beloved master's dugout, heard the shots, saw the officer exit, rubbing his shoulder. Tears welled in his eyes as he realized his lover, his master, was dead. Rage took over. He let out an insane scream.

Bukov's bayonet ran Ian through, slamming him back and down onto the trench floor. The shock was total. Ian looked up in amazement, helpless, as the Russian deliberately pulled the bayonet out. Several shots fired at once...voices drifting far off in the distance. Blackness engulfed him, peaceful now, no pain, just coldness. Ian could feel the leopard fading slowly away in the tall grass. He thought, *how curious. I'm cold, but I can still feel the warmth of the sun. How oddly gentle it feels to die.*

Epilogue

It was November 1857, in a rather large room at Windsor Castle, empty of furniture. Selected officers of the Guards Brigade were in line, with their families. Her Royal Majesty, Queen Victoria, entered with her entourage, which included the Duke of Cambridge. The room was pressed into awed hush. This was one of a few personal presentations Her Royal Majesty was making to her soldiers who fought in the Crimea, but this was special, exclusively for her beloved Guards Brigade.

She walked from one group to the next, saying a few personal words, then presenting each officer with the light blue and yellow-ribboned Crimean War Medal, containing bars for each battle fought: Alma, Inkerman, Balaklava, Sevastopol, and so on.

Her Majesty said to the older distinguished-looking man standing next to the chair, "Lord Dunkairn, it is so very good to see you."

"It is always my greatest pleasure, Your Majesty," the Earl replied, bowing.

"And you Lady Dunkairn." She bowed in reply.

"We presume this is your son, Peter?"

Peter bowed, "Your Majesty."

She turned to the young man in the wheeled chair, "Captain Carlyle, we've heard a great deal about you. It is a pleasure to finally meet you."

Ian blushed, "I'm honoured, Your Majesty."

"Allow us to congratulate you, and present you with this inadequate, but heartfelt medal in appreciation for your service and your sacrifice." Ian accepted the campaign medal, head bowed.

Her Highness continued, "We trust you're mending?"

Ian's head came back up, "I'll be back on active service soon, Your Majesty, thank you for asking."

"We understand there's more recognition to be performed this day, Captain Carlyle. We're told you put someone's name forward for a particular award."

Ian said, "Aye, Your Majesty, indeed I did."

"We're told this brave guardsman is here this day. His citation reads: 'Under withering enemy fire, wounded himself twice, personally dispatched several of the enemy, retrieved the Scots Fusilier Guards regimental colour from a fallen ensign and rallied the men to successfully charge a strongly held Russian position near Sevastopol, the taking of which saved countless lives.' Is that approximately correct, Captain Carlyle?"

Ian was amazed. The Queen had memorized the citation, word for word, "Your Majesty, that is absolutely correct. I was there."

"Excellent. Will Private Broderick Swann, 1st Battalion, Scots Fusilier Guards, please step forward." She reached back, and the Duke handed her a medal.

Swann was dumbfounded, had known nothing of this. His own wounds mended; he'd come along only to take care of his still-recovering officer. The young lad almost tripped over Ian's wheeled chair getting out from behind it, limping slightly. He stood in front of the Queen of England, seriously shaken.

The ribbon on the metal the Queen held was not blue and yellow, but a rich dark red. Not unlike blood. Her Highness said, "It is with the utmost pleasure and gratitude, Private Swann, that we award you the Victoria Cross, our nation's highest decoration, for your unflinching bravery and loyalty to the Crown." She pinned the medal to his uniform jacket, and smiled warmly at the proudest private in Her Majesty's Army.

THE END